Regal
God of Wai
By Victoria B

Edited by Jeff Jones
Cover art by Tabatha Füsting

To Dave
Thank you for buying my book!
I hope you enjoy it.
Merry Christmas + best wishes,
Victoria
xx

Pitsa (Prologue)

'Thousands of years ago, eight mortal beings were born on a planet named Earth, inhabited by a race called the Humans. The beings were not Humans; they were the only people of their kind and they called themselves the Gaiamira. Their names were Kala, Taka, Gonta, Tomakoto, Tangun, Lanka, Donso and Mokuya. The Gaiamira grew amongst the Humans in a cruel and corrupted world filled with conflict and confusion; they saw that the Humans were lost in a world of war, and that one day they would destroy themselves and the planet Earth. The Gaiamira tried to save the Humans but the Humans would not listen, and after many years of struggling on Earth the Gaiamira realised that they were not meant for the Humans, and that they were destined to be part of something more. They felt the universe calling to them and they knew that their place was not on Earth, and so they left in search of their true home.

The Gaiamira travelled for many years through outer space, until they found a small planet similar to their own. The planet was sparsely populated and wasn't yet corrupted or confused. The people of the planet saw the Gaiamiras' ship appear in the sky. The ship flew down to the planet's surface and landed with such force that it split into two and became the moons of the planet. The people of the planet raced to see the Gaiamira, but as soon as the Gaiamira landed they felt the life of the planet calling out to them. They fused their bodies into the planet's core and became one with the planet, turning themselves into immortal beings.

The Gaiamira were so exhausted from their journey that they remained inside the planet for a hundred years. They rested in a realm called the Gaiamirarezo in the centre of the planet, and built up the strength they needed to one day appear to their people.

When the Gaiamira finally awoke they found that their bodies had dissolved into the planet and they existed as spiritual beings. They looked up to the planet's surface and saw that its inhabitants had multiplied into their thousands and although they had grown as a people, they were now lost, without belief or direction. The people were at war with each other and the world was becoming corrupted,

3

and the Gaiamira knew that they would soon destroy themselves and the planet.

The Gaiamira felt the calling of the planet and they knew that their purpose was to save this world, and so they raised a mountain named Mount Gaiamira and they appeared to the people on top of it, showing themselves as the new gods of the planet. They said that this was a new age and a new world for the people; they promised to rid the world of confusion and to give their people belief and guidance. They promised to make the people great, and they promised that as long as the people believed in them and followed them they would never be lost. The people of the world could feel the warmth of the Gaiamira and they knew their promise was true, and so they named themselves the Gaiamirákans and they named their planet Gaiamiráka, and they faithfully followed the Gaiamira into the New Age, and the planet Gaiamiráka was born.'

-       Extract from the Gaiamirapon: 'The Beginning'

*

'King Mokoto Sota-Rokut was born on 15-06-20103G in Meitona Palace. He was the youngest child of his father and predecessor King Taka Sota-Rokut, and the only male out of King Taka's thirteen children. King Mokoto is typically remembered for his role in causing the Gaiamiráka-Earth War of 20144G - 20147G, also known as the Mokotoakat War, which claimed the lives of millions worldwide and led to the Malat Punishment of 20147G; a Punishment that threatened to wipe out the Gaiamirákan race.

However, even before the start of the Gaiamiráka-Earth War Mokoto had a reputation for being a cruel and aggressive leader, obsessed with conflict and dictatorship. Although he was a Hiveakan and largely influenced by his father, Mokoto was surrounded by Outsiders during his post-Hive upbringing and he chose to take an Outsider wife, who gave him an Outsider son.

For the most part, Mokoto seemed to have a civil and perhaps even friendly relationship with his non-Hiveakan relatives, which has

4

caused many historians over the years to wonder what it was that turned Matat (Prince) Mokoto into the most cold-hearted, ruthless and bloodthirsty king in Gaiamirákan history.'

-       Extract from history textbook: 'The Mokoto Era: 20103G - 20147G', 20160G

I.

It was 15-06-20103G; the fifteenth day of the sixth month of the year 20103G, on the planet Gaiamiráka. It was the month of Taka the God of War, and the mortal King Taka, the ferocious ruler of Gaiamiráka whom was named after the God he so admired, could not ask for a better month to welcome the birth of his first son.

The child, who would be named Mokoto, was only an hour old when his yotuna, the Gaiamirákan birth celebration, had started in his home and birthplace, the royal palace in Meitona, Keizuaka. Mokoto was born in the holy room, a temple in the palace basement that paid tribute to the eight gods of Gaiamiráka, the Gaiamira. Holy scripts were carved delicately into the walls of the room, extracted word for word from the Gaiamirapon, the Gaiamirákan holy book. The entire length of the Gaiamirapon was embedded into this room; every word the Gaiamira had ever uttered and every story they had ever told existed here. The energy of the Gaiamira flowed through Mokoto's body before he was even presented to them; he felt their spirit before he even heard their names. Even at an hour old he could sense what an honour it was to be born there.

᛫ Mokoto's yotuna was being held between the statues of Tangun and Taka. Each member of the Gaiamira had their own territory within the holy room, decorated with their own colours and idols. Mokoto's mother Keika (king's wife) Teima had been in Tangun's realm when she was birthing the child, aided and blessed by Tangun the God of Birth and Reincarnation. She longed to hold her son, but the king wouldn't allow it. It was a blessing of the Gaiamira that he'd even permitted her to stay there – her determination to witness her baby's yotuna had been her only saving grace. King Taka had been impressed by her courage, and he hoped that it would be passed onto his son. It was the only thing about Teima that he wanted Mokoto to embrace.

King Taka thought little of Teima. Teima was an Outsider; someone who was raised outside of the institution known as the Hive, and therefore deemed weak and unworthy by anyone who had been subjected to the Hive's life of pain. King Taka had been subjected to

6

this life; he was a Hiveakan, as was everyone else in the room. This was a Hiveakan yotuna; Mokoto would be a Hiveakan child. As soon as Mokoto's yotuna was over he would be sent to live in the Hive. He would have no contact with his family; he would never so much as see their faces or hear their voices until he was considered good enough to leave – to graduate, and return home. He would spend his entire childhood fighting for survival; he would be tortured day and night both mentally and physically; he would be malnourished and denied sleep for days on end; he would be forced to excel in every aspect of his life and beaten brutally if he ever failed. He would learn to take comfort in pain; he would come to embrace darkness and shed all manner of weakness. He would be a monster; he would be a tyrant. He would be cruel. He would be heartless. He would be strong. He would be a Hiveakan.

It was in keeping with Hiveakan tradition that Mokoto's yotuna was being performed before both the God of Birth and the God of War. The mighty god Taka, after whom King Taka was named, was the God of War and the God of the Hive. The Hive was his creation; it was the mortal world's tribute to their warrior lord. Every Hiveakan that had ever lived had been presented to the Gaiamira in front of Taka; every Hiveakan that had ever walked the world carried the darkness of the God of War. They called it the Footprints. The Footprints were at the core of every Hiveakan's being. They were the spirit of Taka. They were the mark of the Hive. They were darkness and they were fierceness. They were a concept and they were a virus. They existed in the souls of Taka's children, and they existed in the walls of his Hive. They were breathed into a Hiveakan's lungs and they were felt on their skin. They were in the eyes of every Hiveakan that existed and they were in their blood. They bonded a Hiveakan to his comrades; they fuelled them with the spirit of Taka and they flooded a Hiveakan's body with the strength and fierceness of the God of War. The Footprints carried Taka; the Footprints carried darkness. The Footprints were the embodiment of the Hive.

The Footprints were what made the room cold. All around the holy room there was a tingling darkness; there was an icy heat that told everyone that Taka was there. He was being summoned for the yotuna,

7

and he was drawn to the dark auras of the Hiveakans that dominated the room. King Taka had invited them for that darkness; he hoped that their ferocity and fearlessness would be absorbed by his child. He wanted their blood to stain Mokoto's soul.

He had only invited three members of his family to join him for Mokoto's yotuna; he didn't want too many bodies to contaminate the room. Standing at King Taka's side was Keika Suela, his fifth and only Hiveakan wife. Members of the royal family were permitted to marry multiple times, and King Taka had taken eight wives in his life. There were only four that were still alive today, and as the only Hiveakan Suela was the strongest. She was his favourite, and the only wife King Taka had come to respect. She was his comrade, and the closest thing a Hiveakan could have to a friend. In their ten years of marriage Suela had given King Taka two Hiveakan daughters, Lanka and Anaka, both of whom were still in the Hive and were excelling as well as any Hiveakan parents could wish. They would be Mokoto's competition. They were the only two people that could challenge Mokoto's right to the throne, and both Taka and Suela were keen to see who would earn possession of King Taka's crown.

Standing alongside Suela were Malatsa (sub-king) Thoit and his wife Keika Haliku; they had arrived in the palace the previous evening to await Mokoto's birth. Thoit was King Taka's older brother; he was forty-eight years old and ten years Taka's senior. He was one of three brothers to King Taka, the others being Malatsa Omota and Malatsa Toka, neither of whom were present today. Omota and Toka had not been invited; Thoit was the king's only Hiveakan sibling and therefore the only one worthy of being witness to Mokoto's yotuna. He was the ruler of Hu Keizuaka, one of the four continents of Gaiamiráka, two of which, Haniaka and Aoutaka, were ruled by Omota and Toka. The remaining continent, Mokoto's birthplace Keizuaka, was ruled by King Taka himself. After his younger brother, Malatsa Thoit was the most powerful man in the world.

Thoit lived in a country named Soan in Hu Keizuaka, of which his much younger wife Haliku was a native. Thoit and Haliku had one child between them, a Hiveakan daughter named Teisumi. She was still in the Soanakan Hive, and would one day rule over Hu Keizuaka under

8

the authority of her newborn cousin, the same way Thoit ruled under Taka's reign. Thoit was respectful to his brother; he had lost his right to the Gaiamirákan throne in a battle that had occurred when they were matats. Their late father, then king of Gaiamiráka, had considered both of his Hiveakan children worthy of taking his place as ruler of the world, and so he had made them fight for the throne. Thoit had almost murdered his sibling before he was defeated. He was a large man with a wide muscular build, and it suited him well that his name was the Gaiamirákan word for 'mountain'. Thoit had tried hard to win the throne but he bore no grudge against his brother; it wasn't the Hiveakan way. There was honour in victory and there was honour in defeat, and bitterness was an Outsider's emotion. Thoit took pride in his brother the way he would his own child, and he would be stirred by Mokoto's cries of pain the same way he was stirred by Teisumi's screams.

Mokoto wasn't crying. Not yet. He soon would. No Hiveakan yotuna was pain free, and the level of the infant's screams was a testament to how strong a Hiveakan they would make. Lanka had been a terrible screaming baby while Anaka had barely uttered a whimper; in fact Anaka had bitten her father. If he was to impress his father at all Mokoto would have to be silent throughout, and if he screamed it would have to be with anger and ferocity. Suela held her gaze sternly on the child in King Taka's arms. Judging him. She resented the baby. He was half Outsider and nothing compared to her pure blooded girls. Suela expected him to scream. She expected Mokoto to cry pleadingly, begging his father for mercy. She was looking forward to seeing her half-breed stepson in pain.

"Taka..." A meek voice caught the attention of the Hiveakans. They moved their eyes to look at Teima. She was sitting down, too weak from childbirth to stand. Her pale yellow Gaiamirákan skin had practically turned white; her usually bright green eyes were dim and drained. She looked like she would cry. She looked afraid. She knew what a monster her baby was about to become.

"What?" Taka answered gruffly.

"Please..." Teima whimpered. "Can I hold him?"

9

"Teima, you will spoil him," Taka growled. "Do I have to tell you again?" He turned away from her and looked at the Hiveakan priest that would present Matat Mokoto to the Gaiamira. Teima lowered her eyes and crumbled into her own despair, trying her best not to cry. She wouldn't hold him... He was her baby and she wasn't allowed to hold him. Why did Taka have to be like this...? Why couldn't he just give her one minute with her son? That was all she wanted. It was all she asked for... Why could she not have it?

Suela smirked to herself at the thought of Teima's despair; she thought so little of Outsiders and she loved to see them suffer, especially at Taka's hand. She took pride in the fact that she was the head mate of the alpha male, and every time King Taka broke someone's heart it felt like a personal victory to Suela. Her name was the Gaiamirákan word for 'victory', and she lived her life in honour of it. Suela finished first in every aspect of her life, and she was certain that her daughters would be no exception. Suela had every confidence that when it came to the fight for the throne, it would be Teima's child that failed.

"If we are ready..." The priest uttered. He met eyes with King Taka and nodded at the king, acknowledging his silent order to begin the service. "Tangun-zozo," the priest began. "Banka dlitomoko nono Mokoto mi ottaka mikita loka fitomoko gan mi Gaiamira-akot sinto." (Lord Tangun, please accept this child Mokoto into your world and welcome him into the arms of the Gaiamira.)

Teima closed her eyes, reluctantly awaiting the Hiveakan side of the prayer. It was the plea to Taka; it was the verse that would turn Mokoto into a monster. Maybe it wouldn't work... Maybe the God of War didn't want Mokoto. Maybe it would all be okay... "Taka-zozo," the priest spoke. "Banta teimamoko gin nono zon ottakot zen loka aourat loka dumoko gan juokosa fomakamozoko. Tiamoko gan gitta, zenzo, tan loka sutan, loka hilakotmoko gin yunatyo loka zerimoyo." (Lord Taka, please bless this child with your blood and strength and help him become a fearless warrior. Give him courage, bloodlust, loyalty and honour, and rid him of all compassion and weakness.)

The priest looked over at Taka. "It's time, Sire." He smiled.

No, Teima thought. *No... Please.* Her prayers were not answered. Nobody heard them, and even if they had they wouldn't have paid any attention. This was happening no matter what. Mokoto was going to be possessed by the God of War.

Taka approached the font that stood between himself and the priest. It was a large stone object finely decorated with images of the eight members of the Gaiamira, more dominantly Taka, the God of War and his yotuna partner Tangun, the God of Birth and Reincarnation. They were carved delicately into the font's surface; they were blessed by the priests of the past and they harnessed all the energy and devotion of their artist. Scattered around the images were holy scripts and verses, some of which would soon be uttered by Mokoto's priest. They were extracted from the Gaiamirapon and they held within them the life and wisdom of the Gaiamira.

Taka took a moment to look at his son before he surrendered him to the Gaiamira. He stared down at Mokoto with dark dominating eyes that made the child wince in fear. Mokoto looked away; the Footprints in his father's soul were too powerful for him to withstand. He closed up in his father's arms and whimpered, pained and terrified by the energy of the God of War. Taka smirked as he watched the baby. Mokoto was only an hour old and he already feared King Taka. That was good. That was how it should be. Any Hiveakan parent should be able to frighten the living soul out of their child with just one glance. Taka hoped that his child wouldn't have any fear left by time the Hive was done with him. He didn't want Mokoto to be afraid; he didn't want him to be capable of weakness. He wanted Mokoto to be filled with the God of War; he wanted him to be possessed by the Hive.

Taka continued to stare down at Mokoto for a moment, waiting to see if the child would dare look up at him. Mokoto shrank and shrivelled in his father's arms, whimpering and flinching as Taka's eyes burned onto him. Taka was torturing his son. He was sending waves of anger and hatred into the baby's soul; he was allowing his own Footprints to trample Mokoto's being. His Footprints were too powerful. They were hurting Mokoto; they were blinding him with their darkness. Another cold smirk formed on Taka's lips as he watched the boy quiver and the smirk grew wider at the sound of

11

Teima softly sobbing. He knew she wanted him to show her son mercy. He knew this was upsetting her. It somehow pleased Taka that Teima was hurt by this; her tears were a clear indication that he was doing this right.

The priest cleared his throat and took a step closer to the font, as did Taka himself. He looked down at its contents, admiring the beauty of the Takákot Seho, the Water of Taka. A font filled with water was part of many yotuna traditions, but only Hiveakans used Taka's water, and only Hiveakans used Taka's flowers. In this instance it was the suna flower, one of the many flowers of Taka. Inside the font floated an array of leaves and petals cut from young suna plants, symbolising new life in the traditional Gaiamirákan way. The suna was a poisonous flower and one of the many dangerous species used in Hiveakan yotunas.

The leaves and petals floated in water taken from one of the planet's purest and clearest rivers; only clear water could be used for a yotuna, as it was believed that any impurities in the water would be passed onto the child. It was the suna flowers that turned the water into Takákot Seho; it was their poison that summoned the God of War. Their petals were coloured a deep purple; it was the colour of Gaiamirákan blood and it was the colour of Taka. The purple dye of the petals floated through the water as fiercely and as powerfully as the Footprints flowed through a Hiveakan's soul. They corrupted the purity of the water; they dissolved away its innocence and they made it look like blood. They made it represent the Hive.

Just underneath the bowl of the font were two small dipped shelves. One held a sharp yotuna knife and the other shelf was empty; this was reserved for the yotuna water, following another Gaiamirákan tradition where the water could simply be poured over the child. King Taka had chosen to have the yotuna water fill the font, to surround Mokoto with the God of War and to make the child more uncomfortable. The priest watched as Taka placed Mokoto into the font; he handled the infant harshly and with a brutal force. Mokoto whimpered a little as the cold water touched his skin. He had never felt cold before; he didn't like it. It wasn't long before the poison of the

12

suna flowers disturbed the infant. Mokoto cried out as the water burned his skin; it ate away at his flesh and made him blotchy and purple.

Suela smiled when Mokoto started to cry; he couldn't handle the pain of his yotuna. He couldn't handle the venom of the Hive. Taka exhaled impatiently and shot his infant son an angry glare. The glare silenced Mokoto instantly; his fear of his father was greater than his intolerance to pain. Mokoto whimpered softly and closed his eyes, shielding himself from the burning of his father's stare. He would never quite become accustomed to the way his father looked at him. He would never lose his fear of his father. That was what made Taka a good Hiveakan, and he hoped that one day Mokoto would be able to silence his own child's cries. The priest held his eyes on Mokoto for a moment, ignoring the infant's whimpering, and began to utter the rest of the yotuna prayer.

"Tangun-zozo, banta dlitomoko gin nono Mokoto Sota-Rokut mata ottakan thit. Somikomoko gan zon Gaiamirákanakot hara laka blata loka teimamoko gan zon ottakot aourat." (Lord Tangun, please accept this child Mokoto Sota-Rokut as one of your people. Grant him with the Gaiamirákans' life and soul and bless him with your strength.)

"Bless him," Taka and his clan all repeated in unison. The priest scooped up a little of the water in his hand and placed it along Mokoto's lips, encouraging the child to drink. Mokoto held his lips together, reluctant to accept the liquid that hurt him. The priest frowned at Mokoto's disobedience and pried the infant's mouth open with his fingers. He poured water into Mokoto's mouth and stopped when Mokoto started to cough. Mokoto spat out some of the liquid but he swallowed what he could; it burned his lips and scarred his throat. He wanted to cry. He whimpered loudly, begging for someone to ease the pain on his flesh and the burning on his tongue. Nobody wanted to help him; nobody except his mother. Teima closed her eyes and listened in agony, praying to the Gaiamira to help her baby.

"Asa ottakot hana butonamo mi gin seho loka gin fala dan honno butonamo mi Mokoto loka itt bunko ott jaetamoko gan loka jetmoko mi gan jeko gan miji nuntomozoko Gaiamira. Yomena." (Just as your spirit lives in this water and these flowers it now lives in

13

Mokoto and we beg you to watch him and stay in him until he too becomes part of the Gaiamira. Forever.)

Teima forced a small smile as she listened to the priest's words. For a moment she pretended Mokoto wasn't in pain. She pretended the water wasn't poisoned; she pretended it didn't hurt Mokoto to touch it. She couldn't pretend for long; she couldn't deny that the God of War was there. He was taking her baby.

The priest moved his eyes up to King Taka for the second part of the service. He took the yotuna knife from its shelf and handed the blade to the king. Before the service he had asked if Taka would like to make the cut himself – Taka had said he would, as most Hiveakan parents did. The king nodded at the priest and took hold of the sharp yotuna knife; he took a moment to gaze at it and smiled inwardly at its image. Taka felt proud to hold this knife. This was the knife of his family; it was part of his heritage and it was his birthright. This was the knife that had welcomed him and Thoit into the world. This knife had welcomed Suela's daughters; it had welcomed Taka's and Thoit's father and grandfather, and countless kings and queens before them. This knife had been in Taka's family since the birth of the Hive and he was pleased to see it would now be used on another addition to his family: his one and only son. The knife was freshly sharpened, ready to draw blood. It had a thick wooden handle that held upon it the fingerprints of Taka's ancestors. Their energies were encased in this handle; their strength would help Taka welcome his son into the world. The blade itself was made of pure silver and held the image of the almighty God of War upon it. The god stood boldly and fiercely on the blade, eagerly awaiting the moment when he would pierce the king's skin. Perhaps it was the name Taka that invoked such fierceness in the king, as King Taka himself was keen to cut into his own flesh.

The priest watched in admiration as King Taka made a deep cut in his hand, without so much as flinching as the blade pierced his skin. King Taka was happy to do this; just as he had been at Anaka's and Lanka's yotunas. Like all Gaiamirákans, Taka was a strict believer in tradition and folklore, and it was a common belief that any sign of weakness shown by the parents at this stage of the service was passed

14

on to their child. Mokoto was about to receive Taka's blood and Taka had to make sure it was pure, free from fear or debility.

Taka moved his eyes down to the pale shivering infant and placed his hand over Mokoto's mouth, forcing him to drink some of the thick purple blood that was spilling onto the child's lips. Mokoto flinched away as the blood stung his burned lips. He opened his mouth in protest and a drop of blood fell onto his tongue. Mokoto whimpered at first, but as the blood seeped into his taste buds he warmed to its flavour. He opened his eyes and drank the blood willingly, as hungrily as if it were his mother's milk. It was the spirit of Taka that drove his hunger; Mokoto had been blessed with a bloodlust that only a Hiveakan could possess. It was a bloodlust that would grow stronger with every minute he lived as a child of the Hive. A dark smile crept across King Taka's lips as he watched a black cloud form in Mokoto's eyes. It was the Footprints; they were coming to him. The God of War had answered King Taka's prayer.

"Taka-zozo," the priest uttered. "Fentimoko Mokoto goneimoko ganakan beilaakot aouratyo loka ni ganakan beilaakot zerimo. Fentimoko gan musutamoko ganakan beilaakot aouratzo loka gutmoko dan ganakot, loka tiamoko gan ottakot aouratzo tonna gan watmoko oreisaka Keizuakan fomakamozoko. Fentimoko gan ritzamoko juko, aouratzomo loka zenzomo, loka dutago fenti jonala hott juoko nata ganakot nuzo. Fentimoko gan juokoko ottsa, loka fentimoko gan fletei gan za Gaiamirasa." (Let Mokoto inherit all of his father's strength and none of his father's weakness. Let him take his father's power and make it his own, and give him your power so that he can become a true Hiveakan warrior. Let him grow strong, powerful and bloodthirsty, and never allow love or fear to enter his heart. Let him fear only you, and let him devote himself only to the Gaiamira.)

"Benota," (Amen) the Hiveakans all chanted.

Thoit glanced over at Suela and winked at her. They both knew this was the beginning of her rivalry with Teima and it was the beginning of her daughters' rivalry with Mokoto. Suela smirked at Thoit arrogantly, rising to his challenge. It wasn't much of a challenge to her. Teima was weak, and no amount of Taka's blood would be able to purify her son. She didn't care if the Footprints made their mark on

15

Mokoto's soul; they were nothing compared to the darkness that lived in her daughters. Suela glanced over at Teima challengingly but Teima was avoiding everyone's gaze. She had her head down with her eyes shut tight, and for the first time she wished for Mokoto to cry.

Please, Teima silently begged. *Please don't be a Hiveakan.* Her prayers were not answered. Her heart froze as the sound of her son giggling, a sound that just moments ago would have warmed every inch of her being, filled the room. Now she despised it. She feared it. That sound – that cold, dark laughter – it meant that he had become one of them... Taka's spirit was in him now. There were Footprints in his soul. He was a monster.

"Congratulations, Sire." The priest smiled at King Taka and lifted Mokoto out of the font. He tried to dry the boy with his robe but Mokoto had stopped shivering and bore his tiny teeth at the fabric, irritated by the feel of it on his skin. King Taka smirked at Mokoto's boldness; he could feel the child's urge to tear at the robe and bite into the priest's flesh. He was pleased to see Mokoto reject help at such a young age. The God of War had blessed him; Mokoto was a fighter. Mokoto was fierce. Taka took Mokoto from the priest's arms and stared down at the boy with the same cold stare Mokoto had cowered away from before. Mokoto simply returned the gaze, looking into his father's dark eyes as callously as Taka looked into his. He felt the Footprints of his father burning onto him; he felt their darkness travelling through his soul. It hurt Mokoto, but he wouldn't look away. He wouldn't succumb to his fear. He had his own Footprints now.

Taka uttered a short, faint laugh and clutched the baby in his arms. It was a success. The God of War had answered him. Matat Mokoto Sota-Rokut, the most cold-hearted, ruthless and bloodthirsty king in Gaiamirákan history, was born.

II.

'The people of Gaiamiráka raced to Mount Gaiamira where their new leaders appeared to them. The first of the Gaiamira to step forward was Kala, the Goddess of Marriage and Unity. She preached about a world of love, peace and unity, and asked the people to live as timid beings who would never lay their hands upon another. Half of the people followed her willingly, and became known as Outsiders who turned their backs on the world of violence and devoted their lives to pacifism and kindness.'

-        Extract from the Gaiamirapon: 'The First Encounters'

*

"So Teima is pregnant again?" The memory of Suela's words echoed around King Taka's mind as he sat alone in his meeting room, recalling the conversation he'd had with Suela almost a year ago to the day. Mokoto was barely a cell in his mother's womb when his entire life was decided.
        "Yes. She is." Taka had answered his wife boldly. Challengingly, even.
        "Another half-breed? Even if it is a boy what do you hope to get from him? Teima's blood will ruin him before he's even hatched. Think about it, Sire."
        "I have, dear. Teima has a lot of males in her family. You have given me two daughters. Believe me, if that child is a boy I'll make him the greatest Hiveakan king that ever lived."
        "Better than you, Sire?"

"Yes." Taka spoke his answer aloud. Of course Mokoto would be better than him. Every Hiveakan king should surpass his predecessor; otherwise what point did his existence have at all?
        "So… Why don't we make a game of it?" Suela had spoken silkily, and she had looked at him with wickedness in her eyes. The way she always looked at him.

17

"Hm?"

"The girls are on different programs, aren't they? It's perfect. If this half-breed is going to be as good as you say he will he'll be the smartest and strongest Hiveakan that ever lived. He should have no problem defeating the pair of them."

"So he has to beat Anaka in brains and Lanka in strength?"

"Mm-hm."

"Fine. What do I win if he does?"

"Pride."

"Pride? ... I already have plenty of that." Taka smiled as he recalled his response and the way Suela had laughed at him. They always got on so well; they always had. The Footprints of the God of War bonded them, and they were close enough in age to have almost everything in common. There was only a year between them; exactly a year. Suela had been born on Taka's first birthday and they had lived in the Meitonákan Hive at the same time, although they had never met as children. Their relationship was an adult one; it was sexual and dangerous. Suela was skilled in the art of seduction and manipulation and she knew how to hold the king's interest in a way that none of his other wives could. In turn he ruled with power and authority, and spent every second of the day reminding her that he was the ultimate Hiveakan mate. The very least they did was get along; even their sense of humour was shared.

Taka tilted his head back against his chair and closed his eyes. He heard the door click open and listened closely to the sound of footsteps; there was not a single part of him that did not know who it was.

Speak of the evil. The footsteps belonged to Suela. Nobody else would ever dare enter his meeting room without knocking first; nobody else would dare stop in front of him without kneeling or speaking. She was challenging him, like she always did. Taka could feel her eyes on him; he knew the weight of her stare. He knew the thoughts in her mind.

Suela smirked down at Taka and folded her arms as she examined his form. Her playful eyes never tired of his image. Taka. *King* Taka... His name always sent shivers down her spine. Suela

18

adored how terrifying he was. There was not a single mortal in the world that wasn't afraid of him; there wasn't a single person in the palace that didn't freeze and crumble every time he met their eyes. He was powerful. He was dangerous. He was a born leader; Suela believed Taka had been destined to win the battle for the throne. He possessed something; it was an energy Thoit never had. It was a passion; an ambition. Taka *wanted* the throne more than his brother or anyone else could ever imagine. He had become one with it, and he would rip the throat out of anyone that tried to get within a mile of it. He could be such a violent man; Suela adored how easy Taka found it to shed another's blood. He was attractive. As if the Footprints in his soul weren't sexy enough, Taka possessed a handsome face and a muscular build. He was tall, around the same height as Thoit. Taka wasn't quite as wide or as bulky as his older brother; he had a naturally slimmer frame that would make him look weaker if he wasn't so much more aggressive than Thoit. Thoit could be violent, but he spent most of his time playing the role of a gentle giant. Taka on the other hand was an animal, and he looked his best when he was coated in another's blood. It was usually Suela's. Theirs wasn't the gentlest of sex lives, and Suela treated their encounters like a battle to the death. She loved to injure him, and she loved it when he slayed her.

Suela allowed her eyes to travel down the king's frame and they finally settled on the large glass of liquor in his hand. She sneered at him spitefully.

"That won't help you get your blood back," Suela sniped, highlighting Taka's one weakness and the only thing about him she did not adore. Nobody would think it to look at him, but Taka was a big drinker. This particular liquid, known as tetsa, had become his favourite over the past couple of years; it was almost pure ethanol and he drank it like water. His drinking had been getting worse and worse ever since he had become king, some ten years ago. Suela didn't know why, nor did she ever want to find out.

"He's welcome to it." Taka opened his eyes and stared up at her, a smirk forming on his coarse lips. "He needs it more than me."

"The half-breed?" Suela raised an eyebrow. "He needs ten pints more than you have in your whole body, just to cancel out hers."

19

She sat down in the chair opposite him. They were seated away from his desk, in front of a fireplace. The fire wasn't on right now; the room was warm enough. There was always a sense of burning in the air when Taka and Suela were alone together; it was as if their Footprints sparked a fire.

"Well, you of all people should know how much blood I have." Taka watched her laugh softly; she was amused by his remark. Suela liked Taka's wit, although she had to admit Thoit was always funnier. Thoit wasn't as good looking as Taka though. Very few people were.

"Where are the guests?" Taka asked his wife.

"Having an argument." Suela replied. "Thoit offered to walk Teima back to her room... Haliku wasn't impressed."

"Oh fantastic..." Taka closed his eyes again and let out a sigh. "Why did I let him bring her?"

"Because you're too soft." Suela was greeted by a half-hearted glare that made her grin vindictively.

"Soft?"

Taka chuckled to himself when he heard Thoit's angry voice entering the room.

"Trouble in paradise, brother?" he questioned.

"When I fucking go I'll fucking tell you." Thoit grumbled, taking a seat amongst his siblings. "You know... some people believe kings don't deserve paradise."

"Who believes that?" Suela questioned. Thoit looked at her and winked.

"Me."

"Oh, really?" Taka laughed, opening his eyes to look at Thoit.

"It's a fact." Thoit moved over to the fireplace and set it alight. "I don't know how you can sit here in this cold. It's fucking freezing."

"You've been in Hu Keizuaka too long," Suela teased.

"I don't care what the reason is. If I'm cold I'm cold. What does it matter why?" Thoit retreated back to his chair and settled into the warmth of the fire.

"Thoit," Suela began, looking at her brother. "You say kings don't deserve paradise? What about me? I'm not a king."

Thoit met her eyes with a mischievous grin and uttered,

20

"Accessories count."

Taka began to laugh loudly as Suela swung out her arm to strike Thoit. Thoit took the blow with a victorious grin, half-heartedly holding up his arm to defend himself.

Suela rolled her eyes and calmed down, and her lips formed into a small smirk.

"So, how is your wife?" she asked, watching Thoit's reaction. She was trying to get under his skin, as always. Suela found great pleasure in tormenting others, and she made no exception for her family and friends.

"Still fucking alive." Thoit growled. "Why did you have to mention her? I was enjoying myself."

"Haha!" Suela laughed. "You only have yourself to blame. Why did you even talk to Teima? You know what Haliku's like."

"The girl could barely stand!" Thoit protested. "She almost passed out during the yotuna – what was I supposed to do, leave her to the Gaiamira? She was fucking pregnant this morning."

"Tch. So what?" Suela scoffed. "I was in the gym four hours after giving birth to Lanka – and I was in the gym two hours after Anaka."

"Well, why don't you save yourself some time, Su," Thoit replied. "Have your next child in the fucking gym."

Suela shot Thoit a nasty glare, ignoring the sound of Taka's laughter. The pair of them were idiots when they were together. All Thoit seemed to do was make stupid remarks and all Taka seemed to do was laugh at them. Thoit winked at Suela, silently asking for her forgiveness before turning his attention towards his clothing. He dipped his hand into his pocket and looked at Taka inquisitively.

"Can I smoke?" Thoit asked.

"Why are you asking, Thoit?" Taka replied, his tone turning serious. He narrowed his eyes at the older man and spoke with caution. "Are you carrying something you shouldn't be?"

"Yes." Thoit smirked at Taka and pulled out a packet of cigarettes. They contained tonito; it was an illegal drug in Keizuaka, as it had been in Thoit's continent until he'd started smoking it. Taka had permitted Thoit to legalise the drug in certain areas across Hu Keizuaka, with Thoit's home country Soan being one of them. Taka looked at his brother sternly and then sighed.

"Go on." He spoke with a mature authority as if he were a headmaster and Thoit were a disobedient schoolboy he'd decided not to cane. "But if anyone comes in, it goes out."

"Yes, Sire," Thoit replied and withdrew a cigarette.

"Is your life really that bad, Thoit?" Suela playfully taunted. "It's your nephew's yotuna and you still need to get high?"

"It makes you wonder, doesn't it?" Thoit answered, raising an eyebrow at her as he put the cigarette packet back in his pocket.

"Don't worry, Thoit," Taka soothed and took a large sip of his liquor. "One day you'll be dead."

"Taka… Have you ever thought about joining the Kala temple? You'd be a fucking hero," Thoit replied, causing Suela to laugh.

*

'Reports from the palace this morning have confirmed that the next child of King Taka will be a boy! Keika Teima returned from her three-month scan two days ago which confirmed the sex of the baby, who will be born later this year. The matat remains unnamed at the moment, but as he is King Taka's first son there is little doubt that he will be given a traditional Hiveakan name. A spokesperson for the royal palace has confirmed the matat will be put in the Hive immediately following his birth.'

\-   News report, 20103G

*

Elsewhere in the world, Mokoto was being held a prisoner in the dark depths of the Hive. He was so close to his family. The Hive was built in a circle around Meitona Palace's grounds and Mokoto had no idea how close he was to the warmth and comfort of his mother's room. He didn't need to know. He wouldn't feel his mother's warmth. Not here. He wasn't entitled to warmth; he wasn't entitled to comfort.

22

Such things would make him weak. Pain and suffering would make him strong; and they were all he would be given for as long as he lived there. Mokoto was alone in his room. He was freezing. The air had been chilled around him; the smell of death and blood flooded his nostrils. He needed to become accustomed to it; he needed to learn not to be afraid of death. He needed to learn how to withstand the cold. Mokoto heard noises sometimes; he heard voices. He cried out to them but they didn't answer. They weren't here to speak to him; they were here to frighten him. There was no light in the room; light would ruin his training. His tutors wanted him to listen. They wanted him to feel the movements in the air. They wanted him to be fully aware of his surroundings even in the darkest of darks. His eyes would become a luxury; he would learn how to live his life blind.

Mokoto was hungry. His lips hurt. He screamed mercilessly, infuriated by the pain of his hunger and the tightness of his burned skin. His setules were raised. Mokoto's, like every Gaiamirákan's body was covered in tiny setules. They grew along his palms and fingers, on his knees, and on the undersides of his arms and legs. They were designed for climbing walls and gripping slippery surfaces and couldn't usually be seen when they weren't being used. Their erection was a response to stress; it was a response to fear. Eventually he would learn to keep them under control.

He was being closely monitored. Mokoto didn't know it, but he was being watched by a team of Hiveakan tutors who knew just how much torture he could withstand. They knew he was hungry; they knew he was screaming to be fed but they wouldn't feed him. Not yet. They were starving him deliberately. It was one of the many tactics they would use to create obedience; Mokoto had to learn that he wouldn't get anything by asking for it. He would be fed when it suited his tutors no matter how loud he cried or how hungry he felt. They wouldn't kill him, but they would hurt him. They would make it feel like he was dying. Eventually Mokoto would become accustomed to this level of torture and he would grow immune to it. When that happened his tutors would use other means to make him suffer.

Mokoto's night guardians came and went; they left him wailing for as long as he could manage until he finally cried himself into a troubled sleep. He slept for just a few hours before he was abruptly awoken the next day. The lights came on and the room was filled suddenly with an intense brightness that stung Mokoto's eyes. A tall man harshly grabbed the infant; he held him firmly in his arms and pinched Mokoto's skin to snatch the child from his dreams. Mokoto was tired and whimpering; he closed his eyes and flinched away from the light. The man pinched him again, forcing Mokoto to pay attention to the bottle in his hand. He was offering Mokoto food, and the infant's starved body told him he had to take it. The Hiveakan nanny shoved a cold bottle into Mokoto's mouth without uttering a word. Mokoto spluttered a little at first, startled by the cold. He took a disliking to the bottle and resisted the feeding in an attempt to get back to sleep. His efforts were futile. The nanny crushed Mokoto's body in his arms, sending a heavy pain through the child's limbs. He held Mokoto firmly and continued to push the bottle into his mouth, almost choking Mokoto until the infant finally started to drink the ice-cold milk he'd spent hours crying for. The young matat sucked on the bottle; his eyebrows furrowed slightly as the coldness of the liquid hurt his injured tongue and he tried to cry. He attempted to pull his head away and uttered a hostile snarl at the bottle he had so quickly learned to hate. The nanny held Mokoto in place and glared down at the child with the same dark look Mokoto had received from his own father. Mokoto met the nanny's eyes and he backed down, reluctantly submitting to the nanny's demands. He was too weak to argue. He drank the cold milk until he was full and he tried to pull away but the nanny wouldn't allow it; he pushed the bottle further into Mokoto's mouth and tilted back the infant's head to force him to swallow the rest of the liquid. Mokoto coughed, almost choking on the unwelcome milk. Its taste was hideous. It didn't taste like mother's milk; it wasn't something Mokoto's body had been programmed to crave. It was foreign to Mokoto. It was disturbing. It was all he was allowed.

Mokoto started to growl as his carer made him finish the bottle, still not uttering a word of kindness or comfort to the distressed infant. Mokoto didn't understand that he had to drink it all; it was laced with all the drugs, vitamins and minerals needed to make him into a strong Hiveakan man. The child started to sob in agony, but his nanny simply

24

gazed down at Mokoto without a scrap of sympathy. He grew more and more impatient with every second it took for Mokoto to finish his breakfast. It was taking too long. Something had to be done about it. If Mokoto couldn't finish the entire bottle in less than a minute by the end of the week his skin would be ripped off and he would be starved of food until he could learn to eat more quickly. King Taka had been adamant he only wanted the best treatment for Mokoto, and the best treatment was exactly what Mokoto was going to get. He would have only the cruellest tutors and he would eat only the most poisonous of foods, and he would grow to believe he had spent the first years of his life in the Hive's version of luxury. It was a luxury that had been given to his father and his Hiveakan sisters; it was a luxury that was part of his birthright; it was his reward for being of royal blood. His blood would entitle him to only the very highest levels of pain. His blood broke his mother's heart.

Teima had never felt such regret in her life. She had never wished so much that her husband could be poorer and her son less entitled to the sort of high class treatment he would receive. She had been watching Mokoto all night with tears in her eyes. She was exhausted and weak; her eyes were red and her skin was so pale she looked as if the Goddess of Death would claim her at any moment. Her entire body cried out for rest and nourishment but she didn't dare take her eyes off her son. She couldn't leave him there, and she didn't care that her baby had no idea his mother was so close to him.

Teima could only look at Mokoto from a private observation gallery above his room. All parents were entitled to view their children as often as they wished, but from a distance. They couldn't enter the child's room; they couldn't talk to them or touch them, and the child would never have any idea that they were there. They watched from above, separated from their child by a one-way mirror. It broke Teima's heart that she couldn't be with him. She wanted to feed him herself; she wanted to hold him. He was her baby. He shouldn't be with anyone except her. She watched him with damp eyes and quivering lips, traumatised and drained by the cruelness of the Hive.

"He's had enough…" Teima whimpered and turned to her husband. "Tell that man he's had enough!"

25

"He hasn't had enough." Taka didn't meet her eyes as he watched his son feeding. He hadn't been here long. Teima had spent the night in the observation room but Taka had only joined her a few minutes ago, accompanied by Suela. "That tutor knows what he's doing. How many children do you think he's raised here, Teima? You only have one."

"That's the same man that took care of Anaka and Lanka." Suela stepped towards the glass wall and gazed down at her stepson's nanny with admiration in her eyes. Suela never forgot a face, and she held a certain warmth for anyone that managed to gain her respect. She looked at Teima with a cold smirk, her dark eyes twinkling with malice. "Don't worry. He's good," Suela said. "Anaka spat out some of her food once and he peeled off her skin. He did it so carefully it didn't even scar. It was just the top layer." Suela's smirk grew wider as she watched a wave of terror sweep across Teima's face. The life drained from the younger woman's eyes and she looked as if she would die. She started to shake; her lips turned colourless.

"Oh…" she choked. "You –"

"Hey." Taka moved over to put his arms around Teima, catching the weight of her body as her knees collapsed under her. He held Teima against him and trailed his claws lightly through her hair. Taka shot Suela an angry glance, his Footprints burning with rage. "She might be carrying another boy soon," he seethed. "Don't make her infertile." He turned his attention back to Teima and listened to the soft sound of her sobs, irritated by the fact that he now had to deal with her. "Don't cry." Taka spoke soothingly, as if her happiness was a genuine concern of his. "She's lying. You know how Suela plays."

Suela watched the scene in amazement. She was gobsmacked. That couldn't have just happened… Had Taka really scolded her for tormenting an Outsider? He never did that. He had no right to do that! Suela's cheeks burned a little as she started to feel embarrassed. Taka was making her feel like a fool. How dare he do this! Suela hadn't done anything wrong; it wasn't her fault Teima was weak. It wasn't her fault the feeble little Outsider couldn't handle the ways of the Hive. The Hive was nothing to be ashamed of, nor was it anything to lie about. Suela really had witnessed that man rip off her daughter's skin

26

with her own eyes – was she supposed to pretend that never happened just to make Teima feel better? Why should *she* accommodate Teima? Suela was here first. This was her territory; their home was her palace. Teima was the one that needed to adjust. Teima was the one that was too weak to handle her own husband – and her own son. Teima was the one in the wrong.

Suela moved her eyes to Taka. He was looking down at Teima softly, waiting for her tears to stop rolling. Impossible… Suela felt her stomach tighten as she tried to make sense of the scene in front of her. Taka never behaved like that. He wasn't gentle; he wasn't compassionate… He was a violent Hiveakan animal! That was part of his charm! That was why Suela liked him! It was also why he liked her… Taka had never chosen Teima over Suela before; he had never chosen anyone over Suela before. Why would he? Suela was his best friend; she was his comrade. She knew how to please him; she knew how to speak to him. She knew how to treat him, and she had given him two Hiveakan children. Why was he taking Teima's side now? What possible reason could he have to choose Teima over *anyone*, let alone Suela? Suela tensed a little as a troubling thought entered her mind. The baby… Nothing else was different, except that Teima had given Taka a son. He'd always wanted a boy. Was that what this was about now? Was Teima suddenly worth more because her baby had a penis? Suela couldn't believe it. She couldn't believe that Taka was going to make her – *her* – fight for her right to rule the palace. Did he really want to start this war? Surely he knew that Suela wouldn't lose? She never lost anything! Well, fine. If Taka wanted to play rivals, then rivals they would play. It seemed fitting actually; Teima's son was a rival to Suela's daughters, so why shouldn't Teima be a rival to Suela? This would be fun. Suela liked to play games, and there was no doubt in her mind that she would win.

Suela braced herself and moved closer to Teima, putting a gentle hand on the woman's shoulder. She didn't wear her best fake smile; she made a point of not wearing it. That was how easy this would be.

"I'm sorry," Suela uttered sincerely. She could feel Taka's eyes on her. She knew he was judging her. Of course he was; he

27

wanted to make sure Suela would obey him. Naturally. Suela wanted Taka to watch this; she wanted him to see how quickly she could manipulate Teima. She wanted to show off how easily she could make friends. Suela squeezed Teima's shoulder lightly and spoke with a soft tone. "You do know I was joking, right? I just… thought you would find it funny."

"Oh…" Teima swallowed, wiping her eyes. "Well… No, I… I thought you were…" She shifted slightly and offered Suela an awkward smile. She was embarrassed. How adorable. "I'm sorry," Teima whimpered sheepishly. "I guess I – I don't understand…"

"My type?" Suela raised an eyebrow at her.

"Sorry!" Teima gasped, her eyes widening. "I didn't mean –"

"Don't worry." Suela smiled warmly. She stroked Teima's arm and lightly squeezed the younger woman's hand. "It's okay. I know we're different. Maybe you'll understand your boy more. Look." She nodded down at Mokoto, who was now being placed back in his crib; the milk bottle was empty. "He's eaten all of his breakfast. They'll reward him for that."

"Really?" Teima looked at Suela hopefully, her eyes sparkling.

"Of course," Suela lied to her. No. They didn't give rewards in the Hive, only punishments. Teima didn't have to know that though. Sweet, naïve little Teima had to believe everything was okay, otherwise her head might explode and she might drown in her own blood. Why would anyone want that?

Suela looked over at Taka and he met her eyes with a pardoning glance. He uttered a low grunt and removed his arms from around Teima.

"Come on," he instructed. "Now that we're all friends again… I have work to do." He moved towards the door and waited impatiently for them to join him. They only had a few seconds before he would leave without them.

"Coming, Sire," Suela purred with a slight sarcasm to her voice. She took a step towards him and stopped dead in her tracks. She could feel something… Teima had grabbed her hand. Suela turned to look at the younger woman and Teima greeted her with large

28

welcoming eyes and a bright smile. It was the kind of smile that Outsiders sang about; the kind that Suela detested.

"Friends?" Teima beamed.

"Mm." Suela could barely formulate a response. It took every ounce of strength in her body to make her smile back, but she did it successfully. It warmed Teima, so much that Suela could feel the gentle heat of Teima's soul smothering her being. She could feel the softness of Teima's skin burning her hand as if she were allergic to it. Suela's claws itched and her tongue tingled with bloodlust as she mercilessly battled every Hiveakan instinct in her body, forcing herself to resist the urge to rip out Teima's eyes and feed them to her half-breed son.

III.

'Taka smirked down at his child and uttered darkly, "Love is a weakness, but it is not a curse. A good Hiveakan is not one who never falls in love, but one who overcomes it. If you can free yourself of love then your heart will turn to stone, and you will be even stronger than before".'

-    Extract from the Gaiamirapon: 'The Communications'

*

It was early in the morning, two days after Mokoto's yotuna. The autumn air chilled Suela's skin as she stood in the vast piece of land that was Meitona Palace's garden. She was with her husband; they had come outside to bid farewell to Thoit. It would probably be another month or two at least before they saw him again; the New Year festival would be their next compulsory reunion. Suela liked seeing Thoit; she was always guaranteed some form of entertainment when he was around. Thoit and Haliku were arguing again. He had followed her into his jet just a few minutes ago, shivering in the Meitonákan cold and cursing wildly at her. Now they were on their way home, and Suela wore a small smirk on her lips as she watched her marital brother disappear into the distance. There would be an atmosphere on that jet all the way home; Suela almost felt sorry for the pilot. Almost. Thoit's and Haliku's constant bickering never failed to amuse her, especially when they bickered about such trivial things. Haliku wanted to visit their daughter Teisumi in the Soanakan Hive when they got home, and she wanted Thoit to accompany her. It wasn't an unreasonable request... but Thoit had said no, and Haliku hated that word. Thoit had no plans to see his child today; he knew his presence in the Hive would have no impact on Teisumi's life or wellbeing. His animals on the other hand had gone for two days without him, and apparently they were pining for him as much as Thoit was pining for them. Thoit had thousands of animals; the once beautiful gardens of his palace had become no more than a wild jungle that was home to a vast array of

30

rare and exotic creatures, most of them dangerous. He had an aviary on his roof and he had several rooms in his palace that were unfit for any Gaiamirákan to inhabit. The rooms were filled with fish tanks, vivariums, loose reptiles, dog baskets, cat toys, straw… A large portion of Soan Palace wasn't fit for people anymore, but the parts of it that were, were without doubt some of the most breathtaking examples of architecture in the world. The building was mesmerising, even if it was nothing more than a beautiful zoo.

Haliku hated the zoo. She adored the beauty of Soan Palace and she detested the mess that Thoit's animals made of it. If she had the chance she would slay every one of them and burn their bodies to ash, and that was precisely what she told Thoit when he refused to see her daughter. It was what she told Thoit on a regular basis, every time his animals got in her way. Thoit always responded with aggression, much to Suela's amusement. They were as bad as each other, and they got a little worse every time.

"How long do you think before he kills her?" Suela asked as she watched Thoit's jet disappear from the Meitonákan sky.

"He won't kill her. He's not the type," Taka answered from his wife's side. "But give it a few more years… He might kill himself."

"Haha!" Suela laughed. "That would be very dishonourable, Taka."

"I think he would rather die in dishonour than live in it," Taka replied. "Either way the Gaiamira won't forgive him."

"I suppose you're right…" Suela smiled. She waited for a moment, deliberately giving Taka enough time to feel comfortable with her. Then she looked at him with seriousness on her face; with caution. "Do you think they will forgive you?" Suela questioned.

"Me?" Taka looked at her.

"It's easier than you think for a Hiveakan to lose his way," Suela said. "Especially when certain… 'things' get under their skin."

"What are you talking about?" Taka growled. He followed Suela's eyes towards the Outsider woman that was sitting on the grass a few feet away from them. It was Teima. She was with her eldest child, Taka's four-year-old Outsider daughter Oreisaka, helping her make a necklace out of the autumn flowers that grew beneath them. Taka

31

rested his eyes on Teima for a moment and looked back at Suela. He stared at her angrily, daring her to speak another word. He knew what she wanted to say. Of course Suela would think of something like that! Anything to discredit Teima. Taka wondered if Suela would have the courage to say it. How dare she make such an accusation of him! How dare she even *think* such a thing!

"You invited her to see Thoit off." Suela spoke calmly, not the least bit intimidated by Taka's powerful demeanour. She wanted to unnerve him.

"So?" Taka snarled. "He's her brother. He's that child's uncle. What's the problem, Su?"

"Nothing, Sire," Suela replied. "I'm just wondering... You barely speak to her. You never invited her to anything before. Why are things so different now?"

"They aren't different!" Taka barked. "But she is valuable. She can give me a son – that's more than you could ever do!"

"If that's all it is then I suppose you have nothing to worry about," Suela answered with a precarious turn to her lips. "I'm just warning you, before it becomes a problem..." She moved closer to him and trailed her claw up his arm, so delicately it didn't even cut the fibres of his shirt. She looked into his eyes and held her lips slightly apart, nurturing the venom of her tongue. "Be careful, Sire," Suela uttered. "Girls like that can get under your skin."

"... Shut up," Taka spat. "You're talking shit, and I have work to do." He shrugged her hand off him with such force it made Suela flinch. She wore a smirk on her lips as he stormed past her towards the palace. That was it. He was paranoid. Suela didn't need to say another word; all she had to do now was wait. Taka would do it all on his own.

Suela turned her head to the feeling of soft eyes on her. She looked over to see Teima smiling at her brightly, with a hint of concern on her face.

"Everything okay?" Teima mouthed. Suela grinned to herself. How cute. Yes, Teima. Everything was okay. Everything was *perfect.* Suela nodded at her new best friend and flashed the woman a reassuring smile, and then she turned to escape into the palace before Teima could invite her to play family.

'A spokesperson for the royal palace has finally confirmed the name of the soon to be born son of King Taka. The matat, who will be a Hiveakan, will be named Mokoto (Invincible), certainly a fitting name for any Hiveakan king. Matat Mokoto is due to be born next month, and palace officials have confirmed he will be one of three heirs to the throne, alongside his older sisters Meitat Lanka and Meitat Anaka, the Hiveakan daughters of Keika Suela.'

-　　　News report, 20103G

*

"Isn't he cute?" The Hiveakan tutor Suna sighed as she watched the infant Mokoto. They were in the depths of the Hive; she and her colleague Aourat had been standing over Mokoto since the early hours of the morning, carefully watching him for signs of heart failure. It would be up to them to determine whether he was worth saving; the king had given them that power. Mokoto was lying in a crib of ice. He was shivering wildly and his yellow skin was pale. His setules were raised and he flinched occasionally, trying to break away from the machine that monitored his vitals. He was connected to the machine with a band that was strapped tightly to his wrist; he had been reluctant to wear it and had spent the first few minutes of his torture session trying to chew it away. Sometimes he still battled it, and Suna giggled every time he did. There was another band strapped around Mokoto's head; it didn't seem to bother him, but it was the source of his pain. Upon the band were several metallic nodes that occasionally sent tiny jolts of electricity through his skin, causing Mokoto to snarl and hiss into the air. He gritted his teeth and waved his claws, trying to fight the unseen force that was hurting him.

　　　"Cute?" Aourat looked at Suna.

　　　"I like them at this age." Suna smiled. "They don't argue. They just cry for a while, and then they submit."

"So do the older ones." Aourat frowned.

"But you know the older ones are thinking," Suna replied. "These don't."

"You don't want them to think?" Aourat looked at her questionably, disturbed by her response.

"I don't want them to judge." Suna looked at Aourat with a stern glance, telling him to back off. Aourat rolled his eyes and looked back at Mokoto.

"If they're judging you badly then you aren't teaching them right," he scolded. "You remember your tutors don't you? Do you think any of them ever did anything wrong?"

"No…" Suna mumbled.

"See." Aourat smirked a little. "You're paranoid, love."

"It's not my fault!" Suna argued. "I think too much. My parents wanted me to be paranoid – they asked the Hive to make me that way!"

"That's creepy." Aourat shook his head, frowning in disapproval. "Some people just shouldn't have kids." He approached Mokoto's monitor and looked at the figures on the screen. "His tolerance to pain has risen."

"By how much?"

"Thirty per cent…" Aourat let out a sigh. "Still not good enough. The king wants us to make his kid immortal."

"How are we supposed to do that?" Suna moaned. "We aren't magicians."

"No," Aourat replied confidently. "But we're engineers." He grabbed one of the two chunky dials on the machine and turned it up, increasing the frequency and the intensity of the jolts to Mokoto's head. Mokoto screamed in pain and burst into tears as the pain became unbearable. He started thrashing his arms and legs violently, hissing wildly at his attackers. His eyes burned with anger as they struggled to withstand the pain; he bore his tiny fangs fiercely and his setules trembled under the power of his rage. "Wow, what a fighter!" Aourat exclaimed as he watched Mokoto's berserk flailing. He sneered down at Mokoto and pinched the infant's foot, causing Mokoto to kick back

with all the ferocity of the God of War. "Sorry, Your Highness."
Aourat grinned. "It's for your own good."

"How cute…" Suna smiled at the infant, her eyes glowing with
a twisted sort of maternal warmth.

*

'Although their relationship was strained at first, shortly after
Mokoto's birth Keika Suela formed a small friendship with Keika
Teima. This friendship was short-lived however, when King Taka
started to develop inappropriate feelings for Teima.'

-      Extract from history textbook: 'The Wives of Taka', 20174G

*

Tap. Tap. Tap. Taka's foot patted harshly against the floor; his
claws banged rhythmically against his desk. He was frustrated. He was
angry. He was concerned. Three days had gone by since Suela had
made her ridiculous remark. Taka knew it was ridiculous. He knew
Teima was no threat to him or his brutality… but he hadn't been able
to shake the thought of it out of his mind. Suela's words had clung to
him like poison, travelling viciously through his blood and spreading
their bile into his soul. He wondered why she had spoken them. He
wondered what had possessed her to make such a remark. Suela like to
play. She liked to torment those around her; she liked to manipulate…
but she wasn't a traitor. She wasn't a liar. She was a comrade. She was
a friend. She had been a loyal wife to Taka for ten years. Her words
had value, even when they were spoken in bitterness or jest. That was
the core of Taka's concern. How much could he believe her? Or more
importantly, could he afford not to?

Taka hadn't spoken to Suela about it, nor had he spoken to
anyone else. The last thing Taka wanted was for people to know he
might be… suffering. What if he wasn't? This could all be a
misunderstanding; Suela could be wrong. She was definitely wrong;
Taka didn't do things like that. He wasn't capable of it. Then again…

35

did he really know what it felt like? Did he know the signs? Would he be able to recognise if he was infected, even if he was? He couldn't take the risk. He had been trying for three days to convince himself Teima was worth the risk. Teima was valuable. Teima could produce boys. Teima was easy to control… Teima was sweet. Teima had weak blood… and Teima had poisoned him. And more importantly, she would poison their son. *His* son. She would destroy the hardness of Mokoto's heart; she would wipe the Footprints from his soul. She would betray him, the same way she had betrayed Taka. It was treason. To make a Hiveakan weak; to make a Hiveakan feel love or… other Outsider things… it was illegal. It was against the God of War and it was against the laws of the mortals. It was treason when committed against a king, and treason was punishable by death. Did Teima deserve to die…? That depended on whether or not she had tainted Taka; it depended on whether or not he loved her. He didn't know. He had no idea how he would know. All he knew was that lately he had been kinder to her, and he didn't know why. He hadn't even noticed – Suela had noticed, and it was a blessing from the Gaiamira that she had. How much would Teima have tainted Taka's soul if Suela hadn't been there? How much of him would Teima have changed if Suela hadn't been there to warn him of what a danger she was? How far would it have gone? Would it have reached Mokoto? Teima could destroy Mokoto. Taka couldn't allow that. It was unacceptable that she had started to destroy him – it was unacceptable that she had even been able to destroy him. Taka was angry at himself for being so weak; he was angry at himself for allowing her to… 'get under his skin'. It wouldn't happen again. It shouldn't have happened at all. He had to fix it. He had to do something to regain his brutality and repent to the God of War. If he didn't, he didn't deserve to bear Taka's name.

Taka let out a heavy sigh and looked down at the empty glass in front of him. He poured himself another drink from the bottle in his hand and drank it slowly, and then he started to pour again. The bottle was half empty; he'd consumed a large amount in the two hours he'd been sitting there. It was justified. He could think more clearly when he'd had something to drink. When he was in the right state of mind the tetsa tasted like blood… It was Teima's blood now. Taka brought the glass to his lips and threw the liquid into his mouth. It was thick and sweet, like the liquid he would drain from her. His bloodlust burned inside of him as he thought about his decision; his Footprints rose excitedly and danced with anticipation at the thought of taking another's life. The more he thought about it the more appealing it became... Taka wanted to do this. He longed to spill the blood of an Outsider, and what better Outsider than her? One who had betrayed him; one who threatened to destroy him and his child... Taka licked the tetsa from his lips and pulled his phone out of his pocket. He called Suela and waited impatiently, his anger rising with every second it took for her to answer the phone.

"Hello, Sire," Suela's silky voice greeted him after far too long a wait.

"I'm going to kill Teima," Taka said bluntly. He waited for a moment and smirked at the sound of her silence. He could hear the shortness of her breath; he could feel the parting of her lips as she uttered a single word.

"Now?" Suela breathed.

"Soon," Taka answered. "Do you want me to save some of her blood for you?"

"Yes." Suela spoke with gratitude; she was becoming captivated by his power. He knew the thought of Teima's murder would drive her wild.

"Okay," Taka replied calmly. "See you later." He hung up on her and poured himself another drink, then called out to his aide. "Rozo!" Taka roared. "Come here! Now!"

IV.

'Then, after Kala's Outsiders had chosen their paths the sky darkened, and with a bolt of lightning the mighty God of War, Taka rose from the depths of the earth with the blood of the weak upon his hands. He stood beside her and preached about a world of battle, strength, victory and loyalty, and with a mighty roar he commanded all the warriors of the world to follow him and worship him, and to raise their children to serve him. The rest of the people followed him willingly and devoted their lives to becoming undefeated warriors who would never be afraid, and who would lead their planet to greatness; and thus, the Hive was born.'

-        Extract from the Gaiamirapon: 'The First Encounters'

*

Clink. The liquid fell like a waterfall cascading down the mountain's face and crashing onto the rocks below; the rocks that were the ice in Taka's glass. He poured the dark tetsa from its bottle with impatience and desperation, angry at how long it took to fill the glass. King Taka didn't have a great deal of patience at the best of times, and especially not now. Not now that he had blood on his mind. Taka had barely stopped pouring before he downed the full amount of the drink with the bottle still in his hand. He didn't even stop to breathe before he filled the glass again. He filled it with more patience this time and he drank with less desperation, as if he had suddenly become aware of himself and was trying determinedly to keep his hated weakness under control. It was a struggle, but he managed it. Taka drank slowly and calmly, breathing away the bloodlust that had flared up in his soul. He couldn't do anything yet… He needed Rozo's help first.

As Taka seemed to calm slightly his fearful aide Rozo began to relax. The man attempted a smile, and looked at the king with concern.

"Forgive me for commenting, Sire…" he began, "but perhaps you shouldn't drink so quickly. Tetsa is so strong –"

"I do not recall asking for your advice on this matter, Rozo." Taka shot the smaller man an angry glare that made it quite clear the aide would not be given a second chance. Rozo swallowed nervously and nodded, his eyes flooding with panic.

"I – I'm sorry, Sire," he whimpered. "Please forgive me."

"No. I won't," Taka answered. "But I'll let you live. How's that?"

"Thank you," Rozo uttered. Taka smirked at him mockingly, feeding on the smaller man's fear. Rozo was pathetic; so much so that it was amusing. How could anybody live like that? How could anybody be so afraid?

"I always was a good negotiator," Taka stated, still holding his bold expression. "Wouldn't you agree?"

Sire, you're famous for getting your way, Rozo thought. He didn't dare say it. He simply nodded. "Of course, Sire."

"Good…" Taka turned his attention back to his drink and topped up his glass. He didn't drink any of it. He just stared at it, as if it held the answer to something. He was playing on Rozo's fears.

Rozo's tension grew as he watched his master; the king's silence was unnerving. There was something wrong; Rozo could feel it. Ever since Malatsa Thoit had left, King Taka had been drifting in and out of thought. He never told Rozo what he was thinking about and he never paid attention when Rozo tried to coax him out of his daze. Not that Rozo tried very hard. Rozo knew better than to rush the king, or try to control him. Rozo had only survived this long by being patient and submissive; it was the way Taka liked all his employees. It was the way Taka liked everyone.

Rozo's eyes shifted when Taka finally took hold of his glass. He raised his glass to his lips and spilt the entire contents of it into his mouth. He swallowed the liquid slowly and with caution, careful not to allow any of the ice cubes to slip down his throat. Taka held the cubes on his tongue and crunched them between his sharp teeth. The sound sent a shiver down Rozo's spine; somehow it felt like the king was practicing for something. Why was he eating the ice cubes? He crunched them firmly but slowly, as if he were savouring them. Why was he doing that…? Why had he called Rozo in here? There were no

39

papers in front of him; there was no political matter that needed to be urgently discussed. Why was Rozo here…?

"Rozo," Taka echoed, pushing one of the cubes forward to hold it between his lips. He seemed to enjoy the coldness; he almost looked comforted by it. Perhaps it reminded him of the Hive. Why would he need to feel the Hive now? What was going on…?

"Yes, Sire?" Rozo obediently replied.

"Do you trust me?"

"What?" Rozo blinked in confusion. "Sire –"

"You heard me, Rozo," Taka cut him off. He looked at the younger man sternly and swallowed the last of the crushed cubes, before refilling his glass. "This is very important," he said. "You have known me for thirteen years. You served my father – he was good to you, wasn't he?"

"Yes, Sire." Rozo nodded. "I only wish I had known him longer."

"And have I been good to you?" Taka questioned.

"Well… Yes, Sire. Of course." Rozo answered nervously, his tension growing. This didn't sound good… Why was the king asking him these questions?

"So…" Taka began. "If I tell you something that is… rather delicate, can I rely on you to trust my judgement?"

"Yes…" Rozo answered. "Of course, Sire." He didn't trust the king. No, not at all! The fact that King Taka was even asking for Rozo's trust was proof that he could *not* be trusted! But what else could Rozo say? The king would kill him if he argued.

"Good."

Taka leaned back in his chair and let out a sigh. "I believe one of my clan is betraying me," he stated. "What do you suggest I do?" Ah… Right, okay. Rozo calmed a little, relieved that he finally knew why he was here. The king wanted his advice; he probably wanted Rozo to recommend the execution of a traitor. Who could that be? Who could possibly be foolish enough to betray King Taka?

"Could you…" Rozo cleared his throat. "Could you explain, Sire?"

"Teima," Taka answered. "She's trying to destroy me."

40

"Oh... Sire!" Rozo started to laugh. "You know – for a moment I thought you were –" He stopped in mid-sentence when he noticed the look of seriousness on Taka's face. "... You aren't serious?" Rozo's jaw dropped. Gods, had the king gone mad? *Teima*? She didn't have a nasty bone in her body! This was a joke, wasn't it? It had to be!

"She's trying to stain me, Rozo," Taka said. "That would be classed as treason, wouldn't it?"

"Well... yes," Rozo awkwardly agreed. "Under Act 1 of the global Hiveakan law it is an offence to try to stain a Hiveakan's character –"

"To knowingly and willingly cause a Hiveakan to think, act or behave in a way that is contrary to the Hive's teachings; whether by force, manipulation or any other means in which the Hiveakan is unaware of the controversial consequences of such means." Taka smirked at Rozo, after quoting the law word for word. "Isn't that right?"

"Yes..." Rozo nodded. "But, Sire, I really don't think Teima – "

"She is changing me, Rozo," Taka said. "I know my own mind. And I know recently it... hasn't been the same." He paused for a moment and lowered his eyes. "This is a very delicate matter... You understand I don't want anybody to know about this?" He moved his eyes up to meet Rozo's. "This could be very... 'damaging' for me – and therefore, damaging for you."

"I... I suppose it could..." Rozo shrivelled under the weight of the king's stare. Damaging for him? What was that supposed to mean?

"I am not just concerned for myself," Taka continued. "You have to understand... If she can do this to me, what could she do to my son?"

"Sire..." Rozo sighed. "I appreciate your concern, but I simply can't picture Teima as a traitor. Surely this is a misunderstanding?"

"Mm," Taka grunted. Rozo swallowed nervously as Taka turned his attention down to his drink and stared at it. He just stared at it, without speaking or moving. Why was he doing that? Did the king want Rozo to say something? What was Rozo supposed to say?

41

Taka waited for what seemed like an eternity; he waited for as long as it took to unnerve Rozo. He wanted his aide to feel uncomfortable. He needed Rozo to agree with him; he needed Rozo to recommend Teima's execution. It would make it so much easier for Taka if his advisor told him to murder his wife. Rozo wouldn't do it though. Not easily, anyway. Taka had suspected as much. There wasn't a single Outsider in the palace that didn't adore Teima, and Rozo was one of her biggest fans. The man would need some… 'unsavoury' convincing. It was a shame. Taka had hoped he wouldn't need to resort to that; he had hoped that Rozo's loyalty to him was great enough that Taka wouldn't need to play on the man's fear… But Rozo wasn't loyal enough. Clearly. Perhaps he himself deserved to be executed. Taka smiled slightly as the thought crossed his mind. No… As much as he would like to take Rozo's life, he needed Rozo. Rozo was useful, and he was a good aide, and Taka's late father would curse him if he ever tried to murder Rozo for such a low form of treason. For now, Teima's blood was enough.

Taka took a small sip of his drink and continued to stare at it as he held it against the desk. He spoke calmly and quietly, carefully selecting each and every word. "Like I said…" Taka began. "I know my own mind. I know she has changed it… and I think she wanted to. That would be classed as treason."

"Yes…" Rozo nodded. "But, Sire –"

"And my biggest concern is for my son." Taka looked at his aide. "I was hoping you could understand that, Rozo. You have a son of your own, don't you? An infant?"

Rozo's blood froze as a sudden jolt of fear shot through his heart. Why… Why was the king saying that? What did this have to do with Rozo's child…?

"How old is your son?" Taka asked, his eyes fixed on Rozo. He was studying the smaller man; he was watching his reaction. Rozo looked afraid.

"F… Four months," Rozo choked. "Sire –"

"And he is your first son, isn't he?" Taka questioned. "What is his name? Rozo, isn't it? After you?"

"Yes…" Rozo answered robotically, his body numb with fear.

42

"A good name for your first born," Taka commented. "So what would you do if you were in my position, Rozo?" he asked. "If someone was a threat to your son. You would want to do whatever it takes, wouldn't you? To ensure that they do not harm him." He looked at Rozo sternly and forced himself not to smirk as he saw a look of horror engulf the man's face. Yes, Rozo... This is what it has come to. Is Teima really that important to you? "And she won't just threaten me and Mokoto," Taka said. "She's befriended Suela – which means she is a threat to Suela as well. My wife. Imagine having someone that didn't just threaten you, but they threatened your son, and your wife... Rozo and Toloki." He raised his eyebrows at Rozo. "I am remembering her name correctly, am I not?"

"Yes..." Rozo whimpered. No, no... This couldn't be happening! Please... The king was *not* saying this!

"And if they were in danger, would you not do whatever you could to protect them? Even if it was something you did not feel entirely comfortable with?" Taka questioned. "After all, my friend, what choice would you have?"

Rozo remained silent. He couldn't answer. How could he? He could barely even believe what was happening. This... this couldn't be real... Was the king really *threatening* his family? Was he really offering to trade Teima's life for theirs? Rozo couldn't... He couldn't authorise her execution! She had done nothing wrong! She was innocent! But what if he didn't agree with King Taka? What would happen then? Teima would understand, wouldn't she? She wouldn't want to be a risk; she would *want* Rozo to do whatever it took to save his family. She would happily give her own life... That was the kind of person she was. Wasn't she? She was sweet and pure and kind...

Or maybe she wasn't. Maybe she really had committed treason. How well did Rozo really know her? Maybe the king was right. Maybe she was trying to stain him; maybe she really did deserve to die. Yes... Yes, that was it. Those were the only two choices. Either Teima really was as pure and innocent as Rozo believed, in which case she would want him to recommend her execution to save his family, or she really was a traitor, in which case she had deceived both Rozo and the king, and she deserved to die. Either way it wouldn't be Rozo's fault. He couldn't be blamed for this. He had no reason to feel guilty. He was just being a good husband and father, and a loyal servant to his king. He liked the king! He had known King Taka for decades longer than he had known Teima – he had known King Taka when he had only been a matat. Rozo had seen the birth of almost all of King Taka's children and he adored them as if they were his own; he had been one of the first people to meet six out of King Taka's eight wives. He was part of this family! His loyalty lay here, with King Taka and his children. Rozo had to appreciate that. He had to honour that. Teima would understand. She would understand that he didn't have a choice… If she didn't, then she deserved to die.

"Rozo."

Rozo met the king's eyes as Taka stared at him sternly, growing impatient with Rozo's silence. "Do you understand the situation?" He watched as Rozo nodded, and uttered a low grunt. "Mm. So I need your advice. What should I do?"

"Sire…" Rozo spoke hoarsely. "I think…" He swallowed and closed his eyes for a moment, afraid of the words he was about to utter. "She isn't worth my family… and she isn't worth yours." Rozo opened his eyes and looked at the king. He could feel tears forming in his own eyes; he knew he was crying. He was sentencing her to death. It wasn't his fault though… This wasn't his fault.

"I see." Taka nodded. "I thought as much." He took another sip of his drink and looked at Rozo. "So," he said. "What do you recommend I do, Rozo? As my advisor."

"As your advisor, Sire…" Rozo cleared his throat. "I… I think she has committed treason against you, and I recommend you execute her before she harms anyone else."

"Mm." Taka paused for a moment, as if he were considering Rozo's words. He wasn't. Rozo knew he wasn't. It was all for show. "And you are sure about that? If anyone were to question my decision, you would be happy to say that you felt her execution was justified?"

"Yes," Rozo answered quickly, becoming embarrassed by his tears. He knew the king would think less of him for this. Part of him didn't care. Rozo would hate himself if he didn't cry – what sort of monster could authorise the murder of an innocent woman and not even care? No, he had to stop thinking like that... This wasn't his fault. It *wasn't* his fault!

"Good," Taka said. "Thank you for your advice, Rozo. You have been a great help to me, as always." He finished his drink and waved a dismissive hand at Rozo. "You may go."

"Thank you, Sire!" Rozo breathed. He practically flew towards the door; he had never been so eager to leave a room. He had to warn Teima – he had to tell her to escape while she still could!

"Wait." Taka's cold voice stopped Rozo dead in his tracks when he was only an inch away from the door. Rozo uttered a short gasp and turned around to face the king. Gods, what now? What could he possibly want now?

"Y... Yes, Sire?" Rozo whimpered nervously. His entire body was tense; he didn't like the atmosphere in that room. It was too dark. The king was too calm; he was too happy. It made Rozo feel sick to his core.

"Tell Teima to come here," Taka instructed. "Tell her to come alone."

"S-Sire..." Rozo choked. Oh, no... No, he wasn't.... Was he going to do it now? Right now? No... Of course not. He wouldn't. He needed to arrange an executioner; he needed to charge Teima... Was he going to charge her now? Shit... What if the king imprisoned her right away? How would she escape...?

"I want to get this over with," Taka said. "In extreme cases of terrorism, where I feel myself and my family are in immediate danger, I can skip right to the execution, can't I?"

"Yes." Rozo's heart stopped. No... This wasn't fair. Teima was innocent! She had a right to be charged! She had a right to defend herself!

"And remind me..." Taka continued. "Who does the law state must perform the execution?"

"Anyone as chosen by the king, Sire," Rozo answered.

"That's right," Taka nodded. "And on this occasion, I choose myself."

"What?"

45

Taka chuckled slightly at the look of horror on Rozo's face. Rozo stared at him with wide eyes and an open jaw, standing there in utter disbelief. What a fool.

"As an Outsider, Rozo, I'm sure you don't understand how much fun it is for a Hiveakan to draw another's blood." Taka smirked darkly at Rozo, his hand clasped firmly around his glass as if it were an extension of his crown. "Especially the blood of his enemy. So…" He took another sip of the cold drink before narrowing his eyes at Rozo. "Bring her to me."

"But…" Rozo stammered. "But, Sire –"

"Rozo." Taka narrowed his eyes at the man. "Don't argue with me now. Think of your family, hm?"

"Yes, Sire." Rozo obediently withdrew his protests. The king was right. He couldn't save Teima. Even if he had time to, if the king ever found out it would be Rozo's family that would die. He couldn't take the risk. He couldn't… She would understand. If there was anything genuine about her, she would understand. "Right away, Sire." Rozo feebly bowed to the king, and left the room.

Taka leaned back in his chair and waited patiently, steadily sipping from his glass. It wouldn't be long now… Poor Rozo. He liked Teima, didn't he? Everyone did. Maybe that was the problem. She was so likeable; she was so easy to trust. Nobody hated her enough to realise what a danger she was.

After a few moments of silence Taka raised his head to the sound of the door opening. In walked Teima as he expected. She had come alone. Hmph. Rozo didn't want to see this, did he? Well… Taka could hardly blame him. The Outsider race was a feeble one, after all. Teima closed the door behind her and knelt before her king, staring at him with warm, bright eyes.

"You wanted to see me, Taka?" Teima smiled. 'Taka'… Thoit had got her calling him that. Not 'Sire' or 'My King' as Taka preferred. Thoit had told her to say 'Taka'; it was his idea of a practical joke. It wasn't funny. Not in the slightest. Yet Taka minded it a lot less now than he had when it had started. He had never thought anything of it; he had simply assumed it was the nature of things; that he was simply growing immune to the word… but maybe he had been wrong. Maybe

46

Taka didn't mind it because he had grown to like Teima more… It was unacceptable. After he murdered her he would punish himself.

"Yes," Taka answered bluntly and gestured for her to stand. Teima stood obediently and awaited his instructions, never once removing the smile from her face. She always smiled at him… She was scared of him, but somehow she wasn't scared enough to wipe her affections away. Perhaps she could sense that she had poisoned him; perhaps her smile was her weapon and her warmth would burn a Hiveakan's Footprints to ash. She was deceitful. Not innocent, not naïve… Deceitful. Taka could see it now.

The king took a moment to gaze at his wife, his eyes slowly travelling across her frame. She was such a small thing. Even after carrying two children Teima's was one of the tiniest figures Taka had ever seen. She had barely grown during her last pregnancy, so much so that it was a wonder how Mokoto had managed to fit inside her. Taka liked Teima like that. It was her smallness that had attracted him to her. She was so delicate, so frail… Her skin was so smooth and so unfamiliar with the world of conflict; it was so pale it made her look weak… Taka craved her. His Footprints craved her. He was like a starving wolf to its prey; as soon as he laid his eyes upon her, everything that was Hiveakan about Taka yearned to unleash its fury upon Teima's soul. The tininess of her frame made him feel powerful; the perfect smoothness of her skin made him want to cut his name into her flesh. Teima had cried during their first few months of marriage; her weak body couldn't bear the pain Taka inflicted upon it. Taka used to enjoy the sound of her tears; he enjoyed seeing what a mess his Footprints could make of her innocent being… but she didn't cry anymore. Sometimes she even welcomed him. She was terrified of him, but she opened her arms out to his wrath as if it didn't hurt her at all. Taka had thought she was getting stronger; he thought that perhaps his Footprints were stepping into her soul and giving her the strength to endure him… But he was wrong. Teima wasn't getting stronger. He was getting weaker. So weak he could barely make her whimper anymore. She would whimper now. She would scream.

Teima watched as Taka rose to his feet, finally setting the glass down on his desk. He steadily made his way over to her and stopped close to her body. Teima raised her head to meet his eyes as he stared down at her, his Footprints burning in his soul.

"Teima…" Taka began. He spoke coarsely, almost lustfully. He could already smell her blood.

"Yes, Taka?" Teima's smile was almost torturing. Taka gazed at her firmly, amazed by the level of her innocence. It couldn't be real. How could anyone be so kind? Even for an Outsider she seemed purer than he could ever imagine. She was the opposite of everything he believed in. Maybe that was how Taka had become so poisoned by her; perhaps a combination of her own gentle aura and his willingness to embrace the unknown. He remained silent for a moment to study her face. Teima had a beautiful face; she was a very attractive woman. Taka only married pretty girls. Her light green eyes were soft and brimming with life and she had fawn-shaded hair that hung loosely down her back. Teima wasn't wearing make-up; she seldom did. It made her feel false. She had a couple of lilac freckles under her left eye that somehow made Teima look much younger than her years. Teima would always look young; her face possessed a youthful glow and her skin was free of creases or scars. Her facial bones were rounded slightly, to such an extent she almost looked like a child. It suited her personality. She was like a tiny bird or a little mouse, the kind that hid from winter's cold and made its home in the smallest place it could find, terrified of being captured by its predator's claws. Taka's claws always itched when he thought of her in that way. He had been so disappointed when she'd stopped crying; it took the fun out of being a predator. Still… Teima had her uses. In so many ways she was worth keeping around. It was a shame this had to happen. Teima was Taka's best chance of having another boy. He had hoped to have at least one more, to make even competition for Suela's girls. Still. Never mind. What was done was done and what would be would be. The God of War would curse Taka if he did not do this, and Teima would continue to poison his soul.

Without a moment's thought, Taka cleared his throat and stared down at his prey.

"Most Outsiders don't know," he began, "but under Act 1 of the global Hiveakan law it is an offence to try to stain a Hiveakan's character. In the case of a king, this is classed as treason."

"What...?" Teima blinked. Her eyebrows furrowed into a frown as she stared at Taka. "I – I don't understand," she uttered, laughing slightly. "What does that mean?"

"'To knowingly and willingly cause a Hiveakan to think, act or behave in a way that is contrary to the Hive's teachings; whether by force, manipulation or any other means in which the Hiveakan is unaware of the controversial consequences of such means.'" Taka flawlessly quoted. He held a small smirk on his lips as he recited the law to Teima, as if he were proud that he knew it and she didn't.

Teima stared at him, dumbfounded. Her eyes widened as she tried to make sense of what he was saying. Why was he telling her this...? Did he think *she* had done that?

"I... I haven't!" Teima gasped, a look of confusion sweeping across her innocent face. "Taka, I would never want to make you act – if I have I didn't mean to!" She grabbed his hands only to have them callously snatched away from her. Teima whimpered; her eyes were glistening as she stared up at him. Taka simply stared back, unfazed and emotionless. "Please..."

"You know the penalty for treason is death, don't you, Teima?" Taka said.

"No!" Teima begged. "Taka, please! You're wrong –"

"You will address me as Sire!" Taka grabbed Teima's throat in one hand and ruthlessly slammed her into the wall. He held her throat firmly, enough to hurt her, but just loosely enough to keep her alive. He could already smell her fear.

"Sire... Sire..." Teima choked. She met his eyes and trembled under the darkness she saw in them. He looked so alive... "Please..."

Taka yanked his hand off Teima's throat and watched her take a breath, smirking at the look of horror on her pretty face. It was captivating. He licked his lips as he battled to keep his bloodlust at bay. He wanted to savour her death; he wanted to make it last as long as he could. Taka moved his hands and banged his palms into the wall, holding them at either side of her head. He watched her quiver and yelp

49

under him; he stared at the tears forming in her eyes. They told him everything there was to know about her. They told him she was frightened; they told him she was weak. They told him she was helpless. Taka uttered a low grunt and pushed his arms against Teima's chest, crushing her bones. He listened to the soft whimpers that escaped Teima's lips and smirked darkly at their sound.

"Sire…" Teima squeaked. "You're hurting me."

"I know," Taka answered. "I've done this before, Teima."

"I'm sorry," Teima sobbed, scrunching her eyes shut. "I didn't mean to hurt you. Please…" She opened her eyes and looked at him desperately, begging for her life. "Please let me go! Think of Mokoto – "

"I am, dear," Taka replied. "I can't allow my only son to become ruined by you, can I? What sort of father would that make me?"

"But I didn't do anything!" Teima screamed. Her face became flooded with tears; she grew more and more hysterical with every second that passed. Her setules rose all over her body; her breathing became fast and frantic. How could he do this to her? Why was he doing this? She was his wife! She loved him! He knew she loved him, he knew! "I wouldn't do anything to you, Taka! I love you!" Teima wailed.

"Stop calling me Taka!"

Teima screamed as Taka smacked his hand across her face so hard he almost broke her jaw. He held his palm firmly against her chest and watched her struggle underneath him, his bloodlust growing with every beat of her heart. It was so fast; so forceful… It was begging to be destroyed.

"I – I'm sorry!" Teima breathed. "Please! Sire…" She tried pitifully to push his hand off her. It was no use. The strength she had in both her arms was no match for the power he held in one hand. Taka watched as Teima stared up at him, tears rolling down her cheeks. She was so frightened. He could feel her fear in every beat of her pounding heart and every quiver of her skin; he could smell it in every one of her breaths. She was helpless.

Taka grunted angrily, disgusted by how pathetic she was. How in the Gaiamira's world had he ever found a place in his heart for her? And a big enough place for Suela to notice. How had he allowed himself to be poisoned by someone so weak? It was disgusting. It was an offence to the God of War. It needed to be rectified. *Now.*

Finally, Taka surrendered to his bloodlust and shoved his fist deep into Teima's chest, using the entire force of his body to snap past her ribs. Teima screamed as he plunged his hand into her, her eyes bulging and her body shaking with fright. She breathed frantically, desperately trying to stay alive. Her body was in shock; she was trembling violently. Taka wore a cold smirk on his lips as he grabbed hold of her heart. He held it in his hand, and exhaled, savouring the feel of the organ in his palm. He felt it pounding rapidly against his skin; he felt Teima's blood surround his hand. He went to meet Teima's eyes but they were closed. She wasn't dead. Not yet. She was praying. Teima kept her eyes scrunched tight, praying to every one of the Gaiamira that this was a dream. She tried to ignore the coldness of her body. She tried to ignore the feeling of his hand around her heart. She prayed that this wasn't real and then she forced her eyes open. More tears flowed from Teima's eyes when she realised she was still in pain. He was still killing her…

"P-Please!" she choked. "Help! Taka! I – I love you!"

"You love me?" Taka raised his eyebrows at her and dug his claws into her heart, cutting it open. He watched the life drain from her eyes; he watched her skin fade to white. He moved his face close to hers and spoke against her ear; he wanted her to hear what he had to say. "Love, Teima… has no place in my home." Taka spoke softly. "And nor does the girl that spreads it." Taka watched her face carefully; he knew she had heard that. He knew how long it would take before she was dead; before her hearing vanished. Taka almost gasped when he saw her reaction. Stunned, he kept his eyes fixed on her, not daring to look away in case he was mistaken. She was smiling. Why…? Taka's eyebrows furrowed in confusion.

"Teima…" he uttered. "Why are you smiling?"

51

Teima didn't answer. She simply continued to smile, and her eyes remained locked onto his until he felt her body grow limp… and the life escaped her eyes.

She was gone. Just like that. She hadn't even had enough strength to scream. Pathetic. Taka gazed at her for a moment, and shrugged off his curiosity. Of course she was smiling. In her last moments her pain would have subsided; she probably thought he was saving her. Idiot. Taka removed his hand from the fatal wound on her chest, allowing Teima's body to fall clumsily to the floor. He looked down at the thick purple blood that covered his hand and smiled to himself as it reminded him of a passage from the Gaiamirapon. "And with a bolt of lightning the mighty God of War Taka rose from the depths of the earth…" Taka recited, walking back over to his desk. He took a seat in front of his glass and started to lick the blood off his hand, enjoying the sweetness of the liquid. This was his trophy; it was his reward for being a good Hiveakan warrior and slaying his enemy. Taka didn't shy when he heard the door open; he knew who it was. Who else would dare enter without knocking?

"With the blood of the weak upon his hands." Who else would say that…? A smooth female voice joined Taka, its owner walking past the body on the floor without so much as flinching at its sight. They weren't shocked; they weren't disgusted. They were impressed. The woman took a seat opposite Taka and watched him drink Teima's blood from his hand. She looked into his eyes with a fiery darkness and smirked seductively as she spoke the words, "He stood beside her and preached about a world of battle, strength, victory and loyalty, and with a mighty roar he commanded all the warriors of the world to follow him and worship him, and to raise their children to serve him."

"The rest of the people followed him willingly, and devoted their lives to becoming undefeated warriors who would never be afraid, and who would lead their planet to greatness…" Taka continued, meeting her eyes. "And thus, the Hive was born." He looked calmly at his wife. "Suela…" he said, glancing at Teima's body. "How in the Gaiamiras' names did you know I was killing her now?"

"I saw Rozo crying," Suela replied. "And I know how impatient you are. I knew you wouldn't be able to stop yourself…" She raised her eyebrows at him and looked at the blood on his hand. "Did you save any for me?"

"I said I would," Taka answered. "Come here."

A victorious smirk made its way across Suela's lips as she rose from her seat and approached him. Taka extended his hand to her and watched as she trailed her tongue along his thumb, lapping up Teima's blood.

"So, are you pleased with me?" Taka asked, his gaze fixed on Suela's lips as she withdrew her blood stained tongue into them. "Sire…" Suela met his eyes once more. "I'm always pleased with you." Taka laughed as Suela reclaimed her seat opposite him. "She needed to die," Suela stated.

"I know," Taka nodded. He reached for the bottle of tetsa and refilled his glass. "You were right. She tried to stain me."

"And did she?" Suela raised her eyebrows at him. Taka paused for a moment, carefully considering his answer. He didn't know. Really. He just knew it was possible; he suspected it might have happened… but he didn't know for sure.

"No," Taka answered bluntly. "But I can't afford to take the risk. She should have known."

"Yes, she should have," Suela purred. "I knew you wouldn't allow yourself to be poisoned by her. She was a fool to think she could defeat you."

"When has anybody ever defeated me?" Taka replied arrogantly, pushing his glass towards her.

"Precisely." Suela took hold of the glass and raised it to her lips. "That's why I married you." She winked at him. "*Sire.*"

"It's good to know you only want me for my throne." Taka smirked playfully and drank from the tetsa bottle.

"Well… Don't feel bad," Suela teased. "You do have a few other good points, even if they don't interest me."

"Ha." Taka laughed a little and held the bottle of tetsa towards her. "So," he began. "To… victory, my gold digger?"

"To victory, My King." Suela smiled. She raised her glass to his bottle, and they drank to her name.

V.

'After Kala's Outsiders and Taka's warriors had chosen their paths the God of Knowledge and Wisdom appeared. His name was Gonta and he held in his hand a book containing all the knowledge in the world. Gonta told the people to become educated and wise; he cursed the world's fools and blessed anybody that wanted to learn.'

\-   Extract from the Gaiamirapon: 'The First Encounters'

*

"Hey." An impatient voice echoed off the walls of the Hive as Mokoto's nanny pinched the infant's foot. Mokoto's eyes snapped open and he awoke with a snarl, infuriated that someone had disturbed him. He was growing angrier by the day; the engineered nutrients in his food and the harshness of his living conditions only served to enhance the Footprints in his soul. He glared up at his nanny, fully aware of who to blame for the pain in his foot and the stinging in his tired eyes. "Don't look at me like that," the nanny growled. He pulled the infant from his bed and held him tightly, shoving a milk bottle into his mouth. Mokoto drank the milk hungrily, undisturbed by its coldness and its unnatural taste. In a matter of days he had become accustomed to it; he had grown to like it. The bitter substance that Mokoto had once despised now tasted like the sweetest thing in the world. "Okay." The nanny sneered. "For being cheeky…" He pulled the milk bottle away when Mokoto was only halfway down it. Mokoto let out a cry and flailed wildly in the nanny's arms, screaming for the return of his food. "No," the nanny said, placing Mokoto back in his crib. He placed his palm on the infant's head and pressed down on his skull. "You don't look at me like that. You show me respect." The nanny watched mesmerised as the infant grabbed hold of his hands and almost gasped when Mokoto sank his teeth into his flesh. "*No!*" The nanny smacked Mokoto's face, causing the young matat to wail in agony. Mokoto looked up at his nanny with regret in his eyes; he could sense that he had done something wrong. "Little shit," the nanny snarled. He looked

54

down at his hand and was shocked to see blood. Gods… How had a baby managed to do that? This child was possessed by Taka! He looked down at Mokoto and smirked slightly. "Your Highness…" he uttered, causing the infant to soften his cries. "You will be a murderer before you are even married." He flicked the infant's nose and ignored Mokoto's screams as he made his way over to the door. He turned off the light before exiting the room, leaving Mokoto to sulk in hunger and darkness.

*

'On 20-06-20103G Keika Teima was executed for treason. Although her death was sudden and unexpected, there was little doubt over the genuineness of King Taka's accusation of treachery, and the vast majority of the Meitonákan people, including Teima's fellow keikas and children, believed she deserved to die.'

-        Extract from history textbook: 'Battle for the throne: A history of treason and threats to the Meitonákan monarchy', 20150G

*

"Mama!" Oreisaka screamed loudly into her sister Maika's clothing as the older girl comforted her.

"I know… I know…" Maika soothed, biting her lip to hold back her own tears. She had adored Teima. Maika was eighteen; she was Taka's first child and the eldest daughter of his first wife Kaeila. She had only met Teima five years ago, when over half of her childhood was already gone, but Teima had always felt like more of a mother to Maika than any one of Taka's wives. She had always spoken to Maika with such patience and warmth, the kind Maika had never known from her parents. Teima didn't resent Maika; she didn't blame Maika for taking away her youth. Teima loved her. Teima loved everybody; she couldn't have committed treason! It was a lie. Maika knew it. Teima had done something her father didn't like – whatever it was, it was no doubt stupid and trivial… and this was how the king had

55

chosen to punish her. By murdering her and destroying her name. It was how he worked; it was how he had always worked. Everything was his way, and if he didn't like something he erased it. This palace wasn't a home to Maika. It was a prison, and everyone inside it was King Taka's slave.

"Maika." The sound of her biological mother's voice caught Maika's attention. Maika was alone in one of the common rooms with Oreisaka and Kaeila; the three of them were tightly squeezed together in the middle of a large sofa, struggling to deal with the news of Teima's death. It had been Rozo that had informed them; he had told Kaeila, and she in turn had told Maika, who had decided they should tell Oreisaka before any of Taka's other children. Now Kaeila was regretting allowing Maika to become involved in this; she was obviously growing more upset with Oreisaka's tears.

"Leave her with me," Kaeila instructed. "You go and…" She paused for a moment as she tried to think of something to take her daughter away from the grieving child. "Pray for Teima, okay?"

"Why?" Maika hissed. "She doesn't need it! The Gaiamira know how good she was! Why would she need my help?"

"Is she…" Oreisaka sobbed. "Is she coming back? Is Mama coming back?"

"Of course!" Maika said, hugging the girl. "She'll be reincarnated, just like your book says, hm? All the good people in the world come back to live all over again."

"Will she come back here?" Oreisaka looked at Maika, baffled by the Gaiamirákan belief of reincarnation. She was still too young to fully understand it.

"No, sweetheart…"

As Oreisaka burst into tears again the door opened. Kaeila and Maika looked up to see who had joined them, and both women uttered an angry sigh at the sight of Suela. She was standing in the doorway with her hand on her hip, wearing a disgusting smirk on her face as she looked at the screaming child.

"My, what a tantrum," Suela sniped. "What's wrong with her?"

"What do you think?" Maika snapped. She rose to her feet and glared at Suela. "This is your fault, isn't it? You made him kill her!"

"Yes, that must be it," Suela retorted. "I managed to overpower a man that's twice my size. It's amazing what these hands can do." She made her way over to Maika and towered over the girl, glaring dominantly into her eyes. "Your father chose to do it himself. Do you know why? Because she betrayed him, and she deserved what was coming to her. Now show some respect!" She threw out her arm and slapped Maika before kicking the young girl to the floor. "She wasn't your only mother!" Suela snarled. "You will bow to me as well! Do you understand –?"

"Suela, please!" Kaeila shrieked. "You're scaring Oreisaka!"

"Oh…" Suela's face softened as she turned her attention towards Oreisaka. She watched in amusement as the child stared back, her loud wails turning into soft sobs as she became unnerved by Suela's presence. Oreisaka had barely spoken to Suela in her life; the Hiveakans and the Outsiders tended to live separately in the palace. Suela scared her.

The Hiveakan woman looked down at Maika and became angered by the aggression in the teen's eyes. What was wrong with her? She had a bad attitude! "Your sister looks upset," Suela hissed. "I thought you were supposed to be comforting her. Here, let me."

"Leave her," Maika growled. Suela simply smirked and moved past Maika to sit down beside Oreisaka. She smiled at the girl and noticed that Kaeila was pulling the child closer to herself.

"What, don't you trust me?" Suela looked at Kaeila. "She's my daughter as well."

"Since when did you care about her?" Kaeila frowned.

"Since I married her father," Suela replied. "A wedding can turn water into blood; why don't you Outsiders ever think of that? I thought you were family-orientated."

"I think we have different views on what a family is," Maika snarled, rising to her feet. "I don't torture mine."

"You're doing it to me now," Suela muttered. She glanced at Maika and frowned. "I didn't say you could stand."

"So?" Maika spat. Suela paused for a moment, and then moved to strike the girl.

"Maika!" Kaeila snapped. She shot her daughter a warning glance, ordering her to obey Suela. Maika hesitated, then let out an angry sigh and returned to the floor. Suela grinned triumphantly and looked back at Oreisaka, stretching her arms out to the child.

"Come here," Suela beckoned. Oreisaka hesitated. Her entire body was tense as she stared back at Suela, shrinking into the familiarity of Kaeila's warm body. "I know…" Suela smiled. "You're scared of me, aren't you? It's okay. You should be."

"Suela!" Kaeila gasped. "Stop it!"

"But you can trust me, Orei," Suela continued, ignoring Kaeila's remarks. "Come on. Come here."

Oreisaka remained silent and looked up at Kaeila for advice on what to do. Kaeila nodded at the young girl and gave her a gentle nudge.

"It's okay. Go on," she said. Oreisaka looked back at Suela and reluctantly crawled over to her, her eyes filled with dread.

"That's a good girl," Suela soothed. She put her arm around the child and pulled Oreisaka against her. "Now… I know you're very sad about your mother. It's understandable, she was very nice to you wasn't she?" Kaeila and Maika looked at each other, unsure of how to respond. Why was Suela being like this? She was never nice to Taka's children – she never wanted anything to do with them! She was up to something…

Oreisaka looked up at Suela and nodded timidly. "But…" Suela continued, "you need to know. Your mother did a very bad thing."

"What!" Maika gasped, her eyes widening.

"She needed to be punished – and the punishment for being *that* naughty is death." Suela smirked at the horror that swept across Oreisaka's face.

"Get out of here!" Maika screamed, jumping up to grab Suela as Oreisaka burst into tears again.

"Don't touch me!" Suela hissed, slashing at Maika's cheek. She stood up and sniggered silently to herself at the sight of blood

58

running from the cut. Pathetic. She had barely touched Maika! Outsiders had such weak skin…

"Get out of here!" Maika roared again, taking a swing at Suela.

"*Suela!*" Kaeila cried out, wide-eyed as Suela caught Maika's arm. Kaeila watched in horror as pain shot across Maika's face. Suela was breaking her wrist!

"I thought you didn't believe in violence, Maika?" Suela raised her eyebrows. "Not in front of the child. Don't you think she's been through enough?"

"You bitch…" Maika snarled.

"Maika, shut up!" Kaeila barked. She stared at Suela, half angry and half terrified. "Suela please – let her go!"

"Of course," Suela said calmly. She released Maika's arm and watched as the younger woman retracted it instantly, gritting her teeth in pain as she rubbed her wrist. "You could have asked me at any time, Maika," Suela scolded. "After all, you are my daughter."

"I'll have to remember that the next time I hurt *your* girls!" Kaeila spat. Suela looked at her with a dark smile, her eyes twinkling excitedly.

"Good," she purred. "I don't want you being too kind to them." She moved her eyes back down to Oreisaka, who had once again grown silent – this time with fear. Suela crouched down in front of Oreisaka and smirked as the child pressed her back against the sofa, trembling slightly as she looked nervously into Suela's eyes. Suela laughed a little and mockingly blew the girl a kiss. "Don't worry, Meitat. You won't end up like her, will you? You'll be a good girl and leave your father alone."

"Get *out!*" Maika screamed.

"Don't worry, I'm going." Suela rose to her feet and shot Kaeila an angry glare. "Your daughter has an attitude problem. I suggest you fix it or her father *will*." She turned and left the room, nudging Maika harshly on the way out.

"Why does she have to be like that…?" Kaeila mumbled.

"Hiveakans. They're all the same, Mother! Why did you even marry him?" Maika snapped.

"I didn't want to," Kaeila growled, cruelly reminding Maika of why she had been forced to marry the king.

"Well I'm sorry I ruined your life," Maika snarled. She sat back down beside Oreisaka and smiled at her. "Promise me something, okay? Promise me you won't listen to the Hiveakans. Don't ever listen to them and don't *ever* be like them. Okay?"

"Okay…" Oreisaka whimpered. She wiped her eyes, and continued crying.

*

'What happened to Teima is very sad; it's always a shame for a baby to lose their Hiveakan parent… which is why her death was necessary. Now Matat Mokoto can live in safety, thanks to King Taka's willingness to do what needed to be done. I always did like a good father.'

\-   Keika Suela, 20103G

*

"Really? And what does that mean in terms of his development? … Mm. … Good. Well, don't be afraid to break his arm if you think it would be appropriate." Taka leaned back in his chair as he spoke to a tutor at the Hive, keen to get an update on Mokoto's growth. He moved his eyes towards the door when he heard it opening, and he nodded at Suela as she walked into the room. "Did he?" Taka laughed. "Good. Well… I'll leave it up to you, Gutari, but please don't hold back on him. … Mm. Alright. Speak to you soon. Bye." He looked over at Suela; she was seated opposite him, patiently waiting to be spoken to. "Mokoto bit someone," Taka grinned. "He drew blood."

"He sounds like he doesn't know his place," Suela remarked, unimpressed by the infant half-breed's aggression.

"He will kill your girls," Taka taunted.

"What is he going to do, bite them to death?" Suela spat. "I'll break his teeth."

60

"You do that," Taka replied. He looked at her. "What?"

"You have a problem," Suela stated. "Guess who."

"Mm." Taka's mind swept across the members of his family. His other wives were Kaeila and Geith… Geith remained isolated most of the time; she probably wouldn't care about Teima's death… Kaeila would be upset but not enough to do anything about it. The children…? Most of them were still quite young; the eldest were Maika and Beina. Beina… She was the favourite of Taka's Outsider children. It was as if she had been born straight out of the Gaiamirapon itself; she was a young nun and one of the few hundred people in history that had regular communication with all eight members of the Gaiamira. Beina would never be a problem; she was a blessing. That only left Maika… As always. Taka sighed. "Maika." He ran his hand through his hair and closed his eyes. "The only regret I have is Maika."

"Really?" Suela laughed. "Your *only* regret? I know you've done plenty of things to be ashamed of."

"I know, and I learned from all of them!" Taka protested. "What can you learn from her?" He made his way over to his drinks cabinet and pulled it open, reaching for a bottle of tetsa and two glasses. "What has she done?"

"She's not happy with you," Suela said.

"So?" Taka shrugged, pouring himself a drink. "She never is."

"But she's telling everyone," Suela replied. "She thinks Teima was innocent – and she's telling Oreisaka." Her face moved into a frown. "She wouldn't bow to me. She kept arguing – your Outsider child tried to attack me."

"Attack you?" Taka looked at Suela in surprise, shocked that any child of his would dare do such a thing to its superior.

"She had an attitude problem. Her mother obviously didn't hit her enough when she was young," Suela said.

"Her mother barely spoke to her," Taka answered, making his way back to Suela. "But I suppose I didn't hit her enough myself…" He let out another sigh and placed a glass down in front of Suela.

"So I have you to blame?" Suela teased.

"To some extent," Taka admitted, filling her glass only half as much as he filled his own. Suela wasn't much of a drinker. Not

compared to him, anyway. "Alright, leave her to me. I'll talk to her."
He took a sip of his drink and looked down at Suela, smirking slightly.
"Are you alright?"

"Alright?" Suela questioned.

"When she attacked you... she didn't hurt you, did she?" Taka
taunted. He touched his claw against a mark on Suela's cheek. "You
have a bruise here."

"Shut up!" Suela snarled, batting his hand away. "That's from
you!"

"Are you sure?" Taka teased. "It looks small."

"Well, you've lost your touch," Suela smirked.

"Have I?" Taka replied, raising his glass to his lips. "So you
won't want to sleep with me anymore, then?"

"I'll lower my standards just this once." Suela winked. Taka
sniggered into his drink.

"Thank you," he uttered.

*

'I am a good mother. If my boys do something wrong, I beat them and
they don't do it again. You can see how good of a mother I am by how
well they've turned out, and I hope that when they are older they beat
their own children... If they don't then I have failed.'

-      Keika Denna Mikon-Rokut, 20084G

*

The sound of chaos and laughter filled the palace nursery as
Kaeila and her assistant Geith entertained the children of the palace. As
Taka's wives it was their job to raise his children; they had chosen their
marriages to the king over their careers and freedom, and had nothing
better to do now than to adopt the role of live-in nannies. Taka had a
total of nine Outsider daughters, six of whom were in this room. The
eldest was Maika, who was assisting her mothers along with her
fifteen-year-old sister Beina, and the youngest was Sukaru; she was

three years old and the only child of Taka's most recent wife Geith. She was timid and well-behaved, as were all of Taka's children, but like the majority of them she became loud and excited when accompanied by her siblings. It was playtime now, and nothing could silence the children's blissful screams.

Nothing except their father. As soon as he stepped through the door the nursery was encased in silence. The children closed their mouths in fear and threw themselves into a bow at his presence, not daring to look up or move a muscle until he told them to. Taka stood with his arms folded, smiling in satisfaction at the scene before him. Obedience... Silence. It was all he expected from his children. It was all they ever showed him... If only they could show the same amount of respect for his wives. Not one of his children had the right to argue with any of their mothers – even Matat Mokoto would have every bone in his body broken if he ever so much as glared at Kaeila. It was a matter of hierarchy; it was a matter of respect, and it disappointed Taka greatly to learn that one of his children was not behaving as they should. Taka moved his eyes to his first wife Kaeila, and he spoke to her without so much as glancing at Geith. Kaeila was married to him first; she was Geith's superior.

"I hope I'm not interrupting?" Taka asked. It wasn't really a question. It was his way of acknowledging that he had disturbed her afternoon, and he didn't particularly care that he had.

"No," Kaeila answered flatly. She knew what this was about. Taka never visited the children unless he wanted to punish them, and then he would take his anger out on Kaeila and Geith for having to do their job for them. *Just take her, already,* Kaeila thought. Taka scanned the room for Maika and his eyes rested on the young nun he saw next to his eldest child. He was glad Beina was there... He needed to speak to her as well, as it happened.

"Beina..." Taka said. "May I have a word, Meitat?"

"Of course, Sire," Beina smiled. She obediently rose to her feet and joined him out in the corridor.

"I suppose you have heard about Teima's death?" Taka began, placing a gentle hand on his daughter's back as he closed the door behind her.

"Yes, Sire," Beina nodded. "The Gaiamira told me before it even happened."

"I thought as much," Taka replied with a proud smile. He had a small fondness for Beina; she was the only one he cared to speak to outside of orders or scolding. As a nun she did wonders for the family's reputation, and her closeness with every member of the Gaiamira was nothing short of a miracle. It was a blessing the world may never see again, and Taka felt honoured that the Gaiamira had chosen his child to bless. "What exactly did they tell you?"

"Only what I cared to ask," Beina answered. "Teima needed to be executed, for committing treason…" She lowered her eyes and chose her words carefully, only too aware of her father's pride. "Kala was involved somehow…"

Taka paused for a moment as he considered Beina's answer. Kala… She was the Goddess of Love and Marriage. In not so many words Beina was acknowledging that the Gaiamira had told her of Teima's attempt to stain Taka, and its potential success… It didn't bother Taka that she knew about that. It wasn't the kind of thing that he would ordinarily share with anyone – and much less his daughter – but the Gaiamira knew everything that happened in the world, and they had every right to share with their nuns and priests whatever they saw fit. Taka had no right to question their decision, nor did he have the right to deny anything they said.

"Mm," Taka grunted in acknowledgement. "Well…" He paused again, and looked at her sternly. "I hope I don't need to ask you to keep some of the details to yourself, Meitat?"

"Of course not, Sire." Beina smiled almost cheekily, charmed by her father's embarrassment.

"I want to ask you," Taka began. "Did the Gaiamira happen to mention what they thought of my actions?" He met Beina's eyes, and she held the same knowing smile. She knew he didn't mean the Gaiamira as a whole. He meant Taka, the God of War. The god he was terrified of displeasing. Beina giggled inwardly and nodded at her king.

"Taka is very pleased with you, Sire…" she assured. "And he hopes Mokoto will turn out like you."

"Hm." Taka smirked arrogantly, satisfied with her response. "I hope he will turn out better. Alright." He squeezed Beina's shoulder and nodded towards the door. "You are dismissed, Meitat." He waited for her to finish bowing and opened the nursery door for her, gesturing for her to enter before him.

Taka followed Beina into the room and listened as the quiet murmuring of his nervous family once again turned into silence at the sight of him. His eyes barely moved; he had memorised Maika's position and as soon as he entered the room he greeted her with a cold glare. "You!" Taka barked. "Come with me!" He didn't wait for her to respond. Taka stormed out of the room and started to travel down the corridor towards his meeting room. He could hear Maika following him; he could tell by the sound of her shuffling that she was nervous. She was dragging her feet; she was walking much slower than she needed to. She knew she was in danger. She was terrified. Good. She ought to be. She knew she had done wrong. At least she was walking behind him, in accordance with Gaiamirákan etiquette. It was a great sign of disrespect to walk alongside someone who was superior to you, and even more offensive to walk past them. Everyone in this palace had to walk behind King Taka, even if it was only a footstep away. At least Maika had not forgotten her place when it came to her father; perhaps the distance between them was a reflection of how inferior she felt to him... She wasn't far away enough. If she walked on the other side of the world the girl would still be too close to King Taka.

Taka stepped into his meeting room and waited impatiently for Maika to catch up to him. She stopped in front of him and awaited further instruction. Taka didn't speak to her; he simply held the door open and gestured for her to enter the room. Maika obeyed reluctantly, trembling as she walked past her father. A small smirk formed on Taka's lips as he noticed the quivering of her skin. It amused him to see her so frightened. She deserved to be frightened. He followed Maika into the room and locked the door behind them. He turned to face her, and studied her frame. She was standing awkwardly with her knees slightly bent, unsure of whether or not he wanted her to bow. She was as pale as the morning sun; Taka hadn't even started yet and already he'd managed to drain the blood from her face. Where was her blood now? Where was the fire she had used to strike her mother? She was pathetic. She was weak. She was a problem. "Sit down," Taka ordered.

Maika obediently sat down at his desk. She sat in silence with her eyes on the floor, not daring to look up. Taka made his way over to her and looked down at the glass of tetsa he'd purposefully left on the desk. It was placed within her reach, freshly poured and ready to be consumed. It would be much too painful for any Outsider to drink, especially a woman as young as her. It would scar her throat and burn the lining of her stomach, but if she was Hiveakan enough to fight Suela... "Drink that," Taka ordered, pointing at the glass. Maika looked up to stare at the liquid in front of her and raised her head to him, a look of confusion sweeping across her face.

"But... Sire..." she uttered. "Won't it be too strong for me?"

"Yes, it probably will," Taka nodded. "But if you are strong enough to disrespect my wife then you are strong enough to drink my alcohol." He narrowed his eyes at her. "*Now.*"

He watched with stern eyes as Maika reluctantly raised the glass to her lips. She had barely allowed any of the liquid into her mouth before she started flinching. The strength of the tetsa burned her lips; its smell flooded her nostrils with such force that she thought she would vomit. She coughed and whimpered and shook her head wildly, holding the glass as far away from herself as she could.

"I – I can't!" Maika whimpered. She looked up at him with tears in her eyes, terrified of what he would do now. "Please –"

"Do it," Taka snarled. "Or I will pour the whole bottle down your throat and it *will* kill you." He wasn't joking. Maika knew he wasn't. She was so afraid she could barely breathe; her blood ran cold with dread and her setules stood on edge. She paused for a moment to try to calm herself; then she took a breath and briefly closed her eyes before forcing the liquid past her lips. Maika whimpered loudly as the tetsa burned her mouth. She managed to swallow a few drops before her gag reflex forced her to spit the rest of the liquid out, leaving her screaming at her father's mercy. "I'm sorry!" Maika shrieked. She looked up at him desperately, begging for his forgiveness. "I'm sorry, Sire!"

"Hm," Taka uttered. "It's not easy being strong, is it?" He grabbed the tetsa bottle from his desk and took a large swig of it, glaring down at her as the liquid smoothly flowed past his callous lips. It was his way of demonstrating his strength; of showing her how much he was capable of and how much she wasn't. She was a child. An Outsider child. It was foolish of her to forget that. "Perhaps you should remember that the next time you decide to disrespect your mother."

Taka threw out his arm and struck Maika across her face, causing the girl to shriek in fright. He watched his daughter sob in front of him; he stared at the mark he'd made on her cheek. It wasn't enough to rectify what she had done. Nor was the scarring on her lips or the burns on her tongue. Not yet. "Now…" Taka uttered calmly, placing the tetsa bottle back on the desk. "When your superior enters a room, you bow. That is me, your mothers, your uncles and your aunts, and anyone else in this family that is older than you. You bow to all of them and you do not stand until you are told. Is that clear?" He watched Maika nod; she moved her head frantically, overcome with panic. "And," Taka added. "You do *not* lay a finger upon any of them! If you do I will break all of your fingers and both of your arms. Is that clear?"

"Yes!" Maika cried. "I… I'm sorry, Sire."

"Good," Taka answered. "Now... This business with Teima. I know you are upset, Maika. I know you liked her, and I am sure you think she did nothing wrong…" He let out a sigh. "And you are almost nineteen. You are an adult, and you are entitled to your opinion…" He narrowed his eyes at her. "But it is *your* opinion. You will keep it to yourself, is that clear?" He watched her nod again, and continued, "A lot of your sisters are still very young – especially Oreisaka. She is a child, and she is easily influenced. I don't want you to ruin her by filling her head with your ridiculous beliefs. Do you understand?" He waited for Maika to respond, but she remained silent. Taka inhaled angrily, his fists clenching as his body became flooded with rage. How dare she not answer him? How *dare* she? "Do you understand, Maika?" he roared.

"Yes!" Maika protested. "Yes, Sire!"

"Good!" Taka growled. "I don't want you to mention Teima to any of my children again. She was a traitor, and she needed to be punished, and that is what I will tell your sisters and your brother, and that is what you will tell your sisters and your brother. Are we clear?"

"Yes, Sire." Maika answered almost robotically. She hated this… She hated him! Nothing that he was saying was true! Teima *wasn't* a traitor! Her daughter deserved to know the truth! This wasn't fair… This wasn't fair! It made Maika feel sick. She knew she was helping him… She was helping him cover up Teima's murder. Why was she such a coward…?

"Good," Taka said. "Your mother Suela thinks you have a bad attitude; it's time for you to prove her wrong."

"She isn't my mother…" Maika muttered angrily, without fully being aware of what she was saying. As soon as she heard her own words her eyes widened and her body filled with dread. She didn't mean to say that… *Dammit* why had she said that?

"Not your mother!" Taka's voice thundered around the room as if he were possessed by the God of War; his rage tore through the air with so much force it felt as if his Footprints were kicking Maika's stomach. She almost vomited as she cried out to him, terrified of what he was about to do.

"Sire –"

"Do you think she is not my wife?" Taka roared. "Do you think your sisters Anaka and Lanka are bastards?" He grabbed hold of Maika's head and ruthlessly slammed her into the desk, without so much as flinching at the sound of Maika's cracking skull or the screams that followed. "Suela is your mother!" Taka snarled. "Anaka and Lanka are your sisters! And if you ever so much as *think* about disrespecting any of them ever again, I will break your legs! Do you understand?" He held her shoulder against the desk and grabbed hold of her arm, yanking it harshly to pull it from its socket. Maika screamed in agony but she didn't speak to him; she wasn't giving him the answer he wanted. "Maika!" Taka's voice echoed through her mind; she could feel his rage ruthlessly beating every part of her soul. "Do you understand?"

"*Yes!*" Maika wailed, her trembling body flooding with pain. "Yes, Sire! I'm sorry! I'm sorry!"

"Good!" Taka pushed her away from him and pulled back her chair. " Now get out of here before I slit your throat!"

Maika didn't need to be told twice. She leapt to her feet and ran towards the door. Taka smirked darkly as he watched her struggle to open the door with one hand and a dislocated arm. She was in such a panic she could barely grip the door handle. Maika screamed as she ran out, so loudly that Taka could hear her cries all the way down the corridor. She was heading for the palace medical bay, where she would no doubt spend hours shaking and wasting the nurse's time. It was pathetic. All she had was a bump on her head and a dislocated limb. They could both be easily fixed, without tears or trembles. It wasn't even considered more than a light scolding in the Hive.

VI.

'After hearing Taka's orders the king of the Gaiamirákans, Mukon Joga built the Hive. He worshipped Taka greatly, and ordered the Hive to be built around his own home so that he would always be close to the God of War and his children. The Hive was small at first but little by little it grew, and one year later it surrounded the entire palace. From then on, every Hiveakan king and queen was destined to be blessed with the spirit of Taka.'

- Extract from the Gaiamirapon: 'The Communications'

*

"Taka! *Taka!*" The mighty Thoit's voice almost destroyed the beams of Meitona Palace as he screamed his brother's name. He stormed through the palace corridors with his fists clenched and his aura burning like a volcano about to erupt. He was furious. He was beyond furious; he was so enraged his Footprints had almost exploded under their own power. He had no idea if Taka would still be alive ten minutes from now; he had absolutely no intention of controlling his own bloodlust. Taka had pissed him off. Big time. Now it was up to the God of War to decide how much damage Thoit was going to do.

An almighty bang echoed through the palace as Thoit swung open the door to Taka's meeting room with such force it crashed into the wall beside it. His eyes instantly locked onto the monarch sitting at the desk, and then they quickly moved to Rozo who was stood at his king's side. "Fuck off!" Thoit barked.

Rozo didn't argue. He knew Thoit was a calm and mild-mannered man most of the time, but a tyrant when he was angry. If Thoit was going to kill the king, Rozo didn't want to be there to watch. He briefly glanced at his master but Taka and Thoit were already engaged in their battle and the king's eyes weren't about to move from Thoit's. Rozo offered a quick bow to his king and ran out of the room, struggling to close the battered door behind him.

"Thoit," Taka uttered, calmly. "You're here late." He glanced at the clock on the wall; it was almost midnight. "Did you come all the way from Soan?"

"Eventually!" Thoit growled. "All this technology and I still have to wait four hours to see my own family!" He marched over to Taka like an avalanche cascading down the mountain's face, his entire body throbbing with rage. "I heard Teima is dead," Thoit snarled.

"Yes," Taka nodded. "She committed treason."

"I heard that too!" Thoit yanked out a chair from under Taka's desk and slammed himself down opposite the king. Taka frowned as Thoit glared dominantly at him. Anyone would think Thoit had forgotten his place, but he hadn't. He knew his place damn well. He was Taka's *older* brother, and he was about to lay down the law.

Thoit reached into his pocket, not taking his eyes off his younger sibling.

"Give me your hand," he demanded.

"Who told you?" Taka asked, ignoring his brother's instruction. He hadn't made Teima's death official yet; only Rozo and the girls knew... One of them must have told him. *Maika.*

"Not Maika!" Thoit snapped, reading Taka's mind. "I saw what you did to her! She may be foolish enough to argue with you but she isn't foolish enough to come crying to me about it! Now give me your hand!"

As requested Taka let out a sigh and extended his arm out to Thoit, his mind scanning through the names of people that might have told Thoit about Teima. Taka would find out who it was eventually; Thoit would tell him when he was finished throwing his weight about. Taka watched his older brother with a slight curiosity, waiting for the man's next move. As expected, Thoit made his signature move of pulling out a lighter and a packet of his illegal cigarettes – this time without asking. He lit one without saying a word, his eyes still on Taka's. Taka watched as Thoit took a long drag from the piece and exhaled slowly, blowing the smoke in Taka's direction.

Thoit paused for a moment, and then all of a sudden he threw out his arm and grabbed Taka's hand, digging his claws maliciously into Taka's wrist with such force it spilt Taka's blood. Taka didn't

71

respond, but he knew this wasn't the worst of it. He kept his eyes on Thoit, refusing to look away or speak a word as Thoit increased the pressure on Taka's wrist. Taka could feel his own blood spilling onto his skin; he could feel Thoit's claws against his veins; he could envision the thick purple stains forming on his shirt… He gritted his teeth and forced himself to remain silent, ignoring the pain in his wrist and the growing wetness of his hand. He refused to lose to his older brother. He could *not* lose to Thoit.

Thoit held his grip for a moment, watching Taka's reaction with an almost mentor-like gaze. He knew Taka would put on a brave face. Cocky little shit. Thoit could rip his arm off and Taka wouldn't dare break his stare. It was Thoit's fault; he'd spent too much time toughening Taka up when they were younger, and now there was almost nothing that Taka couldn't endure. Almost. Thoit placed his free hand on the cigarette in his mouth and took another drag, then removed it from his lips. He watched Taka for a moment more and Taka stared back, challenging his brother to rip open his arm. Thoit smirked a little, then in another sudden movement he yanked his claws off Taka, tearing open Taka's wound. Before Taka's blood could even begin to spill Thoit ripped apart Taka's sleeve and slammed his cigarette down onto the flesh of Taka's wrist, sealing the wound shut with such an intense burning it caused Taka to cry out and snatch his hand away. Taka glared at Thoit angrily, enraged that he had lost to his brother.

"What did you think I was going to do, smoke the whole thing?" Thoit scolded, leaning back in his chair. "I'm already fucking stoned."

"Are you drunk too?" Taka protested, angered and amazed at the shockingly warm blister he felt forming on his wrist. His skin was still burning; he could feel his own veins pulsing beneath his flesh. "Why was that so hot?"

"Fuck knows," Thoit shrugged. "It always burns hot. If a tonito forest ever caught fire we would never need radiators again."

"Is that how you heat your palace?" Taka retorted, standing up. He shot Thoit another angry glare and made his way over to the drinks cabinet, assessing the damage Thoit had done to his clothing. Thoit…

What a dick. He was always a dick, but at least most of the time he was funny as well. What was he doing here anyway? What did he want to say in person that he couldn't say over the phone? "So did you come here to tell me off?" Taka demanded. "Or did you just want to ruin my wardrobe?"

"Both," Thoit answered, calmed by the pain he had inflicted on Taka and the extent of his brother's anger. "She didn't commit treason," Thoit stated. "If she had you would have told me first. You would have come to *me*!"

"Are you jealous, Thoit?" Taka sneered, pouring himself a drink.

"Jealous?"

Thoit stood up and advanced on his brother, squaring up to the younger man like an angry dog. "I don't care who you appoint to babysit you!" he snarled. "I've served my time as your guardian; Suela can have you now! At least I thought she could." He snatched the glass from Taka's hand and hesitated for a second to give Taka a chance to respond. Taka remained silent, so Thoit carried on. "She let you kill Teima! The most adored keika on the planet! Everybody liked her!" He downed the drink. "*I* liked her." He shoved the glass forcefully into Taka's chest, almost shattering it against the king's ribs.

"Don't worry, Thoit. Give it a day and you will get over her," Taka answered mockingly, taking hold of the glass. He refused to be intimidated by Thoit. Thoit wasn't even right – he was ranting over nothing! "And she didn't let me do anything! Teima was my decision. She was poisoning me."

"Was she?" Thoit replied. "And did Suela notice it first?"

"I am grateful that she did," Taka answered coldly, unimpressed by his brother's demeanour. What was his problem? Thoit liked Suela; why was he suddenly against her now? Maybe Teima had poisoned him as well. Bitch.

"And what about your people?" Thoit argued. "The billions of people that you will have to explain yourself to? Will they be grateful that she made up this shit? Do you think they will be happy with your decision?"

73

"It wasn't made up," Taka argued. "And no, they won't be happy. But what can they do about it? She made a fool of us all, Thoit. She deserved to die. Even Rozo agreed – actually, it was his idea." He poured himself another drink and waited for Thoit to respond.

"What did you do, threaten his family?" Thoit narrowed his eyes at Taka. "Is that what you do now? You kill people until you get your way?"

"I kill traitors," Taka stated, and downed his drink.

"Of course…" Thoit nodded. "Fine. Label her a traitor. Force Rozo to back you up, nobody will dare to question you." He watched in disgust as a smirk formed on Taka's face; the king was finally agreeing with Thoit. Great. He was agreeing with the wrong thing! "You can't use fear to control them forever!" Thoit protested. "You need allies, Taka. You need friends – people that will back you up not just because they are scared of you!"

"Allies?" Taka looked at him. "I am the most powerful man on this planet, Thoit. Nobody with half a brain will question me." He poured himself another drink. "And there are plenty of people on my side. *All* of the Hiveakans will support my decision, and the Outsiders will always argue no matter what I do. This is just… another difficult situation. I've never had an issue with difficult situations before, and I won't with this one." He took a sip of his drink. "You need to stop watching over me, friend. If you wanted the throne you should have won it yourself."

"I don't want your throne – I saw what it fucking did to you!" Thoit bellowed. "What I want is for you to think with your head! You never would have decided to kill Teima on your own, the thought would have never even occurred to you if it wasn't for Suela!"

"Shut up!"

Taka locked his eyes sternly onto Thoit, threatening the older man. He was tired of this. Thoit was stepping out of line! He had no right to come in here and start speaking ill of Taka and his wife! No right at all! "She helped me!" Taka snarled. "She noticed Teima was committing treason – and given time I would have noticed it myself! Do you think I am a fool?" He watched Thoit scoff and he clenched his fists, advancing on the older man. "Thoit, do *not* start anything with

Suela. I mean it," Taka threatened. "This was not Suela's decision – it was mine, and mine alone!"

"Oh, fucking wake up," Thoit scolded. "*Everything* is Suela's decision. Everything is my decision. Fucking Toka's, fucking Anaka's, fucking Lanka's, fucking *Mokoto's*. You hold your family too close. Just because they have your blood it doesn't mean they want the best for you – you need to figure out who you can trust, Taka! That's always been your problem! One look at someone's Footprints and you think they are your fucking soulmate!"

"Oh, shut up!" Taka scoffed. "This coming from a man who treats all of his people like they are his best friends! You practically live among your people!"

"It doesn't matter how I treat them; what matters is whether or not I trust them." Thoit narrowed his eyes at Taka. "You are a cunt, Taka, and you are not a fool, but you trust every Hiveakan that lives under your roof. You need to be careful about where your loyalties lie – the scars of the Hive don't always make a friend for life."

"I know that, Thoit!" Taka frowned. "Don't talk to me like I am a child! Suela has been a loyal wife to me for ten years! She has given me two daughters – she is your friend! And Toka's! I think she has earned my trust, don't you?" he scoffed. "Teima didn't. She was a threat. I don't like threats."

"You don't have to kill everything you don't like," Thoit spat. He turned and retreated back to the desk, sitting down. "If I did that you would be fucking dead. A million times over. Every time the Gaiamira put you back in the world I would fucking kill you again."

Taka laughed slightly and downed the rest of his drink, then took out another glass. He gazed at his brother for a moment, studying the older man's body language. Thoit seemed to have calmed down. Perhaps he'd finally realised that Taka *had* thought this through, and that no harm would actually come of this decision. Good. It had taken Thoit long enough. Not that Taka needed Thoit's approval anyway. Taka exhaled to relax himself and joined his brother at the desk, setting the glasses down between them. He took a seat and began to pour himself another drink, looking at Thoit invitingly.

"Mm?"

"No, I don't drink!" Thoit snapped, his face crumbling in disgust as if he were being pestered.

"Liar," Taka argued. "I've seen you drink."

"We aren't children anymore. You just said so yourself," Thoit mumbled, reaching into his pocket for another cigarette. He lit it and placed it in his mouth. "And I'm not trying to get a girl to sleep with me."

"I never tried the sleeping part," Taka smirked.

"You should." Thoit blew his smoke out to his side, away from Taka. "That way you don't have to hear them fucking arguing with you."

Taka laughed again and sighed, his eyes relaxing on Thoit as he drank.

"Well, brother... If there is nothing else you would like to say... I was actually in the middle of revising the global laws, and I would like to get it finished. So do you think I have learned my lesson?"

"You've learned fuck all," Thoit hissed. "You can't teach a child that will not listen."

"But you can beat him until he does what you want." Taka winked.

"Mm. That's true," Thoit said and filled up Taka's glass. Taka nodded at Thoit gratefully and reached for his glass, then gasped as a heavy jolt of pain shot through his shin. That bastard Thoit! He'd kicked him! "You're beaten enough for now," Thoit said with a triumphant smirk. He tapped his foot into Taka's leg again, not as hard this time, and laughed at the angry look on Taka's face. "Do that again and I will *break* your legs."

"I'm not promising," Taka growled. "And I'll break your neck before you can even touch my legs!"

"Taka..." Thoit sighed, a look of sincerity creeping onto his face. "I'm only looking out for you. You do know that? I didn't come here for the views, brother."

"Yes... I know," Taka replied reluctantly.

"No, you don't," Thoit said, taking another drag of his cigarette. "You don't have a younger sibling. You don't know what a

76

fucking burden they are." He exhaled slowly, his eyes resting on Taka. "All I ever heard from Mother and Father..." He placed the cigarette in his mouth and locked his hands together in the symbol of the Gaiamira, his thumbs touching tip to tip and his fingers entwined to represent the eight members of the Gaiamira looking over the world; it was a sign of respect when talking about the dead,. "... Was how much of a success I had to make of you." He removed the cigarette from his mouth and continued talking. "Everything you've ever done was down to me. If you fuck up, I fuck up. Every time you stepped out of line and Mother broke your legs – she broke my legs and my fucking arms as well."

"I'm sorry I was such a burden to you, Thoit," Taka answered. "Still... I turned out alright, didn't I? I suppose my success is your success?"

"You would think so," Thoit said. "But apparently that's down to the fucking Gaiamira."

Taka laughed at his brother's remark, amused even more by the tragedy of how true it was.

"Well... You don't have to take care of me anymore, Thoit," Taka assured. "When I took the crown I relieved you of your babysitting duties. You can't be responsible for your superior, can you?"

"I'm sorry," Thoit replied, taking another drag of his cigarette, "but only those that place the curse can lift it. Until I go to the Gaiamirarezo and our parents say you aren't my problem anymore, you are my problem." He looked at Taka. "... And so it should be. I was ten when you came along; I was old enough to know my duty... You are my baby brother, Taka. I don't want to see you fall."
"I know, Thoit," Taka sighed, forgiving Thoit for the dull pain he could still feel in his leg. "I appreciate that; and I have listened to you."

"No you fucking haven't," Thoit growled. "You never do. I have failed as your leader." He stubbed his cigarette out on his own arm, his fist clenching as he did so. "My best hope now is to make something of that boy it took you twelve daughters to make." Taka laughed slightly and watched Thoit in confusion. Thoit always stubbed his cigarette out on his arm, and Taka had never found out why. "You know, Thoit, I've been meaning to ask you..."

"You've never smoked this, have you?" Thoit asked. Taka shook his head. Thoit smirked, and then sniggered a little. "One side effect is that it converts pain into pleasure…" He leaned back in his chair. "It makes acid showers feel as good as getting away with murder."

"Thank you for that choice of words, Thoit…"

*

'Children are easy, because you know that eventually they will grow up. Siblings are a fucking nightmare.'

-       Malatsa Thoit, 20098G

*

Suela played around with her phone as she wandered towards her bedroom. She had just finished a heavy training session and her skin was still raw from the acid shower that had followed. Every step burned a little, but she enjoyed it. Only Hiveakans could withstand the pain of an acid shower, and only Hiveakan skin was thick and toughened from being drowned in acid as part of an endurance ritual. The intensity of her own training had caused Suela to wonder how her daughters were doing, and she searched her phone for the number of the Hive. Suela was about to turn a corner when a large figure caused her to stop dead in her tracks. She flinched slightly as Thoit leapt out in front of her with a cigarette in his mouth and a deadly playfulness in his eyes.

"Thoit!" Suela huffed, annoyed that he had surprised her. "Where did you come from? Were you waiting for me?"

"No," Thoit answered, taking a drag of his cigarette. "I was looking for you."

"Oh… I'm flattered," Suela teased. "I heard you were in the palace. Did you come just to visit me?"

"You and that child you married," Thoit answered calmly.

"Well," Suela smiled. "It's good to see you –"

78

"Stop your bullshit," Thoit snarled. Suela paused for a moment, taken aback by Thoit's outburst. Why was he so aggressive? Actually, she could guess why, but she wanted him to say it. She dared him to. Suela put a hand on her hip and raised her eyebrows at him.

"Have I upset you?" she purred.

"I don't want you manipulating Taka again," Thoit stated.

"I don't know what you're talking about." Suela shrugged, forcing back a smirk.

"Well that makes fucking two of you," Thoit retorted. "Am I the only one around here that knows Taka loves you more than his fucking tetsa?"

Suela laughed a little at Thoit's choice of words and shook her head.

"You're talking about Teima," she said, giving in. This seemed to be one of those rare occasions where a small surrender would give her more enjoyment. She wanted to hear what Thoit had to say about Teima, and she was desperate to know what part Thoit thought Suela had played in Teima's demise.

"Mm," Thoit nodded, taking a drag of his cigarette. "I heard she committed treason."

"She was poisoning him," Suela answered.

"She might have been," Thoit said. "But not half as much as someone else."

"Really?" Suela replied. "So you don't think he was..." Suela paused for a moment, choosing her words carefully. "Infected?"

"I do," Thoit answered. "But when Kala rang her bells over Taka's head, it wasn't with Teima in mind." He narrowed his eyes at her. "And I think you know that, and I think you played on that. You could tell him the sky was fucking green and he would believe you."

"So what are you going to do?" Suela challenged. "Execute me for treason? He *was* growing soft around her, whether it was actually a problem or not. A man in his position can't take the risk."

"Mm." Thoit nodded again. "And I think a part of you believes that, which is why I'm not going to kill you. It's just fucking handy that Teima happens to be your only threat." He removed the cigarette from his lips and towered over Suela, glaring down at her. Suela didn't

79

move. She stared back up at him challengingly, waiting for him to make his next move. "I like you, Su," Thoit said. "You are a good girl, and you are good for him... But Teima did not need to die. I might never be able to convince Taka of that, but I can at least tell you to *not* manipulate my brother again. You know how fucking stupid he is when it comes to you – and next time you try to take advantage of him, I will kill you."

"How sweet," Suela teased. She didn't care if Thoit slit open her throat. She was fully aware that he could. Easily. So let him, if he wanted to. Taka would never forgive Thoit if he did, but Thoit knew that. Teima wasn't worth losing his brother over, even if he did want to tear Suela apart. Still... It was a warning. Suela knew full well that if her next action called for it, Thoit would murder her. "It's nice that Taka has someone to take care of him, Thoit," Suela taunted, maintaining her Hiveakan demeanour. "Your parents would be proud."

"Shut up!" Thoit barked. "It isn't sweet, it's fucking nature. He is my younger brother – my responsibility. Of course I'll take care of him." He half-smirked down at her. "And he made you my sister, so I'll take care of you as well. Do you understand?"

"Every word, brother." Suela answered, accepting the silent truce. Thoit was so simple that way... Family was family, enemies were enemies and friends were friends, and Thoit never confused the three. Even if he hated Taka with every bone in his body he would give his last breath to save the man's life. It was almost naïve... It would be, if Thoit was ever foolish enough to trust anyone.

"Good." Thoit opened up his clenched fist and extended his arm out to Suela. "So you won't do anything stupid again? I don't want to leave you without legs. Are we clear?"

"Yes, Sire. Very clear," Suela nodded, taking his hand. "... *Ow!*"

Suela jumped and snatched her hand back, staring in shock at the blister that was forming on her wrist. She glared at Thoit. "You bastard!"

"Don't misbehave again," Thoit scolded. "You see what happens."

"Why is it so hot?" Suela demanded, not at all amused by Thoit's choice of punishment. She would have preferred it if he had tried to kill her! Thoit smirked and chuckled lightly.

"Ask your husband. Here." He moved closer to her and pulled her into a hug. "Su... I adore you. You are the best thing that ever happened to him, and in a few years you will be a mother. When those girls come out of the Hive you should teach them how to be as much of a manipulative bitch as you." He looked down at her and smiled darkly. "But don't practice on their father. Promise me, sister."

"Yes," Suela sighed, still annoyed at him for burning her wrist.

"You'll be a good parent," Thoit stated.

"Thank you," Suela growled. She watched him cautiously, trying to establish whether or not he was still angry at her. He probably was. She didn't care.

"I have to go, I'm not staying. It was good to see you, Su." Thoit broke off the hug and looked at her.

"You too," Suela mumbled and watched as Thoit winked at her and walked away, leaving her standing there feeling stupid, and that made her feel angry.

VII.

'Following Gonta, the young God Tomakoto appeared; he was the God of Ambition. He had the face of a child and he held the brightness of the future in his eyes. Tomakoto knew no limits and he encouraged others to be the same; he held in his hand a globe that held all the possibilities in the world and he blessed every one of his people with his ambition.'

-        Extract from the Gaiamirapon: 'The First Encounters'

*

Thud. Another chilling sound brought life into the beast that was the Hive. The walls breathed at night; the echoing sound of screams and angered voices seemed to come from the Hive's own foundations. Mokoto used to be frightened by it, but he wasn't anymore. Five dark years had gone by and Mokoto could only hear so many screams before the sound of pain and torture became nothing more than a soothing lullaby. Now there was just one sound that frightened him. One sound, out of the thousands of noises that would make any Outsider sick to their stomach. It was the sound of his bedroom door.

Mokoto's blood ran cold when he heard the deadly thud. He knew who it was. Of all the thuds this was the only one that scared him. Of all the cold-blooded tutors that visited Mokoto's room this was the only one that could send a shiver through his soul. *Teikota.* He had a way about him; a darkness. Somehow it was different to the others. There was something evil about him; something immortal. Something that Mokoto could never bring himself to destroy.

Mokoto always knew Teikota was there even before he entered the room. Mokoto could sense him; he could feel him. Suddenly the room would grow cold; the lights seemed to dim, and even in the brightest of lights Teikota always managed to turn the world black. It was as if the cold Goddess of Death followed him, accompanied by the God of War and the very soul of the Hive. Everything that lived in

82

nightmares followed Teikota, and Teikota was without a doubt the creator of nightmares.

"*Mokoto.*" The man's dark, booming voice echoed through the room. There was blood in it. Not his own. It was never his own. "Face me, please."

Mokoto looked at the blank wall in front of him and he obediently turned to face his tutor. He knelt down and stared fearfully into Teikota's eyes, waiting for further instruction. He didn't dare move until he was told. He didn't dare breathe. Teikota took a moment to stare back, like he always did. He was judging Mokoto; he was making the boy feel uneasy. He liked to unnerve his students.

Mokoto had no idea, but Teikota was a fairly new face at the Hive. He was young; he was twenty-one and he had only been a tutor for three years, but his students didn't know that. They thought he was older. They thought he had been training children before even their parents were born. It was Teikota's Footprints that gave them that impression. He had a darkness and a bloodlust that was more powerful than most; it ignored his age and how little experience he really had. Teikota didn't need experience. He was a born tutor; he was a natural maker of monsters. Even as a child he had been a living nightmare; he had so much anger and fire in his soul that it had shaken the nerves of even his strongest Hiveakan tutors. It had been the only time in history that a Hiveakan tutor had been frightened by a child. Teikota wasn't just a product of the Hive. He hadn't just grown in the depths of darkness; he had been fathered by it.

Teikota's frame alone was a terrifying sight for any child of the Hive. He had thick muscles, the kind that could split a spine in two without even being strained. They were partially hidden under his clothing; clothing that always smelt of blood. Upon Teikota's talon-like feet were large heavy boots; he always used them to break his students' bones. Mokoto could see traces of blood on the boots; it was fresh. It didn't belong to Teikota; the blood on Teikota's clothing was never his own. It belonged to a child. A child just like Mokoto. Mokoto could hear their screams; he could envision the fear in their eyes. He could see them now, half alive and cowering in darkness after just a few minutes with the evil that was Teikota. The stench of the purple liquid sent a sharp wave of fear through Mokoto's soul. That would be his blood on Teikota's boots soon. It was only a matter of time. Those boots were made for Mokoto's blood.

Mokoto felt his body shrink as Teikota made his way over to him and stood over Mokoto, staring down at the child with cold, dead eyes. He had very dark eyes; Mokoto knew what that meant. As a toddler he'd been told of the Gaiamirákan belief that the darker your eyes the colder your heart, and the darker your soul. Mokoto had never forgotten that, or anything else he'd been taught. He wasn't capable; he would be beaten if he ever forgot a thing. Teikota's soul had to be black. Even black wasn't dark enough – if there was anything beyond black it would be the colour of Teikota's soul. His Footprints had to be giant in size; they had to be bigger than the Hive itself. The darkness wasn't just in Teikota's eyes; his eyes alone weren't big enough to contain the blackness that lived in Teikota. Even his skin was dark. Teikota was a deep scarlet colour; Mokoto had been told that meant he was from a hot country. That wasn't the reason though. Not in Teikota's case. Even if Teikota was a Meitonákan his skin would still be stained by the darkness of his Footprints. His biology was a disguise. Teikota was from South Heikato; it was the only personal thing about him that Mokoto knew. He had grown up in the Southern Heikato Hive, towards the bottom of Meitona's neighbouring country Heikato; it was a few thousand miles from King Taka's palace and Mokoto's Meitonákan Hive home.

Mokoto knew the world map better than he knew his own claws; he could name any town, any country, and any landmark in the world, but he had never seen them. He had never set foot outside of the Hive, and he had barely set foot within it. Mokoto's life here was limited to three rooms – his room, a common room where he mixed with other children, and a gym where he was forced to train and exercise until his muscles were falling from his bones. He had to enter the gym when he was told, and he couldn't leave until he was ordered to.

The tutors at the Hive controlled everything in his life. They controlled when he would eat; they controlled when he would sleep; they controlled when he would exercise; they controlled when he would see other children, when he would wash and dress... Nothing about his life was within Mokoto's control, and if he died in here that too would be at the discretion of the Hive.

"Now..." Teikota began, causing Mokoto to freeze again. Mokoto looked into Teikota's dark eyes obediently, not daring to break his gaze. Teikota had a scar under his left eye. It was only small, but it made him look more frightening. It told a gruesome tale; it meant Teikota had been in a fight, and the fact that he was still alive now meant that he had won. Mokoto could only imagine what he had done to his opponent; he must have mutilated them. He must have torn them apart; he must have ripped off their limbs and shattered every one of their bones – while they were still alive. He must have let them bleed to death, and before they had taken their last breath he must have crushed their skull with those blood stained boots. That was what Teikota was like. That was what he had done, and he had enjoyed doing it, and now there was nothing left of his victim except a scar under his left eye.

That was the rumour the children of the Hive had spread. Teikota let them believe it. If it made them fear him it was useful to him. It was more useful than the truth. The scar wasn't anything significant; it was simply what was left of a wound Teikota had obtained when he himself was a child in the Hive. He had a second scar on his top lip that told a similar tale, and many others around his body. It pleased Teikota so much to hear what wild and ludicrous stories his students made up about him. They really thought he was evil itself; they thought his Footprints were the leader of all Footprints. Teikota was evil, but he didn't have half as many tell-tale signs as the children claimed. The true extent of Teikota's darkness was hidden from their young eyes, and the children would die on the spot if he ever unleashed it upon them.

"Get up," Teikota ordered. Mokoto obeyed, almost tripping over himself as he frantically climbed to his feet. "I have an assignment for you, Mokoto," Teikota continued. "Maths. You like maths, don't you?"

"Yes, sir," Mokoto choked.

"You don't have to lie, Mokoto." Teikota stated. "I do not like liars. Little matats should not lie."

85

"I – I'm sorry," Mokoto stammered, trembling slightly. "I… I don't like maths."

"Good boy." Mokoto relaxed briefly as Teikota spoke approvingly. Mokoto had been good… He wasn't going to get beaten. The Gaiamira were taking care of him – he was being watched by the God of War. The god's name was Taka, like his father. Taka was watching over Mokoto. He watched over all the children of the Hive. "However…" Mokoto's heart stopped. Oh, no…

Teikota knelt down to Mokoto's level and stared into the boy's eyes, his breathing turning deep and feral; almost like a growl. "You lied to me the first time, didn't you?"

"I… I…" Mokoto's lip quivered. Without even realising, he took a couple of paces back, terrified of what was about to happen to him. "I thought you wanted me to say yes!" he pleaded. "I thought –"

"I understand, Mokoto." Teikota nodded, rising to his feet. He followed Mokoto and once again towered over the frightened child. "But you shouldn't ever lie to your superiors. Am I not your superior, Mokoto?"

"Y-Yes," Mokoto whimpered. "Yes you are."

"Good boy." Teikota smirked. "It is a shame that I have to punish you for lying, it was obviously a mistake…" He watched as Mokoto's eyebrows furrowed slightly. The child was confused. He couldn't read Teikota. *Perfect.* "But bad behaviour must be punished, no matter what."

"Please –"

Mokoto's words were cut off as Teikota slammed his boot hard into Mokoto's stomach, forcing from the child a breathless cough.

"I – a –" Mokoto gagged, clutching his stomach in agony. Teikota simply stared down at the boy.

"Are you sorry, Mokoto?" he asked. Mokoto nodded desperately.

"Y-Y –"

"Hm?" Teikota kicked him again, this time in the side of his head, causing Mokoto to fall to the ground. Mokoto scrunched his eyes closed, gritting his teeth to fight the pain that was shooting through him. "*I didn't hear you, Mokoto.*" Teikota's words echoed through his mind;

they sounded so far away. Mokoto knew he had to fight back. If he stayed down he was vulnerable. At least if he stood up he might be able to protect himself...

"I'm sorry!" Mokoto cried as he used all the strength in his body to push himself to his feet. He stared up at Teikota, assuming a weak fighting stance. His body was shaking, but nevertheless Mokoto held his stance firmly and forced himself to face up to his attacker. The God of War would be angry at him if he didn't. Teikota gazed down at Mokoto, examining the child's efforts. Hm... admirable. He was coming along well. Teikota never had a problem getting Mokoto to fight; he just needed a little encouragement here and there, to wake up the boy's Footprints. They were good Footprints; the strongest Teikota had ever seen.

"Good," Teikota uttered, slamming his boot down on Mokoto's foot. "You won't do that again."

"No, sir!" Mokoto screamed, almost choking on his own cry as pain shot through his foot.

"Now." Teikota made his way over to the small desk that was in the corner of the room and switched on Mokoto's laptop. "We have some more assignments for you." He scanned through the laptop's programs and opened up a series of completed maths exercises. Mokoto watched as Teikota typed into the laptop, inputting various codes and passwords to allow him access to the latest assignments. After he had got everything ready Teikota stepped away from the desk and pulled out Mokoto's chair. He motioned for the young matat to sit down. "You have ten minutes. I expect one hundred per cent."

"Y-Yes, sir..." Mokoto nodded. He steadily made his way over to the desk and took a seat in front of the laptop, placing his eyes on the screen. It was an advanced machine; Meitona especially prided itself on its technology and computers these days were completely touch-free, with no physical mouse or keyboard and a simple hologram in their place, tailored to the size of the user's fingers. It read Mokoto's movements with a motion detector that was built into the screen. This technology was designed to be more user-friendly than the older, more cumbersome models, but not for Mokoto. The keyboard was programmed to be too small, to force him into building his precision.

One wrong movement of his fingers would earn Mokoto a beating, but Mokoto wasn't overly worried about that. His precision was quite good. Mokoto had other concerns. He tried not to let it show, but he was nervous. Maths was never his strong point and he wasn't sure if he could do it. Ninety-eight or ninety-nine per cent maybe... but full marks? That wasn't likely... Not in ten minutes.

"Your time starts now."

"Yes, sir." At the sound of Teikota's voice Mokoto hastily made a start on the questions, terrified of what would happen to him if he got a single answer wrong.

*

'What do I think of Meitat Lanka's graduation? I think she will make a wonderful addition to King Taka's collection of daughters.'

-      Malatsa Thoit, 20108G

*

Elsewhere in Meitona, Mokoto's older sister Lanka was sitting under the painful stare of her own Hiveakan guardians, her mother and father. She had graduated the day before, at the acceptable age of thirteen. Her mother had escorted her home from the Hive and hadn't hesitated to emphasise to Lanka how important it was for the young meitat to defeat her brother and claim the Gaiamirákan throne. It was something Lanka had been told throughout her life, and at the young age of thirteen she already resented the child Mokoto. She hadn't met him, but she had been shown photographs of her brother and she knew everything there was to know about him. Lanka knew Mokoto's blood type; she knew his mother's name and birthplace; she knew his birthday; she knew his strengths and weaknesses; she knew the colour of his eyes and hair; she knew the marks on his skin... She knew he was the only thing that stood between her and the throne. He and Anaka. Anaka was different though. Anaka was another child of Suela, and Lanka was not arrogant enough to believe that she was the only

88

one of Suela's children worthy of taking the throne. If Anaka could defeat Mokoto first then Lanka would gladly step aside without quarrel or question… but Lanka had made it her mission to spill Mokoto's blood before Anaka could so much as utter the matat's name. All she had to do was wait. She had to wait until he graduated, until he came to meet her… Then she would kill him.

"You seem nervous, Meitat," King Taka commented, sending a sharp jolt of fear through Lanka's heart as the king looked across the dining table at her. Lanka battled against her fear of him and lowered her eyes, ashamed and angry at her body for betraying her. She was nervous, but she wasn't supposed to let it show. She would be classed as a failure if she did it again. This was the first time Lanka had been alone with both of her parents; upon her arrival she had been welcomed by her father's other wives and their Outsider children. She had met her father briefly during her welcoming ceremony, but business had called him away before his Footprints had managed to make a heavy impression upon her soul. Now though… it was different. It was terrifying.

Lanka was alone with her mother and father, eating the kind of food she had always been denied in the Hive and trying her best to say what they wanted to hear. She was terrified of saying or doing the wrong thing; she had no idea what wrong word or action would put her back in the Hive. It was impossible for Lanka to return there; everybody knew it except her. A graduate was a graduate for life, but their tutors liked to insinuate that with incorrect behaviour, they could return to the Hive. They liked the graduates to think the threat of the Hive was still very real; it stopped the graduate getting too comfortable with life outside of the Hive and it encouraged them to maintain their Hiveakan strength and discipline. Lanka had no idea how safe she really was now, and she had no idea how amusing her parents found her fear.

"I should hope so." Suela looked at her husband. "She should be afraid of you."

"And you," Taka replied. He moved his eyes back to his daughter. "What did you think of your sisters?"

"They are… pleasant," Lanka answered awkwardly. They were boring, was what she wanted to say. They were weak and foolish. They were the sort of people she had been taught to loathe. They were pleasant, yes. That was precisely what made them so loathsome.

"Don't worry, they'll keep out of your way," Suela smirked. "If they don't, you have our permission to kill them." She glanced at Taka challengingly, daring him to defend his children. He simply rolled his eyes and remained silent, indifferent to Suela's callous remark.

"Thank you, Mother…" Lanka replied quietly.

"They won't be much help," Taka commented. "Tomorrow your mother will spend the day with you – if you want to kill a Hiveakan you will waste your time practising on Outsiders." He smirked slightly and gestured towards Suela. "If you can harm her, you might just be able to break your brother's skin."

"She'll do more than that," Suela replied with confidence. She looked at her daughter, judging the girl's very existence. Lanka would kill Mokoto. She would. She was nothing if she didn't. Suela hadn't given birth to a failure. "Your father's throne will be yours. You won't disappoint me, will you?"

"No, Mother." Lanka shook her head frantically, desperate to convince her mother that she was worthy of the life she had been given. She knew her life depended on how much of a success she could make of it, and she was determined to become not only a queen, but the best queen the world had ever known. "I swear to you – when my brother comes out of the Hive, he will be dead within the year."

"A year?" Taka gasped, raising his glass to his lips. "I thought you said a week, Su."

"I'll train her," Suela growled, annoyed by the smugness in Taka's eyes. "Your half-breed won't even last a day."

Lanka listened to the sound of her father's laughter and shrank into her seat, terrified of the beating she expected to receive for setting herself a longer deadline than her mother had desired.

*

'Well... I am a Hiveakan, so to me the word 'comrade' actually means someone I am madly in love with but can't admit it because it goes against my beliefs. So in answer to your question no, there are not any people that I consider 'comrades'; I am one of the few Hiveakans that actually is a heartless cunt.'

-        Malatsa Thoit, 20094G

*

"How is your son doing?" Suela's sniping voice came from somewhere behind Taka.

"Are you worried?" Taka replied teasingly, sliding his shirt from his shoulders. It was late into the night, and King Taka and his favourite wife were in his bedroom, readying themselves to put an end to the day. He examined his bare flesh in the mirror that stood before him, as he always did when he undressed. Every day Taka liked to make sure he was still just as Hiveakan as he had been the night before. Every day when he awoke and every night before he slept he checked the density of his muscles; the thickness of his scars; the lack of blood as nobody had the skills to harm him... Not without his consent, anyway. Taka glanced at his wife in the mirror and met her eyes with the same level of darkness he found in hers. Suela was lying in his bed, her naked body stretched out under the sheets and hidden from his sight by the most expensive fabrics in the world. She was staring at him with a sinister cockiness in her face, the kind that taunted Taka for still believing his son could ever compare to her daughters. Taka wouldn't back down from the challenge. He actually believed she was wrong. "You'll be away from Lanka for two months," he stated with confidence, running his hand across his scalp to check the thickness of his hair. "Do you think she will keep on top of her training?"

"Why not? I barely train her these days anyway," Suela replied.

"Mm," Taka grunted. She was right. Lanka hardly needed her mother anymore; perhaps not at all. It was now two years since Lanka had graduated, and the girl was growing stronger by the day. Her once tiny and starved Hiveakan body had become a gallant display of

91

victory and strength; it was a body only suited to the very finest of Hiveakan queens. Her once timid new graduate eyes had become dark and hard, and her Footprints so strong that even her own mother and father could barely stir her soul. Lanka trained all day every day, usually unsupervised and with minimal food and rest. She was determined to fulfil her mother's wishes; she was determined to claim the throne regardless of how much pain she had to endure. It was because of Lanka's determination that Suela felt confident enough to leave.

Suela was going on a pilgrimage, and was due to leave the following day. It was something that most Hiveakans did at some point in their lives; a pilgrimage was a test of endurance and a tribute to the Hive and the God of War. Suela would set off into the most northern part of Meitona, into a restricted area of the world known as Takáka Eia, Taka's Wilderness, where she would spend two months alone, accompanied only by the harsh whispers of the wind and the Goddess of Death following closely behind her. If she was to succeed in her pilgrimage Suela would have to brave the elements and endure any trials the Gaiamira and the Guardians of the Wilderness chose to set upon her. The Guardians were believed to be the cruellest Hiveakans in the world; they were a group of priests so blessed by Taka and so at one with his being it wasn't quite known whether they were even mortals themselves. They had been, to begin with, but it was an ancient belief that only a god could test a mortal's true strength, and only in Takáka Eia was a mortal's strength truly tested. As such, nobody could say for certain if the Guardians were mortal anymore, or if they even had physical bodies at all.

Suela couldn't leave her pilgrimage early; she had chosen to make her pilgrimage last for two months and she wasn't permitted to leave Taka's Wilderness alive until she had endured two months' worth of trials. She would have no phone and no communication with anybody until the day she returned. Suela would need to find her own food; she would need to build her own shelter and she would need to fight off any predators with her bare hands. She would come back scarred and hungry, beaten and bruised, but she would come back a warrior who had honoured herself and her family more than any other mortal in the world could. To successfully complete a pilgrimage was the greatest tribute to the God of War that a Hiveakan could offer, and it would guarantee only the very best of blessings to their family. Likewise, to fail a pilgrimage was considered a bigger offence to the Gaiamira than blasphemy. If Suela returned home even a day late she would bring dishonour upon the palace, and anything more than a month late would put her and her family to shame for all of eternity. It was a great event for the palace, and an exciting event, and neither Taka nor his wife had any doubt that she would succeed.

Finally satisfied with his image, Taka turned around to face his wife and smirked a little. "Well... Mokoto is doing well. Thank you for asking. He'll be living here by the time you get back."

"Ha! If he graduates in two months then I'll kill the girls myself," Suela retorted. Taka laughed and moved over to join her in the bed.

"We'll see," he purred.

"Mm." Suela watched as Taka reached over to his bedside table and grabbed hold of the tetsa bottle that sat upon it. It was his bedtime drink. It was his bedtime drink, his morning drink, his afternoon drink... Taka was only sober when he was asleep, and he barely slept. Suela let out a sigh and moved to lean against him, her claws trailing themselves along the thick muscles that coated Taka's bones. She always liked to toy with his body; she teased his muscles to emphasise the fact that they were there; it soothed his ego and therefore his confidence, and Suela knew just how confident Taka liked to feel. She was always careful not to overdo it; she always made him feel just secure enough so that he listened to her without question, and without thinking for a second that her many acts of flattery were only a way for her to make him do whatever she wanted. "So," Suela began. "Will you miss me?"

"Miss you?" Taka looked down at her. "I have two more where you came from."

"Shut up!"

Taka laughed as Suela swiped at him, placing a fine cut across his chest. "They can't satisfy you."

"They'll do." Taka took a swig of the tetsa bottle and yawned, putting a possessive arm around her. "You're only going for two months, Su. It's hardly death."

"Only two months?" Suela raised her eyebrows at him. "Well, if it isn't that long... perhaps you could do something as well."

"Mm?" Taka grunted.

"That shit you mistake for water." Suela spoke bluntly. "Give it up."

"What?" Taka looked at her, frowning in confusion. "Why?"

"Because it's not that long. Apparently." Suela smirked. "And I want to see if you can do it."

"Of course I can do it," Taka growled. "I'm not an alcoholic."

"Yes you are," Suela answered. "But I want to see if you can handle the withdrawal..." She looked at him wickedly, her eyes glimmering with a playful darkness. "To see if you are still worthy of me."

"Ha!" Taka sniggered. "Fine." He held the bottle to his lips and drank thirstily, not stopping to breathe until he had consumed every last drop. He held the empty bottle in front of Suela and dared her to not believe him as he placed it back down on the bedside table. "If that's what you want, I won't open another until you return."

"Do you think you'll be able to help yourself?" Suela taunted.

"Shut up," Taka growled. "It's only a drink."

"Fine," Suela replied. "But..." She moved up his body and held her face close to his, the flesh of her lips almost touching the flesh of his. "When I get back, I don't want to taste a single drop of it in your blood."

"When you get back you won't have chance to taste my blood," Taka purred. He moved on top of her and sank his teeth into her cheek, then silenced her cry with a firm kiss. He pulled away briefly and smirked at her. "And I will miss you. To some extent."

"Shut up!" Suela scolded, reacting exactly how he'd hoped. "I hope that's the drink talking – you're starting to sound like an Outsider." She let out a sharp gasp and smiled at the sudden pain of Taka's claws sinking into her thigh, determined to prove her wrong.

'After bidding farewell to her family in the palace, Keika Suela embarked on her pilgrimage earlier today. She is due to return in two months' time, and will no doubt be welcomed by the Hiveakans of Meitona with a very well deserved honour and respect for both herself and our king.'

\-   News report, 20110G

*

"Okay," Suela said. "Stop there." She hid her breathlessness from her daughter as well as she could, pleased with how good of a fighter Lanka had become. They were in the gym; Suela had decided to squeeze in one last training session with Lanka before she departed. Time had run out now. She had to go. Suela looked down at the fresh marks on her arms and smiled. "Good," she said. She looked at Lanka. "Keep it up."

"Yes, Mother," Lanka nodded, panting.

"I mean it." Suela approached Lanka and stared at her forcefully. "Don't let me down, Meitat. You have the makings of a great queen."

Lanka remained silent, shocked at the words that had just left her mother's mouth. Her mother had never complimented her before – not to that extent at least. Why was she being so kind...? Perhaps she felt sentimental because she would be leaving for so long... No. That was ridiculous. The last thing Keika Suela is is sentimental. Maybe she was just testing Lanka's reaction... Yes. That made more sense. Lanka nodded and cleared her throat.

"Thank you," she uttered obediently, wiping all emotion from her face.

"Hm." Suela smiled a little, and raised her eyes to the sound of the door. Her face fell. She looked angry all of a sudden. Lanka turned round to see who had offended her mother so, and was surprised to see it was her uncle. What was he doing here? Lanka bowed before

95

Malatsa Thoit and stared up at him questioningly, wondering why he had come to the palace. She didn't know he was due to visit… Usually her parents notified her so that she had time to prepare for his arrival. Was everything alright in Hu Keizuaka? "What are you doing here?" Suela's cold voice came from behind Lanka. Obviously this visit was unexpected… Lanka started to grow concerned. It had to be something to do with Hu Keizuaka – something urgent. Or her cousin… Uncle Thoit's daughter Meitat Teisumi was still in the Hive; had something happened to her?

"Forgive me for interrupting, ladies…" Thoit began. He gestured for Lanka to stand and she stood obediently, awaiting his answer to her mother's question. Thoit narrowed his eyes at Suela. "I need to speak to you," he uttered. "In private." He sounded angry as well…

"Whatever you want to say you can say in front of my daughter," Suela replied.

"No," Thoit growled. "I can't." He looked at her sternly. "And I would hope you wouldn't want me to."

" Lanka." Suela's voice caught her daughter's attention and Lanka looked at her mother obediently. "Wait here," Suela instructed, and looked at Thoit. "I'm leaving in ten minutes. This had better be quick."

"Just come!" Thoit barked. He moved towards the door and led Suela out of the room, then slammed the door behind her.

Lanka waited for a moment, unsure of whether or not she should spy on them. She knew she shouldn't. It would be disrespectful, wouldn't it? Whatever they were discussing it obviously wasn't for Lanka's eyes or ears. What could it be, though…? Lanka felt nervous. Surely if it was important then her father would be speaking to them as well? Then again, if it wasn't important then why couldn't it wait until her mother returned home? Maybe the king was out in the corridor with them… Maybe it was something to do with politics; perhaps there was something happening between Keizuaka and Hu Keizuaka… But Lanka's mother wasn't a legal advisor; would her father and Uncle Thoit really need to consult with her? Surely not now that she had to leave soon? Maybe it was Teisumi… Lanka remained still for a minute, her body tense and ready to move as her anxiety grew. She had a bad feeling. She didn't know why. This was nothing to do with her! It was obviously something spontaneous – her mother hadn't expected to see Thoit. But that was yet another cause for concern… Uncle Thoit rarely visited the palace unscheduled. He had no need to; the majority of his political dealings could be done by phone. He only came to Meitona for family visits, and this obviously wasn't a family visit. What was going on…? What was going on?

Lanka couldn't fight her curiosity any longer. She didn't want to, for the sake of her planet. If something was going on she had a right to know – this would be her planet someday! She cautiously approached the door and stared out through its window, expecting to see her father talking with her mother and Uncle Thoit. Lanka's eyes widened at the king's absence. He wasn't there… Her mother and Uncle Thoit were standing away from the door; Lanka could barely see them, but she could see enough to know that her father wasn't with them. They were talking alone… They seemed to be arguing. Her mother was standing defensively; Uncle Thoit was speaking with aggression and force… Lanka stared at their lips, trying to make out what they were saying.

"Su… Please," Uncle Thoit mouthed, his body softening. What was going on…? Fuck!

Lanka moved away from the door as her uncle moved his arm out to gesture towards her. Had he seen her? Had he even looked? She was being talked about… They were talking about her! What was it? Was it the rivalry? Did Uncle Thoit object to Lanka and Mokoto's battle for the throne? No… No, he adored it! Whenever it came up in conversation he seemed so amused by it – it was all he ever spoke about with Lanka. Anyway, he wouldn't fly all the way to Meitona just to talk about that. What was it…? Lanka hesitated for a moment, and looked back through the window.

They weren't arguing anymore. Lanka's eyes widened at the sight before her. They were hugging… They were hugging like Outsiders! They were clinging to each other, like lovers in an over-emotional movie! Why were they doing that…? What was going on? Lanka watched as her mother and uncle pulled away from each other and stared at each other for a moment, their eyes soft and their bodies loose as if they were Outsiders. Why were they doing that…? Her mother was saying something; Lanka couldn't make out the words. She was too shocked to concentrate. Whatever it was, Uncle Thoit nodded and replied, and then… Shit!

Lanka ran away from the door and returned to her position in the room as Suela and Thoit turned back towards the gym. She waited nervously, terrified of what they would do if they had seen her. Her mother would break her legs; there was no doubt about it. Within seconds Lanka's mother and uncle were back in the room, and Lanka looked at them anxiously. Her mother's eyes… They looked strange. They were glistening. She hadn't been crying, had she? No. Lanka was angry at herself for thinking such a thing. Her mother couldn't cry – she wasn't capable of it.

"Okay," Suela uttered. "I'm out of time." She looked at her daughter. "Be a queen, Lanka."

"Of course." Lanka nodded. "But… He won't graduate before you return."

"I suppose." Suela half smiled. Why was she doing that? She wasn't as arrogant as usual… What had *happened* out there?

"I won't walk you out, Su," Thoit said.

"I wouldn't expect you to," Suela replied. She looked at him. "Bye, Thoit. Watch over the palace for me."

"I'll fucking have to," Thoit growled. Suela laughed a little and left the room, her cockiness returning.

Lanka stared at her uncle, waiting to see if he would offer some sort of explanation as to what had just happened. Thoit looked back at her and sniggered. "I suppose you were watching?"

"No!" Lanka gasped, a jolt of panic shooting through her soul. *Shit!* "I –"

"It's fine, Meitat," Thoit soothed. "Just don't tell anyone else what you saw – including your father. I'm sorry, darling… That's all I can tell you."

"Okay…" Lanka answered cautiously. She didn't like this… Something was going on, and her father wasn't involved. What was it?

"Come on." Thoit beckoned Lanka towards him. "Take a break from exhausting yourself. Should we see your sister? I think your father is already there with Mokoto."

"Mm." Lanka nodded. She cautiously followed her uncle out of the room, and accompanied him to visit Suela's youngest child in the Hive.

VIII.

'After the young god Tomakoto appeared the peaceful god Tangun rose from the earth, and brightened up the sky. He was a gentle man with a calming face and an aura that brought energy to the world. Tangun said he was the God of Birth and Reincarnation; he wore around his neck a necklace made of buds and flowers and he told the people it was his mission to breathe new life into the world. Every newborn baby would be blessed by Tangun, and every living thing no matter how great or small would carry his spirit within them.'

- Extract from the Gaiamirapon: 'The First Encounters'

*

Mokoto sat nervously as he watched his tutor. It was a female tutor this time; she was sitting at his desk and checking through his latest assignment. Her name was Hara, the Gaiamirákan word for 'life'. It was typically an Outsider name, but there was nothing Outsider about Hara. She was very strict and very cruel, so much so that she had earned herself a nickname in the Hive. She had two sons of her own in the Hive, and this had caused the students to name her Heia Keila, or Hei-kei for short: The Evil Mother. They didn't dare call her Hei-kei to her face, only to each other, but Hei-kei knew of the name. She found it amusing; she was a lot like Teikota in that respect. She prided herself on how much the children feared her.

"Mm." Hei-kei hummed as she checked through Mokoto's work. Mokoto fixed his eyes on her, not daring to pull his gaze away until she told him to. He keenly awaited her feedback; he was desperate to know how well he had done. He was desperate to know how much or how little she would beat him. He wanted time to brace himself; time to plan his defence if she did come at him. Hei-kei let out a short sigh and closed the assignment down. She turned to face Mokoto with a difficult look on her face. "Well done. You answered all of the questions correctly."

Mokoto felt himself relax at the sound of her approval. That was good. It was what he had expected. The work subject had been history; he liked history. He always found it interesting, maybe because it was mostly about his family. Mokoto liked learning about his ancestors. "But," Mokoto's heart sank. 'But'... why did she have to say 'but'? Hei-kei looked at Mokoto sternly. "You completed this assignment in sixteen minutes. Didn't we agree on fifteen?"

"Yes," Mokoto uttered angrily. He was angry at himself. He knew where he had gone wrong – he'd spent too long on the second question; he'd put in too much detail...

"You know why, don't you?" Hei-kei said, reading the expression on the young boy's face.

"Yes," Mokoto nodded.

"Mm," Hei-kei replied. She sighed again and rose to her feet, moving closer to the child as she spoke. "It's a shame, Mokoto. That second answer was very good, but you wrote too much. This wasn't an essay – you aren't at an essay writing level yet. I know you keep trying..." She smirked down at him. "I think a little self-discipline is needed here, isn't it? Very few people can run before they can walk." He always heard that... Lately Mokoto's tutors had been scolding him for trying to do more than he could. He wrote too much in his history assignments; he tried to draw things that were too difficult in his art classes; he tried to hit too hard or endure too much in combat and he ended up injured... He couldn't help it. Mokoto's Footprints were growing, and as much as he tried to contain them he couldn't fight their impatience. They were dragging him into something he wasn't ready to be dragged into, and they didn't care how much he got hurt. "Mokoto," Hei-kei's voice pulled the matat's eyes up to meet hers. "Sort it out." Mokoto didn't flinch as she kicked him hard in the stomach. He crouched down breathlessly but he didn't whimper; he didn't cry out or curse even though he felt a terrible pain in his abdomen. Mokoto was better than that. He knew better than to show pain or weakness. He didn't need to show his tutors that he felt punished; they knew it. They would only lose respect for him if he cried like a child. Hei-kei's silence meant he had done the right thing; she didn't attack him again. "You have nine minutes to yourself – I'm deducting that minute you

101

owe me. Don't leave this room." Her voice came from somewhere over his head and Mokoto listened to the sound of his tutor's footsteps as she left the room, leaving the young matat to have a reduced ten minute break. Mokoto closed his eyes and waited for a moment for the pain in his stomach to subside, and then he moved over to his computer and started to browse through the internet for articles about his Hiveakan sisters. It was almost all Mokoto ever did in his free time. He liked to get to know his rivals.

*

'Outside Meitona Palace this morning people have gathered in their thousands to welcome Keika Suela home. Keika Suela is due to return later this afternoon after a two month pilgrimage to Takáka Eia – something that has no doubt brought a great deal of honour onto the royal family within the Hiveakan community. The crowds started forming in the early hours of the morning and even now people continue to join the masses that are waiting outside the palace; newspapers are already naming it the most exciting royal event of the year.'

-       News report, 20110G

*

"Well… He's coming now." Elsewhere in Meitona, in the basement of King Taka's palace, Mokoto's older sister Meitat Beina was in the prayer room. She was talking to the Gaiamira as she often did; being a nun gave her that privilege. Sometimes she didn't appreciate her gift… not that she would ever dare say that in front of her father. Beina knew that her relationship with the Gaiamira was something that benefitted Meitona Palace greatly, and she would never dream of taking that away from her only living parent. Beina adored the king, as much as many people didn't. He was on his way here now; she could hear his footsteps. King Taka was always so heavy footed, as if the burdens of the throne added weight to his frame. Actually, he had

102

gained weight recently. He wasn't fat – not at all. He was just more muscular than before. He had given up alcohol at Suela's request; he hadn't touched a drop since her departure, and in place of the tetsa he'd actually started eating real food and drinking more water. He looked healthier these days; his skin practically glowed and his always rigorous training regime seemed to benefit his body more when it didn't have the alcohol to compete against. The king was two months older but he looked a year younger; he looked handsome. He was handsome anyway, but now more than ever. It was good… Beina liked to see her father like this. She wondered how long it would last. A part of her feared it, in fact. Beina looked at the visions of the Gaiamira she saw before her, fully aware that they knew of her concerns, and she bowed her head. "I have to go." She rose to her feet and awaited her father's arrival.

King Taka entered the room almost immediately, and offered his daughter a polite smile.

"Sorry Meitat," he apologised as Beina knelt before him. "I hope I'm not disturbing you?" Taka gestured for Beina to stand and looked around the room cautiously, sensing the Gaiamiras' presence.

"We're finished, Sire," Beina smiled. "I was just leaving."

"Right. Good," Taka uttered and walked past Beina, towards the statue of the God of War. Beina couldn't help but smile as he walked past her; he smelt nice. He was wearing cologne. His wedding chains were glowing. It was Gaiamirákan tradition for couples to exchange jewellery during their wedding ceremony; necklaces and pendants were a popular choice and King Taka had received a chain for each of his eight weddings. He didn't wear them all now; Teima's chain had been destroyed when she had betrayed him, as had the chain he'd received from his late wife Kala, named after the Goddess of Love. Kala had committed suicide when Taka had put their daughter Korana in the Hive, and suicide was a great offence to the Gaiamira. That act had done Taka's reputation a lot of damage, especially within the Hiveakan community. It was still undetermined whether or not Taka would even let Kala's daughter return home. Regardless, he only wore six chains now; three in honour of the three wives he had lost to illness, one of whom was Beina's biological mother, and his surviving wives

Kaeila, Geith and Suela… It was Suela's chain that had caused the collection to glow. Beina knew her father had wanted to have it cleaned in time for her return home, but of course he had been too Hiveakan to admit the reasons why, even to himself. So he had cleaned all of them, in the hope that it would disguise the cuteness in his heart. It was cute, as far as Beina was concerned. Beina found it adorable. He was wearing cologne; he'd cut his hair; he'd cleaned Suela's chain… It was all for Suela, because she was coming home today. King Taka would never admit it. He put up a good act, probably because he believed it himself. He had no place for Suela in his heart. Strictly no place. Of course, Sire. Of course that was the truth. Who would dare argue? Certainly not Beina, although she was the only person in the world that didn't believe him. She was the only mortal alive that wasn't fooled by her father's ruthless Hiveakan demeanour, and the only reason she hadn't fallen victim to his flawless façade was because she had inside information from the Goddess of Love. Even King Taka was oblivious to the bells that rang within his own heart.

"I'll leave you to it, Sire," Beina said.

"Alright. See you later," Taka answered lazily, indifferent to his daughter's presence.

"Suela is due home today, isn't she?" Beina forced herself not to giggle as she awaited her father's response.

"Mm, at some point," Taka replied. He didn't sound interested; he didn't sound excited… He didn't seem to care. "I think your mother Kaeila is making arrangements for her homecoming – I want you girls to greet her, but you probably won't see me. I doubt I'll have the time to deal with that."

"No, Sire." Beina smirked. "Of course not." She left the room with a smile on her face, charmed by the extent of her father's denial.

*

'Thousands of Hiveakans all over the world were greatly disappointed today when Keika Suela failed to return from her pilgrimage on time. The majority of people waiting outside Meitona Palace have now returned home, however there is still a significant crowd outside the gates and people are expecting her to arrive shortly after midnight, if not before.'

-       News report, 20110G

*

Within a matter of hours the atmosphere in the palace changed from warm and exciting to icy and angry. Suela was late. It was past midnight now, and she still had not returned home. Taka wasn't impressed. Not in the slightest. Besides the fact that his daughters had interrupted their lessons and activities to greet Suela; besides the fact that the media and millions of members of the public had been keenly waiting for her to return home, Suela had shamed Taka. She had shamed him greatly, in front of the entire world. To return home late from a pilgrimage was an offence to the Gaiamira, even if it was only by a day – it was an offence even if it was only by an hour. Suela had brought a great deal of embarrassment upon Taka and Meitona Palace by not returning home on time. She had made Taka look foolish; she had made their marriage and their children look weak, and she had damaged the family name. Taka wouldn't let her get away with it. Nobody made a fool out of him! Suela was sure to return in the morning; she wasn't weak enough to return more than one day late, and she would be too proud to even think of it. She would be angry at herself for missing her deadline... Not half as angry as Taka was. He would beat her when she came home. If he wanted to he could have her executed for treason. He might... Or he might make her go on another pilgrimage to prove her worth and repent to the Gaiamira. It would depend on how ashamed she was, and how much she begged for his forgiveness. Taka smirked slightly as he thought about it. He was looking forward to it in a way; Suela was always so arrogant, so sure of herself... Taka couldn't even begin to imagine how her face would look tomorrow morning; there was no way she would be able to look him in the eye. He wouldn't let her forget this. Never. He would enjoy reminding her; this was a guarantee that he would always, under every circumstance in every situation, win over her for the rest of their lives.

Not that he didn't win anyway. Of course he won over her. He was the king.

"Rozo." Taka moved his eyes to his aide, noting how sleepy the man looked. Poor Rozo... Taka never usually kept him up this late. The king had wanted to stay awake until midnight, to see if Suela really would be a day late. He had been tending to a few political matters with Rozo to pass the time, and the time had taken its toll on Rozo's face.

"Mm?" Rozo answered, holding back a yawn. "Yes, Sire?"

"Get me some water," Taka ordered. "Then you can go to bed."

"Water, Sire?" Rozo seemed surprised by his king's request. Why? What was he expecting the king to say?

"Of course," Taka said. "Suela and I had an agreement. I will keep my word, even if she cannot keep hers."

"You may want to remind her of that, Sire," Rozo replied, joining in with the king's attack on Suela. "She will feel all the more ashamed for being late."

"Mm," Taka smirked, nodding in agreement. "Go on. Get my water. Then bed."

"Yes, Sire." Rozo nodded and left the room.

*

'It isn't like Suela to be late for anything – but she's tough. I am not worried about her... Not yet, anyway. I am worried about what my brother will do to her when she does come home!'

\-   Malatsa Toka, 20110G

*

"Very good..." Hei-kei's voice relaxed Mokoto as she read through his latest essay. She moved her eyes to look at the matat and held back a smile. "You stopped waffling, I see – and look." She checked her watch and moved her eyes back to Mokoto. "You have a

106

minute to spare." Mokoto forced himself not to grin smugly at her remark; he rarely received praise and when he did it made him so arrogant. Mokoto was six years old now, soon to be seven, and as a well-educated Hiveakan boy he was old enough to appreciate that he was the only male heir in a family of twelve girls, and through his limited access to the internet and the voices of the media Mokoto had come to learn at least to some degree the true value of his being. It had made him arrogant, but not half as much as he could have been. His tutors made sure Mokoto's confidence never soared too high. Praise was damaging, and Mokoto absorbed it more than most.

Hei-kei didn't dare compliment the matat without also saying something to deflate his ego. "So… in that minute, do you think you could have written more?" Hei-kei narrowed her eyes at Mokoto, and the boy's heart sunk at the sound of her disapproval. "I told you not to write too much, but it's still an essay. I gave you that time for a reason – you were supposed to use all of it." She rose from her seat and made her way over to Mokoto, amused by the look of self-disgust on his face. Hei-kei adored Mokoto; she barely had to touch him at all. He tortured himself so much; he took the words of his tutors so to heart that even the slightest disapproving remark practically led him to suicide. That was because he valued himself so highly; he knew his own standards should be set higher than other people's. It was good. He should think that, and he should live by it – he was probably going to be king one day. He should set himself high standards, and he should consistently achieve them. If he didn't then he had failed the world. Hei-kei was pleased to see that Mokoto seemed to understand that. He was a very intelligent child. "I'm going to take two minutes off your break," Hei-kei said. "Maybe then you'll learn how to count the time, hm? I hope you aren't going to need a clock – that would put you down two levels. You do understand that, don't you?"

"Yes…" Mokoto nodded angrily. No. He didn't need a clock! He hadn't used a clock since he was five years old; he could count minutes in his head. He *could*!

"Good," Hei-kei said. She flung up her foot to kick him in the jaw, causing the young matat to gag and grunt loudly. His jaw cracked. Maybe she had broken it; Hei-kei didn't particularly care. There would be no real damage, not with the force she'd used. Hei-kei laughed a little as she watched Mokoto trying to hold back his pain; he was pretending not to be bothered by the blood he could taste in his mouth. "I suggest you use your break to get better. You aren't getting any meals until you can write an essay properly." She moved past the boy and left the room, knowing full well that he would follow her advice.

Mokoto spat the blood from his mouth and clutched his fractured jaw as he made his way over to his essay. He scanned through the piece, trying to work out what he could add in a minute. He used his break to rewrite the whole thing.

*

'What was once dubbed the most exciting royal event of the year was finally declared a failure on 01-05-20110G. At 10:00, exactly one month after her expected arrival, Keika Suela was declared a korota.'

-        Extract from history textbook: 'The Wives of Taka', 20174G

*

"Sire…" The word fell on deaf ears, as if they were spoken by a spirit to the living… or perhaps the other way round. King Taka looked dead now. He didn't look like a mortal deceased; he looked like a soulless creature that had never felt the warmth of worldly blood. Anger was not the word. There was no word for this – this vision Rozo saw before him. It was horrifying. It was petrifying. It was a wonder the walls of the palace had not turned black. They would crumble soon; they had to. Nothing could withstand the force of whatever it was that embodied the king at this very moment. This was the scariest Rozo had ever seen him. Rozo had no idea a mortal could even look like this. He wasn't a mortal anymore; that much was clear. The king was named after the God of War, and right now the God of War was all he was. "Sire."

"It is brave of you to speak, my friend." King Taka finally spoke in a voice that didn't sound like his own. It sounded dark… Evil.

He was a god. "If your parents had put you in the Hive, perhaps you would have graduated early..." Taka said. He grunted a little, almost laughing. Almost. "But then... that doesn't mean anything. Obviously not. A Hiveakan means nothing these days. Apparently a Hiveakan can be the biggest traitor in the world."

Taka reached for the bottle of tetsa that was situated on his desk, just where it used to be. It was almost empty, as it had been when Rozo had entered the room. He'd only left the king alone for an hour or so; he'd thought it would be in the king's best interests to be alone to... 'process' the news. Suela hadn't returned. It was a month later, and she had officially failed her pilgrimage. Only an hour ago she had been declared a korota, someone that had failed their pilgrimage and betrayed the Gaiamira in one of the most blasphemous ways they could. Rozo had thought the king would react better if he was left alone, but now the aide was regretting his decision. The king was drinking again, obviously. He hadn't touched a drop before today – he hadn't touched a drop before Suela's failure had been made official. Now... What had he become? Rozo didn't even recognise the man anymore.

"Sire..." Rozo breathed as he watched the king drink. "There is no dishonour in being a Hiveakan. She was one of billions – countless Hiveakans have completed their pilgrimages without becoming korotas."

"*Shut up, Rozo!*" Taka's voice thundered around the room with such tremendous force it was as if the God of War had sent an earthquake through the palace. Rozo screamed in fright at the power of King Taka's anger, his body jumping into the air.

"I'm sorry, Sire!" he shrieked. "Please forgive me!"

"What?" Taka snarled. He looked at the fear in the man's eyes and it seemed to soothe him. He calmed himself a little and retreated back to the bottle in his hand, emptying it. "You are forgiven," Taka grunted. "I will give to you the forgiveness I will deny her." He smirked a little. "If I ever see her again... her blood will paint this room."

"Yes, Sire..." Rozo gasped, his heart racing in his chest.

Taka looked at his aide and sniggered. Pathetic. What did Rozo think he was going to do, kill him? Kill him for something Suela had done? That wasn't very fair... It wasn't very Hiveakan. It wasn't honourable. Taka would never let an innocent man die for something a traitor had done, regardless of who they were. Taka still had honour; he still adhered to Hiveakan morals even if she didn't. 'She'. That was what he would call her. Nobody in this palace was permitted to speak her name, not ever again. It would put a curse on the walls.

"The next person that mentions her will die." Taka vocalised his own thoughts. "Her name will never be spoken in this palace again. If you hear it, you will tell me, and whoever says that name will be executed by me. Do you understand?"

"Yes, Sire." Rozo nodded.

"I want everything of hers destroyed," Taka ordered. "I want all of her possessions destroyed – not given away – destroyed. Set fire to them."

"Yes, Sire."

"And pictures of her..." Taka moved his eyes to the painting on the wall. It had once been a stunning masterpiece created by one of the finest painters in the world. It was a painting of Taka with Suela and Lanka; the first ever painting of Taka with one of his heirs. Now... it was a wreck. Suela's face had been slashed out by Taka's own claws; her body mutilated and destroyed. She was unrecognisable now, as she would be to her children. In a few years they would have no idea what she even looked like. "Burn them all," Taka said. "Every photo of her, every painting – starting with that one." He gestured towards the destroyed picture on the wall. "I don't want any trace of her in this palace. As far as this family is concerned, she never existed. Do you understand?" He looked at Rozo sternly.

"Yes, Sire..." Rozo answered carefully. "Whatever you wish." He didn't dare argue. It was pointless. Taka wouldn't listen; not even the Gaiamira would be able to convince him not to erase Suela from history. To some degree Rozo agreed with the king. He was not a Hiveakan, but he had lived with them long enough to understand their culture. Suela had done a great deal of damage to the family's reputation, and she had betrayed the king and the Gaiamira in the worst way that she could. Why should she be remembered? Why should she be honoured? Rozo for once was actually siding with the king in his acts of cruelty.

"Go." Taka waved a dismissive hand at Rozo. "I have things to sort out. I will call you when I want you."

"Yes, Sire." Rozo nodded and reluctantly left the room, concerned as to the king's next move.

Taka stared down at the empty tetsa bottle in front of him and sighed. To think he had given it up for her, as part of some idiotic challenge. He had promised not to touch a drop until she had returned home... Well she wasn't coming home! She had broken her promise to him, and to the Gaiamira. Taka was drinking to spite her; he pictured her anger with every drop. He hoped she could see him now; he hoped she could see him breaking their vow. Her word meant nothing. Her existence meant nothing. She wasn't his comrade; she wasn't his loyal wife. She was a korota that had betrayed him. She had failed him; she had betrayed the Gaiamira. She had betrayed their marriage and she had betrayed their children. She had made a fool of them all... and Taka had let her. That was the foundation of his anger. King Taka was infuriated with himself, because he had actually believed Suela to be a true Hiveakan. He had believed that she could never fail; he had believed that she could never betray him, not in any way at all... and he had been wrong. He had been fooled. By her. Her entire existence was a lie, and he hadn't seen through it. It wasn't acceptable. Taka was weak. He could see that now. He was weak, and a failure... and perhaps beyond saving.

His mind raced, desperately trying to come up with a way to fix this. What could King Taka do to repent for his weakness? He couldn't kill her; he had no idea where she was, and it was against the Gaiamira to look for a korota. She wouldn't come home, not now. Taka would never be able to rectify the failings in his own soul with Suela's blood. He could make something of the girls, perhaps... Lanka had already been stained by her mother; perhaps even she could not be saved. Anaka was still in the Hive, though. When she came out Taka could mould her into a worthy Hiveakan. He could erase all trace of her mother from Anaka's existence; he could make the girl resent her mother the way that he did now. The way the world did now. Perhaps

Anaka could grow to be something… but she would still have her mother's blood. Taka could only hope to purify it; he had no idea if he actually could.

He leaned back in his chair and tilted his head back, staring at the ceiling for a moment before moving his eyes around the room. There was a portrait of his own mother and father in here, King Keizu and Keika Denna. They were always watching him. Judging him. What would they possibly think of him now? Taka had brought a korota into their family. He had trusted her, and believed in her, and he had made two children with her. What would his parents think of that? If they were here they would kill him themselves. There was no doubt in Taka's mind – no doubt in the world's mind that King Keizu and Keika Denna had never wanted their son to turn out like this. They had never wanted him to become so weak, so easily fooled. Nor did Taka. He didn't want it for his own children – what parent did? Mokoto wouldn't turn out like this. Never. Even if it meant the boy would not trust even his own father, then so be it. As long as Mokoto could never trust a korota; as long as Mokoto could never allow himself to be so fooled… Taka didn't care if the boy hated him. Anything to keep this from ever happening again. Maybe Taka should have been beaten more as a child. Perhaps they were too gentle with him in the Hive; perhaps that was why he had ever been capable of trust in the first place. That wouldn't happen with Mokoto. He would be stronger than that. Taka would make sure of it. Mokoto's loyalty would belong to the Gaiamira and to his people, and he would not allow himself to be fooled by anyone else. He would be beaten too much to be capable of it. Yes… that was it. That was how Taka would repent. He could not be saved, but he could save his children. He could save his son and heir. He would give Mokoto a soul fit for the God of War himself. Yes… that was how. Taka stared at the portrait of his parents on the wall and closed his eyes, praying to the Gaiamira to bless his son with strength. That was how he would repent. He would save his son's soul. Taka opened his eyes and rose from his seat. He was going to the Hive.

*

'I, King Taka Sota-Rokut hereby declare that I have consented to subject my son Matat Mokoto Sota-Rokut to a gross level of physical training, to be conducted by a qualified employee of the Hive, against the advice and guidelines of the Hive and its employees. I confirm that I have been advised of the risks involved and that I fully understand the potential fatal consequences of my decision to subject Matat Mokoto Sota-Rokut to this level of training. I therefore waive all responsibility in regards to the Hive, its employees, its representatives and its associates, relating to any and all possible outcomes of this gross training including but not limited to temporary or permanent mental or physical disability, temporary or permanent injury above that which is expected of a typical Hiveakan student, temporary or permanent loss of consciousness, temporary or permanent loss of physical or mental function, or death.'

-      Legal document signed by King Taka, 20110G

*

Mokoto almost flinched at the evil aura he felt coming his way. He wouldn't be scared. He refused to be scared! Teikota was looking more mortal every day... One day maybe he wouldn't affect Mokoto at all. That was what the boy hoped. He stood and turned towards the door and braced himself, his mind soaring through the many ways Teikota could torture him. Mokoto was prepared... He would withstand it. He wasn't going to back down!

The door opened and in marched Teikota, filled with bloodlust. Mokoto had barely taken a breath before the man threw his boot into Mokoto's jaw, and in that fleeting second all of Mokoto's bravery crumbled into dust.

"Is that all he can do?" Taka spoke from the observation gallery above Mokoto's room. He watched the scene with dead eyes, angry at how unharmed his son remained.

"Sire..." A senior representative of the Hive stood beside him, looking at the king with concern. "Any harder and he would have fractured the matat's skull."

113

"And?" Taka shrugged, not moving his eyes from the scene before him. He watched his son struggle; he watched Mokoto try to fight against Teikota's attacks as the man beat him brutally, as if he were trying to murder the child. "I already signed your waiver – if he dies, he dies. You have nothing to worry about." Taka grunted. "He is my only son – my heir. I put him in your care because I didn't want him to be weak." He moved his head to look at the Hiveakan man for the first time. "But if you are telling me he can't survive this, he doesn't deserve to live. Tell your tutor to stop holding back."

"But, Sire –"

"Do it!" Taka roared.

"Yes, Sire." The man looked down at the scene before them and held onto his earpiece, speaking into Teikota's counterpart. "Teikota, don't let him defend himself. Try to kill him."

Mokoto had no idea he was being watched; he had no idea Teikota was following orders. The thought never even crossed his mind; as far as he was concerned this was all Teikota's idea. Why wouldn't it be? Teikota was evil. He was darkness in its mortal form. Teikota was crazy. He wanted to harm Mokoto; he wanted to *kill* him! He didn't care who Mokoto was; he didn't care what the king would think of Mokoto's death. He was a monster. He was a murderer!

Mokoto took a breath while he could. For a split second Teikota seemed to hesitate, and Mokoto took the chance to lunge at his attacker. He charged at Teikota with all his might and managed to strike a heavy blow before he was greeted with the man's fist. Mokoto cried out as Teikota threw his weight down onto the boy, smacking him to the ground. He didn't let Mokoto get up; he didn't give Mokoto a chance to defend himself against any more attacks. Teikota beat him mercilessly, using the weight of his own body to keep the matat trapped. Mokoto couldn't escape. After all his years of combat training, after he'd allowed himself to believe that he was actually a good fighter, he couldn't escape. Teikota could kill him now. Teikota *was* killing him now. Mokoto felt pain everywhere; he felt every thud of Teikota's fists echo through his body like an earthquake. He couldn't get up; he couldn't protect himself. Mokoto was powerless. He hated that he was powerless! He couldn't be powerless; he was the matat of

114

Gaiamiráka! He had to prove his worth! He couldn't die now – he couldn't let this soulless monster kill him! He had to survive!

"S-stop…" Mokoto choked. He could taste his own blood; he could hear his own heart pounding fiercely in his ears. He felt his veins throb under his skin; he saw a dark cloud appear before his eyes. It wasn't just Teikota's darkness; it was his own death. Mokoto knew it was coming for him; he couldn't let the darkness take over his eyes. He had to stay awake – Mokoto knew the second he closed his eyes he would die. He felt cold… The Goddess of Death, Lanka was nearby; she was coming for him. He couldn't see her – he *couldn't*!

Teikota let out a harsh breath as Mokoto firmly grabbed his arm. He locked his eyes onto the child's and battled him, shocked by the strength that had suddenly arisen within the matat. The God of War was with him. Teikota could feel the darkness in Mokoto's soul; he could see the Footprints of Taka burning in the child's eyes. They were angry; they were powerful. They were determined to defeat Teikota. Mokoto was blessed. The God of War was helping him… Sadly, not enough. Teikota grabbed Mokoto's head with his free hand and slammed it harshly against the floor. He saw the boy's eyes widen; he saw the Footprints in Mokoto's eyes drain away. The hardness of Teikota's attack was too much to bear. Teikota felt Mokoto's grip on his arm loosen, and the matat's body slowly fell limp below him. Mokoto's eyes were closed. The room suddenly felt cold… The Goddess of Death was nearby. She was waiting for Mokoto.

Teikota checked Mokoto's pulse, listening in annoyance to the voice in his earpiece.

"Is he dead?" Teikota's superior asked.

"No," Teikota answered, looking up at the mirrored part of Mokoto's bedroom wall. He knew they were behind there. "But he will be. He needs a doctor." Teikota waited for his superior's reply, angered that there was even a question as to whether or not Mokoto's injuries would be seen to.

Behind the observation wall the senior Hive employee looked at the king for an answer, hoping it would be the one he wanted.

"No," Taka said, staring down at his son's body. "Let him bleed. If he isn't worthy of Taka, then Lanka is welcome to him." He left the room before the man could answer, and let the Hive's employees worry about the ethics of killing a child. He knew he had just saved his son's soul.

IX.

'Tangun stepped aside as the sky darkened once more, and the air become cold. Lanka was the sixth to rise from the earth; she was the Goddess of Death and she said she would carry the souls of the dead to the Gaiamiras' Realm. She wore around her neck a key that opened the door to this realm, the Gaiamirarezo, and she said all who felt a sudden cold should be warned, as it meant that Lanka was nearby.'

-        Extract from the Gaiamirapon: 'The First Encounters'

*

"Moko... Moko..." The young matat heard a female voice calling to him. She was calling softly... She sounded nearby. He hadn't opened his eyes yet, but Mokoto could already see the woman. He could feel the movements in the air; he could hear the distance in her voice. She was standing over him. There wasn't anybody else there; he couldn't hear anything except her. The room was still cold... *"Are you going to open your eyes, darling?"* she asked him impatiently. Who was she? The last thing he remembered was Teikota... Teikota attacking him. Teikota knocking him to the ground... Was Mokoto unconscious? Was she one of the medical staff? Mokoto opened his eyes as she requested and stared up at the woman. He didn't recognise her. She wasn't a tutor, but she wasn't dressed like one of the Hive's medical staff... She wore blue. Like the Goddess of Death, Lanka. She wore a chain around her neck; a chain that held a key... like the key that opened the door to the Gaiamirarezo. Why did she look so much like Lanka...? Was he dead...? The woman smirked a little and knelt down over Mokoto with a playful wickedness in her eyes. "Taka doesn't think I should take you," she uttered. "But if you don't get up soon, I'll have no choice. I can't make you die, and I can't make you live. Did they teach you that?"

"Yes," Mokoto answered. The room was freezing! It grew colder with every second that passed; Mokoto could feel the floor

117

beneath him turning to ice. It was her. She was making it cold. She was Lanka!

"So what do I do?" Lanka questioned. "If I don't make people die?"

"You wait," Mokoto answered, staring up at her. He tried not to shiver; he tried not to be afraid of her. He wasn't afraid... Not really. He was just so cold. "You wait for them to die on their own." Mokoto spoke confidently, as if he knew everything there was to know about the Goddess of Death. He knew all about the Gaiamira, like any properly raised Gaiamirákan child. He knew Lanka couldn't kill him. She never killed anyone; she just claimed their deceased souls. "You only take the ones that aren't strong enough to survive."

"That's right." Lanka nodded. "Are you strong enough?" She moved her hand to almost touch him, holding her fingertips close to his skin. "Do you feel cold?"

"No," Mokoto answered stubbornly. He couldn't let her take him. All he had to do was fight it; she couldn't take him as long as he fought against the cold. He didn't want to die. He *wouldn't* die!

"That's a start," Lanka spoke. "So. Am I going to have to take you?"

"No!" Mokoto argued. He battled against the ice that tried to touch his skin; he fought against the chills that crept up his back. He wouldn't feel it. He wouldn't!

Mokoto gasped as he suddenly started to feel pain; the kind of pain he'd felt during Teikota's attack. It burned through his entire body; he felt his blood pulse through his veins. He was in so much pain... but she couldn't take him away from it. If she took him, he'd never be able to go back. He wanted to stay in agony – he wanted to stay alive!

"Doesn't it hurt?" Lanka's voice echoed through Mokoto's ears; she sounded further away.

"I don't care!" Mokoto snapped. He gritted his teeth and forced his body to move. He forced his arms to push him up; he forced his legs to stand. He stood in agony and let out another breathless gasp, struggling to fight through the pain of his injuries. He looked at Lanka;

118

she was at his level now. He stared right into her eyes, refusing to back down. She started to smirk.

"Good boy," Lanka purred. "See you in a few years."

Mokoto let out a scream as he felt a great force thunder through his body, as if the God of War had punched him right through the heart. The world changed before his eyes; suddenly he wasn't standing anymore. He was lying on the ground; his body was motionless but he was gasping for breath. His heart was racing in his chest; the veins in his arms and legs were pulsing wildly. The room felt so warm... Even the coldness of the Hive's floor felt like fire compared to the coldness the Goddess of Death had brought. Mokoto stared up at the ceiling and then moved his eyes around the room, looking for any sign of her. She wasn't there. There was no ice; no cold air; no haunting voice... Every last trace of her was gone.

Mokoto lay motionless for a moment, trying to make sense of the world around him. He could smell his own blood; he could feel the pain of his injuries all over his body... Why wasn't he standing anymore? Where had Lanka gone? Why had she suddenly disappeared? ... It must have been a dream. Had it been a dream? Had she even been here? Mokoto suddenly recalled something he'd learned in his lessons about the Gaiamira; the Gaiamira and the spirits of the dead could appear in dreams. They only appeared to nuns or holy people when they were awake, but in dreams everyone could see them. Had Lanka really been in his dream...? Had she really come to take him...?

She hadn't though. She couldn't. Mokoto smirked a little, his young body suddenly overcome with arrogance. Lanka hadn't been able to take him. He had been too strong. He had conquered death. He had escaped from a goddess! The God of War had blessed him... Mokoto felt Taka's strength now more than ever. His Footprints burned within his soul, stronger now than they ever had been. He couldn't die. Mokoto knew that now. He felt it. He would survive here; Teikota couldn't kill him. No matter how hard that evil man tried, he couldn't kill Mokoto. Mokoto was too strong, and he would get stronger. Maybe one day he would even kill Teikota himself. Yes... Yes – he could! He could kill Teikota! He had to get stronger. He had to train harder. That

119

was his new goal; that was his mission. He would do it in the name of Taka, to thank him for letting Mokoto live. It was his destiny. When he was old enough, Mokoto would be the death of darkness.

*

'First Teima, then Suela, now Geith. I don't know what's happening in that palace, but Kala must be pretty pissed off at someone to send our country three traitors.'

-        Interview with a member of the public, 20110G

*

" Meitat Lanka…" The teenage Meitat Lanka stopped the treadmill at the sound of her name. She was angered to do so; any distraction from her rigorous training regime annoyed her greatly. Her annoyance was justified; Lanka's Hiveakan exterior depended on the strictness of her gym schedule, and any sort of break in her routine could damage her development. Lanka was proud of her body; she was the strongest and fastest woman in the palace now and her face was beautiful. Lanka was aware of how appealing she was, and she took advantage of it. Her mother had taught her to take advantage of people; she had taught Lanka how to use her looks and her skills in combat to achieve anyone and anything she desired. It would be foolish of Lanka not to; the Gaiamira had blessed Lanka with a gift, and as a mere mortal she had no right to not accept it. Lanka knew how to seduce men and she knew how to make friends, and she had no doubt that she would make strong allies of the world's entrepreneurs when she inevitably became queen. Lanka was intelligent and flirtatious; calculating and manipulative… Her mother would be proud. Lanka hoped her father was. His opinion mattered more than anyone else's in the world, especially now. King Taka was the only man who could terrify Lanka; he was the only man she could not manipulate or murder. He reduced her to a frightened child, when to every other male in the world she was a dominating mate, far too good for them and far too

120

desirable to forget about. King Taka was the only man in the world that was immune to her looks and charms, and he was the only man that would be oblivious to them if they did not so often force themselves into his life.

Taka received multiple propositions a month when it came to Lanka; any high class couple old enough to have a son within a few years of Lanka hounded King Taka for his daughter's hand in marriage, even offering to make all the arrangements themselves without once bothering the king. Taka didn't surrender Lanka's hand; he saw no need to. The most valuable young man in the world was Taka's own son and the matat was already in the king's collection of assets, and so Taka left it up to Lanka to decide who and when she wanted to marry. Lanka had no interest in it; she had no interest in marriage or dating at all. The only man she was interested in was Mokoto, and it would only be until she could end his life.

Meitat Lanka had spent the last two years of her life training and pushing herself mercilessly, not caring about anything in the Gaiamiras' world except the mission she had been given the day of his birth. She would defeat Mokoto. She would take the throne. There was no doubt about it. Lanka didn't believe for a moment that she would ever fail, but her success depended on her training; she had no time for anything else. She had devoted her life to perfecting herself; she spent every spare second turning herself into the woman who would kill the matat. It was her destiny, and until she was queen, Lanka had no time for marriage or friendship or romance. Until she was queen, she didn't deserve them. Lanka believed that firmly, and she made others aware of her beliefs in as tactless a way as she could… Not that it stopped the boys pestering her.

Lanka climbed off the treadmill and turned around to face the young man that was stood there; it was one of the palace's servants. His presence angered her all the more; he had no reason to be there. He didn't want anything; Lanka could tell. The only thing he wanted was to be in the same room as her; there was no palace news or message from her father or anything else of importance on his mind. He was wasting his time, and hers. Actually Lanka was surprised he had waited this long to pester her – he must be a coward on top of being worthless.

Lanka recognised this man; she had no idea of his name but she had seen his face countless times before. He was one of those boys that looked at her a certain way, one that carried Kala whenever he was near her. Lanka could always tell when an Outsider liked her; it was so easy. Even if they hid the signs of their body they still told her with their eyes. Outsiders never knew how to control their eyes. Hiveakans on the other hand... They were harder to read. Sometimes Lanka didn't know if a Hiveakan really liked her or if he was just trying to manipulate her the same way she was trying to manipulate him. Hiveakans were a challenge; they were interesting to her. If Lanka was to marry, she would marry a Hiveakan. Not a weak little creature like this. She could only pray to the Gaiamira that this servant's visit would be a short one.

"*Yes?*" Lanka snarled. "What do you want?"

"I... I just wanted to see if you were alright, Meitat," the man replied sheepishly, stiffening slightly.

"Fine. Why not?" Lanka glared at him fiercely. 'Alright'? What did he take her for, some sort of Outsider? Why would someone like him *ever* need to check on her wellbeing? Why was it even any of his concern? "What is your name?" Lanka demanded.

"Um... Torin, Meitat," the servant answered nervously.

"Torin?" Lanka sarcastically repeated. It was the Gaiamirákan word for 'cloud'. "No wonder you have such an empty head." She sniped. "Why would I not be alright?"

"Well..." Torin swallowed. He shook nervously under Lanka's cold stare, partly fearing for his life. "You've just..." Torin bravely continued. "You've been here for a while –"

"So?" Lanka growled. "Mokoto will be seven next month, and he is already having combat lessons designed for ten-year-olds! I have to keep up with him. Don't you understand that? I promised my mother." She narrowed her eyes at Torin and sneered. "You do understand the concept of loyalty, don't you, Torin?"

"Well... that's why I'm worried," Torin replied. "I'm a little concerned her death might be... affecting you."

"Why?" Lanka snapped at him again, angered that he could suggest such a thing. How dare he apply such trivial emotions to her!

She wasn't some lunatic that was having a breakdown! How could he be so ignorant? Her mother had failed a pilgrimage; so what? Her mother was presumed dead – did that mean Lanka's honour had to die with her? Lanka was born to be queen, and nothing would change that! Whatever had happened to her mother, it was *irrelevant* to Lanka's mission! It wasn't about her mother! Was this pathetic excuse of a man really too stupid to understand that? "People die all the time," Lanka ruthlessly stated. "I am not an Outsider. Why would her death concern me?"

"But... she's a korota –" Torin stopped dead, frozen by the ice-cold glare Lanka was giving him. A korota... Lanka hated people calling her mother that. She hated to think of it! It had been two days now since her mother had been officially named a failure. It sickened Lanka to think of it. One month ago Lanka had waited eagerly for her mother's arrival, so keen to show her how much she had grown... Her mother had never shown up. Presumed dead by the cold hand of Taka's Wilderness. Whatever. Lanka didn't care. They could call her mother whatever they wanted – it didn't matter. Lanka had made a promise to a Hiveakan woman, to her father, to herself and to the Gaiamira, and if it cost her her life she would keep it. She could not care less what anybody else had to say.

Torin looked at Lanka with sympathy, which seemed to anger her more. Her face twisted in fury; she didn't need his pity! She didn't need anything from him except to get out so she could carry on with her training! She wasn't just Mokoto's rival. It had become more than that. With her mother gone it was up to Lanka to guide her younger sister Anaka when she came out of the Hive. Lanka had to prepare herself not just for Mokoto's graduation, but for Anaka's as well. She had to make sure that Anaka too fulfilled their mission to defeat the matat. Lanka wasn't permitted to live until Mokoto was defeated, and that was the case whether her mother was dead or alive – so the events of the past month really didn't matter. Nothing mattered except Mokoto.

"I just think..." Torin pressed on, ignoring the growing anger that burned in Lanka's eyes, "with Keika Geith being executed, and now this –"

"Geith!" Lanka spat. "*Geith!*" She almost laughed as she recalled yet another recent drama in the palace. The media would be paid well this week. First Lanka's mother had been named a korota, and earlier this morning one of her father's two remaining wives, Keika Geith, had been executed for treason for forging King Taka's will and attempting to kill the king, all to make her daughter Sukaru, queen of Gaiamiráka. It was ridiculous. Geith for some reason had decided to take advantage of the king's 'vulnerable' state. Not that he was ever vulnerable – Geith deserved to be killed just for thinking that. With Lanka's mother out of the picture Geith seemed to think she had a chance in the world of taking over the palace. It was stupid. For a start the king *wasn't* vulnerable, nor was he capable of being vulnerable, and secondly, Geith had the handwriting of a child and even a newborn baby would be able to tell that the document she had created, naming Sukaru as heir to the throne and supposedly 'signed by King Taka' was fake, and thirdly… even if her writing had been a perfect match for King Taka's, who in the Gaiamiras' world would believe that King Taka would ever hand his throne to Geith and her Outsider daughter? Geith would *never* run this palace! The king would rather see her dead! Which was what had happened actually. He had even executed her himself. "You mean my father's pathetic excuse of a wife?" Lanka snarled. "Sukaru's pathetic excuse of a mother! Ha!" Lanka smirked. "Sukaru always was an idiot. Now I know why."

"It's much more serious than that, Meitat!" Torin gasped. "Geith forged your father's will! She tried to kill your father and Keika Kaeila –"

"I know. To make Sukaru heir to the throne." Lanka smirked again, folding her arms. "How in the Gaiamiras' world did she think that would work? She couldn't kill Kaeila even *after* she poisoned her. It's laughable that she thought she could take on my father, don't you think? If she wasn't so stupid I would admire her for trying."

"It was horrible, Meitat…" Torin whimpered. "Kaeila nearly died. She's still in hospital –"

"*Nearly* isn't dead," Lanka growled. "Besides, what would I care? It's no concern of mine if Kaeila dies. My father didn't die."

"They said he could have –"

124

"Plenty of things *could* have happened, Torin," Lanka replied. "You *could* have left me alone in here, and I could be a lot stronger now. But no, you came in – and here we are. Wasting my time!"

"I… I just…" Torin lowered his eyes. He felt like crying. Lanka was such a harsh woman. Why did she have to be so nasty? He was just trying to help… "I care about you, Meitat…" Torin looked at her, his eyes glistening a little. "I don't think you understand how many people –"

"Oh, *get out*!" Lanka roared. "Before I cut open your throat."

"Yes, Meitat," Torin mumbled. "I'm sorry. Forgive me." In defeat he left the room with Lanka's eyes burning into him all the way. After he had gone she let out an angry sigh and got back on the treadmill, muttering angrily to herself about the sheer patheticness of the Outsider race. She couldn't wait until Mokoto's graduation, even if it was only to balance out the population of Outsiders in the palace.

X.

'Following Lanka two beings arose, wearing crowns upon their heads. They were the twins Donso and Mokuya, God and Goddess of Kings and Queens. Their bodies touching, they said that they would watch over the royal family and bless all future monarchs of the world, and they would help and guide them throughout their reign, and give them the strength to become fair and great.'

\-   Extract from the Gaiamirapon: 'The First Encounters'

*

Mokoto cracked his knuckles for the tenth time that morning. He didn't like to feel nervous; it wasn't a Hiveakan emotion. If anyone found out he was anything that even remotely resembled nervous, he might not be permitted to leave. Time had passed as fiercely and as ruthlessly as any nightmare in the Hive, and like all nightmares this one had to end. Now was the time for it to be over. After thirteen years of suffering in the dark depths of the Hive, Mokoto was finally being set free.

He was waiting in his room; any moment now one of his tutors would bring him his graduation certificate and escort him out of the Hive. The longer he was left waiting the more Mokoto's nerves grew. Why were they taking so long? Had they changed their mind? Had they been displeased with his early morning training sessions? They could go back on their decision anytime they wanted to; they could keep him here for another year if they saw fit… That bothered Mokoto most of all. He was aware of his age and how it made him look to his tutors and to his father the king. Mokoto was thirteen… That was acceptable, for now. The average graduation age for a Hiveakan student was between fourteen and sixteen years, so right now Mokoto was above average, but what if they decided to keep him here? He was already annoyed at himself for even making it to thirteen. Mokoto had turned thirteen just ten days ago; if he had only been a better student he might have graduated at age twelve… Twelve would have been better. The

126

younger the better. His older sister Lanka had been thirteen. Mokoto knew her graduation date, 20-07-20108G. It was a month before her fourteenth birthday, so she had been older than Mokoto. Anaka's graduation date was 17-02-20111G, a week after her fifteenth birthday. So far Mokoto had beaten them both… but was that enough? Was his father angry that he had not graduated ten days earlier? Just ten days earlier would have made Mokoto a twelve-year-old graduate. He was the only male heir to the Gaiamirákan throne; there was no doubt that the world was hoping for Mokoto's release at a young age, and no doubt they were disappointed when he only just missed his twelve-year deadline… Shit! Would his father beat him when he arrived at the palace? Would he even speak to him?

Mokoto tried to picture the royal building. He knew its exterior like the back of his hand; there was no shortage of images of the palace on the internet. The inside was different though… Mokoto knew the layout but not the décor. He wouldn't recognise it, not all of it anyway. Would he be permitted to sleep in an heir's room? There were three bedrooms in Meitona Palace reserved for the heirs to the throne. Lanka and Anaka had claimed two, and to his knowledge Mokoto held the rights to the third, but had he lost them by graduating too late? Well, it didn't matter. He would win back his right to the third heir's room. He was determined to. Mokoto cracked his knuckles again and stared at himself in the mirror he had earned some years ago. He was strong. He looked strong. If his father was angry at him, Mokoto could repent. He would work hard; he would become whatever his father needed him to become, no matter what he had to do or how much he had to sacrifice. Mokoto was strong enough to earn his father's respect, and he would earn it. He had to. He would die if he didn't – by his father's hand.

Mokoto raised his head to the sound of the door opening. He knelt down before the man that entered the room; it was a Hiveakan tutor. He had Mokoto's graduation certificate in his hand. "Come on," the man said, gesturing for Mokoto to stand. "Your ride's here." He waited for the young teen to rise to his feet and led Mokoto out of the room.

They moved down the corridors of the Hive; Mokoto could feel the other students' ears on him. They could hear him walk past their rooms; he knew they could. Mokoto could always hear footsteps moving past his room. Did they know he was leaving? Mokoto had been told about other students' graduations from time to time, but not always. He never cared anyway. These students wouldn't care. They were too busy concentrating on making themselves fit for their own graduations.

The man led Mokoto into a room he had never been in before. There was another man stood waiting there, in front of a closed door. He wasn't an employee of the Hive. He was an Outsider. He smiled warmly at Mokoto, making the teen flinch a little. How was he supposed to respond to that? Mokoto moved his head to the feeling of a sharp nudge into his back. The Hiveakan tutor was looking at him, holding out his graduation certificate. "Congratulations," the man uttered. "Good luck, boy."

"Thank you, sir," Mokoto responded, taking the certificate from the man's hand. He didn't have time to look at it before he was shoved towards the Outsider and ordered to follow the man through the closed door, where Mokoto saw the outside world for the first time.

The morning sun hit him like lightning striking as Mokoto walked through the door of the Hive. He had seen the sun before; when his tutors had been pleased with him Mokoto had been permitted to explore the Hive's garden. This was different though. Somehow this wasn't the same sun; it seemed more real. It seemed brighter. The air seemed fresher; the breeze seemed cooler… Was this what Meitona really felt like?

Mokoto was conscious of his surroundings; his senses were more alert than ever and he was preparing himself for any last minute trials he might have to endure. He was aware of the Outsider man in front of him and the distance between them; he was aware of the Hiveakan guard that was following them closely behind. They moved from the Hive's entrance onto a car park; Mokoto recognised the layout from pictures he had seen. They moved through the car park towards an expensive looking vehicle, the kind that only royalty and the world's wealthiest people could afford. Mokoto looked up to see another young boy with a Hiveakan guard and his parents. They made eye contact, and they instantly knew each other. They had never met before, but they each knew what the other had gone through to get here. Mokoto knew this boy's life story as well as he knew his own, and as well as the boy knew him. Maybe they would meet again at some point in their lives… It wasn't completely impossible. The boy's vehicle looked expensive; his parents were well groomed and healthy looking. This car park was reserved for families in the higher part of society; if Mokoto would ever meet anyone his own age outside of his family there was a chance it would be this boy, at some sort of political gathering. Maybe they would become allies… Or maybe Mokoto would kill him.

"Here we are, My Matat," the Outsider man spoke for the first time. Mokoto looked at him and the man offered him another warm smile before opening the door to their vehicle. The man nodded at the Hiveakan guard. "Thank you."

"I'll wait here," the guard answered, unwilling to let the matat leave his sight until Mokoto was out of the Hive's territory. It was for legal reasons, Mokoto knew. Until he was off the premises completely he was still under the Hive's care, and they had to look out for his wellbeing in the minimal way that they always did.

"I thought you would," the Outsider smirked. He looked at Mokoto and nodded towards the open car door. "In you get."

Mokoto obediently climbed into the vehicle and sat unfazed as the Outsider closed the door, locking the matat in. He kept his eyes on the Hiveakan guard as his Outsider escort climbed into the driver's seat. Mokoto clutched his certificate tightly in his hand; it was the one thing that told him he deserved to be in this car. He kept his eyes on the guard as the car started to move away, not daring to avert his gaze in case the man tried to attack him. He didn't. Mokoto had been told he wouldn't; he had been told there would be no tests in the car park, but his instincts told him to be ready to fight at all times, even if he had been guaranteed he wouldn't need to. Mokoto knew every inch of his surroundings; he took in everything around him as the vehicle started to move. He saw the guard getting smaller and smaller; he saw the other stationary vehicles as they passed; he felt the momentary stop and start of his car as more Hiveakan guards opened the gates to the car park to let Mokoto through… He saw the second car that was following them closely behind. It contained armed guards from the palace, sent to escort him home and warn off anyone that might try to attack Mokoto. Mokoto had been told about them, and he had picked out their vehicle as soon as he had been shown his own. He could see the distance between his vehicle and theirs; he could see the speeds at which they were both travelling… Everything was recorded. Everything was memorised. Everything was a part of him being set free.

"I'm sorry your father couldn't pick you up, My Matat," the Outsider apologised sincerely. "But you can imagine how busy he is – my name is Rowan, by the way. I'm the driver." Yes… Rowan. Mokoto recognised the name now. He was one of the palace's chauffeurs, responsible for taking members of the royal family anywhere they desired. "I suppose you're feeling quite nervous about today, Your Highness?" Rowan glanced at Mokoto in the rear view mirror, keenly watching the teen's reaction.

"No." Mokoto recited his answer. He couldn't let his nerves show, and certainly not to an employee of the palace. His father would never let him through its walls if he did.

"My, you are brave," Rowan chuckled. He didn't believe Mokoto. Mokoto could tell. Whatever. Mokoto couldn't care less about Rowan's opinion; it was one of the least important in the world. "I suppose this is quite exciting for you? They don't take you into the streets, do they?"

"No, sir… They do not." Mokoto answered politely, aware that for the moment at least Rowan was still his superior, even if he didn't care much for the man.

"Take a look while you can; your sisters won't let you leave their sights for a good few days now." Rowan spoke half-jokingly. Mokoto nodded silently and turned his head to look out of the car window, staring in wonder at the sights of the world outside the Hive.

He didn't need to be driven home. There was a private sector in the Hive known as the Gateway that led directly into the palace gardens; it was heavily guarded and impossible to access without the correct authorisation, but it allowed members of the royal family to safely come and go as they pleased, without having to visit their relatives via the 'public route'. It was convenient for the royal students' relatives, but the Hive never recommended the Gateway as a going home route for new graduates. The Hive always advised that even royal graduates should return to the palace via the public route, passing through the streets of the outside world. The public route helped graduates adjust to the outside world better; it allowed them to get a view of society from the safety of their vehicle before they were thrown mercilessly into it. It was a filter Mokoto didn't think he needed, but he was grateful for it all the same.

The young matat stared in fascination, captivated by the visions before his eyes. Streets, shops, traffic, Outsiders… They were all things he had seen before, but only in literature. It was amazing to see them in reality. The Outsiders caught his interest the most. They were like another species. They walked so carelessly, so openly, as if the notion of being hurt at any moment just wasn't familiar to them. The children looked different… Mokoto saw them walking down the street with their parents, without a scratch on their bodies. Mokoto had never seen a child that wasn't scarred. Even from this distance and through the glass of his car Mokoto could see how innocent the Outsider children were. They had every trust in their parents. They loved their parents. They loved their friends… It was so bizarre to him. It was foolish.

"Different, aren't they?" Rowan's voice broke Mokoto's concentration. "You'll see more Outsiders than Hiveakans now, Your Highness."

"I know," Mokoto answered almost fiercely. What a ridiculous thing to say! Mokoto had nine Outsider sisters, an Outsider mother and a palace full of Outsider servants; of course he would see more Outsiders! Even now, just minutes after his graduation he was sat alone with one. Were they all this unbearable? Why did Rowan feel the need to make conversation? They had nothing in common; they had nothing to talk about. Why couldn't he accept that and perform his duty in silence? When Mokoto became king this man would be out of a job.

Mokoto flinched at himself for thinking such a thing. No… That was wrong. His father had hired this man for a reason; perhaps Rowan was good at his job. Perhaps his skills as a chauffeur outweighed his need to make small talk. Mokoto's father was right to employ this man. The king was always right.

"I expect you're tired, My Matat."

Mokoto looked up to meet Rowan's eyes again in the mirror. How he would love to kill Rowan right now... How could Rowan misjudge him? Mokoto wasn't tired! He was never tired!

"Tired?" Mokoto repeated questioningly.

"I heard you Hiveakans aren't allowed to sleep much," Rowan smiled. "It'll be about half an hour to the palace yet, Your Highness, I've been ordered to take you all over the city... But why don't you get some rest?" He winked, and Mokoto caught a glimmer of sympathy in Rowan's eyes. He was going to disobey his master out of the kindness of his heart. "You can see the city anytime. I won't tell if you don't."

"Thank you," Mokoto uttered. He was angry at Rowan for saying such a thing; Rowan shouldn't have disobeyed the king's orders... but a small part of Mokoto was grateful for it. He was permitted sleep, and sleep was a luxury he wasn't often granted. It wouldn't be wrong to sleep, would it? Mokoto's tutors had told him to obey Rowan; for now at least Rowan was Mokoto's superior and Mokoto was to do what Rowan said until his father or anyone else of higher authority stated otherwise. So... if Rowan permitted Mokoto to sleep, then he could. Couldn't he? Yes. He could. It was Rowan's wish. Mokoto quickly closed his eyes; he didn't dare waste any time. Thirty minutes was a long time, but Mokoto had no idea when he would be allowed to sleep again. He wanted every second he could get now, and he was asleep in an instant. Within seconds he was dreaming.

"I hope you're being good, Mokoto."

Mokoto's heart stopped at the sound of a dark voice echoing around his mind. He hadn't heard that voice in years, but he knew its owner well. Every nightmare he had was built around that man; every angry thought and every dark desire... It was Teikota. He wasn't just darkness anymore; he was blood. He was blood that Mokoto hadn't seen since he was a child, but he saw him now as clear as the marks on his own hands. Teikota was here. He had come for Mokoto. He had come to take him back to the Hive!

132

Mokoto looked around desperately, suddenly terrified by his surroundings. He wasn't in the car anymore; he was in his room in the Hive. Teikota had brought him here. Why? Why was he here again? He'd been set free! He deserved to be free!

"The others made a mistake," Teikota spoke as he slowly made his way towards Mokoto. Every one of his movements was emphasised; Mokoto could hear the scraping of Teikota's clothes against his dark skin; he could hear the thud of his bloodstained boots against the floor… He could feel the movements in the air as Teikota reached his hand out to him. "You don't deserve this."

Mokoto let out a short gasp as Teikota snatched his graduation certificate from him, staring down at Mokoto with evil eyes. He was so tall… Mokoto had grown, but Teikota was still bigger than him. This didn't make sense. Teikota couldn't be this tall! He couldn't be this frightening! Mokoto had grown; he wasn't the child Teikota had tried to murder anymore. He was a graduate! He had been set free! He couldn't let Teikota destroy that.

"They let me go!" Mokoto snarled, taking up a fighting stance in front of his enemy. "That's mine!" He swiped his hand out to try to grab the certificate but Teikota pulled his arm away, chuckling darkly as he stared down at the matat.

"Prove it," Teikota said. "Show me what you have learned."

Mokoto let out an angry cry and threw a clenched fist at Teikota's jawbone. He moved quickly, but his efforts to harm the man were futile. Teikota grabbed Mokoto's arm with ease before the matat's fist could even come near to his face. He held his grip firmly on Mokoto's arm and twisted the limb, causing Mokoto to cry out in pain. Shit…! Why was he screaming? Mokoto was angry at himself; he hadn't screamed in years, why was he doing it now?

"I'm not impressed with this," Teikota said calmly. He clenched his fist around Mokoto's arm, snapping the matat's bones. Mokoto gritted his teeth and closed his eyes in a vain attempt to block out the pain. Why was this so hard…? Why couldn't he beat him? He *could* beat Teikota! He had been set free! He deserved to go home!

Mokoto took a breath and threw the weight of his body into his free arm, this time evading Teikota's hand. He struck Teikota hard; the

133

crack of Teikota's jaw echoed around the room as if lightning had struck above them. Teikota flinched and backed off, releasing his grip on Mokoto's arm. He stood in front of Mokoto and remained motionless, staring at the teen with dead eyes. Mokoto held his stance firmly, ignoring the pain in his arm and preparing himself for another attack.

"Come on," Mokoto challenged. He waited for Teikota to move, but the man didn't. He continued to stare at Mokoto with his cold, dead eyes, not moving a muscle. Mokoto shifted a little, uncomfortable with the perfect stoniness of Teikota's stance. Why wasn't he moving? "Come on!" Mokoto screamed. Nothing happened. Teikota didn't move, but somehow Mokoto's graduation certificate fell from his hand. Mokoto watched as it hit the floor and he moved his eyes back up to Teikota. He was smirking...

"Come on." Teikota repeated Mokoto's words, his eyes twinkling with menace. "Come and get it."

Mokoto paused for a moment, and then leapt towards the certificate on the floor. He had almost grabbed it when he suddenly became startled by a voice calling his name.

"*Matat Mokoto!*"

Mokoto's eyes snapped open, instantly focusing on the man that was looking at him. It was Rowan. He was smiling sympathetically.

"You fell asleep, Your Highness," Rowan said. "I hope you weren't having nightmares?"

"No," Mokoto mumbled. Nightmares? Rowan said it as if they weren't normal. Did Outsiders have good dreams? "Did I wake up right away?" Mokoto asked. The car was stopped... Had Mokoto not noticed it stop? His heart started to fill with dread. Maybe he didn't deserve to be here...

"Hm? Well... I stopped the car, and then I spoke to you once," Rowan replied. "But you started to wake up when the engine stopped." He offered Mokoto another warm smile. "Don't worry, Your Highness. You deserve to be here."

"Thank you," Mokoto uttered, unsure of what else to say. How did Rowan know what he was thinking? Maybe Lanka and Anaka had had the same concern when they'd graduated. Mokoto felt his graduation

134

certificate in his hand, assuring himself that he had earned it. He deserved to be here.

"Well, Your Highness, should we go inside?" Rowan offered. "Your sisters are very excited to meet you. I suppose you've memorised all their names?"

"Yes, sir," Mokoto answered. He obediently began to list the names of his sisters and their biological mothers, stopping at Lanka and Anaka. He wasn't supposed to speak their mother's name, was he...? He'd been told about that woman when he was young. Her name was forbidden in the palace, and under *no* circumstances was he to ever mention her in his father's presence... or at all. "Daughters of... a korota..."

"Mm," Rowan nodded approvingly. "Very good. Don't say any more than that, whatever you do. I wouldn't even talk about her at all if I were you."

"Yes, sir." Mokoto nodded, relieved that he hadn't said too much. Good. He was off to a good start. He cleared his throat and continued to list his siblings. "Oreisaka," Mokoto spoke. "From my mother..." He hesitated for a moment, recalling what he'd been told about his biological mother. She was another traitor. Not as bad as 'that' woman, but still... Mokoto was already at a disadvantage just for having her blood; he would have to work twice as hard to earn his father's respect. He would earn it though. He had to. "Sukaru, daughter of Geith, and Korana, Hiveakan daughter of Kala." He looked at Rowan. "Kaeila is the only mother left."

Rowan stared at Mokoto for a long moment. Mokoto kept his eyes fixed on Rowan, waiting for him to respond. He had just started to wonder if he should say something else when Rowan chuckled.

"Well... it's good to know the Hive have taught you well." He half-smiled. "But be careful not to mention Geith, Teima or Kala either – your father can be quite sensitive about those three. All of them traitors, I'm sure you know."

"Yes, sir." Mokoto nodded obediently.

"And I... I wouldn't bother much with Korana, if you ever meet her," Rowan went on. "The poor girl is an outcast, really. Your father probably won't let her speak to you – and you shouldn't seek her out. Just... pretend she doesn't exist. That's what the rest of us do."

"Of course, sir." Mokoto kept his obedient tone. He had been told about Korana, and Rowan's words weren't a surprise to him. Korana was the daughter of someone who had committed suicide, a very serious offence to the Gaiamira. Although she had been raised in the Hive she wasn't a Hiveakan, not as far as the rest of the Hiveakan community was concerned. Mokoto had already been told Korana would never be part of his life. As far as he and his tutors were concerned, she did not exist.

"Good." Rowan beamed. "Well then, shall we go?"

Mokoto stepped out of the car, taking a look at the driving seat as Rowan let him out. It had occurred to Mokoto that Rowan had driven the car manually; he'd seen Rowan hovering his hands over the steer pad, a motion-sensitive area of the dashboard that detected the driver's hand movements. Mokoto had always been told that most cars these days drove themselves, particularly the more expensive models associated with families such as Mokoto's... but Rowan chose to drive manually? Why? Surely the palace had auto-drive technology in their cars?

"I know, Your Highness." Mokoto looked at Rowan to see the man smiling at him knowingly. "Call me old-fashioned, but I don't trust a car to drive itself. I'm not entirely happy about this motion sensor stuff either – have you seen a car from a hundred years ago? They had a steering wheel, and I can guarantee they were much safer." He shut the car door. "Well then. Come on." Mokoto watched Rowan walk away, annoyed by his remark. What a foolish man – had he no education at all? Motion-sensitive steering *was* safer, that was why it was invented! It stopped idiot drivers hitting the steering too hard; if Rowan drove an old car he would kill himself with it – and other people. It was fools like that that had made auto-drive a necessity in the first place, didn't Rowan realise that? Mokoto sighed inwardly, and followed Rowan down the path of the front garden, towards the palace.

As Mokoto moved he took in his surroundings, matching them to pictures he'd seen and what he'd been told of his home. Just as he'd been told, there was the Hive. It was a great wall that surrounded the

136

entire length of Meitona Palace's grounds, acting as a barrier between the palace and the outside world. Mokoto had never seen the Hive from the outside before; somehow it looked even more intimidating now than it did from the inside. It was two storeys high, and on top... Mokoto's jaw almost dropped and he struggled to keep himself calm. He could see it. He could see Eilaháka. It was like a legend to him – it was a fascinating place that up until now Mokoto had only heard about. Eilaháka was a town on top of the Hive that was literally named 'Sky's Place'. Mokoto had seen a few pictures of Eilaháka, but to see it in reality was an entirely different experience; it brought the legend to life in a way that only the Gaiamira could put into words. The town was one of the greatest parts of Meitona; it was a tourist attraction that brought thousands of visitors from all over the world. Eilaháka's shops and buildings alone were worth almost as much as Meitona itself, not to mention the value of its residents. It cost millions to own a house in Eilaháka, and its residents were all strictly vetted before they were permitted to even buy a property there, regardless of whether or not they planned to live there themselves. The town was surrounded by security, who would not hesitate to kill on the spot anybody that they so much as suspected as trying to get into Meitona Palace's territory. Eilaháka was one of the most difficult places in the world to move to. It was the strictest, most exclusive location in Meitona – in the entire world, in fact – but the residents of Eilaháka did have the privilege of having the royal family as their neighbours, and the best view of Meitona in the whole of Keizuaka. Mokoto wanted to go there. He wanted to see Keizuaka from its height. One day, when he had earned it, he would.

Mokoto brought his eyes back down from the top of the Hive and looked back to see a gap in the wall behind him, maybe twenty feet wide, exposing the streets of the outside world. This was the only way to get to the palace from the other side of the Hive. It was closed off now by a large steel gate that was almost as old as the palace itself, surrounded by guards. There were guards all over the palace gardens, as to be expected. Mokoto turned back to face the front of the palace to see more guards positioned on either side of the palace door. The palace door... He felt nervous just looking at it. Beyond that door was a new home, a new life… and the king. The only man in the world that could legally kill Mokoto would be living in the same building as him, perhaps only a couple of rooms away. It was terrifying. What if Mokoto did something wrong? He could die here.

Rowan smiled a little from a few feet away, watching the young matat with warmth. He was such a child. Rowan didn't know what other people were so afraid of; the young Hiveakan standing before him was no less mortal than anyone else. The boy was wide-eyed and nervous, like any Outsider child would be. Perhaps Mokoto behaved slightly differently to other boys his age, but he was still just a boy. He had a long way to go before he really did become a monster. It was a shame so few people saw new graduates that way.

Mokoto felt Rowan's eyes on him as he stared up at the palace. He took his time to look at the building; he knew Rowan would come and get him if he was stood there for too long. Silence was permission. The palace looked as Mokoto had expected; Mokoto had been shown countless pictures of this building over the years and he probably knew its details better than some of its residents. Still… Like Eilaháka it seemed so much more amazing in real life. The palace was only three storeys high but more than double that in width. It was built from ancient bricks that were thousands of years old; they had obviously been well looked after, even if they had been replaced here and there over the years. The bricks were painted a pale yellow – the trademark colour of the God and Goddess Donso and Mokuya, the twin deities in charge of crowning and watching over kings and queens. Even without going in Mokoto could feel their spirits surrounding him. It was comforting.

Every member of the Gaiamira watched over this palace; Mokoto could see them now. On the roof of the palace there they stood, the famous eight giant statues of the Gaiamira – they were nicknamed the 'Lookout Statues'. They were the only part of the palace that was completely original; the only piece of artwork that hadn't been replaced or refurbished over the years. They held the spirits of the Gaiamira within them, and the more time passed the stronger they became. It could even be said that because of them this palace was one of the most holy places in the world; the energy of the Gaiamira here was overwhelming. It was certainly one of the most blessed buildings in history.

Mokoto moved his eyes down the palace's face, keen to see its next famous feature: the Royal Balcony. The entrance to the palace's ground floor was laid out like a conservatory, extended away from the rest of the palace. The extension travelled up all three floors and from the third floor grew one of the most important features of Meitona Palace's history – the Royal Balcony. It was a solid structure, more like a bridge than anything else. It was a stone walkway that travelled across the palace's front garden and over Mokoto's head, stopping just shy of the gate that cut through the deep walls of the Hive. It was from this balcony that all the kings and queens in the history of the palace had addressed their people; they'd stood before the world at its very tip and spoken to the thousands that had gathered outside the gate to hear what their leader had to say. It was an amazing sight to see, and it was something that still went on today. Mokoto's father had spoken to his people from the end of the Royal Balcony countless times over his reign; to announce the birth of his children, to welcome in the New Year, to connect with the people of Meitona… The Royal Balcony was the first mass communication tool that mortals had ever made, and just by existing it had written history.

"Is it anything like you expected, Your Highness?" Rowan's voice interrupted Mokoto's gazing. The teen lowered his eyes and looked at Rowan, then nodded.

"Yes," he answered. "Exactly."

"It's quite a sight though, isn't it, when you see it in the flesh?" Rowan smiled.

"Yes…" Mokoto quietly agreed. Rowan laughed.

"Come on," he said. "Let's meet your family." He nodded at the guards that were stood either side of the palace door, loyally awaiting Rowan's instructions. They nodded back and opened the door to the palace, and they held back their smiles as they watched Rowan accompany the nervous teen inside.

XI.

'It wasn't until they met Gonta that the people of the world learned to count the time. Before the Gaiamira arose the people argued about the length of the days and their society was falling apart, but the God of Knowledge and Wisdom, Gonta gave them a system that would be used by everybody in the world. He declared that there would be sixty seconds in a minute and ninety minutes in an hour, and there would be sixteen hours in a day, eight days in a week, eight weeks in a month and eight months in a year.'

-        Extract from the Gaiamirapon: 'The Communications'

*

Rozo watched his master curiously, surprised at how calm and distant the king seemed. He cleared his throat and spoke reluctantly.

"Sire…" Rozo began.

"Mm?" Taka grunted from the depths of his paperwork.

"Matat Mokoto has arrived in the palace, Sire," Rowan stated.

"I know. I ordered his car," Taka replied, not looking up from his work. He extended his arm out and reached for his drink, sipping it between his words and barely noticing as the liquid touched his lips. "The guards have reported journalists outside the gates…" He let out an angry sigh. "Mokoto's graduation isn't public news yet – what are they doing, stalking my drivers?"

"I wouldn't put it past them," Rozo commented bluntly. "Shall I bring the matat to you, Sire?"

"No," Taka answered. "Let the girls terrorise him for a while, let him get settled in… I'm sure our paths will cross at some point." He wouldn't tell Rozo, but he was reluctant to meet this one. When his other Hiveakan children had graduated, namely Lanka and Anaka, he hadn't bothered with Korana… Taka had summoned them to his meeting room for a formal introduction. Now though… This was different. The thought of meeting Mokoto was somewhat daunting. Mokoto was the only other royal male in the palace, and he had

140

graduated at a younger age than his siblings. So far Mokoto was the second most dominant member of Taka's tribe, and that meant that Taka had to assert his dominance all the more over the matat. He couldn't meet Mokoto yet; he couldn't let Mokoto think he was worthy of meeting the king – it would place him too close to Taka's throne. They would meet, eventually. Either by chance, or when Taka felt Mokoto had earned it. Regardless, it couldn't be today.

"As you wish, Sire." Rozo nodded obediently. He paused for a moment, and then smiled a little.

"What's wrong?" Taka growled, sensing the change on Rozo's face. He raised his head to look at Rozo for the first time that day, and impatiently waited for the man's response.

"Oh – it's – it's nothing, Sire," Rozo stammered.

"*What?*" Taka boomed.

"It's just…" Rozo whimpered. "He… He looks like you – as you did, when I started working for your father."

"I was twenty-four then," Taka replied flatly. "I had two wives and three children. Are you saying that when I was a twenty-four-year-old husband and father I looked like a thirteen-year-old graduate?"

"No!" Rozo shrieked. "I – I didn't mean that, I just - -" His voice softened as he noticed a cruel smirk forming on the king's face. The king was amused…

"I always did look young," Taka stated. He moved his eyes back down to his papers and continued his work. "He does look like me, yes… But I hope that will be the end of our similarities." He sniggered slightly and reached for his drink. "Otherwise I'm going to castrate him."

"Yes, Sire…"

*

'Although his graduation was not officially announced until the following day, journalists started to gather outside Meitona Palace on 25-06-20116G after a royal car was allegedly spotted exiting the Hive with a security tailgate. It has been suggested that King Taka at the time did not wish to make the matat's graduation public because he wanted to spend time with his son.'

-     Extract from newspaper article, 20116G

*

The décor of the palace fascinated Mokoto. Everywhere he looked he was presented with the images of decorative ornaments, paintings, family photos, holy idols, framed scripts of the Gaiamirapon… Some of them were thousands of years old, others more modern. The surfaces were flawlessly clean but marked here and there, as if they had been the victim of decades of child's play and fights. The walls were made from a pale brown wood and lacked wallpaper, and the floor was coated with a soft cream carpet that remained so well-groomed it looked as if it had never been walked upon. Mokoto paid close attention to the layout of the building, applying what he was seeing to the floor plans he had been shown in the Hive. He tried to work out where Rowan was taking him; he assumed they were heading for one of the common rooms that belonged to the ground floor, but he could have just as easily been led anywhere. Any room in this building would capture Mokoto's interest; every step he took felt as if he were walking through a dream.

They did enter a common room; one of the largest. It was along the front wall of the palace and provided a stunning view of the front garden… Not that Mokoto gave much time to the view when he stepped inside.

Mokoto threw himself to the floor as soon as he entered the room, and he didn't dare stand up again until he was ordered to by the woman that stood before him. It was Kaeila, his only living mother. Mokoto recognised her immediately, just as he recognised the other females in the room – his sisters. He'd memorised every detail of his surroundings; two short seconds had given Mokoto the time he needed to study the overwhelming size of the room, the colour of the carpets, every ornament, and every piece of furniture… The contents of the room alone had to be worth a fortune, but they were mere toys and

142

decorations to the royal family. In a way it was intimidating; this room was worth more than Mokoto's own life.

Kaeila gestured for Mokoto to stand and nodded at Rowan.

"Thank you. You may go," she stated, dismissing him from the room.

"Yes, Your Highness." Rowan's voice came from behind Mokoto and the teen heard his companion leave. He was alone now. This was the next stage of his homecoming. The time had come for Mokoto to prove his worth; he had to impress his family. He would.

"Matat Mokoto," Kaeila addressed the young matat. "Welcome to the palace. I suppose you know that I am your mother?" She smiled politely but sternly, ordering Mokoto to remain silent. "And I am sure you know that these are your sisters?" Kaeila went on to introduce Mokoto to the eleven girls that were standing behind her; Mokoto knew every one of their names before he was even told, but he remained obedient and polite, only speaking when spoken to and bowing respectfully at each of his sisters. It was what he had been told to do; they were all his superiors until he could prove himself to be a greater asset to his father than them, and even then he was to treat them with respect. That would be easy for some, and not so much for others... Mokoto could already tell which of the girls he would soon surpass; it was most of them. The only real threats to him were Beina, the palace nun – he would always be at least equal to her, because of her connection with the Gaiamira. Mokoto didn't mind that. Beina didn't want his throne; she wouldn't jeopardise his future... but Lanka would. Meitat Lanka... the current heir to the Gaiamirákan throne. Mokoto was introduced to Lanka last, but he had been waiting so desperately to meet her. She was his rival. Along with her sister Anaka, she was the only obstacle that could keep Mokoto from the throne. His throne. As far as Mokoto was concerned Lanka was his enemy, and it was obvious that she felt the same.

As soon as her name was uttered Lanka stepped towards Mokoto and smiled darkly at the matat, her eyes burning with an animalistic deadliness that could only come from years of residing in the Hive. Her eyes looked black. They weren't black, but they felt it. Their true colour was black; the dark blue shade that coated them was

143

nothing more than a mask, to hide the true horror of her nature. It wasn't hidden from Mokoto. He could see Lanka for what she was, and she couldn't shield the ugliness of her being from him.

"Hello." Lanka spoke icily, still holding a wicked smile as she looked into her brother's eyes. She was trying to intimidate him. Mokoto could feel the sharpness of her stare piercing into his skin. She couldn't intimidate him. He wasn't afraid of her! He would beat her. The throne was his, and he was determined to let her know.

"Hello, Meitat." Mokoto responded with the same dark smile she was giving him. He offered his hand out to her; she was the first one he had done this to. Mokoto had to make the first move with Lanka; he had to assert his dominance and show her he wasn't afraid. It worked. Lanka stiffened slightly, in a way that only another Hiveakan would notice. She was annoyed that he had beaten her to the greeting.

"So nice to meet you." Lanka spoke coarsely, taking his hand in hers. They shook hands firmly, each of them trying to crush the other. "Sorry Anaka isn't here. I suppose she doesn't think you are important enough. You'll have to forgive her."

"Lanka!" Kaeila sighed angrily. "He's only been here a few minutes – can't you wait?" She looked at Mokoto and sighed again. "Yes, I was going to mention that. Anaka sends her best wishes, but she can't get away from work. She is disappointed that she couldn't be here."

"If you want to speak to her you should phone her," one of the Outsider girls piped up. Mokoto moved his eyes to her. Vari. She seemed pleasant enough. She was an Outsider, but desperate to be a Hiveakan. She worked out a lot and held a strict, disciplined lifestyle. Mokoto had read that she had a good relationship with their father and the Hiveakans in the family... Perhaps Vari would make a good ally to him. "I think the last time I saw her was through the observation window at the Hive."

"Vari, don't exaggerate!" Kaeila scolded, but with a smirk. She looked back at Mokoto. "Anaka works a lot. If you want to see her you're better off going to the Royal – I assume they told you about the Royal?"

"Yes." Mokoto nodded.

He had been taught about it many times, and sometimes in great detail. The Royal Laboratory of Science, or 'The Royal' for short, was one of the planet's largest laboratories. It was the third largest building in Keizuaka. It was funded by his father, and it was responsible for most of the medicines and machines in existence. The Royal had five main departments, which were then split into sub-sections, and researched everything from chemistry and biology to astronomy and engineering; it was even partly occupied by Keizuaka's military, and was home to the majority of their classified creations and experiments. Meitat Anaka worked for the Royal along with her husband Raikun, the head manager of the Royal. It was an intense job, and from what Mokoto had read Meitat Anaka gave herself a heavy workload… It was understandable that she wasn't there, but Mokoto was disappointed. He had been looking forward to meeting his second rival. Would she try to intimidate him as well? She would fail. If Mokoto wasn't afraid of Lanka, he wasn't going to be afraid of her younger sister.

"Good, well…" Kaeila looked across her daughters. "Don't all stare at him, girls. You may go if you wish."

"Finally!" the eldest of Mokoto's sisters exhaled. Mokoto looked at her with a frown. Maika… She had been so hostile when they were introduced; Mokoto had been warned about her. She didn't like Hiveakans, and she felt the need to make that known whenever she could. She had a few marks on her, the kind of marks Mokoto had from spending his life being beaten in the Hive. Maika had obviously been beaten several times in her life, by their father no doubt. Well, it was no surprise. If she was insubordinate and voiced her opinion where it was not wanted, it was no wonder their father had beaten her. She deserved every one of those scars, and they weren't victory scars. They weren't like Mokoto's; they weren't proof of the trials she had endured and overcome. They were marks of shame; they were proof that she was an unruly child.

"Less attitude please, Maika," Kaeila growled sternly. "Do you want me to tell your father how miserable you've been?" That shut her up. Maika looked away and spoke stubbornly, causing Mokoto to inwardly smirk.

145

"Can I go?" she demanded.

"Are you deaf?" Kaeila snapped. "*Yes*. Go."

Maika looked at the girl that was stood next to her and gestured for the younger meitat to follow.

"Orei, are you coming?"

"Actually, I'm going to show Mokoto to his room." The girl smiled. This was Oreisaka... Mokoto's only full sibling. She had taken hold of his hands as soon as they'd been introduced, and she had hugged him as if they were old friends. They weren't friends. When he had earned the right to speak, Mokoto would inform her of that. They shared their parents, and that was all they had in common. It was the only thing that would ever connect them. Why did she feel the need to show him such affection? Even now she was smiling at him so warmly. Why? What did she hope to gain?

"Fine." Maika huffed, and turned her back to Oreisaka. "See you later then."

"Maika, I didn't mean –"

"Bye!" Maika cut Oreisaka off and stormed out of the room like a petulant child.

Mokoto moved his eyes to Kaeila. He was shocked by Maika's behaviour – how could she act like that? Would she still be alive tomorrow? He had never behaved like that in all his life; if he had he would have been beaten to death. Would Maika be punished for that? Of course... She must be. There was no way the king would tolerate that sort of behaviour!

"Right – we are done here," Kaeila snarled. She looked across the girls. "Girls, thank you for acting like adults – and Lanka you can stop smirking!"

"Sorry, Mother." Lanka offered her superior a bow, but she was still smirking. How disrespectful... Kaeila was her mother! Lanka should show respect for her at all times! These girls were too outspoken; with respect to Kaeila, she didn't treat them harshly enough.

"Beina and Orei, you two can stay," Kaeila instructed. "The rest of you are dismissed."

The girls didn't need to be told twice; they were trained to some extent at least. They bowed to Kaeila and left the room

146

obediently, glancing and smiling at Mokoto and murmuring amongst themselves as they walked away. Mokoto met eyes with Lanka one final time as she made her way towards the door. She offered him another nasty smirk; it was challenging him. She was daring him to run after her, knowing full well that he couldn't. Her challenge infuriated Mokoto; he couldn't possibly rise to it! She knew that. She knew he couldn't attack her now, when he had not yet been dismissed. Her challenge wasn't fair. There was no honour in it. It wasn't a real victory for her; Lanka would realise that. The next time they met, Mokoto would make sure she realised that.

Kaeila waited until the girls had left the room and turned her attention towards Beina. "Could you read him, Meitat?"

"I already did." Beina smiled. "He has Taka in him." She turned to face Mokoto and looked at him fondly. "I would know those eyes anywhere... The strongest Footprints I've ever seen." She looked back at Kaeila. "Stronger than Anaka and Lanka."

"Pff!" Kaeila sniggered. "I wish you'd said that five minutes ago." She ran her eyes up and down Mokoto's frame, studying him. "Well... That's something at least. One less thing for your father to moan about."

"Maybe he will have a new favourite?" Oreisaka smiled, almost giggling as she looked at her brother.

"Ha! I'll believe that when I see it," Kaeila scoffed. "He's only blessed by the God of War, he's no Anaka." The other girls laughed at her remark, causing Mokoto to frown. What were they talking about? Was Anaka his father's favourite? But how? Her graduation age was average! She was more of an Outsider than her older sister – she had to be; she worked with Outsiders all the time! Then again, her work in the Royal did benefit the palace's reputation... Of course! How had Mokoto not realised that sooner? He had been foolish; he had only taken her personal attributes into consideration, but Anaka had earned their father's respect by holding a job in his laboratory, and marrying the man that had practically invented modern science. She was certainly a favourite of the public... Mokoto could recall the many articles and biographies he had read about her – and her husband. Raikun had been world famous and a celebrity in his own right before

147

he had even married the meitat; he had been one of the youngest heads the Royal had ever known and he had published his work in various books and magazines across the world... That must be it. It had to be. Anaka's reputation and the reputation of her husband had made her the favourite child of the king. It wasn't just about how strong she was, or how intimidating... It was about her value to the palace. Maybe *she* was the real threat to Mokoto's throne. Well... she wouldn't be for long. Mokoto would make sure of it. Even if it meant he had to kill her, Mokoto would overcome the obstacle that was Meitat Anaka. That throne was *his*! "Go on then." Kaeila twitched her head at Oreisaka, gesturing for the girl to leave the room. "Take him away. I know you're dying to hold his hand."

"Thank you!" Oreisaka giggled. She turned to Mokoto, and as predicted grabbed hold of his hand. "Come on – I'll show you to your room." She bowed at Kaeila and gave Mokoto time to do the same before she dragged him through the open door.

XII

'Taka, the most powerful of the Gaiamira was furious when he found the baby. He rounded up the rest of the Gaiamira, and between them they demanded that the baby be killed. Tangun and Lanka pleaded for the child's life; it was the only time Lanka had been known to cry. The Gaiamira eventually agreed to spare the child's life, on the condition that she was exiled from the Gaiamirarezo. Her parents took the baby up to the mortal world and left her in the care of a doctor, never to see their daughter again. Before they said goodbye, they named the child Aleisa.'

-        Extract from the Aleisapon: 'The Exile'

*

"So here it is." Oreisaka smiled as she and Mokoto stopped outside a pale wooden door on the third floor of the palace – the royal floor, as it was dubbed. It belonged to members of the royal family, and was situated above the servants' living quarters. "Rowan's already put your things inside – you'll find a few extras as well. Father gave you a phone to use, my number is in there." Her eyes sparkled as she grinned at Mokoto. "Call me anytime you want – I can show you around Meitona if you like."

"Thank you…" Mokoto uttered awkwardly. Would their father be annoyed if he told her now that he had no intention of ever speaking to her again? He hadn't earned the right to be cruel to his sisters yet, but Oreisaka had been making ridiculous small talk all the way up there; it was boring and annoying. Why did she think they were friends? They weren't friends! They shared blood – but Oreisaka shared blood with all of their father's children! She had much more in common with the others; why didn't she just stick with them?

"I'll leave you to get settled," Oreisaka said. "Dinner will be at thirteen; someone will come for you this time, but then you'll be expected to attend on your own." She shrugged carelessly. "But to be honest… we all tend to eat separately; Father only wants us to eat together sometimes – on special occasions."

"Will he be there tonight?" Mokoto questioned. This was the first piece of useful information Oreisaka would give him.

"He should be…" Oreisaka answered quietly. "But – if he isn't, don't take it personally. He's very busy."

"I see." Mokoto nodded. Was that a no? Not that it mattered… Mokoto would meet his father when he was ready, and when he deserved to. Still… He was anxious to meet the king. The king was the only person in this palace that really mattered; he was the only one Mokoto had to impress. Maybe Mokoto could still impress his father at dinner even if the king wasn't there, if he behaved well and gave his mother Kaeila only good things to report to the king… Dinner was his second test, after his introduction to the family. Mokoto was determined to pass.

"I'll see you later," Oreisaka beamed. "If you like, we can have lunch together tomorrow?"

"If… He doesn't need me for anything," Mokoto answered cautiously. He didn't want to have lunch with her! But he couldn't say that. His father might beat him if he offended any of his sisters this early on.

"Okay." Oreisaka nodded. She was hurt. Mokoto could see it in her eyes. She knew he didn't want to spend time with her… Why did that even bother her? She was pathetic! "Bye." Mokoto stiffened as Oreisaka hugged him awkwardly, and offered him a tearful smile before walking away.

Finally! Mokoto sighed inwardly and shook his body in disgust. He could still feel Oreisaka's warmth on him… It had taken a lot of his strength to fight his Hiveakan instincts during that hug; his Footprints had wanted to rip her apart. Mokoto's tutors had warned him that his Outsider siblings might try to hug him. He was grateful for that warning now; at least he had been somewhat prepared… Not that it had made the hug any more pleasant. Mokoto let out a short breath and regained his composure, and then he stared up at his bedroom door. Well… This was it. This was his new room. He grabbed hold of the golden handle and cautiously stepped inside.

Mokoto's eyes widened and his breath caught in his throat as he stared at the wonder before him. His room... It was gigantic! It was five, six times bigger than his room in the Hive. He was expecting it to be big, but... This was ridiculous! Was he expected to live here alone? How? He could marry in this room! He could take a hundred wives and they would barely touch the walls. Surely he hadn't been given this room to occupy on his own? His tutors hadn't told him, but he must be expected to share it with his siblings. Perhaps two or three. There was only one bed though... That wasn't just for him was it? No. It couldn't be. It looked as if it were made for a family! He could share it with three other people and there would still be room left. Mokoto had barely had room to move in his bed in the Hive. He had earned it piece by piece; when he was a child he had earned a small bedframe that he had soon grown out of, and after that he had earned a hard mattress, then thin sheets that he had to treat with the upmost care. Mokoto had had to work hard in the Hive to even get an upgrade to a bed that was longer than his own body; he'd spent many nights in the Hive not even using his bed at all; he had grown accustomed to sleeping on the wall, in a hammock made from his own silk ducts. This thing – this object before him, giant as it was, it barely made a mark in the room – it was unreal. It was fit for a king – it was fit for the most blessed priest in the world. Mokoto didn't deserve this... He didn't deserve a room this size; he hadn't earned it. Perhaps he was to share it, or... perhaps it was another test. That might be it... In the Hive Mokoto had started with nothing and he had earned his possessions; perhaps the palace operated in reverse. Perhaps every time he displeased his father he would have something taken from him; perhaps this room at this moment was the best and most exquisite it ever would be. Well it would stay this way. Mokoto would make sure of that. Nothing about this room would be lost – *nothing*! He would never displease his father, not in his entire life. He wouldn't dare.

Mokoto moved his eyes across the objects in the room; it was so perfectly decorated. Everything looked new; everything looked clean. The shelves were mostly bare – of course they were. There was so much space on them! Mokoto's possessions had taken up a large proportion of his room in the Hive; he had been so proud of how much he had earned and how his collection of things had made his room look small… Now they looked pathetic. Mokoto could collect every item he had ever owned in his entire life and gather it on the bed alone – and they wouldn't even fill one side.

He curiously made his way towards a large desk that was situated against the far wall, underneath a window that stretched across the length of the room. There was a laptop here… It wasn't the one Mokoto had used in the Hive; it was new. There wasn't a mark on it; it still shone as if it had just been removed from its packaging. Was Mokoto's data on there? He didn't have much, but he would have liked to keep a few of his old projects and pictures he had downloaded… Still. It didn't matter. He could always do the work again. Mokoto looked over at a small unit on the desk. It contained his holobooks, organised in alphabetical order by author. He had a lot – at least it had looked like a lot in the Hive. Now the collection of small devices that projected a hologram of words looked pitiful in this organiser. They barely took up any space at all; there was room for at least a hundred more in this unit. Maybe he could earn more… Mokoto liked reading, particularly history books. His family was always in them.

Mokoto moved his eyes to look out of the window that resided above his desk. It was the back garden… Finally, he could see it for real! The pictures he had seen and memorised over the years didn't even begin to do it justice. It went on for what seemed like miles; there was so much detail and land. A maze, a pond, an elaborate display of flowers and greenery… The entire place was landscaped so perfectly it was as if it had been designed by the Gaiamira themselves. Part of it was. Mokoto locked his eyes onto another legend of Meitona; he knew exactly where to look for it. He had studied the layout of the palace gardens from pictures he had been shown in the Hive, and this piece was by far the most enchanting thing about the palace's exterior. The Aleisa Tree. This one was never seen by the outside world, except maybe through binoculars in Eilaháka, but it was still one of the most famous parts of Meitona Palace.

There were only five Aleisa Trees left in the world, including this one, and they were all believed to be thousands of years old. They were named after an ancient legend, the legend of Aleisa. According to the legend, Aleisa was the forbidden daughter of Tangun the God of Birth and Reincarnation and Lanka the Goddess of Death. She was rejected by the Gaiamira at birth and cast out of the Gaiamirarezo, and left to wander the mortal world alone. There were so many different stories about her, so many variations on who or what she was. Some said she was killed as soon as she touched the mortal world, and now she only existed in the form of a spirit that appeared only to a chosen few. Others claimed she became a mortal when she left the Gaiamirarezo, and that she grew and lived a normal life, raised by mortals, but died thousands of years ago. Then there were those that said Aleisa was still a goddess, but she walked the world in the form of a mortal to hide her true identity. Some others claimed that she was indeed still a goddess, but rather than having a mortal body of her own she lived dormant in the bodies of others, only awakening when her people needed her... All variations of the legend acknowledged her as a healer though, in some form or another. She was a mortal doctor, or an immortal being that had the power to heal the sick... That was how the Aleisa Tree got its name. The tree leaves contained a chemical that helped boost the Gaiamirákan immune system, and anyone who had a lot of exposure to its leaves would soon be cured of most common infections or diseases. Of course it was nothing more than simple biology, but before science was popular people believed that Aleisa's spirit lived in the trees, and that she healed anyone who came near her.

It wasn't true. None of it. Mokoto didn't believe the legend for a second, not one word. Aleisa wasn't real – she wasn't acknowledged by any of the official temples of the world and the Gaiamira had never acknowledged her existence. It didn't stop other people believing though. She had an entire following of her own; hundreds of thousands, perhaps even millions of people all over the world believed in Aleisa and worshiped her. They built temples and idols in her name, none of which were acknowledged as real holy places by any official representative of the Gaiamira. Aleisa even had her own holy book named the Aleisapon, and her followers believed every word as loyally and as seriously as they believed the Gaiamirapon. There was a name for followers of Aleisa. They were called Aleisákans. ... Or lunatics. They could even be called blasphemers, for accusing Tangun and

153

Lanka of having an illicit child whose existence was never confirmed by any member of the Gaiamira. As far as Mokoto and millions of other people across the world were concerned, the Aleisa legend was a joke; nobody could say for certain how it was started, but it was definitely some treacherous maniac's idea of a joke, and so many foolish people in the world had taken it seriously. It was a shame, and it was insulting to the Gaiamira and their temples. Still… The Aleisa Tree was a beautiful thing. Mokoto was lucky to see it. He was lucky to live with it, even if it was named after a lie.

Mokoto turned to look at another feature of the room; he hadn't even looked at the ensuite bathroom yet. He was still busy taking in the sights of this room! There was a large wardrobe on the same side as his bedroom door, its doors were mirrored. Mokoto had never seen a mirror that big before; he had never seen himself so clearly. He walked over to the wardrobe and looked at himself, studying every inch of his frame. Did he look okay…? A couple of his sisters had called him cute. That wasn't Hiveakan. Maybe he needed to train more; perhaps he should work on widening his body. He was tall for his age, that was an advantage… but he was slim. He had muscles, but he was slim. He wasn't frightening. That had to change.

Mokoto took his focus off his image and looked across the wide depth that was his wardrobe. How would he ever fill this? He could fit a lifetime's worth of clothing in there! Mokoto opened one of the doors and looked at his pitiful collection of clothing. He only had a few outfits; he had made most of them himself, from his silk ducts. He had a few things that had been made from other materials and given to him at various points in his life – those were clothes that he had earned. He treasured them. They didn't all fit him anymore, and they were aged and stained, but Mokoto had never wanted to throw them away. They were trophies to him; they were proof of what he had achieved. Maybe he would be able to get them cleaned now… Mokoto didn't clean these anymore; his washing allowance in the Hive was limited and he had saved his cleaning allowance for garments that he wore every day, so most of his old clothes hadn't been cleaned in years. Maybe he could clean them now though, if he pleased his father enough. It would be nice to restore them to how they had been.

Mokoto turned around again to look at a door that was on the other side of the room, against the left hand wall. It led to another room, one that came away from the back wall and interrupted the giant window that swept across it. Was that his bathroom? It was huge! Even from there he could tell. Mokoto raced over to the door, eager to see where it led. He opened it and was almost blinded by the brightness he saw before him. He never could have imagined a bathroom like this... Every surface was gleaming; the window that had swept across his bedroom carried on into here and the light it let in bounced off every sparkling object in the room. There was so much space in there... This couldn't just be for one person! There was a bathtub... Mokoto had never had free access to one before. The Hive had bathtubs but they were in a separate room that students needed to earn access to. Was Mokoto permitted to use this one whenever he wanted? Or would he need to earn his right to bathe here as well? It was enormous... He could swim in it! There was a shower in there as well – it was much bigger than the shower he'd had in the Hive. Was it acid...? Mokoto approached the shower cubicle and looked inside at the item's controls. There was an acid setting. Yes! How could he be so fortunate? An acid shower was the ultimate training device; it slowly burned away one's skin and increased their endurance and tolerance to pain. Then the skin grew back thicker and tougher than before – in the Hive Mokoto had earned the right to have one acid shower a week, but now... Could he use this every day? If he could, he would. His skin would be practically made of stone by the time he was fourteen! Maybe he could try it now... No. No, not yet. He didn't know if he was allowed. He had to check first; if he used any of these luxuries without permission they might be taken away from him.

Mokoto took a moment to allow his eyes to travel across the room, taking in the sight before him. It was unreal... This was unbelievable!

After a long couple of minutes he finally managed to drag himself away, in search of his Gaiamirapon. It didn't take long to find; it was on the floor beside the bed, according to tradition. It was believed that the Gaiamira should be close to a mortal at all times, in the form of jewellery and idols, and the Gaiamirapon was by far one of the holiest items one could own. It was common practice for one to keep an extra copy of the Gaiamirapon about their person, in their pocket or handbag, in the form of an easy to carry holobook, but by no means should that replace a hard copy. Everyone needed a hard copy, even if they only ever kept it in their room. Next to the bed was the perfect place; it meant that the Gaiamira were still there, even when one was sleeping. It couldn't be placed above the bed – idols could be placed above the bed, but not the Gaiamirapon. The Gaiamira were believed to live in the centre of the world, and so the closer the Gaiamirapon was to them the holier it became. It was for this reason that prayer rooms were typically in the basement of a home, or on the ground floor. Traditionally the Gaiamirapon would be placed on the floor; on a special mat known as the Gaiamirákot Tuna, the Gaiamiras' Mat. Mokoto's Gaiamirapon was here, on its mat next to his bed. It was a beautiful object – of all his possessions Mokoto valued this one the most, and not only because it was the holy book. It was the very best edition of the holy book. It was thousands of years old, and perhaps the only thing of Mokoto's that showed just how much his family could afford. It was printed on paper that was almost out of existence now, with ink that could have been used to paint the temples of the world. Every page was handwritten in the finest calligraphy known to mortals and decorated by the greatest artists in history. Mokoto had only read it a handful of times, from fear of damaging its delicate pages. He had memorised every word of the Gaiamirapon from his holobook edition, and reserved this ancient copy for when he was truly in need of spiritual guidance. Maybe he should pray now, to thank the Gaiamira for his home. Mokoto moved down onto his knees and closed his eyes, interlocking his fingers and holding his thumbs together in the prayer position.

Mokoto hadn't started his prayer before he was interrupted by the sound of knocking on his bedroom door. Was it time for dinner already? No... He knew what time it was; dinner wasn't for another two hours yet. Perhaps this was his father... Would his father knock? No, of course not. Perhaps it was Oreisaka again... Dammit! Mokoto stiffened slightly and rose to his feet, making his way over to the door. If this was Oreisaka...

It wasn't her. Mokoto glanced at the girl in front of him and took a defensive stance as soon as he opened the door. This wasn't Oreisaka. This was Anaka! His rival. He would know her face anywhere! She was dressed in office clothing; she must have just finished work. She was standing openly... Why? Did she think he wasn't a threat? She was mocking him. She would regret that. Sincerely!

Anaka met eyes with her brother and smiled.

"Hi," she said. "I suppose you know who I am?" She raised her eyebrows at him, as if she were expecting him to do something. "Are you going to let me in?"

Mokoto didn't have chance to respond; Anaka pushed past him and entered his room uninvited, looking around with a keen interest. "Hm," she uttered. "It's not bigger than mine... Okay." She turned to face Mokoto and winked. "That makes me feel better." She raised her eyebrows at him again and smirked a little. "Are you going to shut the door? You aren't afraid of me, are you?"

"Of course not!" Mokoto growled. He shut the door and stepped further into the room, keeping his eyes sternly fixed on her. "The others seem to think you are Father's favourite. I thought Lanka was my biggest threat..." He smirked nastily and watched her reaction, trying to assert his dominance over her. "She graduated younger than you, after all."

"She did..." Anaka answered reluctantly. She was annoyed. Mokoto could tell. He was winning! "And yet, they say I'm the favourite," Anaka said, her confidence quickly returning. "It's funny, isn't it?" She made her way over to Mokoto and looked him up and down, studying his frame. "I would have expected a bow. You do know I am your superior? I'm older than you."

Mokoto couldn't answer. He didn't know what to say. She was right. He should have shown her respect... Would their father beat him for that?

"I won't tell if you don't," Anaka whispered, a mischievous smile forming on her face. Mokoto frowned slightly, confused. Was she offering to protect him? Why? What did she possibly have to gain from that? "You can stop trying to be a big boy now," Anaka teased.

157

"You don't seem to suit it – you're a little too cute." She giggled. "Don't worry." She extended her hand to ruffle Mokoto's hair. "You'll grow into it."

"Hey!" Mokoto snarled, pulling his head away. How dare she do that! He wasn't a doll for her to pet! He was the biggest threat to her life that Anaka would ever know! Mokoto glared at her angrily, his Footprints burning. "I graduated!"

"I know," Anaka nodded. "And all new graduates think they're tough, until they actually get tough and realise how cute they were." She smirked again. "You'll see."

Anaka walked past Mokoto and stopped in front of the mirrored wardrobe, as if she owned the room. She started examining her reflection, scanning her eyes over every piece of her appearance. She had a good appearance; Anaka was twenty, and somehow managed to look both mature and respectable, and young and fruitful at the same time. Her face was young and pretty, and decorated with two birthmarks, one under each eye, resting against her cheekbones. They were almost identical in appearance, slightly darker than her pale yellow skin and shaped like petals. Birthmarks such as these were not uncommon amongst Gaiamirákans, but they often faded over time. To still have them apparent in adulthood was considered a blessing, and a sign that they belonged to a body that had been particularly blessed by the Gaiamira. The petal shape of Anaka's was associated with Tangun and therefore with life, and Anaka was full of life. Her hair was Gaiamirákan blonde, an orange-brown mix that was flooded with natural highlights and seemed to capture the essence of autumn. Physically, Anaka's youthful, pretty face made her look her age, but her eyes… They were dark brown, and Hiveakan. They were older than her body; they were harder. Colder, as if they had seen the very face of war. They made Mokoto wary of her, and he watched her intently as she studied herself, seemingly oblivious to Mokoto's presence or the hostility he was expelling from his body.

Anaka wasn't easily distracted, and she liked to look at herself a few times a day. She liked to make sure she was still perfect. Was her skin clear enough? Was her make-up too strong or too plain? Was her hair styled correctly? Was her body the right shape? Did she have the right look in her eyes…? She liked to look like a Hiveakan, and she would never struggle to do so. Anaka could have the warmest smile in the world and her eyes would still make her look deadly.

"Have you decided who your friends are going to be?" Anaka questioned, not shifting her eyes from her own image.

"Friends?" Mokoto repeated questioningly. What did she mean?

"Well… You aren't a normal graduate," Anaka replied. "You're a matat, and an heir to the throne." She moved her eyes to look at Mokoto. "The media will be watching you – for the next couple of months at least. You need to think about how you want to be viewed – who you want to be seen with. They should have told you about this in the Hive!" She let out an angry sigh. "They never think about our family! It's as if they think you aren't going to have a life after them." Anaka looked at Mokoto openly, without hostility or anger, as if she were genuinely trying to befriend him. She wasn't. She couldn't be. They were rivals. "If you want, I'll be your friend. I'm assuming you want them to view you as a Hiveakan? So you should have Hiveakan friends – stick with me and Lanka." She smirked a little. "But just bear in mind that she might try to kill you."

"And you won't?" Mokoto answered back. "You're my rival. If you want the throne, you will have to take it from me."

"I don't want the throne." Anaka shrugged. "You're welcome to it. Sorry. I presumed you knew." She seemed amused at something… Perhaps the look of shock on Mokoto's face. He stared at her with wide eyes, in utter disbelief of what he had just heard. Had she really said that? She *didn't* want the throne? Why…? Why would she not want it? It was her birthright – and what right did she have to reject it? She had no right! No right at all!

"That throne is an honour," Mokoto growled. "It's your birthright – you are lucky to be an heir!"

"I know…" Anaka answered. "But this rivalry… it was started by my mother." She narrowed her eyes at him, her expression suddenly becoming serious. "The korota. I know they would have told you about her – you know what she did to this family. Why would I want to honour her by carrying on with that stupid rivalry? To be honest it

159

annoys me that Lanka still honours it." Anaka turned back to the mirror and stared at her reflection with a look of annoyance on her face. She was angry. Mokoto could feel the hatred in her soul. She was burning. "So you aren't my rival – far from it. I wouldn't give her the satisfaction, and to be perfectly honest I'm too busy to take the throne. The Royal takes up enough of my time, I can't become queen without giving up my career – and I am *not* giving up my career." Anaka turned back to Mokoto and smiled. "So, if you can get rid of Lanka the throne is all yours."

Anaka paused for a moment, studying her younger brother. His body was stiff; he looked hostile. Anaka wasn't surprised. Mokoto didn't believe her, and rightly so. He didn't know her, and there was no doubt in Anaka's mind that the Hive had made him believe he couldn't trust her. He would be a failure if he wasn't suspicious of her now. "I'm telling the truth," Anaka said. "Ask Father when you meet him." She moved over to Mokoto and met his eyes, watching the young matat's body language. He was standing defensively. He was expecting her to attack him. How cute. "My number is in your phone," Anaka stated. "Or you can find me at the Royal – if you want to be friends, I'm here. You should make at least two Hiveakan friends, to compensate for Oreisaka."

"What does Oreisaka have to do with it?" Mokoto growled.

"You'll have to be friends with her," Anaka answered. "Sorry. I know it won't be fun – she is really boring…" She let out a short sigh. "But she's your only full blood relative, and for the next month at least you should at least make it look like you're friends. Go out to lunch with her and get seen – it'll make us look like a happy family. The public will like it." She smirked a little. "Which means Father will like it." Anaka watched Mokoto hesitate again, his stance still defensive. He didn't believe her. Anaka narrowed her eyes at Mokoto and spoke sternly. "Seriously. I'm not trying to fool you. If you want the throne then you need him to like you – and I guarantee he will like you more if you can benefit the family's reputation. You need to learn about politics if you want to be king. Frankly I'm disgusted that the Hive hasn't already told you this." Mokoto didn't comment; he didn't want her to know that he believed some of what she was saying. The Hive had told him... He needed to please his father if he wanted the throne, and of course they had taught Mokoto about politics and public perception... but he didn't trust Anaka, and he wanted her to know that.

"So why have you learned?" Mokoto demanded. "If you don't want to be queen – why do you even care about politics?"

"I don't really," Anaka answered. "I'm just a natural." She winked. "That's why I'm his favourite." She giggled at the disgruntled expression on Mokoto's face, and ruffled his hair again. "Anyway. I have to go. I'll see you at dinner. Call me if you want to look tough."

Mokoto didn't answer. He pulled away from her grasp and held his claws ready to strike, disappointed when she didn't seem to acknowledge his demeanour. Anaka left the room carelessly, completely unintimidated and undisturbed by his anger, as if she hadn't even noticed it. She wasn't scared of him... She should be! Mokoto could already tell that he was physically stronger than her. He could kill Anaka if he wanted to! ... It was pointless though. If she really didn't have any interest in the throne... No. He didn't believe her. That was just a lie to keep him out of her way, Mokoto was sure of it. Who in the world would not want the throne? Anaka was cunning. She was manipulative. She was the biggest threat of all... but she would *not* fool him.

*

'Meitona Palace officially announced yesterday that Matat Mokoto has safely returned home after graduating from the Hive at the age of thirteen. No doubt he has already formed a close bond with his Hiveakan sisters Meitat Lanka and Meitat Anaka, and we all look forward to seeing them together once our young matat has settled in.'

-       Extract from newspaper article, 20116G

*

Dinner had been interesting, and one family gathering Kaeila could have done without. She had spent the evening watching the

161

meitats fuss over Mokoto, and the poor boy had sat there respectfully, allowing them to devour him while fighting the urge to slit every one of their throats. He was a well-behaved boy, but then all new graduates were. Even his father had been at some point. Kaeila was on her way to see the king now; he hadn't been at dinner but he had summoned her to his room shortly after. To discuss dinner, no doubt. If he was really that interested he should have been there! But, obviously Kaeila's time was far less valuable than his own. Jackass.

Kaeila stopped outside Taka's room and knocked, then waited for permission to enter.

"Come." Taka's voice summoned her from inside the room, but the door opened before Kaeila could even touch the handle. She was greeted by a young girl, a servant. The servant was young, and pretty... she was just how the king liked them. She wore a red collar; it was the first thing Kaeila noticed, and an indication of the girl's job description. The red collars were prostitutes; their main role was to clean and make the beds, like all other servants, but red collars were on a higher salary because they were also required to... 'satisfy' members of the royal family whenever their services were desired. Kaeila could have been a red collar, if she hadn't had so much self-respect. Kaeila wasn't born into high society. She had come from a humble home, and had worked in the palace as an ordinary servant many years ago, saving up money to travel the world... She had never been quite desperate enough to be a red collar, but then who was she to judge? These days she used the male ones herself from time to time; they never seemed below her anymore. At least these young girls had their freedom. They were prostitutes, but they could leave. In a way, they were better than her... and Kaeila hated it.

"Is he decent?" Kaeila questioned, looking at the young girl before her with arrogant eyes. She had to make this girl feel like dirt. She had to make herself feel like she still had a better life than this child.

"Very." The girl answered with a smirk, sending a wave of disgust through Kaeila's soul. She wanted to vomit! Gods, she remembered that smirk – she had worn it herself, but at least she had been his age back then. Kaeila had fancied the king like mad, many

162

years ago… How stupid she had been. If this girl knew what life with him was really like, she wouldn't be smirking.

"Right," Kaeila answered bluntly and pushed past the red collar, nudging the girl harshly and slamming the door behind her.

Kaeila looked up to see the king wearing nothing more than a pair of lounge trousers and his wedding chains. Of course. He was doing his usual vanity routine. He was stood in front of his mirror, studying his bare chest and marvelling at his body. He told himself he was making sure he was still at a Hiveakan standard, but Kaeila suspected better. He was just vain. Vain, and arrogant. He liked to look at himself; he liked being attractive. It was amazing… Once upon a time the young Matat Taka had swept Kaeila off her feet. He was a teenage girl's dream – every young female in the palace wanted him, and if they were pretty enough they could have him. Kaeila had been pretty enough. In her younger days she had been as stunning and as vibrant as him. They were children back then. Kaeila had finally saved up enough money, and she was leaving her job at the palace to travel the world… and she just couldn't resist the parting gift that was an encounter with the gorgeous Matat Taka. That was all it was supposed to be. An encounter. They had both agreed on that. They would have their moment, and each of them was to be nothing more to the other than a pleasant memory… Then the morning sickness had started, and these two children suddenly found themselves to be married and parents, seemingly overnight. Kaeila never did travel the world, and before long she hated her husband for imprisoning her, just as much as he hated her for making him grow up. They barely spoke to each other now except to discuss the children. They were rarely intimate, and it was never with Kaeila's blessing. How the world had changed…

"What do you think of him?" Taka asked his wife, not moving his eyes from his own reflection.

"He's good. Obedient," Kaeila answered bluntly. "But give him time to come out of his shell."

"How was he with the girls?" Taka questioned.

"Well Maika hates him," Kaeila sniggered. "But he doesn't seem to care."

"Good," Taka grunted. "He shouldn't."

163

"Lanka's at him already, and he seems to be rising to it quite well." Kaeila looked at her husband. "He isn't scared of her. He isn't scared of anything."

"Mm…" Taka didn't say, but he was pleased with that. He wore a satisfied smile on his face, as if he was ever going to treat his son with the respect the boy deserved.

"Anaka isn't interested in this rivalry," Kaeila stated. "I think she wants to be friends."

"Mm. I spoke to Anaka earlier," Taka answered. "She's always made it clear she isn't interested in the throne." He smirked a little. "She's the only girl that has ever rejected me."

"Yes, I know," Kaeila replied flatly, not amused by his remark.

"She thinks he's cute…" Taka took his eyes off his own image and looked at Kaeila. "I'm not happy with that."

"Well… he is cute." Kaeila smirked a little. "You should see his face."

"He's a Hiveakan!" Taka growled. "And heir to my throne! He can't be cute!"

"Oh, that means nothing!" Kaeila scoffed. "He's only been here a day – Thoit still calls you cute now!"

"That's just Thoit being a dick," Taka muttered, looking away.

"They're all cute to begin with," Kaeila said. "This time next year he'll be hideous – just like his father." She narrowed her eyes at Taka, and he seemed to calm down.

"Hm," Taka grunted. "I hope you are right. Otherwise I'll kill him."

"Wise move, Sire," Kaeila sarcastically replied.

Taka glared at her, warning his wife to watch her tone around him.

"Dismissed," he ordered. Kaeila nodded stubbornly and left the room, silently praying for the king to choke to death on his own ego. It wouldn't even fit in his mouth.

XIII.

'Kala always appears as a beautiful woman, described as bright and pretty, youthful and friendly. Her looks will change from mortal to mortal, as one's opinion of beauty may not be the same as another's. When Kala appears to a mortal she knows them, and she will appear beautiful to them, whatever that may be.'

-       Extract from the Gaiamirapon: 'The Identities'

*

Mokoto paused, and hesitated. It was the following day and he was yet to meet his father. The king's aide Rozo had arrived at Mokoto's bedroom door early in the morning, and told the matat that his father wished him to explore the palace and become accustomed to his surroundings, and his sisters. Reluctantly, Mokoto had decided to take Anaka's advice. It wasn't what he wanted to do… but it made sense. As much as Mokoto didn't want to admit it. He should form a friendship with Oreisaka; it would make the palace look good and strengthen the Hiveakan-Outsider alliance. Anyway, if his father wished him to become familiar with his sisters, Mokoto might as well start with Oreisaka. So now here he was, outside her bedroom door. Mokoto forced himself to knock and hoped she wouldn't answer.

Unfortunately, she did. Oreisaka seemed overjoyed to see him, as Mokoto had expected. Why was he such an exciting vision to her?

"Mokoto!" Oreisaka exclaimed. "Come in!" She practically leapt to one side to allow him access to her room and she kept her eyes fixed on him as he entered. Mokoto memorised his surroundings in mere seconds. Oreisaka's room was slightly smaller than his, which filled Mokoto with a sense of importance. He was the heir… He was above her in their father's eyes. The size of this room was proof. Oreisaka had decorated it tastefully, according to Outsider standards. It was warm and welcoming, and filled with family photos and trinkets she had gathered over the years. Mokoto expected as much.

"You are friends with Maika?" Mokoto commented, looking at a picture of the two meitats together, both smiling as if they were the best of friends.

"Yes…" Oreisaka smiled a little. "But I think we might fall out over you." Great! That was exactly what Mokoto wanted to hear! Perhaps Oreisaka didn't want a relationship with him, if it would spoil the closeness she held with Maika. Perhaps she would be happy to just be seen with Mokoto once or twice; just enough to make them look like a happy family.

"We don't have to meet up much," Mokoto insisted. "If it will upset Maika –"

"Oh, forget Maika!" Oreisaka huffed. "She just doesn't like Hiveakans – it's nothing personal against you, and it's not going to stop me seeing my brother. I've told her that." She offered him a warm smile, much to Mokoto's dismay. "Now – would you like me to show you around the palace?"

"Please," Mokoto answered glumly. Well… a tour of the building with Oreisaka wouldn't be too awful, would it?

Actually, it wasn't. Not too awful, at least. Oreisaka went into great detail as she showed her brother around, pointing out every object and painting and explaining the history behind it. She was too busy acting like a tour guide to act like herself, much to Mokoto's relief. He found the building fascinating and the information she gave him was useful and interesting. Every part of the palace and every object in it had such a rich heritage; it was all so full of culture and history… It still didn't seem real that Mokoto would live here for the rest of his life. He didn't feel like he deserved it. But then, he did have a bigger room than Oreisaka…

"Do you want to have some lunch?" Oreisaka suggested, leading Mokoto into the dining room.

"Alright…" Mokoto answered. He had to make himself realise he was hungry; he had become so accustomed to ignoring hunger. In the Hive Mokoto would sometimes go for days without food. Was he allowed to eat now? Could he eat whenever he wanted? It didn't seem reasonable… Mokoto had only eaten last night; surely it was too soon to eat again?

166

"I'll order." Oreisaka smiled. "What do you like?"

"Anything," Mokoto replied, still surprised that he was eating again after such a short space of time. He was grateful though, and he wasn't picky with his food. He didn't know how to be. In the Hive he only had two options; eat what was given to him or starve. Even if he detested the taste of something he never refused it.

"Alright," Oreisaka laughed. "I forgot – graduates don't have taste buds do they? Well... I'll order a few things, and try to remember what you do like. You can order it yourself next time."

"How often can we eat?" Mokoto questioned.

"As often as you want," Oreisaka said. "If you can find a servant..." She looked around the room, and smiled as an employee of the palace entered. "Excuse me," Mokoto watched as Oreisaka approached the servant, a young man. He bowed before the meitat and nodded as she spoke, taking in her every word. It was amazing... She was ordering food. The servant hadn't approached her. Nobody had told Oreisaka it was time to eat; she wanted to eat so she ordered food – and she could choose what she ate! The concept was bizarre to Mokoto. It was amazing that this was everyday life – they weren't at a restaurant, they were in their own home! Waiter service in their own home... It was insane.

The servant nodded and bowed again, then left the room, and Oreisaka made her way back over to Mokoto. "All done." She smiled. "If you ever want anything, just grab someone and they'll arrange it for you." She gestured towards the table where Mokoto had dined with his family the night before. "Sit down."

Mokoto obeyed and watched with fascination as Oreisaka joined him at the table. She was so relaxed, so used to this style of life... Would he become used to it as well? Mokoto wasn't sure if he wanted to. He had to be careful not to become too comfortable here; he had to make sure he stayed true to the Footprints in his soul. He couldn't relax. He couldn't become weak. If he did his sisters would destroy him. "What do you think of Anaka?" Oreisaka asked, making conversation. "She's nice isn't she? For a Hiveakan." She laughed a little. "I suppose it's working with Outsiders all day... She's very sociable."

"She told me she doesn't want the throne," Mokoto replied. "Why does she think I would believe her?"

"Why don't you?" Oreisaka frowned. Mokoto noticed the expression on his sister's face; she seemed confused. She believed Anaka; she really thought Anaka didn't want to be queen. Anaka had fooled her. Of course. It wasn't difficult to fool an Outsider – and Oreisaka seemed particularly trusting. Anaka could say that there were only six members of the Gaiamira and Oreisaka would believe her.

"She is an heir," Mokoto growled. "Father chose her – why would she not want it?"

"Because *father* chose her," Oreisaka smirked. "The only choices Anaka listens to are her own – and Raikun's. Actually, if Raikun made her heir she probably would take the throne. She practically worships him." Blasphemy... How could Oreisaka say that? Mokoto hoped that for Anaka's sake it wasn't true. Did Anaka really value her husband more than her own father? Were Raikun's opinions really more important to her? They couldn't be. Raikun was a well-respected man, but he wasn't her parent. He wasn't the king. The king's voice should be the only voice Anaka listened to, not one she didn't! If Oreisaka was telling the truth then why was Anaka even an heir at all? Why would their father want to give his planet to someone with such little respect for her king? Perhaps Mokoto should aid their father... Anaka was wild and disrespectful; perhaps Mokoto should do away with her. Would that please the king? Maybe Mokoto would earn an encounter with his father if he killed her. "Why don't you go and visit Anaka at work?" Oreisaka piped up. "I don't really have much to talk about with her, but I'm sure you two could be friends. She seems to get on with Lanka and Vari well. I think she's Lanka's only friend actually..."

"Lanka doesn't have friends?" Mokoto questioned.

"No, not really," Oreisaka answered. "I think she thinks they're a waste of time. She does things with Anaka sometimes, but with everyone else she's too... busy. She just trains all the time – I don't think she really has the patience to speak to people." Oreisaka smiled awkwardly and looked away. "She'd um... rather practice killing you."

168

"Really?" Mokoto sniggered. He had to admire Lanka's determination. She was true to her mission; she had sacrificed her social life and reputation to kill Mokoto... It was a shame that all of her hard work would amount to nothing. Lanka was looking less intimidating by the day; even her reputation was no match for Mokoto. She was an outcast, and easy to outshine. Mokoto just had to work on establishing himself. He looked at Oreisaka and offered a convincing smile. "If you don't mind, I want to train after lunch..." Mokoto watched her nod, and continued, "But do you want to meet again tomorrow, Orei?" Orei... That was what the girls called her, and she seemed to like it. Actually she seemed overjoyed with it now. Oreisaka's face lit up and she nodded excitedly.

"Of course!" she beamed. "Just knock on my door."

"Okay." Mokoto smiled again. Tomorrow would be horrible...

*

'Oh, I like my brother. I think he'll fit in well in the palace; he's very cute, and very keen... Why are you laughing? You don't all think he's cute? Listen, I'm a Hiveakan as well, if I can be the pretty science girl then a thirteen-year-old boy can be cute.'

-      Meitat Anaka, 20116G

*

Mokoto panted heavily and shook the sweat from his face. He could spend his life in this room... The palace gym was like a wonderland, filled with every piece of training equipment Mokoto could ever imagine. He hadn't even seen some of it before – not outside of the internet, anyway. The young matat had been training for hours and he wanted desperately to continue, but his body was ready to give way beneath him. He had trained through pain before; that was easy. Mokoto could ignore the pain. He had trained with broken bones and almost no energy left in his being... but the stage of 'almost' no energy had come and gone. Now he really had to stop. Mokoto knew his limits. He hated them, but he knew them. Mokoto reluctantly

169

scanned the room for the showers, and headed towards them. He was permitted to shower, wasn't he? Oreisaka had explained that every aspect of the gym was for him to use whenever he liked, except for the acid showers. They were in a separate room, and were only accessible with a security code – a code that Mokoto had not yet been given. The water showers would be fine to use; Oreisaka had no reason to give Mokoto false information. He'd decided he could trust her, with trivial things at least.

Mokoto entered a cubicle and removed his clothing. He stared up at the shower settings, surprised once more to see an adjustable water temperature gauge. He could choose his own water temperature? Was it locked? It was often locked in the Hive; Mokoto could choose the temperature of his water depending on how much he had impressed his tutors. How could this one be locked though, when it could be used by anyone at any time? Were there cameras in here? Perhaps the king could see who was using the showers, and activate the gauge lock accordingly. Mokoto looked around the cubicle for signs of surveillance. There had been cameras in the main shower room, but not in this cubicle... not that he could see anyway. Mokoto turned on the water and closed his eyes, surprised at the lack of bitter cold that he felt. The water was lukewarm... He opened his eyes and fiddled with the temperature settings, just to see. It did change. Hotter, colder... the water could be adjusted at any time! Great!

Mokoto tried to rush his shower, before he remembered that he wasn't being timed anymore. He could spend as much or as little time in here as he wanted... It was bizarre. He exhaled, and tried to enjoy the warmness of the water on his skin. It was pleasant... but Mokoto couldn't enjoy it. He wasn't used to it! Mokoto frowned and turned the water to its coldest setting, comforted by the familiar pain of ice cold water. This was better for him anyway. It made him stronger. Maybe next time he would turn up the heat and try to give himself burns.

Mokoto's head suddenly turned to the sound of another body in the room. They had entered, but they weren't moving. Were they listening to him?

"Hello?" Mokoto uttered. He heard the body move closer, until they were outside his cubicle door... What were they planning on doing, jumping in with him?

Mokoto flinched slightly as, surprisingly, his suspicions came true. A great thud echoed through the shower room as the body leapt up and secured its hands to the top of the cubicle door. Mokoto watched as the body pulled itself up and a sinister head revealed itself, smirking.

"Hello," she purred. It was Lanka. What was she doing here?

"I'm naked!" Mokoto growled, turning away from her. She had no right to see him like this! And why did she want to?

"So?" Lanka replied. "I'm not. Who cares, anyway? We're family, and you're still a child."

Mokoto stepped back as Lanka jumped into the cubicle and stared at him with fierce eyes. "If I cut you now, you will bleed more," she threatened.

"You can't." Mokoto pushed her away and frowned in annoyance when Lanka started to laugh.

"I won't," she remarked. She reached over and turned off the shower, then opened the cubicle door. "You may be my enemy, but you are still my brother. I wouldn't give your corpse the humiliation of being left naked." She twitched her head, beckoning for him to leave the cubicle. "Get dressed."

"If you don't want to fight me now then why didn't you just wait until I was finished?" Mokoto snarled. He knew why. She was trying to annoy him. Why? Did she think he would surrender the throne if she pestered him enough? She was infuriating!

"Get dressed," Lanka repeated with a smirk. "I'll be outside." She made her way over to the door and left the shower room.

Mokoto clicked his claws together, enraged with Lanka's behaviour. Who did she think she was? She would never dream of treating Anaka like this. She was trying to bully him, because he was new, or because he was younger than her, or maybe because she actually felt threatened by him. Well she could behave however she wanted, she still wouldn't get the throne! Mokoto grabbed his clothes and quickly got dressed, not even bothering to dry himself. He made

171

his way to the door and pushed it open, ready to fend off any attack Lanka would throw at him.

She swung at him. Literally. Lanka swooped down at Mokoto, holding onto a rope she'd made from her own silk ducts. Mokoto leapt out of the way and threw his claws at the silk, cutting it and sending Lanka to the floor. She landed perfectly; of course she had expected him to cut her loose. Lanka jumped to her feet and looked at Mokoto. "You knew I would do that," she stated, ensuring that he was fully aware he hadn't outsmarted her.

Mokoto remained silent. Of course it hadn't been a real attack – Lanka knew he would be prepared for her to pounce on him. He didn't want to admit it, but he was impressed with how quickly Lanka had made that rope. It dangled from the ceiling; she would have had to climb up there on her setules first, and then the rope would have to have been thick enough to support her weight... Mokoto couldn't do that – not as fast as she could, anyway. He had to get better... He *hated* losing to her! "So," Lanka took a fighting stance and waited for her brother to do the same. "How are you settling in?"

"I –" Mokoto couldn't speak another word before she went for him. He leapt out of the way, narrowly evading her attack before she started bombarding him with quick punches.

"Well?" Lanka impatiently barked.

"Fine!" Mokoto protested. He threw his fist at her and broke through her attack, catching Lanka's jaw. Mokoto smirked slightly as a look of anger swept across his sister's face. Anger... and embarrassment. Wasn't she supposed to have spent the last few years training herself to defeat him? What had she been doing since her graduation?

"New graduates aren't normally as quick as me," Lanka breathed, trying to recover some of her pride. "But Father did say you were advanced."

"He did...?" Mokoto uttered. Had his father really said that? Did that mean the king was pleased with him?

"You're friends with Oreisaka, aren't you?" Lanka questioned.

"It's just for appearances!" Mokoto argued. "I don't like her!"

172

"Obviously not." Lanka replied. "But you don't want to look too weak. I'll be your friend."

"Why?" Mokoto frowned. "I thought you wanted to kill me?"

"I do," Lanka nodded. "But we can still be friends. You, me and Anaka. Won't that be nice?"

Before Mokoto could answer Lanka jumped at him and almost caught him off guard. Mokoto battled to block her attacks; she seemed much better now. Had she been holding back because he was a new graduate? Why would she do that? Why did she think so little of him? Mokoto tried to hit her but she was too fast for him; he could barely protect himself from her attacks, there was no way he could harm her! She was quicker than his tutors in the Hive… Mokoto never thought that was possible. He started to feel tired… He had exhausted himself training; he didn't have the energy to fight her. Shit… She would think he was weak! He wasn't weak, he was just tired! It was no excuse. He couldn't allow himself to be tired; he could battle through tiredness! Mokoto felt his body pulsing. His Footprints battled to pump the blood in his veins; his heart wanted to give up. His body wanted to rest. It couldn't rest; it was in a fight! Mokoto's Footprints never allowed him to give up a fight; they never allowed his body to succumb to fatigue when he was at war. He ached all over as he battled Lanka; every tear in his skin felt ten times worse as her claws grazed against him. He saw purple, and he felt it. He felt the spirit of Taka in his time of need; he heard the sound of blood and war echoing through his soul. Mokoto saw his opponent, and possessed by the God of War, he leapt on her.

Lanka cried out as the young matat knocked her to the floor and pinned her down, mauling her like a wild dog. Where had this come from! Just a moment ago he'd been close to fainting! Lanka clasped her hands around Mokoto's throat, desperately trying to weaken him as he clawed away at her body, the blood from his own injuries spilling onto hers. He started to choke as she tightened her grip on him; he grabbed her hands and tried to pull them away. No. She wasn't going to let go! Lanka dug her claws into Mokoto's skin, locking onto his throat. He was going to die. Today!

Mokoto held his breath and gritted his teeth. He had to break out of Lanka's grasp; if he didn't she would slice his throat open! He

173

closed his eyes and in one quick, agonising movement he yanked his head away, snarling as he ripped himself away from her claws. He jumped off her before she could grab him again and he stood panting, his Footprints subsiding as a wave of cold sweat poured over his face. He was exhausted... Fuck!

Lanka rolled onto her front and looked at Mokoto, holding herself halfway above the ground as she waited for his next move. She could pounce on him again... He was completely drained; if she went for him now she would kill him. Lanka stood up and cautiously took a step towards Mokoto, smiling darkly as she readied her claws. They were already stained with his blood. "Sorry," she purred. "I thought you would last longer."

Mokoto took a breath and readied himself as best he could, trying to stay on his feet. If he couldn't defend himself she would kill him. He couldn't die...

Mokoto twitched suddenly, reacting to Lanka's quick movements as she jerked her head towards the gym door. The sound of the door opening had distracted her; now was his chance! Mokoto could go for her! He started to run towards Lanka but she threw herself to the ground and grabbed his arm when he got close. Mokoto stopped, stunned at her behaviour and clumsily allowed Lanka to pull him down beside her. What was she doing? "Get down!" Lanka hissed. Mokoto frowned in confusion, all the more bewildered in his weakened state. He panted heavily and moved his head to follow her gaze. There were two more people in the room. Anaka, and a man... Shit!

Mokoto's blood froze. All the confidence he had ever gained and all the power in his Footprints crumbled instantly at the sight of this man... The King of Gaiamiráka. His father. Mokoto knew him straight away. He had seen his father's face countless times before, but not a single one of the thousands of pictures and videos he had seen could even begin to portray just how terrifying a sight King Taka was. He was a real Hiveakan. He was tall, as tall as Mokoto hoped to be. He had dark eyes, the eyes of Taka. The eyes of a king. He was muscular, of course. Mokoto could only imagine how many bones King Taka had snapped in his time, and how many times he hadn't so much as flinched when he himself had been hurt. The king's hair was greying slightly – still thick, but greying. That in itself was frightening; it showed just how long the king had been alive and just how much time he'd had to practice being a Hiveakan. He was a good Hiveakan. He was the best in the world. That was why he was king. That was why Mokoto had to do whatever it took to impress him; he knew that if he didn't he would die... Perhaps he would die now. He couldn't meet the king like this! He was so weak; he was covered in injuries... He was no sight for the King of Gaiamiráka!

"See, Sire?" Anaka spoke with a smile as she looked up at the king. "I knew they would be here."

"You did, Meitat," King Taka answered, not taking his eyes off Mokoto and Lanka. "Is there anything you don't know?"

"Not that I know of."

The king laughed slightly. That confused Mokoto. Anaka seemed to be speaking boldly – too boldly for the king's presence – but the king found it amusing. Did Anaka impress him so much that she had earned the right to speak to the king so casually? That was dangerous. She was threatening Mokoto's throne... He had to make himself look more valuable than her. Mokoto sat upright as best as he could in his bowed position. He forced his eyes to stay open; he forced his body to hold itself up through its exhaustion. He had to look strong... He had to look worthy of being here.

"Well..." the king began. Mokoto tensed as his father made his way towards them, stopping in front of the young matat. He moved his eyes to Lanka. "You didn't waste any time, did you? He's nearly dead." He frowned slightly, studying Lanka's injuries. "And he's damaged you... not half as much as you've damaged him." The king turned his gaze back to Mokoto and stared down at the boy. He looked annoyed. "You are breathing your last breath. Why isn't she?"

"I..." Mokoto didn't know how to respond. He felt light-headed; he wanted to vomit. He was so tired, so exhausted, so drained of blood and energy... but he couldn't tell the king that. He couldn't admit how tired he had been at the start of the fight, and how exhausted he was now. He couldn't admit to weakness. If he did he would be murdered.

"Sire…" Anaka spoke, stepping up beside the king. Beside him. Literally, beside him. As tired as he was, Mokoto could still notice that. She didn't stand behind him where she belonged; it was as if she were the king's equal… She really had claimed his throne.

"Mm?" Taka grunted, still studying the pair before him.

"Orei said Mokoto came in to train alone – and that was hours ago." Anaka looked at her older sister and frowned. "Had he already finished when you got to him? He must have been worn out before you could even touch him!"

"Maybe he was," Lanka replied with a smirk, shooting a callous glance at Mokoto. "I thought he had more stamina in him. I suppose I was wrong."

"So it wasn't a fair fight," the king stated. "I'm glad for your sake that you didn't kill him, Meitat. How many years have you been waiting to kill him? Do you really want to do it in a dishonourable way? You would never forgive yourself."

Lanka went quiet. Stubbornly quiet. She knew he was right. Mokoto held back a smirk; she had just been scolded. Good. At least the king's opinion of her had been damaged. "Come on." The king looked at Anaka. "I suppose you are dying to get back to work? I have to as well." He turned away from his children and headed towards the gym door.

Anaka smiled at Mokoto and held out her hand to him.

"Do you want help getting back to your room?" she offered, sincerely but mockingly.

"Leave him!" Her father's voice came from the gym door. "Let him walk on his own. Or bleed to death." The king left the room, and like a shadow to its body, Anaka all too naturally felt compelled to follow.

"Sorry." She smirked at Mokoto. "Maybe next time." She looked at her older sister. "I'm going back to the Royal now."

"See you in a week," Lanka remarked.

"Haha." Anaka pouted and turned to follow her father out of the room.

Mokoto didn't move. He couldn't. He was still traumatised from his first encounter with his father. It shouldn't have gone like

176

that... The king wasn't supposed to see him weak! He wasn't supposed to see Mokoto tired and bloody... This was because Lanka couldn't have a fair fight! If she had attacked him before he had exhausted himself training, Mokoto wouldn't have a scratch on him!

"He doesn't get any less scary." Lanka's voice came from beside Mokoto, and he turned to look at her with angry eyes. "But eventually you learn to deal with your fears." She was smirking... She thought Mokoto was afraid!

"I'm not scared," Mokoto growled.

"Don't let him hear you say that." Lanka rose to her feet and moved her eyes away. She seemed uncomfortable. "I suppose... we weren't in the same condition at the start of that fight. I'm sorry." She met Mokoto's eyes. "But next time, I will expect more from you."

"And there won't be a time after that," Mokoto replied, not daring to break her stare. Lanka simply let out a short laugh.

"Call me when your bruises are gone." She turned and walked away, and as soon as she was out of the room Mokoto allowed his body to fall to the floor.

XIV.

'As Kala appears as a beautiful woman, Gonta appears to mortals as a wise man. His looks will change from person to person. He is young or old, a scientist or a scholar. He is the most intelligent being in the universe, and such a being is intelligent enough to keep many forms.'

-        Extract from the Gaiamirapon: 'The Identities'

*

"We should go out," Anaka beamed. "I've never seen Mokoto drunk before."

"You've barely seen *me* before," Mokoto teased. "You know you can't take your work with you if we go out?"

"I can," Anaka replied.

"And she will," Raikun remarked from beside his wife, earning himself a playful nudge to his side. Four months had passed since Mokoto's graduation, and he had established a small circle of friends within the palace. Mokoto still spent time with Oreisaka; the smallest amount of time necessary to maintain his reputation. She seemed aware of the fact that he was using her, but she didn't seem to mind. Apparently Oreisaka valued time with her brother over her own pride and dignity. It was pathetic, and it ruined any chance she would ever have of earning Mokoto's respect.

Aside from Oreisaka, Mokoto's usual associates had come to be Lanka, Anaka and Raikun. He saw Lanka the most; Anaka and Raikun spent most of their time in the Royal, with the occasional hour or so spared for lunches such as this. Mokoto enjoyed their company when they were around, but for the majority of the time he was left with Lanka, and he didn't really talk to Lanka. They just fought. All the time. Neither one had managed to slay the other yet, but Mokoto was confident it would only be a matter of time before he took his sister's life. The stronger he grew the more arrogant he became, and the more confident he was in his future as the king of Gaiamiráka. It was a certainty. All he had to do was surpass Lanka, and he had

178

already matched her strength. That was it. Just Lanka. Anaka wasn't an obstacle. As it turned out, and as reluctant as Mokoto had been to believe it, Anaka really didn't seem interested in taking the throne. She was so engrossed in her work at the Royal, and her need to act like Raikun's PA, that being queen didn't even seem to cross her mind. Perhaps it was a blessing to the world. In his time in Meitona Palace Mokoto had come to learn that Anaka had been indirectly named after an historical queen, Ana. She was a Hiveakan and famous for starting the Anákat War, a war in which she attempted to wipe out the entire Outsider race. She had defied the Gaiamira in doing so, and her war had been ended by the Korana Punishment, a series of natural disasters caused by the Gaiamira, which cost the lives of thousands of Hiveakans and Outsiders alike. In the end Ana's people had turned on her, and had executed her on the Royal Balcony of Meitona Palace. In fact, her reign had been met with such a shameful end that nobody had been permitted to name their child Ana since her death, thousands of years ago now. When he'd been in the Hive, Mokoto had read that the meitat's name 'Anaka' was supposed to refer to Meitona Palace during Ana's reign. Ana had always been regarded as a strong-willed and brave queen, and though she was an unwanted name in history now, she had been a credit to Meitona Palace once upon a time. The name 'Anaka' supposedly captured her positive traits, without cursing the meitat with her downfall. At least... that was what Mokoto had read in the Hive, and since his graduation Raikun and Anaka had confirmed it to be true. Honestly, it was a risky name... but it seemed to work for her. Anaka was indeed blessed with bravery and a strong will; hopefully the fact that she wasn't actually named 'Ana' was enough to keep her from meeting an unfortunate end. Either way, it was fact that Mokoto would never have to worry about her trying to become queen.

In a way Mokoto was thankful to the Gaiamira that Anaka wasn't the threat she could be... but in another way, he was angry at her. He was angry that she could so easily cast aside the throne, the greatest honour in the world – the seat that other people would literally kill for. Mokoto didn't understand it. It was the only thing about Anaka that he didn't like: her lack of respect for their heritage. He blamed it on the Royal. Working with so many Outsiders all day had to have corrupted her; why else would she deny herself the throne? It was a shame, really. Anaka would have made a great queen. If she wanted to, she could be the only real threat to Mokoto in the world.

"I can do it on my phone," Anaka stated, assuring the group that she wouldn't dare spend an evening away from work. "And if I need approval for something..." She looked at Raikun with a playful smirk. "You are coming out with me anyway."

"I'll be sure to wear my work clothes," Raikun replied, with sarcasm and a warm smile. He always looked like that when he spoke to her. It fascinated Mokoto how close Raikun and Anaka were – yet again Anaka refused to accept an authority that was rightfully hers. She admired him too much. Anaka wasn't the leader of their marriage, not in any way at all. She could be; being a meitat gave her the right to treat Raikun like her slave, and the unwritten laws of what was right and what was natural dictated that Anaka should make a slave of her husband... But she didn't. This was yet another law of etiquette and nature that Anaka seemed to so carelessly and so blatantly break. Wrongly, she and Raikun were equals, and sometimes they weren't even that. They were equals in their marriage, but in the realm of the Royal she was his employee... and she acted like it. Mokoto would be annoyed at Raikun if Anaka wasn't so obviously comfortable with the informal way he spoke to her; she even seemed to enjoy it. Anyway, he wasn't the worst choice for an equal... Mokoto had to admit that. To some extent Raikun was deserving of Anaka's respect; she couldn't have married a more reputable man. He was good company as well; Mokoto found Raikun easy to get along with. They had met at dinner on Mokoto's first day home; Raikun had actually deflected a series of demeaning remarks made to Mokoto by his sisters. Raikun seemed to be good at that; he was a Hiveakan, but a natural peace-keeper. He was an intelligent man. He was well-spoken, with a polite and calming manner – diplomatic for want of a better word. He knew how to handle Mokoto's sisters without being offensive or frightening, and yet as a Hiveakan he had the capability to be both. He didn't look like a Hiveakan. Not to any Outsider, anyway. Raikun was gentle and kind, and all the things he had to be to work amongst Outsiders... but he wasn't one. Not in the slightest. Mokoto could see it in Raikun's eyes;

he could smell it in his aura. He could see the scars through Raikun's clothes. Mokoto could see, that behind that gentle façade that Outsiders found so reassuring, Raikun's Footsteps tiptoed in darkness, and they would be all the more dangerous because they were starving.

Mokoto liked him. For all the above reasons. He liked the way Raikun had perfected his mask, and he liked that Raikun was male. In a family that was overrun with Outsider women, Mokoto had quickly come to appreciate the value of having a brother from the Hive, and he would not hesitate to say that Raikun was genuinely one of his best friends.

"Well then, there's no problem is there?" Anaka laughed, continuing their conversation. She looked at Lanka and Mokoto. "So?"

"Shocking. You can't leave work behind for a night, so you bring your employer out with you," Lanka smirked.

"He doesn't mind," Anaka smiled. "We'll act like husband and wife when we get home." She looked at Raikun. "Won't we, dear?"

"Well, I do enjoy roleplay," Raikun answered calmly, causing Mokoto to almost choke on his food.

"Oh, get a room!" Lanka exclaimed.

"I think that's the idea…" Mokoto mumbled. He watched as Anaka giggled and smiled at Raikun, blushing slightly as if she were a schoolgirl smitten with her teacher. It was absurd; Anaka was practically a child around him! Even after four years of marriage she was still a devoted fan of the legendary Doctor Raikun Eika-Koan.

Lanka made a face and quickly moved on.

"So where are we going?" she asked.

"Well, it's payday at the end of the week," Anaka answered, managing to tear her attention away from her idol. "Everyone from the Royal goes out then – the bar is just a few minutes away. Raikun and I always have to attend, so why don't you two come –"

"Outsiders?" Lanka raised her eyebrows. "Are you serious? I'm not going unless we can go to a Hive bar – and your friends won't get in."

"They aren't my friends!" Anaka protested. "And we only have to start there. People start leaving after an hour or so anyway – and they'll be at least a hundred out. Nobody will notice if we leave."

181

"Fine…" Lanka sighed, as if an evening amongst Outsiders was the greatest chore in the world. "But if *any* of them try to talk to me I am going to cut open their throat."

"You should be flattered if they try to talk to you," Anaka said. "Some of the best minds in the world work with me."

"And yet none of them are intelligent enough to realise that talking to me won't get them a promotion," Lanka growled. She moved her eyes to Raikun and spoke with a cruel smile. "In fact, I will write you a list of everyone that tries to 'make friends' with me – you can fire them in the morning."

"Lanka… I'm sorry. I can't do that," Raikun replied.

"Of course you can," Lanka said. "You are their boss."

"Yes I know…" Raikun answered, reaching for his drink. "But I can't fire them after you have cut open their throat, can I?"

"Ha!" Mokoto sniggered and looked at Lanka, trying to read her mind. She seemed to be struggling to decide which she would prefer, an end to her pesterers' careers or an end to their lives. They all knew that ultimately it would come down to how she would feel in the moment, and how many witnesses there were.

*

'When you compare King Mokoto of the Mokotoakat War to Queen Ana of the Anákat War, you do start to see similarities in their characters. Both had lost close relatives at the hands of their targeted group. Both were highly motivated by revenge, and both seemed to have an inability to see the wrong in their actions. Now considering they were both products of the Hive, an institution that should have trained them and raised them with the ability to know right from wrong, and to put their personal feelings aside, it does beg the question… did these unfortunate monarchs fail society, or were they simply the products of a society that had failed them?'

-       Historian Aeika Ron-Morat, 20150G

*

Mokoto cracked his knuckles again. In a way he knew what to expect. He knew what a bar was; he knew what Outsiders were like, and he could imagine what sort of an evening he would have amongst them. It would be boring mostly; he might be able to engage in a vaguely interesting conversation with some of the scientists, but science was never one of Mokoto's great interests. He was good at science, but he preferred history and literature. Things that he could change. Things that would be written about him.

Mokoto stared intently out of the car window, watching and memorising every corner they turned and every building they passed. He didn't need to, but he couldn't help it. Mokoto memorised everything, and he was more observant now than ever. He didn't know why. He somehow felt the need to distract himself with the sights of the journey. Why? It wasn't like he was nervous. He had no need to be. It was just a bar. Just a place full of strangers, just like the palace had once been. This was different though… These people weren't members of his family. These were real people – people with jobs, people that didn't think being in his company was normal. People that would treat him like a matat. He had to assert his authority over them. He couldn't appear weak, but they weren't servants. Mokoto had to treat them with respect. It was a delicate balance. Everything he did tonight mattered; the way he acted, the way he spoke… It would all no doubt be reported back to his father, and if he acted wrongly Mokoto's very future as the king of Gaiamiráka could be at risk.

"Are you nervous?"

Mokoto turned his head to see Lanka staring at him, smirking mockingly as usual. It was just the two of them, and this was the first time she had tried to make conversation in the ten minutes they'd been driving.

"No!" Mokoto answered fiercely. Of course not. Of course he wasn't nervous! And he wouldn't admit it to her even if he was.

"Good," Lanka replied, looking away from him. "You have a lot riding on tonight."

"We're late," Mokoto stated, changing the subject. "Anaka will be angry."

"I don't care," Lanka growled. "The sooner we arrive the more likely we are to get spoken to by her friends – especially you."

"Really?" Mokoto almost laughed. "But they aren't her friends, are they?" He glanced at his older sister, half looking for an answer.

"Well… She says not," Lanka answered. "But she goes out with them every payday. I think she likes them to think they're her friends. That way she looks like Miss Ordinary and the public like her, which means Father likes her… and Anaka likes to be Father's little treasure."

"You aren't bothered by that?" Mokoto questioned, watching Lanka's reaction closely. He had hoped to hit a nerve, but she seemed unfazed.

"Tch! Why would I be?" Lanka scoffed. "She isn't interested in the throne, and even if she was I would rather lose it to her than you." She looked at Mokoto and sneered. "I'm not really cut out to be a daddy's girl… She can have his eyes and I will take his throne."

"A daddy's girl?" Mokoto couldn't help but laugh. "You think that's what she is?"

"Well… If there was any such thing as a Hiveakan daddy's girl, it would be Anaka," Lanka smirked. "You should thank the Gaiamira that you are a boy, otherwise you really would have no chance of winning the throne."

"Whatever." Mokoto grunted, and turned back to the window. He could feel Lanka watching him, wearing her usual sinister smirk. Bitch.

Rowan looked back at the pair in the rear view mirror and smiled.

"Don't you two look wonderful?" he commented, trying to lighten the mood between them.

Mokoto glanced at Rowan briefly, unsure of how to respond. He hadn't chosen his own clothing; actually Lanka had told him what to wear. It was the latest fashion, and appropriate for the night they would have. He was dressed casually enough for an Outsider bar, but he wore weapons around his body. A thick metal bracelet coated in spikes, trendy but heavy footwear, a discreet but effective spiked choker… It was fashionable battle clothing apparently, worn by

184

everyone that entered a Hiveakan club. Mokoto didn't see the point of it. It looked nice, but he didn't need weapons. Actually to rely on weapons was an insult to his tutors in the Hive; he was surprised that Lanka had dressed him like this, and that she wore similar accessories herself. "You'll be popular tonight." Rowan smiled. "As always."

"My father is not paying you to talk," Lanka spoke.

"I'm sorry, Your Highness. Forgive me," Rowan said, and immediately looked away. He seemed insulted.

"How long is left?" Mokoto questioned.

"Ten minutes or so, Your Highness," Rowan replied. "She doesn't work far away."

"Just as well," Lanka sniped. "If she did we would never see her."

"Maybe there are worse things," Mokoto joked and awaited her response. Lanka sniggered slightly and hit him.

"Don't be disrespectful!"

"Sorry…"

*

'It was at the age of thirteen that Mokoto first publically demonstrated his inability to control his desire to kill. At what was considered to be a normal social event he attacked a fellow Hiveakan whom he had never previously met and had no prior issue with; witnesses at the time claimed he was trying to kill her despite the fact that he was entirely unprovoked and understood the consequences of his actions. It was this event that has caused many historians and psychiatrists to believe that Mokoto held a diminished responsibility for his actions in starting the Mokotoakat War, as this event was evidence to suggest that he was not properly trained in the Hive, and was allowed to graduate either too early, or with an undiagnosed mental illness.'

- Extract from history textbook: 'The Mokoto Era: 20103G - 20147G', 20160G

*

185

"Come on, let's move on!" Anaka giggled, curling her legs up onto the sofa where she and Raikun sat. It was a couple of hours later and Mokoto and his family had drawn themselves away from Anaka's co-workers into a private room of the venue, protected by a small army of bodyguards that were positioned both in the room and outside, in front of the closed door. They were Hiveakan bodyguards, of course. Outsider bodyguards would be useless against anyone that was skilled or insane enough to attack a royal Hiveakan. Mokoto was having a good evening... now. The new environment of the venue had entertained him for the first few minutes until Anaka had introduced him to her scientist friends... then it had started to bore him a little. They weren't particularly unpleasant company, and they were by far the best Outsiders Mokoto had met... but they were still Outsiders, and Mokoto's interest in them was still limited. He had been relieved when Anaka had finally excused herself, her husband and her siblings, and they had come into this private room. Now they were talking amongst themselves over a series of alcoholic beverages, and Anaka was halfway through her sixth cocktail. She held the drink close to her lips and sipped neatly on her straw, so relaxed with herself it was obvious that she went out a lot.

"Stop acting so drunk! They won't let you in!" Lanka scolded from the across their table.

"Right – like anyone is going to say no to me," Anaka sniped back.

"Because you are the king's daughter?" Mokoto questioned.

"Well, yes..." Anaka answered, looking at him with a mischievous grin. "And because... well, I'm beautiful."

"And if the door staff aren't into women?" Lanka raised her eyebrows at Anaka.

"Oh it's fine – I can turn people." Anaka waved a dismissive hand. "They call me Kala." She giggled and retreated into her drink. Lanka couldn't help but snigger, but she soon set a pair of stern eyes on her sister. "Anaka –"

"Oh, Lanka, I'm fine!" Anaka protested. "I can focus – watch." She placed her drink down on the table in front of them and sat upright, staring at Lanka with pure, undivided concentration. Lanka waited for a moment, and then clicked her fingers close to Anaka's face, hoping to break her stare. It was unsuccessful, and Anaka grinned at her. "See?" She argued. "You forget I am still a Hiveakan!"

"Academics are not real Hiveakans," Lanka sniped back, turning to her drink with her eyes fixed on Anaka.

"Is that a challenge?" Anaka answered.

"Did it *sound* like a challenge?"

"Maybe… leave this for 'The Battlefield', hm?" Raikun laughed a little, amused by their energy.

"Is it really called 'The Battlefield'?" Mokoto asked.

"It's actually the most accurately named club you'll find," Anaka replied. "You can't look nervous though. They *really* won't let you in."

"I'm not nervous!" Mokoto frowned; insulted that she could ever accuse him of such a thing. "Let's go!"

"Alright, drink up!" Lanka ordered. Mokoto obeyed, causing her to laugh a little.

"Are you coming?" Anaka turned to Raikun.

"No… I'll pass," he answered.

"Really?" Anaka teased. "You'll be able to beat someone up for free. You haven't done that since you were my age, have you?"

"Even younger." Raikun looked at her with a small smirk. "Alright then. I suppose I could join you just this once."

"Good. You can watch Anaka," Lanka remarked. "It's been so long since I've seen her fight I know she's forgotten how to do it."

"Shut up!" Anaka barked, and threw ice at her sister.

*

'He's a maniac. I knew this would happen – you can't let somebody out when they're thirteen, I hope they're holding the Hive responsible because you cannot function in society at the age of thirteen.'

-     Interview with a member of the public, 20117G

187

Different. That was the best way to describe it. It was Mokoto's first time in a Hiveakan club, and it was… 'different'. It was packed full of Hiveakans. Real Hiveakans. Ones that had long since graduated, and had been hungering for blood ever since. Mokoto had no idea which was more powerful, the ferocious heat that emitted from their bodies or the smell of fresh blood in the air. The music was loud; so loud it made Mokoto's ears hurt, and he could only assume that as he grew as a Hiveakan the music would become more and more tolerable. The club itself was a test of endurance before the fighting had even started. The room was black, lit only by a series of coloured laser beams that darted around the room. They occasionally turned into white strobe lights, so bright and so intensifying that for a few seconds every being in the room was exposed, their predatory teeth glistening and their Taka-blessed eyes glowing under the intensifying beams of white light.

Mokoto was sitting with his siblings on the top floor of the club, in an enclosed area reserved solely for the highest members of society, waiting to go into the 'battle pit'. That was the reason Mokoto had been dressed in weapons. It was a prominent feature in most Hiveakan clubs, and as its name suggested, it was literally a battle pit. It was a room filled with Hiveakan fighters, all bloodthirsty and ready to hurt each other. Weapons were permitted but food and drink were not, and anyone who entered did so for the sole purpose of letting loose their Footprints and unleashing their battle skills upon a stranger. Murder wasn't permitted; nor was disabling your opponent, but they were the only rules and there was no limit on the amount of blood you could shed.

Mokoto and his family were in a private booth, separated from the other patrons of the club, but that was as far as their differences went. The club staff had still done all the standard checks on them. They had taken a number of medical readings from Mokoto; his weight, his blood type, his blood pressure, his heart rate… all standard things that would determine whether or not Mokoto was deemed fit and well enough to enter the battle pit. He'd had to show his ID to get into the club, despite having one of the most recognisable faces in the world. Mokoto could understand. Anybody could make themselves look like him, and it was all too easy to ensure that he really was the matat. His ID stated his age, his place of birth, his upbringing style – whether or not he was a Hiveakan – and how long he had been out of the Hive. That was the most important part; by law nobody was allowed to go into the battle room of a Hiveakan club until they had been out for at least two months, just in case the sudden change in environment was too much for them and they... 'went crazy'. Mokoto didn't know if he was comfortable with that. A Hiveakan wasn't supposed to graduate at all until they were mentally capable of adjusting to the outside world; in theory a Hiveakan who was ready to graduate should be able to go into a battle pit, or anywhere in the world, immediately after their graduation without having any kind of unwanted reaction. But... there was always that one. That one who had graduated too soon, that one who had slipped through the seemingly flawless net of the Hive, that one who had an underlying mental condition that hadn't ever been noticed during their upbringing, that one that the unfailing Hive had failed... That one that was the exception. That one that was the failure. It disgusted Mokoto. That one maniac that hadn't been properly raised was the reason he couldn't go into a battle pit until two months after his graduation. Mokoto hated him, whoever he was. He was a disgrace to the Hive's name.

Mokoto took a sip of his drink as he waited to be summoned into the battle pit. He could only drink this because he was a Hiveakan, yet another reason why Mokoto and his fellow Hiveakan comrades were superior to their Outsider counterparts. For Outsiders, the legal minimum drinking age was fourteen; when they became a legal adult, but Hiveakans were permitted to take part in any age-restricted activity as soon as they were deemed fit enough to leave the Hive. Hive graduates were adults as far as the law was concerned, even if they hadn't started puberty yet.

Mokoto finished his drink and cracked his knuckles nervously. No... not nervously. Excitedly. He wasn't nervous; he was excited. He was excited to fight someone he didn't know; he was excited to test his skills in a new environment, on a new opponent... How should he do

189

it? Should he wait for someone to challenge him, or should he just run into the battle pit and attack the first person he saw? Lanka had told him to wait for a moment; to study the room, to watch the fighters and pick out the one that looked the most challenging... that was how she did it. Raikun said he would challenge someone his age that looked as if they battled often, to see how his skills compared to a more seasoned fighter than himself. Anaka... She was just going to stand there, and see who approached her first. She and Lanka had a bet as to whether her challenger would be male or female, and how long it would be before they either tried to befriend or seduce her. Well... she was wearing barely any clothes. Anaka always did like to get a reaction...

"Do you definitely want to do this?" Raikun looked at Mokoto cautiously, dragging the boy from his thoughts. "You can cancel if you want to."

"No, I want to," Mokoto said with confidence. He definitely wanted to!

"Alright." Raikun smiled, not seeming particularly concerned. "There will be people keeping an eye on you – you can leave whenever you want, if anyone picks a fight with you just tell them you aren't playing."

"They already explained that." Mokoto said. The battle pit staff had briefed them on this already; did Raikun think Mokoto hadn't listened?

"I know," Raikun replied. "But if the staff ask you to leave make sure you do it – you'll get barred for life if you fight back."

"Yes, sir," Mokoto nodded. Raikun chuckled a little.

A large Hiveakan bouncer approached the group and bowed respectfully.

"Your Highnesses... The battle pit is ready for you," he said. "Please – leave your drinks."

"Finally!" Lanka sighed and stood up. She looked at Mokoto mockingly and reached out to him.
"Do you want to hold my hand?" she teased.

"Shut up!" Mokoto growled and batted her hand away. He heard her laugh, and a dark force deep within his soul carried Mokoto's body towards the arena.

Once inside, Mokoto could do nothing but stare in awe at his new surroundings. The walls were built from a thick grey metal, completely undecorated, and the ceiling was coated with lights. Along the tops of the walls lay a series of mirrors, just like his old bedroom in the Hive. In fact the layout of the room was exactly like his old bedroom, and just like in the Hive the mirrors were actually one-sided windows that hid an observation gallery; behind the windows stood a team of medically trained Hiveakan staff members that were closely observing their guests. The room was filled with fighters... literally. The place was a bloodbath! Mokoto's stomach tingled as he looked around the room; there must have been fifty or so people in front of him and all were brutally beating each other. The floor was covered in blood and shards of ripped clothing and broken jewellery; the smell of freshly cut skin and sweat filled the air... It was exhilarating, and yet at the same time comforting... It felt like home.

Anaka was the first to go. Almost immediately she was approached by a young attractive man who looked as if he had come there just to meet a young attractive woman. He obviously recognised her, and considering who she was he was overly polite and under-confident, downplaying his abilities and experience in a vain attempt to flatter her. It was ridiculous... Did that ever work for him? Mokoto would never behave like that towards a woman, even if she was a meitat! Why would any Hiveakan woman ever be interested in someone that tried to make himself look weak? Still... Raikun seemed amused. He allowed his wife to be swept away by this silver-tongued fool, winking at her as she moved away from him.

"You lost the bet, Lanka," Raikun stated. "I could have told you that."

"I wouldn't have lost if your wife tried putting some clothes on," Lanka sniped. Raikun chuckled again and looked at Mokoto. "You're sure you can handle this?" he questioned.

"Yes," Mokoto frowned, annoyed that everyone kept asking. "Go."

Lanka and Raikun both scanned the room for a suitable opponent, and one after the other they disappeared into the crowd, leaving Mokoto behind. He exhaled. Finally. He could get on with this!

191

No doubt they were somehow watching though... Mokoto could feel his siblings' eyes on him, from wherever they were in the room. How many visits to this battle pit would it take before they stopped watching over him? Mokoto hoped it was just this one.

"Hey!" Mokoto turned towards a foreign voice and was greeted by the image of a young girl. She was about his age, but not fresh. Her visible wounds were too old for her to be as new a graduate as him. The freshest blemishes on her body were clearly from tonight, or a recent night like it – her torture scars were at least six months old. The girl was covered in blood, not necessarily her own. Her black vest was ripped and she had a hand on her hip, birthing a form of arrogance within her. She was looking at Mokoto as if she knew him – and not just from the media. It was as if she knew something about him, or more precisely, about his immediate future. The girl was panting slightly, but still eager to continue fighting. That much was obvious. This was it. This was Mokoto's first opponent. She knew she was. "You're new here aren't you, Your Highness?" The girl bowed quickly, and then looked at him. "Sorry to be informal. If I stay down too long I'll be killed."

"That's alright," Mokoto replied with a slight smirk. She knew who he was. She knew his name, and his title... Obviously. He wouldn't expect anything less, but still... She was the first person outside of the palace to know him. It fed his ego.

"Do you have a date?" the girl asked. Mokoto paused for a moment. She was just asking him to fight, right...? Of course. He scolded himself. Of course! This was a battle room! Mokoto shot the girl a confident smirk, trying his best to assert his dominance over his opponent, and moved into a fighting stance.

"I do now," he stated. The girl grinned back.

"Come on, then!"

She raced towards him and flung her leg into a kick; Mokoto was quick to block the attack but clumsily failed to catch her other foot as it went straight into his head. A sharp pain fired through his skull as her spiked heel pierced his skin; he closed his eyes for a second and clenched his fists at the sound of her laughter. Dammit! He was better than that! Mokoto became angry at himself and used his own anger to fuel him as he leapt at the girl and flung his fists towards her chest. She managed to block the attack with her arms but winced slightly as her limbs absorbed the impact, causing Mokoto to smirk a little. It felt good to know he was inflicting pain; it only made him want to attack her more. This was a real fight... This was what his Footprints craved. This was what he was born to do! Mokoto moved his free hand down to punch her abdomen, cracking his knuckles into her elbow as she rapidly attempted to block his second strike. "Dammit!" The girl snarled as a wave of pain shot through her arm. She seemed annoyed, as if she had expected more from herself. Maybe she had been better, once upon a time...

"You've been out longer than me, right?" Mokoto asked.

"What makes you say that?" The girl frowned.

"You aren't very good," Mokoto remarked, deliberately trying to annoy her. This was his first fight in a battle pit; he wanted to make it as fun as possible. He wouldn't just hurt his opponent's body; he would hurt their Footprints and their pride as well. "I heard you can lose it easily when you leave."

"Shut up!" the girl growled and leapt at him, slamming her fist into the young matat's chest faster than Mokoto could react. She laughed as Mokoto spluttered, stunned by the strike. Mokoto closed his eyes to force himself into focus but he was caught by another blow – this time to his jaw. He gagged and spat out a clump of his own blood as it gathered in his mouth, the taste of it still lingering on his tongue. This was humiliating... Why was he being beaten? He'd only been in here a few minutes and he was already spitting blood. Was she really better than him? No... No, she couldn't be. This girl was weaker than him; she was stained by the outside world. She was *not* better than him!

Mokoto took a breath and allowed himself to be overcome by the dark mist that enthralled him as the girl struck him to the ground. He focused on it as if it were a blanket; he used it to hide himself from distraction, to clear his mind and summon his Footprints to the surface of his being. Mokoto called upon the Taka within his soul and made a vow that he would win this fight. He would not be defeated by this girl. He would not be defeated by anybody! He would become famous for being undefeated, and he would start his legacy here. Tonight. He would start it with this girl. She wasn't winning this – she couldn't. She couldn't alter his destiny; no mortal in the world except King Taka himself could alter the destiny of Matat Mokoto. Mokoto was going to beat this girl. He was going to *kill* her!

In a few flashing seconds Mokoto leapt up off the ground and grabbed the girl, throwing punch after punch into her abdomen. She cried out as she took the blows, throwing her fist into his throat. Mokoto snarled as the small spikes on her gloves pierced his skin, causing him to release her from his grasp.

"Hey!" Mokoto felt a pair of rough hands grab his shoulders and spin him around. "You want to dance with my sister?" Mokoto looked at the man in front of him; he was a few years older than Mokoto, quite tall and slim. He didn't look very strong but he wasn't injured much; he obviously kept up with his training. The man assumed a fighting stance and began jumping on the spot, keeping himself ready for battle. "It's an honour to meet you, Your Highness – sorry to be informal. Would you mind if I joined the fight?"

"I bet you say that to all the newbies."

Mokoto turned to the sound of Lanka's voice and saw her standing there beside the girl. She was looking at the man that had joined them.

"Meitat Lanka." The man smiled. "So you're babysitting?"

"And you?" Lanka looked at the girl. "Are you Toka's sister?"

"Yes, Your Highness…" the girl answered. "Rimi."

"Rimi," Lanka repeated, and moved her eyes to Mokoto. "This is Toka and Rimi – their father is the mayor of Meitona." The mayor of Meitona…? Then he wasn't worlds apart from Mokoto's own father. Each country in the world was overseen by a mayor, who took care of the day-to-day running of their country and who answered only to their continent's malatsa or to King Taka himself. Mokoto had heard of Matatsa (sub-matat) Toka and Meitatsa (sub-meitat) Rimi, but he had never seen their picture. So… This was them? The girl that would start Mokoto's legacy was no less than Meitatsa Rimi herself? What an honour for her… and what a perfect start to the legend that would be Mokoto! He could make it his rule that he would only fight members of

194

the higher class; mortals that possessed only the purest and most worthy of bloods. This was perfect!

"Hm." Toka grunted, eyeing up the young matat. "You weren't kidding when you said he was Taka's shadow, were you Meitat?" He sniggered at Mokoto. "You're wearing big shoes to hold those Footprints, aren't you, Matat?" Mokoto felt his lips form into an arrogant smirk. He didn't know if 'flattered' was the right word... Matatsa Toka was simply skilled enough to recognise the strength of the Taka that lived within Mokoto. Mokoto could expect no less from the famously seasoned fighter, Matatsa Toka. "Still," Toka continued, "I've always believed that even the shadow of Taka will disappear if it steps into the light. Are you sure you are wearing the right shoes, Your Highness?"

"I'm sure," Mokoto growled, angered by Toka's attitude. Who did he think he was anyway? Mokoto was above him!

"So test him," Lanka said. She looked at Rimi. "Girls versus boys?" She spoke, shooting Mokoto a challenging glance. "Brothers always lose, don't they?"

"Sounds good to me!" Rimi beamed, taking her position against the boys. "Let's go!"

"Alright, Your Highness," Toka said, tapping Mokoto's back. "Watch out."

Mokoto leapt out of the way as Rimi and Lanka charged at them, throwing attack after attack at the boys. Mokoto ducked as Rimi moved her focus onto him, determined to win their fight. Mokoto smirked a little as he fought with her; he knew she couldn't beat him. Nobody could beat him! Rimi was a good fighter... She was certainly worthy of falling victim to Mokoto's Footprints. She was incredibly fast and confident in battle... but she wasn't as strong as him. Mokoto saw Rimi wince as she blocked each of his attacks, her defence breaking. Mokoto kept himself focused on her, so much so that the room became nothing more than an empty void, with nothing clear to Mokoto except himself and his opponent. His body felt warm and distant, as if he were being possessed. He felt his Footprints rising within his soul; he felt an overwhelming darkness – a fierceness that Mokoto could only think of as the God of War himself. He was completely unaware of anyone else in the room, or how Lanka and Toka were fighting. No... How could he be unaware? He had to be aware of his surroundings at all times – it was what the Hive had taught him. He couldn't... Mokoto couldn't see them. All he could see was Rimi, and she was becoming distorted. She wasn't a person to him anymore, she was... a victim. A corpse. An immense heat rose up into Mokoto's head; the smell of blood intensified in his nostrils, and the taste of blood spread across his tongue. Mokoto hadn't bitten anyone – he knew that. So why could he taste blood? It wasn't his blood. Somehow, Mokoto knew it. It was Rimi's... He was claiming her. His Footprints... they wanted to take her.

Mokoto let out a snarl and hurled himself at Rimi. He cried out as the spikes from her knuckles pierced holes in his jaw, but he didn't let it stop him. This holy force that was driving him... it wasn't deterred by pain – it wasn't deterred by anything. Mokoto endured Rimi's attacks as if they were nothing; he felt his blood trickling down his face but it didn't stop him. He grabbed her. He grabbed her arms as she tried to punch him, and he threw her to the ground. Rimi cried out as Mokoto dived on top of her and sat over her body. He pinned her down and unleashed his Footprints upon her, viciously punching every inch of her flesh and ignoring the blood that was falling rapidly from his jaw.

"Okay!" Rimi screamed as she held her arms up in a pitiful attempt to protect herself, struggling under Mokoto's weight. "I surrender! Boys win!" Her eyes widened in horror as Mokoto ignored her cries and continued attacking her, ripping at her flesh with his claws like a rabid dog. He was out of control!

"Mokoto!"

Mokoto flinched at the sound of Lanka's angry voice coming from somewhere nearby. Tch! He knew what she wanted. She wanted to win. Well she wasn't going to! This was his victim, and Lanka couldn't protect her! Mokoto ignored Lanka and continued attacking his opponent who was now a bloody mess beneath him, barely conscious and holding up her arms weakly, desperately trying to save herself.

"Stop it –" Lanka leapt towards Mokoto but was pushed back by a large member of the security team who was accompanied by another bouncer.

"Out of the way!" the man shouted as he reached out to grab Mokoto. "Hey –"

"What?" Mokoto snarled, flinging his clenched fist at the man. His eyes widened as the man caught his fist, and he suddenly came to his senses. He looked down at the young girl beneath him; her eyes were closed. No… Mokoto's heart stopped as a horrible wave of dread shot through his core. Had he killed her? No… He couldn't kill her! He was just supposed to defeat her! She was the meitatsa of Meitona! "Rimi –" Mokoto gagged as the bouncer clasped his hand around Mokoto's throat and pulled him to his feet.

"Come with me!" the bouncer ordered.

"Is she okay?" Mokoto asked, allowing himself to be restrained by the bouncer.

"Hey, what's wrong with you?" Mokoto looked up to see Toka glaring at him furiously; Lanka was holding him back as he tried to advance towards Mokoto. "Are you trying to kill her?"

"No – Toka, he's drunk," Lanka insisted as she struggled to restrain him. She glanced at the gathering crowd and then at Rimi, who was now being attended to by the second bouncer.

"Get them out of here!" Lanka looked up at the sound of the first bouncer's voice; he was barking orders at two other men that had now joined him as he made his way towards the exit, pulling Mokoto along with him.

"Wait! That's my sister!" Toka shouted as the two new men grabbed him and Lanka. "Get off me! Do you know who I am?"

"Yes, sir – and Meitatsa Rimi needs you to leave," one of the bouncers replied, and he and his colleague dragged Toka and Lanka out after Mokoto, ordering the crowd to move away from the scene.

"She's fine, sir," one of the bouncers said once they had all exited the room. "This is just our procedure – we have to remove everyone involved." He narrowed his eyes at Lanka. "And, Your Highness – I'm assuming the sooner you get away from witnesses the better?"

197

"Yes. Thank you." Lanka nodded. "Can I trust that you will not speak of this? You will be well compensated, of course."

"You don't need to worry about us, Your Highness," the bouncer replied, glancing at his colleagues. He looked back at Lanka. "But we aren't your concern. That room was full." He gestured towards the seating area, at a private booth. "Please. Have a drink." He moved his eyes to Mokoto. "... Calm yourselves."

Mokoto stood still, unable to move under the weight of his shock. He'd lost control... Something had overcome him – something had possessed him... And he had lost control. His first battle pit... and he had nearly killed someone. It was a cold feeling. A cold, dark... It was him. Mokoto could barely breathe as the horrifying truth struck him. He... he was that maniac that had slipped through the net of the Hive. He was the reason other graduates had to wait two months before they could fight. He was a failure...

"Come," Lanka ordered, grabbing hold of Mokoto's arm.

She violently pulled him into the booth, and threw him down onto the seat.

"Lanka –"

"Shut up!" Lanka snarled, glaring at Mokoto. She turned her gaze to Toka, who had followed them into the booth, and as he took a seat the venue staff drew a curtain around them, cutting them off from everyone else in the bar. "Toka."

"I'm not fucking happy about this!" Toka barked. He turned to Mokoto, and advanced on him. "Do you think you're a man now, Sire? Murdering a kid!"

"Toka!" Lanka threw her hands across the man, pulling him back as he attempted to slaughter Mokoto. "Stop!"

"Get off me, Lanka!" Toka screamed, forcefully shrugging her off. He took a breath, calming himself. Mokoto watched him cautiously. He was angry... Obviously. He wasn't going to attack again, though. He was calming down... He was listening. "I suppose your father will make this go away," Toka uttered, almost to himself. "Even if she dies."

"She won't die," Mokoto said. "They said she wouldn't die."

"Hm," Toka snorted. He looked at Mokoto... angrily. No, not angrily. Threateningly. Spitefully. Arrogantly... as if Mokoto were nothing more than dirt to him. Mokoto was his lesser. There, in that moment... Mokoto was the only one of them that had failed. "She might not die," Toka stated. "Nor will you, Your Highness... but only because of your father." He narrowed his eyes at Mokoto, and gave the matat a cruel, wicked sneer. "Your father is the only reason you are still alive." He looked at Lanka, and growled. "Don't bring him out again, love." He turned and left the booth, not bothering to wait for Lanka's reply.

Lanka looked down at Mokoto, and as soon as he stared back he was greeted by her claws slashing across his face.

"*Idiot!*" she screamed. "You'd better pray to the Gaiamira that nobody knows Anaka came with you!"

"Anaka?" Mokoto snarled defensively, his own shame fuelling his rage. "What does she have to do with it?"

"Because if this damages her, forget Toka – *Father* will kill you," Lanka hissed. "And he won't even give you a funeral!"

"And what if it doesn't harm Anaka?" Mokoto muttered. "He'll let me live?"

"I wouldn't go that far," Lanka replied with a smirk. "But he'll give you a funeral."

Mokoto looked at her, his eyes widening slightly as he tried to figure out whether or not she was joking. Would their father really kill him...? But then, Mokoto had failed... He had brought shame upon his father and his family. A strong Hiveakan king like his father would have no reason to let Mokoto live...

Lanka looked at her brother with just a hint of triumph, her smirking lips damp with arrogance. "It was nice rivalling you, brother," she said, and winked at him. "But I guess I win."

XV.

'A struggling warrior prayed to Taka, and with all the devotion in his soul he asked him, 'Is failure acceptable?' Holding his sword in his hand, with his armour stained with blood, Taka appeared before him from the depths of the Gaiamirarezo, and he replied, 'Failure is not liked, nor is it honourable... but it is acceptable, as long as it is followed by success.'

-       Extract from the Gaiamirapon: 'The Communications'

*

Anaka sat in silence in front of her father's desk, the day after Mokoto's fight. Meitatsa Rimi had survived her injuries and would suffer no permanent damage. However, news of her attack had made it into the media, and therefore into King Taka's ever-growing list of concerns. Needless to say, he was not a happy man.

Taka moved his eyes across her to Anaka's husband, who sat quietly beside her. The king's face was calm. It was stern; dangerous. He was always at his calmest before he was at his most fierce; Anaka had a suspicion he liked to envision what he was about to do to his victims before he actually did it. If she could read his mind now, she would no doubt hear her own screams.

"Raikun," Taka uttered. "Please leave. I want to speak to my daughter alone."

"Sire..." Raikun softly insisted. He glanced at Anaka, who shot him a pleading look.

"Go," she silently begged him, fearing for his safety just as much as he feared for hers.

"I know your loyalty lies with your wife," Taka said, still ever so calmly. "And I am grateful to you for trying to protect her..." He narrowed his eyes at Raikun, his expression growing so cold and deadly that if there was ever any doubt that King Taka was the mortal embodiment of the God of War, it was gone now. "But if you do not leave now, I promise I will murder both of you."

"Very well, Sire," Raikun replied. He avoided Anaka's gaze and rose to his feet, not daring to look back as he left the room. Before he had even gone he cursed himself for leaving.

Taka moved his eyes to Anaka and looked at her sternly.

"What happened?" he demanded.

"I… I don't know," Anaka answered, lowering her eyes. "I'm sorry, Sire. We went to the battle room and –"

"You lost sight of him!" Taka snarled. "I *told* you when you went out – Mokoto was not to leave your sight! Or Raikun's, or Lanka's! And neither you nor Raikun had any idea where he was!"

"He was with Lanka!" Anaka insisted. "She saw him fighting Rimi and she said she wanted to take him alone –"

"So why did you listen to her?" Taka demanded.

"She's my older sister, Father!" Anaka replied. "She's my superior, and I trusted her –"

"*I* am your superior!" Taka roared, slamming his fist down on the desk. "And you will listen to me a hundred times before you listen to her! I told you *not* to let Mokoto out of your sight!"

"I'm sorry!" Anaka protested. "Here." She rose to her feet and took off her blouse, offering her blood. "Beat me."

"Are you asking me to?" Taka growled, narrowing his eyes at his daughter.

"I deserve it," Anaka said, nodding confidently as if she were actually trying to convince him to rip her apart. "I disobeyed you, Sire. I let Mokoto out of my sight… and I shouldn't have. I thought Lanka could control him but obviously she couldn't – and I should have been there with her."

"Yes," Taka said flatly. "You should have."

He paused for a moment, studying Anaka. Anaka remained still, but she felt uncomfortable under his gaze. He was trying to solve her. He was trying to read her mind, her body language, her breathing… Normally Anaka didn't care when another Hiveakan tried to read her. She knew they couldn't, not unless she allowed them to. Her father was different though. She had to let him read her – she wasn't permitted to keep anything from him. She had to let him break down her walls – walls that she had built for a reason. She had to

201

surrender to him. Anaka didn't like surrendering to anybody; not even to the king. She hated it, in fact. The fact that she did it for him was proof of how highly Meitat Anaka thought of her father. "You..." Taka began. "You were not wrong to trust your older sister. It is her duty to be someone you can trust – just as it was yours to be someone that Mokoto could trust."

"I know," Anaka replied. "And I failed him. I made a wrong decision, when I should have known better... I wouldn't accept that from my employees, and I wouldn't ask you to accept it from your child. So." She took hold of the small, sharp letter opener King Taka kept on his desk, and she held it out to him. "Punish me. I would if it were my child."

"Hmph," Taka grunted. "Of course you would." He leaned towards her slightly and reached out for the knife. "You would make a wonderful mother."

Anaka watched in confusion as King Taka took the knife from her hand and trailed it along her forearm; he was drawing blood – just. He was barely piercing the surface of her skin. The pain wasn't even enough to make Anaka wince, and no sooner had he feebly cut her did King Taka set the knife down and relax back into his seat, folding his arms. He sat there in silence and watched her reaction.

"That's it?" Anaka blinked.

"For your honesty, your acknowledgement of what you did wrong and your willingness to be punished." Taka smiled at her slightly. "As always, I think I can trust you." He motioned for Anaka to take a seat. "Sit down. Get dressed. There are many beautiful women I would like to see undress for me, but none of them are my daughter."

"Thank you," Anaka softly uttered and slowly lowered herself back onto her seat. She picked her blouse up from the floor and dressed herself, seemingly lost in her own thoughts as she covered her uninjured flesh. She felt confused... She had deserved to be beaten – she wanted to be beaten. That was it, wasn't it? That was why she was unharmed. The king knew her, and he knew that this 'getting off lightly' would eat away at her... and that was her punishment.

"You can go," Taka said, picking the knife up to toy with it a little. He spun it against his index finger, keeping his eyes focused on it as he listened to Anaka stand. "Tell Lanka and Mokoto to come in. Together."

"Yes, Sire." Anaka nodded and turned towards the door. She remained silent as she made her way across the room, listening out for him.

"Anaka." Anaka stopped dead at the sound of his voice. He wasn't finished. He had something more to say… or maybe he had decided to beat her after all, just to flavour his punishment. Anaka turned slightly to look at her king.

"Yes, Sire?"

"You know…" Taka began. "I didn't tell Lanka to keep an eye on him. Only you. Please do not break my trust again, Meitat."

"I promise." Anaka watched him nod in acknowledgement, and her heart sank as the realisation of his feelings for her weighed heavily on her soul. The one thing that was worse than him breaking every bone in her body was knowing that she had let her father down. It wasn't acceptable. It wouldn't happen again. *Ever.* Anaka turned back to the door. She cleared her throat, and pushed back the feeling of overwhelming guilt as she went outside to greet her siblings.

Lanka and Mokoto were waiting outside, along with a nervous Raikun.

"You're alright…" Raikun sighed, relieved to see Anaka leave her father's company in one piece. He beckoned for her to come closer. "What did he do?" He grabbed Anaka's wrist and looked at the thin line of blood on her arm, then frantically moved his eyes to Anaka's face. He was puzzled. "Is that it?" Raikun questioned.

"I suppose I'm the favourite." Anaka smirked a little, deliberately acting cocky.

"Right…" Lanka mumbled. "If he cut you, think what he is going to do to us." She gritted her teeth in annoyance. "If I ever find the reporter that leaked this, I'll kill them."

"People would have found out anyway…" Mokoto mumbled. "There were witnesses."

"Why did they even care?" Lanka snapped. "People get injured in the battle room every day – more injured than her! Nobody would even care what happened if we weren't celebrities. Why don't they just mind their own business? We don't read about their lives."

"Lanka." Anaka met her sister's eyes. "He wants to see both of you. I wouldn't make him wait."

"Right." Lanka looked at Mokoto. "Come on. You're taking the blame for this." She dug her claws into his shoulder and pushed him towards King Taka's meeting room door, knocking before she entered.

"Come," Taka's booming voice called from inside the room and Lanka opened the door, not looking back as she and Mokoto entered.

Raikun moved his eyes to Anaka.

"What sort of mood is he in?" he asked.

"He's angry," Anaka stated. "They aren't coming out for a while."

"Well... they don't have jobs," Raikun mumbled. "There is no reason why he can't beat them enough to keep them indoors for the rest of the year."

"Yeah," Anaka said. "Do me a favour – would you go back to the Royal? I want to stay here."

"Anaka –"

"I know, I've thought about it," Anaka interrupted. She looked at Raikun pleadingly. "Just go, would you? One of us has to supervise that place."

"*I* have to. You just volunteer." Raikun smirked a little. "Alright, fine. Call me when you're on your way back."

"Alright." Anaka smiled slightly as Raikun kissed her cheek.

"See you later." He quickly squeezed her hand and walked away, leaving her alone outside the door. Anaka sighed and moved closer to the meeting room, half listening to what was going on.

There was silence for a long while. Then the silence was broken by King Taka's voice. He was demanding what had happened and who was to blame. He barely gave his children a chance to explain before he was roaring at them again.

"Do you realise what you have done to this family's reputation?" His thunderous voice cascaded through the closed door as

if a bomb had gone off, sending a jolt through Anaka's body as if she had been caught in the blast. She winced at the thought of what was happening to her brother and sister.

"Please, Father! Please forgive me!" Mokoto's desperate plea came through the door. Lanka was silent, as Anaka had expected. She'd been in this palace long enough. Lanka knew how pointless begging was and how feeble it looked. Lanka was never one for cowardice, especially when she knew she had nothing to gain from it. Anaka flinched again as Mokoto's plea turned into a harsh gagging noise and she suspected Taka had his hand around Mokoto's throat. The gagging was followed by a series of short, blunt cries and the sound of broken bones. Mokoto's quick breathing accompanied the noises and even from out here Anaka could see the fear in her brother's eyes and she could smell the young blood on Taka's hands. Poor thing... Anaka pitied Mokoto. Up to now he hadn't done anything to warrant such a beating, and he had probably become used to the idea of not being afraid every day. Anaka remembered the first time she had been punished here. It was when the Hive was nothing more than a distant memory to her, and she had naively adjusted to the idea of never having a hand laid upon her again. The shock had been so great to begin with that she couldn't feel anything except her own wounds, and then... after a moment, when she had once again become accustomed to pain... she'd felt ashamed. She'd felt so ashamed... Ashamed that she could no longer handle what used to be a perfectly ordinary punishment, and ashamed of the fact that she had been stupid enough to believe that she would never be hurt again. Those things had by far outweighed the shame of doing whatever she had done wrong in the first place. She'd felt like a failure for screaming... And she knew that was how Mokoto felt now.

"Get out!"

Anaka moved away from the door as soon as she heard Taka utter the words. She stood and faced the door, waiting eagerly for someone to emerge from the room. Mokoto quickly came out and desperately shut the door behind him. He moved his eyes up to Anaka's and swallowed, embarrassed to be seen like this.

Anaka looked him up and down. She was a little saddened, but not the least bit surprised by what she saw. Blood. That was all she could see. Her brother was weakly holding his shirt in his hand and his torso was covered in thick indigo bruises and cuts; some were deep knife wounds and others were the work of Taka's own claws. There were lumps all over his body and he was pale and trembling. It wasn't through fear; it was through lack of blood. His body was at the verge of going into shock, and was probably reacting even worse because it hadn't had a beating like this in such a long time. An Outsider would be dead by now... But then again, the king wouldn't have been so rough with an Outsider.

Anaka moved her eyes to Mokoto's free hand, noticing that he was holding it awkwardly.

"Broken?" she asked.

"You're the scientist," Mokoto sniped back, desperate to claw back some of his pride. "You tell me." He moved over to her and threw his hand into her chest, getting blood on her blouse. Anaka ignored her stained clothing and gently took his hand to examine it in hers. Mokoto started to wince in pain as she touched him, but he stopped himself. That was good, as far as Anaka was concerned. He still had control over his actions; he was still aware of what his body was doing... Anaka couldn't help but admire her father. He'd had no formal training, but he could so perfectly pinpoint someone's physical limits. He'd done just little enough to keep Mokoto alive. It really was quite a skill.

Mokoto wiped his face as Anaka examined him; his nose was bleeding and he could feel the blood seep into his lips. His left eye was forced closed as blood dripped onto it from the cut on his brow and he starting using his shirt to get rid of some of the liquid that was blocking his sight.

"Well, it's broken," Anaka concluded. "But if you're careful you shouldn't need any support – you know what to do with a broken bone, don't you?"

"Of course," Mokoto growled. She did know he'd grown up in the Hive, didn't she? Of course he was used to having broken bones! Not that he'd had one since his early childhood... That alone made Mokoto feel ashamed. He was too old for broken bones...

206

Anaka looked down at Mokoto's legs.

"At least he let you walk," she stated.

"Somewhat…" Mokoto turned to show her the backs of his thighs; his trousers were covered in thick patches of blood that had soaked deep into the material. His thighs had been sliced apart; Anaka pitied her brother for having to stand on such damaged limbs. Mokoto lowered his head as he felt his sister's eyes on him, his face burning with embarrassment and shame. He hated being so exposed; he always had. Even when he was in the Hive… The beatings had been terrible, but the worst part was the aftermath. The way his tutors used to look at him… watching him writhing in pain, drenched in blood with not a scrap of pride or dignity to his name. Mokoto had thought he'd seen the end of that…

"Come on." Anaka grabbed his shoulder. "I have things in my room – nobody will know. I can treat you."

"You have medical supplies in your room?" Mokoto mumbled. He turned to face her and watched her nod; she was smiling a little.

"They've come in handy, haven't they?" Anaka answered. "You take your job too seriously," Mokoto said. Anaka laughed, in full understanding of his attempts to make her look small. She beckoned for Mokoto to follow her and they made their way towards her room.

*

'I wouldn't call my father a 'kind' man… Hiveakans aren't kind. But when he could have put me in a wheelchair, he only cut my legs. I suppose that was kind… I didn't really see it that way at the time.'

-      King Mokoto, 20142G

*

Bingo. Another perfect score. Mokoto was sat in front of his computer, in his bedroom, doing a series of maths tests. It was his weakest subject… and he wasn't going to tolerate that. He had barely tolerated it before and he definitely wasn't going to tolerate it now. Not

207

after today. His father thought he was a failure. Mokoto was in danger of losing the throne, and if it did not go to him it would go to Lanka – and he *definitely* didn't want that. He was sat in loose gym clothes with a firm bandage over his broken hand. He'd been in Anaka's room a couple of times before, but he never knew she had a cupboard full of medical supplies. She said she kept them in case she hurt herself training, so she wouldn't lose precious work time going to the hospital or being attended to by one of the servants. It was a little over the top, as far as Mokoto was concerned... but he was secretly grateful. She'd let him use her shower to wash off his wounds and she'd given him some tablets to stop the bleeding, so to any passer-by it simply looked like he'd been training with Lanka. Nobody needed to know. Nobody had any business knowing!

Mokoto looked up as someone tapped on his bedroom door and he made his way over. He opened the door half expecting to see Lanka or Anaka, and was surprised at the sight of Oreisaka. Her eyes sparkled when she saw him and she offered him a small, soft smile. A weak smile.

"You didn't join us for dinner," Oreisaka uttered gently.

"No," Mokoto replied. "I ate in here."

"Oh..." Oreisaka shifted uncomfortably, wondering how to approach the subject. "Lanka looked very injured... and you..." Mokoto pulled his head away as she tried to touch the wound above his eye, scowling a little. Oreisaka withdrew her hand and gave him a sympathetic smile. "It was Father, wasn't it? The two of you did something wrong last night."

"That's none of your business!" Mokoto snapped. Why was she here? He didn't need anybody's sympathy, and certainly not an Outsider's! She wasn't a Hiveakan, she couldn't understand this! Mokoto felt an overwhelming urge to slice open her throat with every soft look she gave him.

"I'm sorry," Oreisaka said, and lowered her eyes. "I just..." She looked back up at him with another pathetic smile. "You're my brother. I don't want to see you hurt."

"I'm fine," Mokoto said flatly. "Don't worry about me, I'm a Hiveakan." He gave her an arrogant smirk. "You don't think I can cope with this?"

"No…" Oreisaka blushed a little, fidgeting in embarrassment. She laughed feebly. "I suppose I forgot how much a Hiveakan can handle. I'm – I'm sorry." She smiled at him again. "You know where I am if you need me."

"Yes." Mokoto nodded, and he watched Oreisaka crumble before him. She felt foolish. Embarrassed. He was doing that to her. Good. Knowing that, satisfied Mokoto… it made him feel big. Who was she anyway? She was his older sister, but she was weak. She pitied him. She loved him. Mokoto didn't need that in his life. Was she really helping? Did their father really like to see Mokoto keep an Outsider's company? He hadn't said either way. Maybe Oreisaka really was useless. Oreisaka nodded at Mokoto politely, and she walked back down the corridor, heading for her room. Mokoto closed the door behind her and sighed. What a weakling she was… Why couldn't he share Anaka's blood?

Actually… Mokoto didn't see Anaka for a few days after that. He moved around the palace as infrequently as possible, still ashamed of his scars. He only left his room to train and battle Lanka, both when he could be sure he would not be seen. After a while though, he thought he should see Anaka… His wounds would take over a month to completely fade and he couldn't stay hidden away for all that time, so he asked Rowan to take him to the Royal.

Within thirty minutes Mokoto found himself stepping out of the lift onto Anaka's floor; he ignored the horrified stare of the receptionist that greeted him. What was wrong with her? Had she never seen a cut before?

"Um…" the girl uttered, averting her eyes from the cuts and bruises that still lay upon Mokoto's face. "Can I… help you, sir?"

"Yes – I am looking for my sister," Mokoto answered bluntly. "Anaka."

"Anaka?" The receptionist looked at him, seemingly bewildered.

"Don't tell me you have more than one person with that name?" Mokoto snorted arrogantly. "Meitat Anaka. My sister."

"Oh... Oh!" The girl's eyes widened and she shot up off her chair. Apparently she'd only just realised who he was. "Matat Mokoto! I'm so sorry, Your Highness!" She offered a frantic bow and looked at him desperately. "This way, I'll take you at once!"

"Thanks..." Mokoto mumbled and followed the girl down the hall. How had she not recognised him? He was the newest graduate in Meitona Palace, and the only son of King Taka! She should have recognised him immediately! Then again, she didn't seem very competent. Mokoto watched the girl walk; she was constantly looking from left to right, always peering through door windows... did she have any idea where Anaka was?

"Sorry, I thought she was in cell biology this morning... She moves a lot," the girl explained. She turned to glance at Mokoto, and flashed him a smile. "You probably know that. If you take the lift down to the ground floor – she's probably in engineering –"

"I see her." Mokoto looked past the girl towards Anaka; she was surrounded by a group of co-workers and talking them through the notes she held in her hand. Mokoto moved his eyes to the receptionist. "Thank you," he said, not that he meant it. He hated being polite to people he thought so little of. It was such a chore. Mokoto pushed past the girl before she could say another word, and approached the group of biologists. "Anaka."

Anaka looked up from her notes, and blinked in surprise.

"Moko?" she uttered. Mokoto shifted slightly as Anaka's companions deliberately avoided his gaze, conscious of his wounds and fully aware of who had inflicted them. They were pretending not to know who Mokoto was. Anaka glanced at them. "Um – can you show these to Leiton?" she asked, and handed one of them the notes. The crowd nodded and walked away, not daring to speak a word.

"Leiton?" Mokoto questioned, looking at Anaka.

"My boss," she answered.

"I thought Raikun was your boss?" Mokoto said.

"Raikun is head of the Royal." Anaka smiled. "He's everybody's boss. Leiton is head of Chemical and Life Sciences."

"You work in engineering too, right…?" Mokoto uttered.

"I have three bosses," Anaka stated, and laughed. "What brings you here anyway?" She gestured for him to follow her and made her way into the break room, stopping in front of a vending machine. "Do you want anything?"

"No," Mokoto answered as Anaka bought a soda. He grinned, deciding to tease her a little. "You have to pay for your drinks here? Why do you work? You don't need the money."

"I know. I don't do it for the money." Anaka shrugged. She made her way over to an empty table and took a seat, followed by Mokoto. "I like biology, and engineering. You know that, Moko!" She laughed again, and lowered her eye. She paused… hesitating. She was deciding whether or not she should say anything more. "I studied astronomy too."

"I didn't know you worked in that field," Mokoto replied, closely watching Anaka's body language. Something was wrong. She seemed uncomfortable all of a sudden…

"I don't," Anaka mumbled. "I'm not interested in it anymore."

"Why?" Mokoto asked.

"No reason." Anaka smiled quickly, and changed the subject. "Why are you here anyway?"

Mokoto didn't answer immediately. He took a few seconds to decide whether or not he should press her further. Astronomy was a science, but a heavily religious one. It was a fact that the Gaiamira had travelled here from another planet – a planet named Earth, occupied by creatures called Humans. According to legend, the Gaiamira had also travelled on Gaiamiráka's two moons, which were once believed to be giant ships in the sky. So, with all their 'other world' connections the Gaiamira played a large part in the study of things outside of this planet. It was by far the smallest area of science, though. The Gaiamira permitted their people to study very little of outer space, and so most of what could be explored with modern technology remained untouched. Was that why Anaka didn't like it? Because she actually had to behave and not study something she wanted to study? If Mokoto knew his sister, that would irritate her to no end. Ha. Typical. He decided to let Anaka go, and allowed her to change the subject.

"I wanted to get out." Mokoto shrugged. He looked at her, and became uncomfortable. He blushed slightly. "And I wanted to thank you… for…" He glanced around him, making sure nobody was listening before he moved his eyes back to Anaka. "For… helping me."

"You could have text me that," Anaka smiled. "Anyway, don't worry about it. Father can be tough sometimes. You should learn to not anger him."

"I learned," Mokoto replied awkwardly, trying not to recall the beating that had left him so damaged. "He didn't do anything to you, though."

"Not physical…" Anaka said. "But he is making me marry again."

Mokoto froze. He was stunned. Had he heard her right? Marry? She was getting *married* again? Since when? Mokoto stared at Anaka in shock.

"What?" he gagged. How had he not heard about this?

"He thinks we need to make a stronger tie with Heikato." Anaka sighed. "Personally I don't, but… Father gets what he wants. He wants me to marry a Heikatoakan."

"Does Raikun mind…?" Mokoto uttered.

"Not really." Anaka shrugged. "He knows it's only politics, and we agreed we wouldn't have children anyway…" She smiled a little. "I suppose this is Father's chance to get a grandchild."

"What – you're having children with him?" Mokoto gasped, even more surprised. This seemed a little rushed, didn't it? Then again… Mokoto almost scolded himself for thinking that. Anaka was right – it was only politics. Mokoto knew he shouldn't be so shocked by this, but… five minutes ago he didn't even know Anaka was getting married again, and now he was learning that he was going to be an uncle!

"Of course." Anaka giggled. "Otherwise everybody will know it's not a real marriage."

"I suppose…" Mokoto mumbled, fully understanding her logic. "But why don't you want children with Raikun?"

"Oh – it's not like that. It's just..." Anaka shifted slightly. "It's just personal." She looked at him sternly, almost dangerously. "Don't ask."

"Alright... sorry." Mokoto looked at Anaka, trying to decode her. Why was she being so defensive suddenly? It had previously occurred to Mokoto that Anaka and Raikun should have had children by now, but he always assumed they hadn't because of their careers – Anaka never wanted to tear herself away from work after all, and childbirth would pull her away for at least a few minutes. Now though, Mokoto was starting to wonder... was it even a possibility? Raikun wasn't infertile was he? If he was, then why would Anaka marry him?

Mokoto felt his sister's eyes on him and he quickly changed the subject, aware that her personal life wasn't really any of his business – or his concern. "Is Father letting you choose the man?" Mokoto asked.

"Yes," Anaka giggled. "I wanted another scientist, but it turns out Heikatoakans are idiots." She smirked. "So I just went to the Hive and picked the best looking one."

"Really?" Mokoto laughed. "Your first husband was older and your second is younger? When does he graduate?"

"He's not a student, you idiot!" Anaka barked. "He's a tutor – actually, he's the best they have."

"Oh really?" Mokoto answered.

"Mm." Anaka took a sip of her soda. "He's the department manager of Childhood Development – and he's the best tutor the Hive has had in years. He's a natural, apparently." She shrugged. "Whatever that means. I suppose some need more training than others."

"He sounds good," Mokoto remarked. "We need more men at home anyway! There are too many girls." He smirked a little, quickly adjusting to the idea of having more Hiveakan brothers to cancel out the Outsider women. This second husband was starting to sound like a good idea – someone that made a living out of fighting would always be a welcome addition to Mokoto's life. This man was a *real* Hiveakan tyrant. Finally, Mokoto would have a Hiveakan brother that was actually interested in fighting! "What's his name?"

"Teikota."

Mokoto froze. Teikota…? He felt a shiver run down his spine at the sound of the man's name. Teikota…? As in…? No. No, that was ridiculous. What were the chances? Mokoto hadn't seen Teikota in years – he didn't even know if he still worked at the Hive. But… if he did, he would probably be a department manager by now… No. No, it couldn't be. It *wasn't* the same man.

"What is it?" Anaka uttered. "You know him?"

"No…" Mokoto mumbled. He looked at Anaka, his stomach tingling as his nerves grew. He felt sick. The very thought of…

"When… when are you marrying him?" Mokoto asked. He was trying to seem calm, and indifferent. He didn't want Anaka to know. He didn't want anybody to know about Teikota. He didn't want this to be real…

"Next week maybe," Anaka said. "I need to meet him first. He said he was going to come this afternoon." She quickly checked her watch. "Actually he should be here soon. Why don't you stay –?"

"No!" Mokoto's cheeks flushed at the look of surprise on Anaka's face. "I – I need to go. Father wants me back in the palace."

"Mokoto…" Anaka frowned, speaking sternly. "You haven't disobeyed him by coming here, have you?"

"No, of course not!" Mokoto protested. He stood up and pointed to his beaten face. "Do you think I want this to happen again?"

"We take a lot of risks." Anaka smirked. "What's wrong?"

"Nothing." Mokoto forced a smile, and equipped his calm face. "I just have to go. Sorry, Anaka. Thanks, again."

"It's –"

"Bye." Mokoto left the room before she could say another word, ashamed of the fear that was racing through his core. It wasn't even fear; it was… disgust. Pure, dark, evil disgust like nothing he had ever felt before. She couldn't do this. She could not bring that man into Mokoto's family! She couldn't make him Mokoto's brother – he was supposed to be his victim! Their father would stop this – then again, their father didn't know. Nobody knew. Mokoto was convinced, that day when Teikota had almost killed him, nobody knew about it. If they had, Teikota would have been murdered for what he'd done. It was up

214

to Mokoto to punish him for it, and he couldn't do that if Teikota was Anaka's husband!

No... No, he wouldn't be. It wasn't the same man. Teikota was a common Hiveakan name. It was a strong name. It was the Gaiamirákan word for 'thunder', and fitting for the amount of fear Teikota could bestow upon a child's soul. There had to be more than one Teikota working at the Hive – and this one wasn't his. Mokoto forced himself to believe it.

He hastily made his way through the lab and towards the lift; he had to get out of here. He had to calm down! That was all he needed. He just needed to clear his head, and relax... It wasn't the same man. It couldn't be. The timings didn't fit – Teikota would be in his thirties or forties, or possibly fifties by now! Then again, Anaka didn't mind them old... *No*! Mokoto forced himself to stop thinking like that. He was making it worse for himself! Mokoto stopped outside the lift and pushed his clenched fist onto the call button on the wall, his nerves growing with every second that he waited for it to arrive. This was ridiculous. It was *ridiculous*. He couldn't be so stressed over this. Just the name of that man, just the thought of seeing him again... it couldn't do this to him! He wasn't a child anymore. He wasn't in the Hive and he wasn't under Teikota's control – he had no need to feel stress, or fear. Anyway – the next time Mokoto and Teikota did meet, it would be Teikota who should be afraid, not Mokoto! Teikota would be the one in danger! But that wasn't relevant now. Teikota and Mokoto's next meeting was so far away it wasn't even worth thinking about, because Anaka was *not* marrying that Teikota!

Mokoto held back a sigh of relief when the lift arrived in front of him and the door opened. *Finally*. He just needed to get out of here. He needed to get that traitor out of his mind. Mokoto stepped forward and moved his eyes up into the open vessel... Then he stopped dead. At that moment, everything went dark.

There he was. That man... The world darkened around Mokoto as he stared at the living nightmare that stood before him. His skin was just as dark as Mokoto remembered; his eyes were just as cold; his stare was just as deadly. He was the one person that had left a permanent mark on Mokoto's soul. He was the only wound that would not heal... He was darkness. Still. He was nightmares. Still. He was a plague whose fever Mokoto had never really overcome. Even now, standing here... He was still that man. After all these years, he was still the face of darkness. *Teikota.*

Mokoto stood dumbstruck, too stunned to speak as the world seemed to collapse around him and sent him falling into oblivion at the sight of that man. What was he supposed to do now? What could he do...? Through the sound of his own blood in his ears Mokoto could hear Teikota's laughter. He would know that laugh anywhere; it had been burned into his mind. That low, dark chuckle... Mokoto could feel the cruelness behind it – he could see it. It was in Teikota's eyes. In Teikota's cruel, dark eyes. They flickered menacingly as they gazed upon Mokoto, and Teikota's calloused lips slowly twisted into that same cold, tormenting smile.

"Mokoto." Teikota's voice echoed through Mokoto's mind, stabbing his soul with a painful coldness as he uttered five simple words. "It's good to see you."

XVI.

'When asked about marriage Taka answered, 'As warriors we do not fall in love, but that does not mean we cannot be united. A Hiveakan marriage is a strong one, because we value strength more than romance. We are comrades, loyal, and fighting together for a common cause. Together we will conquer our enemies, and together we will endeavour to never fall in love'.'

-      Extract from the Gaiamirapon: 'The Communications'

*

Everything was different now. As far as Mokoto was concerned, life was different. He couldn't pinpoint exactly when it had changed, but it was at some point after he had seen Teikota at the Royal. Teikota... His brother. That was what Teikota was now. The wedding ceremony had been a glorious thing; it had been an over-elaborate celebration to mask the sham that was Anaka and Teikota's marriage. As Raikun had put it, nobody looked at the ground when there were fireworks in the sky. The public believed Anaka and Teikota's marriage to be real, and they believed it simply because they wanted to believe that the celebrations they'd enjoyed were real. They were forcing it upon themselves, just as the royal family had wanted. Mokoto had forced himself to enjoy the celebrations as well, because in all likelihood his own future marriage would also be a sham. He could only wonder what his wife would be like... It would be years from now, but Mokoto had a vague idea of what to expect. She would be a Hiveakan, obviously. She would have good blood to make good heirs, and she would be attractive... She might have a temper, but only as much as many Hiveakan women did. Either way, she wouldn't be a psychotic murderer who had attempted to kill any of King Taka's children. There were already more than enough of those in Meitona Palace.

     Mokoto and Teikota had been related for a little over five weeks now, and for over five weeks they had shared a home... and for over five weeks Mokoto had kept Anaka at a distance. He was angry at her. He knew he shouldn't be. She had no idea who Teikota was to him – even if she knew he was Mokoto's tutor she wouldn't know what he had done. She didn't even respect Teikota; she wore his wedding chain under Raikun's, as a reminder to the world that Raikun was her favourite. Still, Mokoto didn't care. He didn't care how little respect Anaka had for Teikota, and he didn't care that she would take Mokoto's side if she knew everything there was to know. The fact was that Anaka had taken Teikota off his kill list, and Mokoto would hate her for it even if she had no idea why. She didn't need to know. Nobody did, that was the point. He couldn't tell anybody… How could he? He didn't want them to know how weak he had been, and he didn't want them to be in a position to protect Teikota. If Mokoto did decide to kill him, it would be when Teikota was unguarded and alone, just as Mokoto had been. Still… in all likelihood, could Mokoto ever get his revenge now…?

"*Good morning!*"

"Mm…?" Disturbed from his troubled slumber, Mokoto steadily opened his eyes at the sound of a familiar voice. He was vaguely disappointed to see Oreisaka standing over him, but it wasn't as bad a sight as it once had been. Mokoto had been talking to Oreisaka a lot more lately, even out of the public eye. For some reason he found her presence comforting. Perhaps it was because he could trust Oreisaka. She wasn't about to do anything unexpected or damaging… All she did was bore him, and these days boring didn't seem as bad as it used to be. Still… Oreisaka was enjoying Mokoto's attention a little too much. She'd started stalking him.

Mokoto didn't bother looking around; he knew exactly where he was. He was in the palace gym, where he had collapsed last night. He'd spent almost all of yesterday training here with barely any food and no breaks, until he'd finally run himself into sleep… and now every muscle in his body was burning. It was a good feeling.

"Why did you sleep here?" Oreisaka half scolded Mokoto as she sat on the floor beside him. "It can't have been comfortable – you could have at least made yourself a web!"

"I've slept in worse places," Mokoto mumbled, sitting up. "And this place is as good as any. It has showers."

"What about your clothes?" Oreisaka frowned.

"I brought some," Mokoto replied. "Do you think I would forget?"

"Alright..." Oreisaka giggled. "Then what about food?"

"That too," Mokoto said. "Don't worry, I prepared – I was expecting to spend the night here."

"It still seems excessive... Why is being strong so important to you?" Oreisaka sighed. "You know... Teikota is your brother now. You're family – it doesn't matter how strong you are."

"What?"

Mokoto stared at Oreisaka, his throat suddenly becoming dry. Why...? Why had she said that...? What made her think of Teikota...? She couldn't know. Nobody knew about him!

"Ever since he moved in you've been training a ridiculous amount," Oreisaka began. "I was worried about you... So I read about Hiveakans online." She looked at him. "It said that a student will always fear their tutor, and they will always try to prove their strength even after they leave the Hive."

"I'm not afraid of him!" Mokoto growled. The nerve of her... She had gone behind his back – *she* had betrayed him as well! Why was she worried anyway? She had no need to worry about him! And she wasn't even right. Why was she assuming he was afraid of Teikota? Mokoto wasn't afraid of Teikota – he wanted to kill Teikota! He *hated* Teikota!

"But you were his student, weren't you?" Oreisaka spoke softly. She was looking at Mokoto with gentle eyes... It made him feel sick. He didn't need her kindness or her pity. She had no idea what she was talking about. She did *not* know him! "I asked him... He was your tutor," Oreisaka said. She smiled at Mokoto, and then reached out to take her brother's hand. "Moko... It's different now. You aren't a child anymore, and he isn't your tutor. You don't have to prove anything to him –"

"I'm proving nothing!" Mokoto snarled, snatching his hand away. How dare she do this! She had no right to act like she knew him

– she had no idea! Oreisaka didn't know anything about Mokoto; she didn't know anything about the Hive! She'd noticed him training more – that was where all this had come from. Why was that a problem? He was still talking to her; they were still 'friends' – why did she feel the need to research Mokoto as if he were a kind of science? Would she do that every time he changed his behaviour? If he started eating different foods, or started listening to different music, would Oreisaka go online and try to explain it with some small-minded web article – an article that was probably written by another clueless Outsider? Why would she do that?

"Alright. If you say so." Oreisaka smiled softly. "Anyway… our mother made me promise to take care of you, so let's go out for breakfast. It's a beautiful day; having a little break from your training won't hurt will it?"

"No," Mokoto grunted. No… going out for breakfast would not hurt anybody, but staying indoors with him might hurt *her*. He was genuinely thinking about ripping open Oreisaka's throat. If she ever did that again… if she ever even attempted to understand him… Mokoto had to stop himself. He was fantasising about killing Oreisaka. He wanted to… Ever since the day he'd met her he'd thought it would be fun, but now he *really* wanted to do it. He couldn't. Mokoto had to remind himself of that. She was valuable to him; she helped him maintain the right public image. It wasn't her fault that she thought she could know him… She loved him, didn't she? Her desire to become close to him had driven her to do what she did, and her Outsider upbringing had left her naïve enough and stupid enough to believe that she could actually understand him. Mokoto would pity her if he wasn't too busy being angry. "After you," he hissed.

"Thank you." Oreisaka beamed and pulled Mokoto to his feet, once again taking hold of his hand. She flashed him another soft smile and he returned it before following her out of the room, growing calmer as the seconds passed.

*

220

'Although he was close with his Hiveakan siblings Meitat Lanka and Meitat Anaka, Mokoto seemed to form a special bond with his Outsider sister Meitat Oreisaka, the only sibling with whom he shared a mother. They were often seen together in public following his graduation, but they seemed to grow particularly close after Meitat Anaka married Teikota, a man who had previously been Mokoto's tutor in the Hive.'

-        Extract from history textbook: 'The Mokoto Era: 20103G - 20147G', 20160G

*

"Here they come," Taka spoke into his phone. He was in his bedroom, looking at a holographic image of Mokoto and Oreisaka returning from their outing. The image was from a security camera positioned above the entrance to Meitona Palace. It transmitted its images to the army of armed guards and security personnel in charge of keeping the royal family safe... and to King Taka, who in his own arrogance and territorialism liked to know what was going on in his home. "She is holding his hand."

"Who?" Thoit's voice came from the other end of the line.

"Mokoto and Oreisaka!" Taka snapped. "Haven't you been listening to anything I've said?"

"Nope," Thoit answered bluntly. "I hardly care to listen to my own idiotic ramblings, so fuck if I'm listening to yours. They're siblings, Taka. What do you want them to do, fight? Try to kill each other? That never worked out well for us."

"He's spending too much time with Oreisaka..." Taka thought aloud, sounding somewhat concerned. "This isn't just maintaining his image."

"Well... as far as he's concerned, his best friend has brought a murderer into the palace. I'm sure he's rethinking his alliances," Thoit replied. "Can you blame him for turning to Orei?"

"I can't blame him for turning from Anaka, but he shouldn't be getting close to Oreisaka. She's an Outsider," Taka stated.

221

"And so is Toka," Thoit said. "And he was our best friend – is our best friend. Did you forget? What, an Outsider is good enough for us but not for your son? Fuck, if you are going to put one of your children above me, at least make it Anaka."

"Oreisaka is nothing like Toka!" Taka argued. "Toka wasn't the daughter of a traitor!"

"Oh, not this…" Thoit sighed down the phone, so clearly that Taka could picture his face and the exhausted look that was upon it. "Taka, I will bury you…"

"You will, will you?" Taka snarled. "Then you are a traitor just like her."

"Brother –"

"No! Listen to me, Thoit!" Taka barked. "Mokoto is a child, and fresh out of the Hive. He hasn't settled yet, he's easily influenced – and she is the last influence he needs!" He ran a hand through his hair, steadily becoming angrier at the thought of… Mokoto's mother. "I never should have let him befriend Oreisaka. She was the best one for the public, but… She is just like her mother. She's manipulative. She'll shower him with kindness, she'll pretend to respect him… and he'll be naïve enough to fall for it – she'll make him weak, Thoit!"

"Oh… Lanka, fucking take me now," Thoit groaned through the phone. "I'm touching the floor, Taka. I hope Lanka will take me away from this insanity."

"Insanity?" Taka growled.

"Yes!" Thoit snapped. "I am smoking now, brother. Can you hear me?" He exhaled through the phone, presumably breathing out tonito smoke. "I am fucking *high* and I think this is bullshit. Teima was no threat to anyone, and neither is Orei."

"Well how can I trust your opinion on this?" Taka argued spitefully. "You did not support me with Teima."

"No, I did not," Thoit agreed. "Because you were being stupid – and you are being stupid now! Think before you act, Taka!"

"I am thinking, Thoit! You are not!" Taka snarled. "Mokoto is my only son, and heir to my throne – and I am not going to put his Footprints at risk – and if you are too high to understand that then call me back when you're sober!"

"Oh... Fucking do what you want, Taka, as always," Thoit snorted. "Kill Orei, kill Mokoto. Give your throne to Teikota for all I care, I am done with this – and I am not calling you back when I'm sober. I'll never be sober around you again; there is not a chance in the world that I am ever talking to you without drugs!"

"Thoit –" Taka's eyes widened as Thoit hung up, enraging Taka further. How dare he? How *dare* he? "Disrespectful little..." Taka stopped himself finishing his sentence. Thoit wasn't worth it. He took a long deep breath and slowly exhaled, calming his nerves. "Wanker." He stormed over to his bedside table and yanked the bottle of tetsa from its surface, downing a third of it without even taking a breath.

*

'Teikota was a good man. He was a credit to the Hive, and to the Hiveakan community. I am very sorry for what has happened to him... I had a great deal of respect for him, and I will continue to respect him for the rest of my life.'

-       King Mokoto, 20144G

*

Teikota smirked slightly as he watched Mokoto; they were in the gym and Mokoto was running on a treadmill, overworking himself and ignoring his body's pleading to end its torture in an attempt to prove to Teikota that he wasn't afraid of him.

"You've improved," Teikota commented. "You can never underestimate the power of fear, can you, Mokoto?"

"Fear...?" Mokoto repeated, struggling to restrain his own Footprints. How dare he? He was mocking him!

"You are afraid of me, aren't you?" Teikota moved closer to Mokoto and looked the boy up and down with his trademark stare. That cold, dark stare and those dead, soulless eyes...

223

"What do you want me to say…?" Mokoto asked quietly. His attempt to restrain his Footprints was working… they were backing down. Mokoto convinced himself it was because he wanted them to. It wasn't through fear, or nerves. He slowed his movements slightly, not wanting to lose his footing in front of Teikota as the evil entity continued to stare at him.

"Nothing. Don't say anything," Teikota answered, and folded his arms. "After all, we are family now."

"Yes." Mokoto avoided Teikota's gaze, trying to remain calm through the anger that coursed through his soul.

"Although… I never knew what a family boy you were." Teikota sneered. "I heard you have made friends with your Outsider sister. That's sweet of you."

"She isn't my friend!" Mokoto growled. "That's just to help my image." He looked at Teikota arrogantly. "If you want to be part of this family, sir, I suggest you learn that." Shit! Why had he just said that? Mokoto instantly regretted it. He shouldn't speak to Teikota in such a way! Teikota was his superior… If he told the king about this… Shit!

Mokoto flinched slightly, taken aback by Teikota's chuckling. He seemed amused.

"I will learn that. Thank you," Teikota said. "But, I suspect this is more than just a public friendship." He met Mokoto's eyes, and there it was again. That dark, evil smirk. "You forget, Mokoto. Brother. I can tell when you are lying."

The pair of them looked up suddenly, yanked away from each other by the sound of the door opening, and they saw King Taka enter the room. Teikota knelt down obediently, while Mokoto desperately switched off the treadmill and leapt off the machine, clumsily throwing himself into a kneeling position behind Teikota. Taka almost laughed as he watched the boy. It was so apparent what a child Mokoto was. But then again, that was part of the problem.

"Very good, Teikota," Taka admired as he approached his subordinates. "Even after all these years you still have him cowering behind you." He chuckled cruelly. "I suppose he wouldn't dare try to walk beside you."

224

"Or in front, Sire." Teikota replied.

"Well of course, not in front," Taka answered. He moved his eyes to Mokoto. "Stand up. Come on!" He folded his arms impatiently and watched as the boy steadily rose to his feet. "Teikota." Taka moved his eyes back to his older son. "A moment with my child, please."

"Of course, Sire."

"There is no need to be so formal, Teikota," Taka commented as Teikota stood up. "You are my son now. Understood?"

"Yes, Father." Teikota nodded and left the room, closing the door behind him.

Taka looked at Mokoto.

"You look exhausted," he commented. "Have you been working hard?"

"Yes, Sire." Mokoto nodded, panting slightly after his workout. He was aware that he was sweating, but he'd hoped to not look exhausted. He wanted to look strong. Resilient. Hiveakan...

"Good." Taka nodded, moving his eyes up and down the teen. Mokoto tried to read the king, and he could do so as much as the king allowed. He was... annoyed? There was something unsettling about King Taka. His Footprints were in his eyes, as if they were waiting to attack. Had Mokoto done something to anger the king...? How? "Do you like being strong, Mokoto?" King Taka questioned.

"Yes, Sire." Mokoto nodded again.

"Do you like being a Hiveakan?"

"Yes." Mokoto answered cautiously, his mind racing as he tried to work out where this conversation could be headed. Something was wrong... He could sense it. He had annoyed the king, somehow.

"You don't give that impression," the king stated flatly, narrowing his eyes at Mokoto.

Mokoto's heart stopped. What...? No... What did that mean? Did the king...? Did he think Mokoto was un-Hiveakan? How? Mokoto tried his best to be strong – no! This couldn't be. Why did the king think that? What had Mokoto ever done to give that impression?

"You enjoy the company of Outsiders."

Oh... So that was it. It was Oreisaka... No. No – it wasn't! It was *Teikota*. He'd even mentioned it just now – he thought Mokoto liked Oreisaka. Had Teikota said something to the king? Had he been badmouthing Mokoto behind his back? Had he told the king, Mokoto was spending too much time with Oreisaka? That bastard... Of course! It all made sense to Mokoto now – there could be no other explanation. Teikota was out to get him; he always had been! And now he was trying to jeopardise Mokoto's right to the throne!

"It's just for my image, Sire," Mokoto insisted confidently. "I only talk to her to give the right impression."

"Who, Mokoto?" the king replied, his cold eyes still narrowed at his child.

"Oreisaka..." Mokoto answered, unnerved by his father's callous staring. "I talk to Oreisaka... to make us look like a family."

"Anaka is your family," Taka stated. "So are Lanka, and Raikun, and Teikota. Why don't you talk to them? If you spent as much time with them as you do with Oreisaka, we would not have a problem."

Mokoto's heart started racing. Problem? There was a problem? Oh, no... No, no! This was awful – his father was losing faith in him! He would take away Mokoto's position as heir – he would give the throne to Lanka! *No!*

"Please!" Mokoto begged, then his eyes widened and he let out a sharp gasp as he immediately realised how pathetic he sounded. He wasn't going to beg. Hiveakans didn't beg for anything, and especially not heirs to the throne! He was making this worse for himself... Dammit! This was all Teikota's fault! What was he trying to do, get Mokoto out of the picture so Anaka could take the throne? Anaka didn't want the throne! And if the king himself couldn't convince her to take it then why in the Gaiamiras' globe did Teikota think he stood a chance? Mokoto looked at his father, frantically trying to think of what he could say or do to prove his worth to the king. His father had to understand... He didn't like Oreisaka! Not really... She was bearable, much more bearable than Mokoto had initially thought, but that didn't mean... Did it? Oh, no... No. No, they were not friends! That was

226

absurd! It was all for show – it was for the benefit of the royal family – the benefit of the king! Why didn't he realise that…?

"Her mother was poison," Taka said. "Oreisaka is as well. You are friends now, aren't you? You like her."

"No…" Mokoto uttered. "No – Sire –"

"My throne is a Hiveakan throne," Taka growled. "And it deserves a true Hiveakan; not someone who can be so easily poisoned by a kind face. Fix it. The crown does not belong on a weak man's head."

To Mokoto's horror, the king turned to walk away. Mokoto had never felt anything like it. This was fear. True fear. Fear that he had lost the throne… Fear that his father would never view him as a strong Hiveakan. Fear that he had failed his mission, his purpose in life… No. No, this was not happening! He had to do something! Mokoto's entire being suddenly became flooded with anger. His desperation, his panic and his refusal to lose the throne awakened his Footprints, and they went on a rampage through Mokoto's soul. He had to prove himself. He had to prove his strength, his brutality… and Oreisaka's insignificance. She wasn't his friend. She was *not* going to poison him. He would show the king that. Mokoto watched as his father opened the door to the gym, but before he could leave through it someone entered the room… and Mokoto's heart stopped.

It was her. Mokoto couldn't believe it. He let out a sharp breath, his throat cold from holding it in. It was Orei… She was here, now. She was kneeling before their father, greeted by a grunt from the king as he looked down at her. He was displeased with her. He was displeased with Mokoto, because of her… It was a sign. It had to be. The God of War Taka had brought her here – he was giving Mokoto a chance to prove himself. *Yes.* He was giving Mokoto a chance to prove himself to the Gaiamira, to the Hive, and to his father… and Mokoto had no intention of letting him down.

"Orei." Mokoto greeted her with a small smile as she rose to her feet with her father's permission.

"Hello!" Oreisaka smiled back, as brightly as ever as she approached her younger brother. "I thought you would be in here. Do you want to get some lunch?"

227

"That sounds good," Mokoto said, watching eagerly as she came far too close to him. Far too close for her own safety. His Footprints raced to the surface of his being like predators giving chase, their steps so powerful Mokoto could hear them thudding through his mind. They were one with his heartbeat; they were one with his soul... They were one with Taka. "Father!"

The king turned at the sound of his son calling out to him, infuriated that Mokoto would demand his attention. He was ready to break the boy's neck. Taka had no patience for begging and especially not from his heir... but he was surprised by what he saw. Mokoto had his arm around his older sister, and he was looking at the king with a sense of triumph. What was he doing? What was he trying to say – was he actively trying to *defy* his king? Taka would kill him!

Slash. All at once, Taka's anger disappeared, as did the breath in his lungs. He almost went into shock. His eyes grew wide as he saw Oreisaka standing beside her brother, with a single bloody line across her throat. She didn't know what was happening to her. She placed her hands on her throat in reaction to the pain, but she didn't even know she was bleeding until she felt the liquid cover her palm... and by then it was too late to save her.

"Orei!" Taka gasped. He raced over to her. He caught Oreisaka as she fell to the floor, released by Mokoto as if she were nothing more than mere waste. Taka held Oreisaka, and he watched the life fade from her eyes. He couldn't look away. She was staring at him, in such confusion... She had no idea why she had to die. It must be such a terrible feeling. "Orei..." Taka repeated softly. Orei smiled slightly; Taka didn't know why. It was the kind of smile he had seen somewhere before, a kind he didn't care to remember. Nor did he care to think about... Then she was gone.

Taka looked up at Mokoto, and as a well-trained Hiveakan boy Mokoto knelt down to put himself lower than the king. "Why?" Taka asked.

"I don't like her, Sire. She isn't my friend," Mokoto answered. "But... if you say she is poison, I had to stop myself becoming tainted." He looked at his father with venom in his eyes, venom that Taka would never have expected from a child of his age, not even his own heir. "I promise you, Sire," Mokoto said. "I will be worthy of your throne."

"You may be right," Taka uttered, with the blood of Oreisaka running down his arm.

XVII.

'Lanka always keeps her form. She is a woman with long white hair; she is thin, and ageless, and she wears the key to the Gaiamirarezo on a chain, over a long blue dress. Some say she looks young; some say she is beautiful, but all describe her features the same. Lanka does not change her face, nor does she alter her appearance for any mortal. She is what she is, and she will be perceived how she is perceived. She does not care for opinion, for she knows that regardless of how she looked, it would not change whether or not those that see her want to die.'

\-   Extract from the Gaiamirapon: 'The Identities'

*

Mokoto did not dare to move as he knelt before his father. He watched the king in desperation, looking for any indication of whether or not Mokoto had done wrong. The king was holding Oreisaka's lifeless body in his arms, her blood running down onto his clothing. Mokoto couldn't help but feel proud. Was that wrong? She was his sister, and as a Hiveakan it was his duty to protect his family, even if he didn't care for them... but she was poison, wasn't she? It was like the king had said – Oreisaka's mother was poison, and so was Oreisaka. She was trying to taint Mokoto; she was trying to make him weak... and she might have achieved. Maybe. If Mokoto had given her the chance. She would never poison him now.

The king locked his eyes onto Mokoto, and the boy listened loyally as his father spoke.

"She was poisoning you. It was treason," Taka said. "I told you to kill her." He narrowed his eyes at Mokoto. "It was under my orders, because I have the authority to make that decision."

"Yes, Sire," Mokoto replied. Oh, no... He suddenly felt nervous. He'd never thought of that. Mokoto had thought executing Oreisaka was the best way to prove himself to his father. He thought it was what his father and the God of War wanted – he thought her being here was a sign! … But he had never thought of that. Only the king had the right to decide if she should be executed. It wasn't Mokoto's place to make that decision. Shit! Would the king be angry? Would he have Mokoto executed? No… No, surely…

"Calm down," the king ordered, seeming to sense Mokoto's nerves. "Killing her wasn't wrong." He looked at Mokoto sternly. "But next time you take on the role of a king, it had better be when you are wearing the crown."

"Yes, Sire." Mokoto nodded, unsure of whether to feel relieved or terrified. "I'm sorry."

"Don't be," the king replied. "When we are young, we all have something to prove." He looked at Mokoto with a small smirk… a smile, even. "You are not young anymore."

Mokoto held his breath as his mind began to process his father's words. They were positive, weren't they? They had to be; there was no other way to interpret them. So was this it…? Was Mokoto forgiven? Had he proved his worth…? Yes. It had to be – why else would the king say that? Yes! Mokoto could barely keep himself from grinning widely as he watched the king set Oreisaka's body down. He had proven himself. The king thought he was an adult! He thought he was worthy!

"Thank you, Sire." Mokoto did not dare say it out loud for fear that it would make him look weak.

*

'The entire planet is in shock. Earlier today Meitona Palace announced that Meitat Oreisaka has been executed for treason. She was reported to have been trying to taint Matat Mokoto, an act which is classed as treason when committed against a king. As Matat Mokoto is next in line for the throne, King Taka made the decision to have her executed before she could do him any permanent harm. Her mother was also executed shortly after Matat Mokoto's birth, for trying to taint King Taka in the same way. Those who were fans of Oreisaka are claiming that her execution was unjustified and 'not thought through', but as her mother was found guilty of the same crime the general consensus

231

across Meitona is that the decision made by King Taka was right. The king's brothers Malatsas Thoit and Toka are yet to give their opinion, but Malatsa Omota, an extremist Outsider, has publically stated he is appalled, but not surprised at his 'barbaric brother's' decision.'

-       News report, 20117G

*

Mokoto smiled eagerly as he watched his father open a large bottle of tetsa. Mokoto had never tried it before. It was an extremely powerful substance that could only be consumed by the alpha males and females of the palace… of which Mokoto was now one. He was a man. He was a Hiveakan man, and more importantly – he was heir to the throne. Taka grinned at his son from the head of the dining table. He sat with Anaka, Raikun and Teikota to his right and Mokoto and Lanka to his left. He had created a room of Hiveakans for a Hiveakan event; the evolution of one's Footprints. It was the awakening of Taka inside Mokoto's soul. It was a Hiveakan child's first step towards becoming truly one with the God of War, and it was something to be celebrated.

"You should remember this day, Mokoto," Taka stated as he poured out a large helping of the drink. He passed it to Lanka. "Hand this to my heir, would you?"

"Of course, Father," Lanka replied bitterly, avoiding his gaze as she took the drink and slammed it down in front of Mokoto. "Congratulations," she spat.

"Thank you. That means a lot to me." Mokoto smirked, almost laughing at the glare she gave him in response.

"Don't be so bitter, Lanka. I am not dead yet – there is still time to take the throne off him," Taka commented half-jokingly as he handed glasses of tetsa to the others.

"Yes there is, Sire," Lanka replied, coldly staring at Mokoto. "And I will."

232

"Well, I will hold you to that." Taka beamed, and raised his glass. "To you, Meitat. If you can surpass your brother, you will certainly make an excellent queen."

Mokoto battled the urge to laugh as they toasted Lanka. He could feel the heat of her anger next to him; it was a wonder she didn't explode. Oh, she was so far behind now, wasn't she? So far behind that Mokoto wasn't even her rival anymore, he was her target. If he were less Hiveakan, he might even pity her.

"Thank you, Sire." Lanka spoke gracefully, as if she weren't screaming on the inside. "Thank you, everyone..." She looked at her younger brother, and she offered him a warm smile that would seem genuine to the non-Hiveakan eye. "And thank you, Mokoto... for making our little race more interesting. When I first met you, I never thought you would do anything as bold as this. For a child your age to graduate so young, and then to prove yourself so soon... It's incredible. Really." She kept her eyes on him, watching Mokoto as he tried to predict her next words. He knew there was an attack coming... it was just like her. "But then again," Lanka said with a smirk. "I never really expected you would have a need to prove yourself so much. I'm so happy for you, for overcoming your Outsider disease. We are all very proud."

The others started sniggering, as discreetly as they could, and Anaka openly giggled.

"You're such a bitch," she said. "Just be happy for him!"

"I just said I was," Lanka insisted.

"Mokoto, *I'm* happy for you." Anaka smiled at her brother. "And not in a political way."

"Thank you," Mokoto replied, attempting to hide the awkwardness that still lingered between them. He was more powerful now; he had no reason to be intimidated by Teikota – not that he was... but he still hated Teikota, and Anaka was still the one that had brought him here. Mokoto wasn't sure how to change how he felt about that.

"Teikota," Taka began, as if Mokoto's own thoughts had drawn the king's attention to the embodiment of darkness. "What do you think? When you were raising this boy, did you think this was what he would become?"

233

"Well… Sire, I expect great things from any child that is raised by me," Teikota replied with an arrogant smirk, causing the king to chuckle slightly. Mokoto's Footprints twisted in disgust. The bastard… Now he was attempting to befriend the king. It wouldn't work! The king had more sense than that. "And… yes," Teikota continued on, "I did expect this from him, Sire… but at least a decade from now." He looked at Mokoto with an odd sort of expression. If Mokoto didn't know better, he would say Teikota was smiling. "I never thought he would become a man so young."

"To Mokoto," Raikun announced, holding up his glass. "History's youngest executioner. May none of us displease him."

"I'm sure we wouldn't dare." Anaka grinned playfully.

Mokoto watched in wonder as the table saluted him, and he was suddenly unable to take his eyes off Teikota. That look on the man's face… What was that? For some reason, it looked like pride. Why was Teikota looking like that? Who was he trying to fool? He wasn't proud of Mokoto – if he was proud of anyone it would be of himself, for creating someone as Hiveakan as Mokoto. He was mistaken, though. He did *not* create Mokoto. Mokoto would have turned out like this, with or without Teikota. He was a natural child of Taka; he was born to be this way – and Teikota had no right to feel responsible for that! Then again… this did feel good. Mokoto had to admit it. To have his tutor praise him, and Teikota of all tutors… and his father. Mokoto knew his face was glowing; it had to be. He couldn't contain the joy he felt at this very moment, and he didn't want to. He *had* proven himself today; he had proven he was worthy of the throne, and worthy of being King Taka's son… and he had every right to feel worthy. He had done something exceptional, and everyone was recognising him for it – and they were celebrating it. Hands down, this was the greatest moment of Mokoto's life.

"Have you told the Outsiders yet?"

Anaka looked at her father questioningly, as always daring to say what everyone else was thinking. "Sorry to bring it up, Mokoto…" She looked at her brother apologetically and back at the king. "But I want to know how much I should say?"

234

"Say what you want, I already told them," Taka replied dismissively, as if he couldn't care less what his children thought of him. Well. He didn't. "They weren't happy."

"Well, that was to be expected," Raikun commented. "Oreisaka was well loved."

"Not by me," Taka said. He looked at Mokoto. "And not by you either, hm?"

"No, Sire," Mokoto answered. He should feel bad. He'd made his sisters grieve… but they were only Outsiders, and as insignificant as Oreisaka. If the other Hiveakans didn't care about her death then nor should Mokoto – and he didn't. That was further proof that he was worthy of the throne.

"Good boy." Taka nodded. "Now…" He looked at Anaka and Teikota. "When are you two going to give me a grandchild?"

"Oh!" Raikun shifted uncomfortably, causing Lanka to snigger.

"Father…" Anaka blushed. "Do we have to talk about that now?"

"We don't have to talk about it at all," Taka replied. "Just make it happen. Mokoto will be getting a lot of interest from now on – I want you to have a child before he gets married."

"Don't worry, Anaka, you'll have plenty of time," Lanka sniped, and looked her brother up and down. "Who'll want to marry him? He's a runt."

"Well…" Taka said with a smirk. "Perhaps he'll start to grow into his Footprints soon."

Mokoto remained quiet as the others laughed amongst themselves. Marriage…? He never thought of that – not so soon, anyway. He wasn't even fourteen yet! He'd never even had a girlfriend.

XVIII.

'Many times have the Gaiamira communicated with mortals, throughout the history of the world. The Gaiamira are the only constant, the only eternal beings. They have observed the past and present, and they will observe the future. As mortals perish the Gaiamira will live on, forever watching and speaking to the people of the world.'

-       Extract from the Gaiamirapon: 'The Communications'

*

Anaka and Teikota had a child the following year, in the month of Tomakoto the God of Achievement and Ambition. The child was a boy. They named him Aourat, the Gaiamirákan word for 'strength', and put him into the Hive just a few hours after he was born. He was doing well, by Hiveakan standards – and average, by Anaka's standards. Apparently it was actually possible to be stricter than the Hive. Mokoto had to be amused. It was easy to find Anaka amusing these days... It was over a year since she had married Teikota. Six months since she had birthed Teikota's child, and over a year since she and Teikota had sat and admired Mokoto for ending Oreisaka's life. Now... Mokoto wasn't angry at Anaka anymore. He didn't know why, or how... It all seemed so far away from the present he almost didn't remember why he had hated Anaka at all. Gradually, Mokoto's feelings of resentment for Anaka had subsided, and he had returned to only hating Teikota. He would always hate Teikota, no matter what. It ended there, though. Mokoto had no quarrel with Anaka, or Aourat, or any other children that Teikota may father. It wasn't their fight, after all. Mokoto was enough of an adult to understand that now.

He'd also lost his virginity. Not to anyone special... but the king's comment about Mokoto's marriage prospects had got the young matat thinking... Girls existed, didn't they? Girls that weren't related to Mokoto. Pretty girls. Hiveakan girls. He'd started wondering what it would be like to have a girlfriend, and not long after King Taka's comment that wondering turned into... discovering. It had been nothing fancy. A red collar; a servant prostitute that worked in the palace. She'd been pretty, and slim... She'd been an Outsider, but good enough. It wasn't as if Mokoto had anything to compare her against. He didn't know her name. He hadn't forgotten it; he'd just never learned it. Mokoto had used the servants a few times since then. It was much safer – he got offers outside the palace all the time, from various members of his own social class, but it was safer to stick to the discreet servants of the palace. That way he didn't risk harming any political relationships if things went sour... as they might well have done with Rimi.

Rimi. That was a name Mokoto would take a while to forget. It was the same Rimi he had almost killed when he was a child. Meitatsa Rimi, of Meitona. Mokoto had dated her, for a while. A short while. They'd met again, at some social gathering. She'd been one of many high society girls there, but the only one Mokoto personally recognised. He'd avoided her at first, assuming that she wouldn't want to see him, but to his surprise Rimi had approached Mokoto and demanded a rematch. Well... what was he supposed to do? He'd wanted to test his new skills, and if they were seen in friendly combat together it would no doubt help fix the damage that 'incident' had done to Meitona Palace's reputation all that time ago. So... they'd met in public, and battled... And then they'd met again, in private... and again... As it turned out, Rimi was good company. She may have made a good wife, if Mokoto had been given time to think about it. They were only together for a short while before King Taka had ordered Mokoto to end it. Rimi was from a good family, whose relationship with Meitona Palace was strong and beneficial to the king... so much so that King Taka couldn't risk letting a couple of children ruin it. Mokoto hadn't wanted it to end. He'd thought he could be careful – he thought he could protect Meitona's politics from his relationship with Rimi... But he couldn't. Of course he couldn't. Rimi's mother was an Outsider; she had Outsider influences. If things had gone sour between Rimi and Mokoto, there was no guarantee she wouldn't hold an Outsider grudge, and then only the Gaiamira knew what she would do. Mokoto told himself that at the time. It was what his father had told him at the time, and he'd forced himself to believe it... but it wasn't until he was much

237

older that he truly believed it. Back then, he'd thought he was a man just because he'd killed Oreisaka – and Rimi had thought he was a man too, and she'd believed herself to be a woman… But she wasn't. He wasn't. They were children. Just children, playing games when their parents were looking away. Mokoto could see that now. Now that he really was a man, and he was as cold as Taka's sword.

"Aii!" The sound of a young child's screams of fear filled Mokoto's heart with elation. This was so much fun…

He was watching the youngest royal resident of Meitona Palace, Meitat Chieit. She was the third child of Anaka. Three years after Aourat's birth, Anaka and Teikota had a daughter, Maida, also a Hiveakan child. Then, after another four years Anaka had Chieit. Chieit was Raikun's child, to the surprise of everyone. She was unplanned, and for a while, unwanted. By her mother, at least. Well… by both of them, to begin with. Then, when she was born, Raikun's world seemed a little brighter because Chieit was in it. He *almost* doted on her as much as he did Anaka, and Anaka… she liked Chieit, but not in the same way. She liked Chieit because she herself was the biggest Raikun fan in the world, and Chieit was essentially a walking autograph. What an honour it must have been, to bear the legendary Doctor Raikun's child. They'd decided to name the baby Chieit, which wasn't strictly in the dictionary. It was the Aoutakákan's pronunciation of 'Kieit', which was the Gaiamirákan word for 'superiority'. Anaka preferred the Aoutakákan pronunciation – it sounded better, apparently. Then, as if her existence itself wasn't surprising enough, Anaka had announced that Chieit would be raised outside of the Hive – which was a shock to the whole family. Chieit would be one of a 'crossbreed' of Outsider-Hiveakans; she had Hiveakan blood and she'd had a Hiveakan yotuna, but she grew up outside of the Hive – under the close guidance and supervision of Teikota. He pushed Chieit to her limits, and to all intents and purposes she was a Hiveakan child, with a few Outsider mannerisms here and there. Like any Hiveakan, Chieit understood loyalty. She was loyal to her family, and she strived to please her parents. She was completely ruthless and arrogant; she excelled at everything she did and she was able to identify the weaknesses in others and play on them like the young predator she was. On the

surface it was hard to believe she'd had any Outside influence at all…
except that she was scared of bees. "Kill it! Please!"

Mokoto folded his arms and smirked slightly as he watched his
five-year-old niece cower into the wall, her eyes fixed on the large
insect that hovered above her head. Mokoto was now twenty-six, no
longer a child and more of a Hiveakan than he ever thought he would
be. The years had made him colder and darker; in fact he was an exact
replica of the men he had feared as a child. He had learned to make
enemies of the Outsiders and friends of a select few Hiveakans, all of
whom were his relatives. His siblings, actually. He rarely laughed
unless it was at the expense of someone's injury or misfortune, and
he'd broken many bones in many fights, none of which were his.
Actually, they were mostly Lanka's. She really ought to give up trying
to defeat him. Chieit had more of a chance of befriending this bee.

Mokoto chuckled as he watched Chieit whimpering up at the
insect. She hissed at it and swatted her hand towards it, trying to shoo it
away.

"Good girl," Mokoto congratulated sincerely. "You should
fight your fears, Chieit."

"I hate it!" Chieit screamed. "Kill it!"

"Do it yourself." Mokoto took a seat on the sofa. He was alone
with her in one of the common rooms; he'd come in here to read while
he waited for his father – they had a meeting soon.

"Please!" Chieit whimpered. She took a deep breath and leapt
up at the bee, smacking the back of her hand straight into its body and
against the wall. "*Ew!*" She cried and yanked her hand away, her eyes
scrunching closed in disgust. "Uncle, I hit it!"

"I know," Mokoto answered as he watched the bee struggle to
get itself off the ground. She'd broken its wings.

"Ew!" Chieit screamed again, wiping her hand on her skirt.
"Uncle!" She opened her eyes to stare down at the bee. "Is it… is it
dead?"

"No. Can't you see it moving?" Mokoto frowned. "Squash it."

"No!" Chieit pouted. She looked at him pleadingly. "You do it!
Please!" She stomped both her feet rapidly on the spot, almost crying
at the thought of touching the bee again.

Hm. Maybe she wasn't all that Hiveakan.

"That isn't my victim." Mokoto shrugged and lay down on the sofa, placing his hands behind his head. He kept his eyes on her and sniggered as he watched Chieit steadily approach the squirming insect. She lifted her foot off the ground and slowly placed it above the bee.

"*No!*" Chieit leapt back and stomped her feet in frustration. "I can't! What if it hits my foot?"

"How? You're wearing socks," Mokoto growled. "Do it! If you don't you will always be scared of them."

"No I won't!" Chieit argued. She threw herself into the corner of the room and gripped her dress, shivering in disgust as she took another look at the bee.

"If you don't squash him, I'll squash you," Mokoto threatened.

Chieit lifted her head to look at him, her face scrunching up into an almost sob.
"I can't..."

"Fine." Mokoto started to get up.

"No, wait!" Chieit screamed and immediately stomped on the bee, closing her eyes as she scraped her sock against the floor. "Ew..."

"Good girl," Mokoto said. "You did it."

"Because I didn't want you to hit me!" Chieit screamed. She sat down and took off her sock to examine it, gagging at the sight of a few black dots that were still stuck to the bottom. "Ew!" She threw her sock as far across the room as she could manage, and she coughed dramatically, as if she were trying to vomit.

"Trust me, I just cured you." Mokoto sat back down.

"I still hate them!" Chieit wailed. She slammed her hand into the floor in frustration and clenched her fists in an attempt to both calm herself and get attention. Mokoto ignored her, and wondered how Anaka and Raikun could have produced such a noisy brat.

Chieit raised her head at the sound of the door opening, and she instinctively threw herself into a kneel. She was well trained, if nothing else.

"Father." Mokoto read Chieit's reaction and placed himself in front of her on the floor, also kneeling with his head down as Taka stood before him.

"Rise, both of you," Taka instructed. He made his way over to Chieit and softly kicked her side. "What's wrong with you?"

"A bee." Mokoto smirked, watching as Chieit's face darkened in embarrassment.

"Oh." Taka looked down at his granddaughter and chuckled. "I thought you were over that now. Should I tell Teikota you are still scared of them?"

"No!" Chieit begged, staring up at him. "Please, Sire!"

"Alright." Taka grazed his fingertips across the top of her head, catching a few strands of her hair with his claws. "On one condition. You know computers don't you? Find me a picture of General Lakuna and bring it to me. I'll be waiting in here." He winked at her. "You have five minutes."

"Five minutes!" Chieit protested, her eyes widening. "No, but I can't —"

"Four minutes and fifty seconds." Taka held back his laughter as he watched Chieit race towards the door. She stopped halfway, and turned around frantically to throw herself into a parting bow. She was panting already; her eyes were wide and riddled with self-hatred as she realised she'd forgotten her manners. She made eye contact with her grandfather, and when he nodded at her she leapt onto her feet and bolted out of the room. When she was well away and out of earshot, Taka allowed himself to laugh. "You know…" He took a seat on one of the free chairs, and ran a hand through his greying hair. "I had almost forgotten what it was like to have an Outsider child in the palace."

"The servants have plenty upstairs, Father," Mokoto commented.

"Oh, not them!" Taka growled. "I mean one that matters."

"She certainly matters, Father." Mokoto nodded.

Taka looked at Mokoto with a frown, his powerful body tensing.

"But too much to certain people?" he asked calmly.

"I didn't mean you." Mokoto's chest tightened as he feebly attempted to withdraw his comment. He would never dare admit it, but Mokoto thought Taka had softened in his old age. The king was now

241

sixty-four. On the outside he was still the ruthless dictator he always had been. He still ruled his planet with a callous hand and he refused to tolerate any kind of crime or rebellion. He could still manipulate his way into popularity just as easily as he could brush his teeth, and his popularity among the Hiveakan community had never faded… but in his personal life, he had softened. Nobody outside of Meitona Palace would notice, but Anaka was more of a daddy's girl now than ever – and it showed in King Taka's softness towards Chieit. He had never once beaten her, and he seldom held back even the brightest of smiles when he watched her move. It was as if he admired her energy. Granted, Chieit had a lot of energy, but she was five years old! As far as Mokoto was concerned she was completely normal and barely earned any of the kindness she was shown. She was a good asset to the family. In terms of her intelligence and abilities, Chieit was 'above average' for a girl her age – but so what? She was *average* as far as Hiveakan standards went, and everyone except Mokoto – the king included – seemed to forget that Chieit was to all intents and purposes a Hiveakan.

Taka's expression darkened as he looked at his son.

"I hope you didn't," he said threateningly. Mokoto lowered his eyes. As soft as Taka had become, he still knew how to punish someone when they spoke out of turn, and Mokoto always seemed to get a harder punishment than everyone else. He told himself it was because he was the next in line for the throne. His father had to test him more than he tested the others. Or… it was because the king knew Mokoto could handle it. Either one would do.

"Of course not," Mokoto assured. He looked at his father. "You wanted to see me?"

"Mm." Taka allowed Mokoto to change the subject, on this occasion. "I was thinking…" He stood up and made his way over to the drinks cabinet to retrieve his tetsa. "You are still a child, Mokoto." He poured out two drinks and handed one to Mokoto, as he always did. Mokoto had earned the right to become an alcoholic in recent years, but he never saw a reason to drink unless it was in a meeting with the king – and then he never refused to. Taka took a sip of his tetsa and sat back down, leaving the cabinet open. "Because you are unmarried." He

242

took a bigger sip. "Well, it's time for you to grow up. I found a girl for you, and I've arranged for you to see her tomorrow night. Unless you find her to be a man or infertile, you are marrying her."

"What!" Mokoto gasped, his eyes widening. What – just like that? This was – so… unexpected! Mokoto had no idea – he didn't know his father wanted him to marry that badly! *Why*? Lanka wasn't married, and she was older! Who was this woman anyway? Couldn't Mokoto at least see her *twice* beforehand? What if he hated her? He found it very hard to tolerate a woman for more than a couple of nights. Dammit. *Dammit*. Marriage. It wasn't like Mokoto never thought he would have to do it, but… He'd never planned to so soon, not before he was king. He wanted to focus on changing the world first. He wanted to establish himself as a leader, and set up the planet the way he wanted. A wife would get in the way.

"Don't worry, she is very pretty," Taka assured him. "She's a Hiveakan, about your age… twenty-one actually. She is the youngest woman to be promoted to her position in the history of the Keizuakákan army."

"You mean –" Mokoto's eyes widened once more as he immediately knew who his father was talking about. "General Lakuna?"

"Mm." Taka downed the rest of his drink and rose to pour himself another. "She was orphaned three years ago in a car accident, so there will be no in-laws to deal with. Just her brother, Gonta – he's an Outsider. Lakuna is his legal guardian."

"And how old is he?" Mokoto demanded, his body tensing at the thought of having *another* half-breed child in the palace.

"Mm…" Taka frowned slightly as he poured his drink, digging out the answer to Mokoto's question. "Eight, I think…" He sat back down, this time taking the bottle of tetsa with him. "Someone for Chieit to play with. She needs another child around here, Anaka told me she doesn't mix well with other children." He sniggered slightly. "She bullies them, apparently."

"That's only what her tutors think." Mokoto frowned. He was annoyed that his father had suddenly started talking about Chieit. So were they done discussing Mokoto's future wife? That was it, was it?

Mokoto was going to be a husband and father to an eight-year-old brat in a couple of months, so they could get back to talking about Anaka and her marvellous family. It enraged him… but in an effort to keep his place as heir, Mokoto bit his tongue. "The Outsiders just don't know how to deal with a Hiveakan child."

"Haha." Taka chuckled a little. "You may be right. Anyway…"

He was suddenly interrupted by Chieit rushing back into the room.

"Sire!" she cried, sliding into a kneel. Mokoto smirked slightly as she winced at the carpet burn on her knees; her eyes glistened a little and he knew she wanted to cry. Chieit bit her lip and stared up at Taka. "Did I do it?" she asked.

"Oh." Taka moved his eyes to the clock on the wall; he hadn't checked the time earlier and he didn't know exactly how long she'd been gone, but it certainly hadn't been five minutes. "You were thirty seconds over," he lied. He sighed deeply and held his hand out. "I am very disappointed in you."

"I'm sorry…" Chieit almost sobbed as she handed him the small hologram device she was clutching so tightly.

"Don't do it again," Taka scolded. He pressed a single button on the device, bringing up the image of General Lakuna that Chieit had loaded onto it. He examined the image, slowly sipping on his drink. "What do you think, Chieit? Is this woman pretty?"

"Yes," Chieit smiled. "She's beautiful!"

"Mm." Taka looked at her. "Would you like her to be your aunt?"

"Aunt?" Chieit blinked.

"Father…" Mokoto sighed.

"Chieit likes her," Taka stated as he passed the device over to Mokoto.

Oh, well if Chieit likes her… Mokoto thought bitterly. He looked down at the image. Hm. She wasn't bad. Mokoto had seen Lakuna a few times before, in magazines and on television shortly after her promotion. She was from North Heikato originally, Mokoto couldn't recall exactly where. Her skin was a dark orange and her hair jet black; her eyes were deep and dark, holding all the trademark

244

coldness and bloodlust of a Hiveakan. Her face was quite attractive, although she was more beautiful than pretty. She was smiling slightly on the picture and Mokoto assumed that was the most she would ever smile; Lakuna was famous for being a hard character, even in the eyes of the Outsider media. Maybe that was why Taka wanted her… He seemed to be intrigued by anyone who didn't conform to the social norms, like there was something fascinating about them. She could do with smiling a little more, if she wanted the Outsider community to trust her with their lives.

Taka watched Mokoto carefully as the younger man examined her.

"What do you think?" he asked.

"She's pretty, Sire," Mokoto answered. He handed the device back to his father, conscious of Chieit's eyes on the two of them. What was she hoping to see?

"You will see her tomorrow," Taka instructed as he topped up his glass. "She already knows about it."

"Yes, Sire," Mokoto uttered flatly. Why bother arguing? Just as long as she did what she was told and didn't go where she wasn't wanted. One more woman in Meitona Palace wouldn't bother Mokoto much. At least she was attractive… Then again, Mokoto didn't deserve any less.

"Can I try some, Sire?" Chieit begged, staring in fascination as Taka drank the thick black liquid from his glass. "Please?"

"Mm," Taka grunted. "Come here." He dipped his finger into the glass and completely soaked it before running the digit along Chieit's lips. Chieit winced in pain and pulled away, her face scrunching at the sensation of the harsh liquid on her delicate flesh.

"It's burning!" she cried, rubbing her lips.

"I know. It does that," Taka replied. He looked at her sternly. "And if you ever ask to drink under aged again it will not just be your lips burning, Chieit. Do you understand?"

"Yes…" Chieit sulked, still trying to get the taste of the alcohol off her lips.

"Go on." Taka kicked at her. "Go and kill some more bees."

"Yes, Sire." Chieit frowned and knelt, before leaving the room. Taka smiled slightly and looked at Mokoto.

"I want you and Lakuna to give me one of those," he said.

"Sire!" Mokoto protested. "Can I at least meet her first?"

"Hey!" Taka glared at his son. "No backchat."

*

'Well, what can I say? It was lust at first sight. I couldn't wait to marry her. I knew she was the one when she looked at me like she was going to kill me.'

\-   Matat Mokoto, 20130G

*

Mokoto stared numbly into his dinner, as if gazing at it for long enough would make this entire evening go away. He didn't want to be here. He didn't want her to be here. He knew Lakuna was staring at him. He knew the restaurant's staff were trying to stare at him, and he also knew that if he hadn't been alone with Lakuna in a private dining booth, there would be other diners wanting to stare at him as well. He hated this evening.

"You don't seem to be having a good time," Lakuna remarked. She looked at Mokoto from across the table, wearing a wicked smirk on her lips. "Don't you like me?"

"Of course." Mokoto grunted, and politely met her eyes. "Why wouldn't I?" Actually, there was some truth to that. By all accounts, Lakuna was perfect. She was a strong Hiveakan woman with a respectable job and plenty to contribute to society. She was intelligent, and attractive, and she came from a healthy bloodline… Why wouldn't he want to marry her? She was everything he had ever planned his wife to be. But.

"Because this isn't your choice," Lakuna answered Mokoto, as if she had read his mind. "You're the only boy in a family of Outsider girls. I bet you're used to getting your way." She spoke maliciously. As

246

if she knew him. Mokoto hated that. "A spoilt brat. I bet if we met in a bar and you never had to see me again, things would be different."

"I'm not spoilt!" Mokoto growled, insulted by her accusations. He *wasn't* spoilt. It was the opposite, actually. Anaka and the Outsiders got away with everything! From the moment he had graduated Mokoto had always been treated with so much more callousness than the girls. He'd always had to prove himself twice as hard as them and he'd had to endure twice as much suffering and scrutiny, all because of how significant he was. He was the heir to the king's throne. He was the future ruler of Gaiamiráka, and so his standards had to be higher than the rest. Mokoto was more valuable than his siblings. He knew that much; but it was this value that made his life so much more difficult than theirs. He was punished for being so important, and he was certainly *not* spoilt.

"Of course you are," Lakuna argued. "I bet the Outsiders were ignored, right? And the Hive girls have nothing on you, not with their mother. Did your father speak to you more than anyone else?"

"None were conversations I wanted to have," Mokoto answered stubbornly. Hm. Actually, he took it back – he'd never planned his wife to be like *this*. He didn't like this woman, not at all. She was too argumentative for a wife.

"Tch. I bet the others are still jealous of you." Lakuna raised her eyebrows arrogantly, not doubting for a second that she was right. "Listen… Your Highness." She looked at Mokoto sincerely, her voice taking a more serious tone. "Neither of us wants this, but we both need it. So let's just go home and tell your father we like each other."

"We *both* need it?" Mokoto repeated.

"Yes," Lakuna answered. "I need your money and you need my womb."

"Oh, do I?" Mokoto snorted, disgusted by her bluntness. She could at least try to earn his affections – there were plenty more women that could take her place. She needed Mokoto much more than he needed her! "Do you think it's worth all my money?"

"Actually, it's worth a lot more." Lakuna quipped. "But I'll let you have it cheap because you're so charming."

***

247

"Haha! I like her!"

Mokoto almost smirked as he watched Anaka laughing. It was two hours later and they were alone in one of the common rooms late at night; she had finally come home from work as he was coming back from his date with Lakuna, and like any good sister she'd wanted to know exactly what had happened.

"I thought you would," Mokoto said.

"Don't you?" Anaka questioned. Mokoto paused for a moment, considering his answer. Hm... Well. Lakuna was more outspoken than he'd like. She seemed to think she could talk to the higher class as if they were equals; Mokoto would have to repair that about her if she was going to be his wife... That being said, it hadn't been a bad evening. Overall. Once Mokoto and Lakuna had agreed that their marriage would be purely for the purpose of social or economic gain, and neither one of them was under the illusion that the other would like them, or even want to be with them. Lakuna seemed happy enough to go along with whatever Mokoto wanted, on the condition that she and her brother remained wealthy. That was all Mokoto really needed in a wife. He didn't need to like her at all, did he?

"She was okay." Mokoto shrugged.

"Okay?" Anaka looked at him. "What was wrong with her?"

"Nothing," Mokoto admitted. He looked at Anaka as the thought was still fresh in his mind. "An... Do you like your husbands?"

"What?" Anaka laughed. "What do you mean?"

"I mean, do you like your husbands?" Mokoto blatantly repeated the question, semi-sarcastically.

"One of them," Anaka said, smirking slightly at his tone. "The one *I* chose."

"Does it matter?" Mokoto asked.

"Well... no," Anaka answered. "Like she said," Anaka yawned and lay down on the sofa. "She's just a womb, isn't she? I only married Teikota to have children and make us closer to Heikato. All you need to do is have sex with her once, Moko. Then you don't even need to talk to her ever again."

"Mm." Mokoto grunted in agreement, fully understanding her logic. He smirked slightly, and looked over at his sister with a playful wickedness in his dark eyes. "Well... just once more. That's what you did, isn't it?"

"Shut up." Anaka smirked back.

"Or didn't you bother talking the second time?"

"Shut up!" Anaka and Mokoto both laughed as she hurled a cushion at him, and he of course deflected it. "Go on," Anaka urged. "What happened next?"

***

"Why do you need the money?"

Mokoto looked at Lakuna across the dinner table and watched her reaction, trying to deduce how uncomfortable the question made her. She didn't seem to mind; she clearly had no issue with talking to him about her finances. She shrugged slightly.

"I want my brother to go to university," Lakuna answered honestly, unashamed of how much Mokoto's money meant to her. "My parents wanted him to become a lawyer or a doctor... someone smart," she explained. "With our three incomes we could give him the best education, but I can't afford it on my own."

"So you want me to pay for an overpriced university?" Mokoto raised an eyebrow.

"And private tuition." Lakuna winked. "I heard your niece's tutors are good."

"They can't control her," Mokoto commented.

"Well... that's just down to discipline," Lakuna replied. "But she's smart, isn't she? That's what counts."

"Yes," Mokoto answered, to both comments. Hm. It was admirable, really... Lakuna clearly understood that marriage would make Mokoto's money hers, and yet she hadn't mentioned that she would spend it on herself. Was that really her only concern? "Is that all you want?" Mokoto demanded. "An education for your brother?"

"If I could afford it on my own, I wouldn't marry you," Lakuna answered. "I think you're all far too stuck up for me."

Mokoto was... horrified! How could she say that? He was the matat! He felt a sickening spark of anger in his core as his Footprints awoke from their slumber, ready to spill blood. How dare she insult him! Not just him, but his entire family as well – her king included!

249

Mokoto glared at Lakuna, trying to decide whether or not it was worth his effort to slit her throat. He wanted to with a passion. What did the king see in her? If only King Taka had heard that himself, she would be dead already.

"Oh... I'm sorry." Lakuna sneered, her eyes twinkling wickedly. "I didn't mean to insult you, Your Highness. All I meant was... if it wasn't for Gonta, I wouldn't be here."

"That's very sweet of you," Mokoto answered with a cruel smirk. He was choosing his words carefully; he'd quickly decided that Lakuna was too valuable to Keizuaka to kill, but he could humiliate her. He had to punish her in some way, even if it was only by attacking her pride. "It's not often a Hiveakan shows such love for her brother."

"That's not it," Lakuna hissed, and Mokoto became filled with delight as she was so obviously annoyed by his remark. She wasn't even hiding it... Did she not know how to? Her parents were Outsiders after all, maybe they'd spoiled her in the short time they were alive. Hm. A pity. And *this* woman was responsible for Keizuaka's army? Mokoto hoped for the continent's sake that nobody started a war. "Listen," Lakuna huffed. "I'm Gonta's legal guardian now – he's practically my son. It's my duty to give him the best life I can – don't you understand that? Didn't the Hive ever teach you loyalty?"

"Of course!" Mokoto growled.

"Well then." Lakuna frowned. "Supposing your sister and brothers died – wouldn't you do the same thing for your niece?"

***

"Would you?"

Anaka looked at Mokoto, eager to hear his answer.

"It's a ridiculous question," Mokoto scolded.

"Why?" Anaka asked.

"Because," Mokoto looked at her with a smirk, and his eyes twinkled. "If you die when Chieit is still young enough to need me, it will be because I've killed you. So the last person she will want to take care of her is me."

"What!" Anaka gasped dramatically. "Baby brother! Why would you kill me?"

250

"I don't know," Mokoto sniggered. "Maybe you tried to take my throne."

"Tch!" Anaka snorted. "That will *never* happen." She looked at Mokoto, still keen to hear his answer. "What did you say to Lakuna anyway?"

"I told her yes." Mokoto sighed, and prepared himself for what he knew would be Anaka's reaction.

"Ah!" Anaka squealed triumphantly, just as Mokoto had expected. A wide grin formed on her face as she looked at Mokoto, her dark eyes suddenly alight with excitement. "You would look after my child!"

"How do you know I wasn't lying?" Mokoto protested. "She's going to be my wife." He smirked a little. "I don't want her to think I'm a dick."

"Moko… if she's spent a dinner's length with you, she already thinks that."

"Hey!" Anaka giggled and held her arms up in defence as Mokoto threw a cushion at her. She smiled slightly and scooped the cushion up off the floor, lightly tossing it back to him.

"So, are you going to marry her?" Anaka questioned.

"Of course." Mokoto sighed, as if the answer wasn't obvious. "It's what Father wants."

"She's pretty." Anaka shrugged. "That's all that matters. You like girls, don't you?"

"Yes! That's the problem." Mokoto groaned, and once again felt the burden of having a woman call him her own. Every time he thought about the marriage he felt so chained; so tied to this other person… He had never loathed a feeling so much. Mokoto didn't want to be bound to anybody so early in his life. It was suffocating. "I don't want to get married yet, I'm…" He leaned back in his chair and purposefully looked away. "I'm a player."

Mokoto couldn't help but smirk at the sound of his sister erupting with laughter. He moved his eyes over to see Anaka rolling onto her side, cackling into the sofa.

"What?" Mokoto protested, his lips fixed into an almost laugh.

"You –" Anaka looked at him, her face still pressed into the fabric. "You are so full of shit!"

"I don't tell you everything," Mokoto insisted. "I've had more girls than you've had men."

"Oh really?" Anaka sniggered, sitting up. Mokoto moved his eyes upwards, pretending to consider her comment.

"Hm…" he uttered, and grinned. "Actually, probably not. You're a whore."

"Hey!" Mokoto leaned to the side, dodging the cushion that Anaka had just hurled at him. "I'm not a whore! I've hardly been with anyone!" Anaka snarled.

"Alright, I was joking…" Mokoto said. Although… as much as he had been joking, he was now starting to think that perhaps it was true. She was reacting much more seriously than he'd expected, and she did spend a lot of time making herself look good…

"Listen," Anaka began, suddenly changing the subject back to Mokoto's marriage. "We're members of the royal family, aren't we? We're the only people in the world that can marry as many times as we want – so doesn't that tell you that you *don't* have to be tied to her? If I were you I'd marry her – Father likes her and she's the best mother you'll ever find for your children." She shrugged. "But if you like someone else, marry them too. Or fuck them. Whatever. You are one of the few people that can actually do that without anyone telling you it's wrong."

"Yes, I thought of that." Mokoto nodded. "But what if she gets jealous? I can't be bothered with Lakuna giving me grief over it."

"Why would she care?" Anaka replied. "She'll still have your money – she isn't an Outsider, Mokoto. She isn't going to fall in love with you. All she wants is your money, and as long as you still give her that I promise she isn't going to care how many other girls you get involved with. Just make sure you make her children heir." She smirked. "The last thing you want is to get some nobody pregnant and give those children the throne – then she *will* be a problem."

"Of course I wouldn't do that!" Mokoto barked. How stupid did she think he was? "I'm not a fool! I'm not about to get some whore pregnant!"

"Perfect," Anaka beamed. "Then what are you worried about?"

"Nothing," Mokoto admitted. Everything Anaka was saying made sense. He knew it. He thought each of her words himself. He just didn't like the idea of marriage... But it was necessary, wasn't it? Mokoto was clearly at marriage age if the king wanted him to wed. To tie himself to this woman... Lakuna wasn't a bad girl, though. Not really. She had a few flaws, but it was nothing that couldn't be beaten out of her, and she was far less flawed than some of the other girls the king could have chosen. As a Hiveakan she probably wouldn't be too annoying either... "She might make a good friend," Mokoto thought aloud.

"Well, maybe. But don't worry if you don't get along – I don't like Teikota much and our marriage still works," Anaka assured. "Just promise me something."

"Mm?" Mokoto looked at Anaka as she flashed him a mischievous smile.

"If you do have other girls, seriously don't get them pregnant. You don't need to be *exactly* like Father."

"Anaka!" Mokoto gagged, half laughing and half insulted by her remark. She should know better! "You can't talk about him like that!"

"Why do you think there are so many Outsiders in our family?" Anaka giggled. "*Nobody* wants that many children."

"I'll take your word for it," Mokoto sniggered. "What if I told him you said that?"

"He wouldn't believe you." Anaka winked. "And you wouldn't dare."

"Mm..." Mokoto mused. Well, she was right. On both accounts.

XIX.

'A Goddess of love, Kala enjoys matchmaking. Whenever she is seen it is around a couple, who are newly wed or newly met. If Kala appears before someone who is single, they are guaranteed to find love soon. She is not judgmental, and she does not discriminate. Kala enjoys matching Hiveakans and Outsiders alike. Even if they cannot love, Kala has said that Hiveakans can form a union, and a union she will make them form.'

-       Extract from the Gaiamirapon: 'The Identities'

*

"So here we are, Your Highness." Lakuna smiled flirtatiously at Mokoto. "I'll admit I thought I would be more nervous, but you aren't half as intimidating as I'd imagined."

"Oh, shut up," Mokoto purred. He roughly pushed her further into his bedroom and closed the door behind him, casting his possessive eyes upon his new wife. "I can't believe you are reciting our first date."

"I'm a good speaker," Lakuna replied arrogantly. "When I say something it can be re-used. I never waffle crap."

"So what are you doing now?" Mokoto made his way over to her and pushed her onto his bed. Lakuna fell down effortlessly, without fight or resistance. She was too preoccupied with her new surroundings

"This is my room?" Lakuna questioned, gazing upon it in awe. It was incredible… Without exaggerating, it could cover the whole top floor of her old house.

"No – it's mine," Mokoto answered. "But you can stay here tonight. Yours is down the hall."

"It isn't common to share a bed with your wife?" Lakuna looked at him questioningly, somewhat taken aback by his response. Of course she'd heard that the royal wives had their own rooms, but she had assumed that Mokoto would let her share his, seeing as they'd started to get along so well recently.

254

"It is…" Mokoto began. He flashed her a wicked smirk, his dark eyes twinkling in a way that Lakuna had come to *adore*. "But how do you know you'll be my only wife?"

"Just leave me your wallet. You can bring whatever you want into this bed," Lakuna teased. She lay down, placing her hands above her head to stretch out her frame. Mokoto watched her intently, studying her. He had been intimate with Lakuna before… In her house, away from the public's eye. Not that his father knew about it. Lakuna and Mokoto had accompanied each other on 'secret' dates, dates that the king had not arranged and the media knew nothing about. So the thought of being intimate with her was nothing new to Mokoto, but… this was different. She was his wife now. He owned her. "So," Lakuna purred from her master's bed, looking at Mokoto with a lust hidden behind the veil of her dark eyes. "Do you want to make a child, Your Highness?"

"Not right now," Mokoto answered.

"Oh." Lakuna grunted. "Then goodnight."

She rolled onto her front and moved onto her hands and knees to pull back the bed sheets, doing it just slowly enough for Mokoto to react before she hid herself into bed. She paused, and grinned triumphantly when she felt a calloused hand brush against the top of her armoured skirt. He pressed down on her, his claws digging into her flesh as he tightened his grip on her clothing.

"I didn't say it was time to sleep," Mokoto stated. Still holding onto Lakuna, he climbed onto the bed and stood on his knees behind her. He shoved her onto her stomach and held her head down with one hand, firmly gripping the bottom of his own bloodstained armour with the other. They'd had a traditional Hiveakan wedding, and it had been a violent one. The service had taken place in a Taka-Kala temple, a joint temple honouring the God of War and the Goddess of Marriage. Once the service was complete Mokoto and Lakuna had proceeded with the Unity Battle, a Hiveakan wedding battle in which the bride and groom fought to determine who would hold the power in their marriage. After a long struggle Mokoto had won, but he'd paid dearly for his victory. His face was still bloody from the blows Lakuna had inflicted on him and she'd made a few dents in his wedding armour.

255

His bare forearms were covered in cuts and his mouth still tasted of blood, both his and hers. His injuries were nothing, however, compared to the mess he had made of her. Lakuna too wore armour, but as she'd wanted to look attractive on her wedding day her arms, stomach and most of her legs were exposed – all of which were now covered in bruises and blood. It was… 'desirable', to say the least. Mokoto was always turned on by the sight of a semi-naked Hiveakan woman, and especially one that was covered in injuries… and especially when those injuries had been caused by his own claws.

Mokoto briefly removed his hand from Lakuna, just long enough to take off his chest armour and the vest he wore underneath. He wasted no time in grabbing her again. He slammed his hands onto her and threw her onto her back, staring fiercely into her eyes. Lakuna held his gaze for a moment before moving her eyes onto his body. She loved to see him without clothes… She never thought he would be able to excite her so, but she had to admit that dating Mokoto had caused her to desire more than just his money. Namely, his Footprints, and his strength… and most of all, his body. Lakuna slowly looked across his steel chest, taking in the sight of his bulging muscles and the dirty yellow skin that stretched across them. He was covered in scars he'd probably had all his life; they were faint enough to prove that he hadn't been hurt recently – that in itself was a turn on. He was strong enough to take an attack, and Lakuna could only imagine the damage he'd done to his opponents. She liked to imagine it. How many people could he kill…? How many before he would even take a scratch? Would he feel guilty? Or would he take pride in their blood, and come home to unleash his Footprints upon her? His powerful, fierce, sexy Foot –

"Hey." Lakuna moved her eyes back up to Mokoto's as the sound of his voice suddenly snapped from her wild daydream.

"Mm?" she uttered, eagerly awaiting his next words. She had a vague idea of what they would be. He was so confident and controlling before their wedding, she was certain he would be even worse now.

"You lost the fight," Mokoto said. He threw himself down on top of her and stared into her eyes, his face so close to hers she could almost feel his Footprints stepping upon her lips. Lakuna could smell the blood in his wounds as his hot breath caressed her skin, causing her to tremble ever so slightly under the immense weight of his being. "I think it's your turn to undress." Mokoto spoke, his eyes flickering with a possessive lust as he gazed upon his powerless prey. "And don't stop until I tell you."

"Yes, Your Highness." Lakuna spoke the words mockingly, just to tease him. She liked to tease him... She liked how he responded. She winced and cried out a little as Mokoto sank his teeth into her neck, drawing out yet more of her blood. As if he hadn't taken enough... He growled deeply, like an animal warning off its foes. He licked her blood off his lips, glaring at Lakuna as the taste of her Footprints danced upon his tongue.

"Don't backchat with me!" Mokoto snarled.

"Sorry." Lakuna smirked again, her heart racing with excitement as she thought of the intimate battle that was about to come. Gods, she'd hit the *jackpot*!

*

'Mokoto was said to have found his perfect wife in Lakuna. She was from a poor background, but had excelled in the Hive and had quickly made a name for herself in the Keizuakákan army, allowing her social status to rise at such an impressive rate it drew the attention of the royal family. Although their marriage was suspected to have been arranged, they seemed fond of each other from the start and shared a bond that was considered genuine. They were often seen in public together, alone and alongside other couples, and had a natural chemistry.'

- Extract from history textbook: 'The Mokoto Era: 20103G - 20147G', 20160G

*

Burning. Lakuna closed her eyes as the acid of her shower tore at her skin. She washed it over her body, her hands scorching as the acid cascaded down from the shower head above her. It bounced heavily off the thick shower cap that protected her hair and the goggles that shielded her eyes, mercilessly attacking every other part of her body as if it were angry that it couldn't blind her. Lakuna had never used an acid shower before moving into the palace; they were too expensive. Now she used it every day as if it were going out of style; her skin had barely grown back before she started annihilating it again. She breathed deeply as the pain of her burning skin started to overwhelm her. How long had she been in here now? Five minutes? Just a couple more... Lakuna bit her lip, bravely enduring the physical torment she was putting herself through to last two more minutes. Five... four... three... two... one.

Gasp! Lakuna reached up and switched off the shower, allowing the acid to slide down and off her body before she took off her cap and goggles. The liquid moved slowly across the tilted panelled floor and slowly disappeared down the steel drain, bubbling slightly as it clumped like bile above the drain hole. Lakuna shook her head to shoo away the pain she still felt, and she placed her protective clothing down in the steel sink below the shower head. She took a moment to relax, smiling slightly at the feeling of her throbbing veins. Her entire body burned as if it were caught in Taka's fire, glowing painfully in a dark purple-orange shade. The top layer of her skin was completely stripped off. It would grow back within a day; Hiveakan skin always did. This time it would be even stronger than before; it would take even longer to burn away. This was why acid showers were so expensive... They were by far the greatest body enhancer and test of endurance modern technology had to offer, and it was no surprise that Mokoto had provided his wife with one. He wanted a Hiveakan woman out of Lakuna, and a Hiveakan woman was what he would get. It was also no surprise that Mokoto himself often used an acid shower... Just one look at him and it was obvious. The thickness of his skin and his incredible lack of response to pain were a dead giveaway. Scratching him was like carving into stone; his skin was rock hard. His shoulders were like concrete; his hands were calloused and firm... Lakuna sighed deeply and leaned back against the wall, closing her eyes in a semi-daydream as she thought about the Hiveakan masterpiece that she was bound to. She turned the shower on once again – this time with water.

Lakuna hissed slightly as the hot water touched her raw, sensitive body, but she soon adjusted to the pain and grabbed the tub of exfoliating body wash that she kept on another wall shelf. More pain shot through her body as she scrubbed at her flesh, removing all traces of dead skin that had stuck to her. She glowed purple, her shade growing deeper and deeper as she scrubbed relentlessly at the wounds. Her body stung with pain. She didn't care. Like all Hiveakans she was used to pain – and recently she'd come to enjoy it. After all, it was *Mokoto* that inflicted the pain... Lakuna's lips parted into a rare smile as she thought about the Hiveakan matat. He was so rough with her, so brutal... She'd had Hiveakan boyfriends before; she knew how rough Hiveakan men could be... but Mokoto was something else! Maybe it was his money. Maybe he'd had a better upbringing, and access to better training equipment at home... Whatever it was there was something that made Mokoto more powerful than anyone she'd ever been with before, and as much as Lakuna tried to fight him she couldn't. She wasn't strong enough. Her body was covered in bite marks, cuts and bruises... All war wounds from their lovemaking, and she adored it.

In an effort to calm herself from thoughts of Mokoto Lakuna snapped her eyes open, and forcefully pushed her husband out of her mind as she reached for her shampoo. She ran the liquid through her hair and fiercely scrubbed her scalp, the only part of her that wasn't burning. The lack of pain annoyed her slightly; it made her feel like her head was weak. Surely there must be something she could use to strengthen her skin without damaging her hair? Lakuna wasn't willing to sacrifice her hair... She might have been willing before, but now she wanted to look beautiful for Mokoto. She wanted to look sexy, and keep him interested in her... *No*! Stop thinking about him! Lakuna frowned at herself in annoyance, disappointed with her own lack of self-control. She applied a second layer of shampoo and focused on washing her hair, and eventually her mind drifted onto Gonta. She was slightly concerned about him... or rather, about what others thought of him. Gonta was settling into the palace life well enough; he got on with Chieit and he mixed well with other children when his strict tutors permitted him to venture out of the palace to socialise. He'd even charmed almost every member of Mokoto's family... except one. Taka. The most important man in the palace. Lakuna and Gonta had come from a modest family; their parents had never been 'poor' as such, but they hardly earned a lot. Gonta had always been a well behaved boy; he was friendly, and outgoing, and polite enough... but his manners were sometimes questionable. They hardly used cutlery in Lakuna's old house; cutlery was always considered to be a formal thing – it was only used in posh restaurants or for special occasions. Lakuna had never thought there was anything strange about eating with her hands, but she could appreciate why Taka might like to use cutlery when dining with his family. Lakuna had been taught how to use it in the Hive and she knew exactly what to do, but Gonta on the other hand... he'd barely had any practice with cutlery at all, and the look on Taka's face when he tried to use it... Lakuna had wanted to rip the king's throat open – and if he ever looked at Gonta like that again she would. She knew Taka looked down on Gonta. She knew Gonta was too informal, too common for him. At least Gonta was capable of being around other children without the parents complaining about him! In fact Lakuna had received nothing but glowing reports that Gonta was settling in perfectly. He was keenly adjusting to the company of his tutors and any other children he came into contact with. He always got along well with others and found it easy to make friends... Not like Chieit! That spoilt little brat that Taka adored so much. Sure, she was intelligent, but she was timid and hostile. How was she ever going to be leader of anything if she couldn't even get other children to like her? Yet Taka acted like she was the perfect child, just because she knew how to use a knife and fork.

"Stuck up bastard," Lakuna mumbled out loud.

"I hope you aren't talking about me."

Dammit! Lakuna's blood froze when she heard Mokoto's deep sexy voice. She hadn't even noticed he was there... Lakuna gritted her teeth and dug her fingers into her scalp, punishing herself for letting her guard down.

"Mm?" she uttered quickly, not wanting to lose face in front of Mokoto. She turned her head slightly to look at him, pretending she'd known he was there all along. "What if I am?" Lakuna purred silkily, her excitement growing as she waited for his response. Her heart was racing already, and he hadn't even touched her yet.

"Why would you?" Mokoto uttered as he approached her. He stepped up behind his wife and wrapped his arms around her, and Lakuna's cheeks flushed slightly when she felt his bare skin against hers. She looked towards the smooth part of the floor, just after the shower tiles. Mokoto had removed his clothes and left them in a pile in front of the closed bathroom door, using her room as if it were his own. He did that a lot; Lakuna didn't mind. She sort of liked it, but... he would never permit her to treat his room like her own. That annoyed her slightly. "I don't have a problem with your brother." Mokoto smirked.

"I find that hard to believe," Lakuna replied. She turned to face him, pulling away from his grasp. "You're your father's boy."

"And who is Gonta like?" Mokoto questioned. "He's certainly different to you."

"I was raised in the Hive," Lakuna answered bluntly. "You're comparing him to Chieit. She isn't a real Outsider. Gonta is."

"I know. That's why I wasn't surprised at him." Mokoto shrugged. "I think Father forgets that."

"He just wants him to be the same as Chieit." Lakuna huffed. "But..." She moved her eyes to Mokoto's, and grinned wickedly. "Do you think he'd care so much if she wasn't *Anaka's* daughter?"

"Why are you obsessed with that?" Mokoto growled.

"Just saying." Lakuna turned her back to him teasingly and grabbed her conditioner, applying some of the liquid to her hair. "I didn't know Hiveakan daddy's girls existed. She's his little gem. I don't know how you can't be jealous."

"Because I'm heir." Mokoto spoke stubbornly. "And you're jealous enough for the both of us."

"Me!" Lakuna protested, her brows furrowing. "Why would I be jealous?"

"Because she's my best friend in the whole wide world." Mokoto taunted, putting on a babyish tone. "I think you're possessive." He grabbed Lakuna's wrists and slammed her against the wall, forcing his body weight onto her to keep her in place. "And you're so used to being the only big sister in the house."

"Tch," Lakuna snorted. "Pathetic." She pushed back against him, causing Mokoto to hum in satisfaction.

"It is isn't it?" Mokoto purred and spun her around to face him, still pressing her tightly against the wall. "You're pathetic." He grabbed her thighs and lifted her up onto his hips, smirking slightly at her giggles as he nipped at her neck.

XX.

'Kala cries when a marriage breaks down. She finds happiness in love and unity, and nothing is more heartbreaking to her than a couple parting.'

-        Extract from the Gaiamirapon: 'The Identities'

*

"Oh… Mokoto!"

The words of Lakuna, screamed so often in passion and elation echoed through Mokoto's mind like thunder through a storm. Heavy, and loud… The angered shadows of lightning, merely echoing a spark that had already been and gone. It wasn't even around long enough to truly be appreciated. Was that a Hiveakan romance? A hot, fleeting passion that was over far too soon, followed by a lifetime of disappointment when the only thing that made you able to look at each other had gone to its grave. Mokoto didn't even know why he was thinking about it, nine long months after the flame between himself and Lakuna had burned so strong. Nine long months after it started to die. Was it dying right away? It never felt that way at the time. It felt like it would last forever… until it didn't. Then again, nothing did. Not even the king of Gaiamiráka – in fact Mokoto's very own future as king of the world depended on his father's life coming to an end. It was sinister, wasn't it? Mokoto wanted to be king, so did that mean he wanted his father to die? Not really. But he didn't want him to live forever, either. Nor would Mokoto's children. Even Mokoto himself would be nothing more than a seat-warmer one day, merely keeping the throne maintained until his own children were ready to take it from him. … That was of course, if Mokoto ever had children. It felt unlikely now. In this situation, where he was waiting outside Lakuna's bedroom for the doctors to finish examining her. All he could do was think and reminisce. Reminisce about a time when Mokoto was sure he'd been happy with his wife. It was useless, wasn't it? Reminiscing. Truly useless. All it did was remind one of the time they'd wasted; wasted on flames that once burned out didn't even leave a decent pile of ash. Still. What else was he supposed to do? Other than relive happiness, and remember that it had once been a part of his life.

"Moko..."

The memory was clear in his mind, clear enough that Mokoto could smell her. The scent of her passion, her lust... it was nothing compared to his own. Lakuna's eyes flickered darkly as she removed her silk bathrobe, revealing her toned, naked body underneath.

"Yes, dear?" Mokoto smirked at her from his seat in the common room. "You know, anyone could just walk in?"

"You'd better make it quick then." Lakuna approached him and placed herself on his lap. Without a second's hesitation she started to unbutton his shirt, hissing in bliss as he slammed his palms onto her buttocks and dug his claws into her throbbing flesh.

"Don't worry, it will be!" Mokoto promised and yanked her shoulders down towards him, desperately pulling her into a forceful kiss.

***

"Okay..."

Lakuna panted heavily as she lay back on Mokoto's bed, sore and exhausted. "I'm done."

"*You're* done?" Mokoto breathed from beside her, their two naked bodies covered in sweat and scars. "I did all the work!"

"You did not!" Lakuna argued.

"You did nothing," Mokoto said.

"Well – you were holding me down! I couldn't move!" Lakuna protested.

"I'm... not placing blame. I'm just saying..." Mokoto smirked slightly, proud of how helpless he'd made her.

"Well then..." Lakuna looked at him, her eyes teasingly flickering. "How about next time *I'll* be the master?"

"No." Mokoto rolled onto his front in escape, and immediately felt her weight on his back.

"That's not a good idea?" Lakuna sniggered as she tickled her claws along his spine. "You can be my bitch."

"Shut up!" Mokoto huffed. He threw his body up and his arm out to violently push her back onto the bed, and the two of them started laughing.

***

"So... your first night with Lakuna."

This was it. One of Mokoto's most memorable moments. He looked across the dining table to his father, as the two of them ate alone.

"Mm?" Mokoto grunted in response.

"How was it?" King Taka blatantly asked, without shame or discretion. Mokoto almost choked on his food. He felt incredibly embarrassed. Did he really have to answer? It was... his father. The king! But he was waiting. King Taka was staring at Mokoto, his patience rapidly running out and his anger steadily growing with every second it took for Mokoto to answer.

"Pleasant, Sire," Mokoto said, and immediately cleared his throat in an attempt to growl away his discomfort.

"How did it compare to the other times?" Taka asked. "Now that she's your wife?" Oh... This was why he was asking. He wanted the truth. How did he know they'd done it before? *Shit!* Mokoto's mind raced as he quickly tried to decide whether or not to admit he had been misbehaving, or to stay loyal to his façade. The façade. Always the façade.

"Sire..." Mokoto uttered. "There haven't been any other times —"

"Oh, come now," Taka huffed. "You are talking to the man who was famous for having sex behind his father's back." He looked at Mokoto sternly. "Do you think I don't know the signs?"

"I... didn't realise there were any signs..." Mokoto mumbled. Fuck. He was in danger now. How many limbs would the king break this time? There couldn't have been a worse time for Mokoto to get found out, right when he was newly wed and he needed his body at its best. Hm... but, actually... the king didn't seem too angry. In fact he looked rather... amused?

"There aren't," Taka sniggered. He took a large sip of his tetsa, and winked at Mokoto. "I just remember what it's like to be young." Then he started laughing. Truly laughing. Genuinely enough for

Mokoto to join in. It seemed wrong, didn't it? That a mutual disrespect for their fathers and a childish lust could be such a good reason to laugh.

***

"What's your problem?"

Lakuna glared at Mokoto. He was seated on the edge of the bed and Lakuna was standing in front of him, her shirt open and her breasts exposed.

"I don't want to." Mokoto shrugged carelessly. He looked at her in disgust, as if the very sight of her flesh repulsed him. "Why should I?" He rose to his feet and stood over her, glaring down at the pathetic sight of his wife. "It won't get you pregnant."

"That's what this is about?" Lakuna seethed.

"Of course," Mokoto uttered flatly. "What the fuck else are you for?" He pushed her hard, sending her backwards a few steps before she caught her balance. Without saying another word Mokoto left the room, and slammed the door behind him. That was the start of it… The start of a great bitterness between them. The world was waiting for Lakuna to conceive. The king was waiting for his grandchild. They had been waiting for almost a year. It was unacceptable. Mokoto looked like more of a failure every day, and it was through no fault of his own. It was her. She couldn't conceive. At least, she was struggling to. She was making a fool of him, and in return he treated her like the filth she was. Mokoto almost considered giving up; he wondered how easy it would be to get her to commit the mildest of offences and have her executed for treason. Then… just as his contemplating was reaching its peak, she was saved. The God of Birth had wanted her to live.

***

"Are you happy now?"

Lakuna threw a nasty, smug smirk at Mokoto, her tone becoming more arrogant with every word that escaped her lips.

"Mm?" Mokoto half-heartedly replied as he looked up from his paperwork, mildly annoyed that she had torn his attention away from something more interesting than her. Even the tedious errands his father delegated to him were more exciting than Lakuna these days.

266

They were always exactly what they were supposed to be, without a trace of disappointment in sight.

"I'm pregnant," Lakuna announced. She folded her arms triumphantly, the spiteful smirk still fixed upon her face. "I suppose sex with me isn't so bad after all."

"Hm," Mokoto uttered. He had to admit, he was surprised. He had become so convinced it would never happen. He had even thought of a way to have Lakuna executed so that he could start afresh with a new wife, without having to deal with her inevitable sniping. Mokoto had found a young, handsome nobody that was willing to say he and Lakuna were having an affair. It would be classed as treason, and punishable by death. Lakuna wasn't wildly popular in the Outsider community anyway, and Hiveakans could not stand disloyalty, so not much fuss would come from her execution. Mokoto was planning on having the young man spread his lies soon, but... this changed things. This little incident. This... child. It saved Lakuna's life, in fact. The Gaiamira obviously didn't want her existence to end, so much so that Tangun had blessed Lakuna. Mokoto had no right to disobey them. He rose from his seat and made his way over to Lakuna, looking down at her form.

"You don't look pregnant," he commented.

"You know how this works, right?" Lakuna raised an eyebrow. "It takes more than a day for it to show."

"How far along are you?" Mokoto asked. Lakuna shrugged.

"A couple of weeks." She shot him another spiteful glance. "Your sperm finally worked."

"My sperm is fine," Mokoto snarled. He looked her up and down again, and forced himself to pull her closer to him. She was different now. With those simple words, Lakuna had become significant again; enough for Mokoto to want to keep her warm, even if the fire between them had long since burned out. He kissed her forehead softly, and trailed the tips of his claws down her spine... then he released her. "Good," Mokoto grunted. "Maybe after it's born we can try for a second."

"Are you flirting with me, Your Highness?" Lakuna smiled, her eyes twinkling slightly.

267

"Hm." Mokoto almost smiled back. For a few short seconds, he almost felt the way he used to about her – that she could be useful for something. "Maybe. Go get some rest." He quietly moved back to his seat, and continued with his paperwork.

***

"Are you excited?"

Mokoto looked at Anaka's gleeful face as she stared at him across the break room table in the Royal Laboratory.

"Sure." Mokoto shrugged. "She finally got pregnant. It only took her a year."

"Oh, shut up," Anaka huffed. "It's not a year yet – all you wanted her to do was get pregnant before your anniversary. She did that."

"Only just," Mokoto stubbornly replied. "It still took too long."

"Well – I didn't become pregnant with Aourat right away," Anaka reasoned. "It took about a month."

"You mean… a month before you found a spare ten minutes to get pregnant?" Mokoto teased, causing Anaka to snigger into her drink.

"Five minutes," she quipped, and Mokoto laughed.

***

"Have you decided on names yet?"

Raikun met eyes with Mokoto, as the two of them shared a rare lunch together in a high-class restaurant, in full view of the public. Mokoto didn't mind having a media-friendly 'boy's lunch' with Raikun. He liked Raikun.

"We've narrowed it down now." He answered. "It's Thozo for a boy."

"Very nice." Raikun smiled approvingly, seemingly pleased with the name. It was the Gaiamirákan word for 'leadership', and very Hiveakan. "It's fitting."

"It is," Mokoto nodded. "And for a girl…" He was interrupted by his phone ringing, and moved his hand into his pocket to retrieve it.

"Anything important?" Raikun questioned.

"Father…" Mokoto replied, staring at the name on screen. He shrugged slightly, and answered the call. "Yes, Sire?"

268

"Mokoto, come home now!" Taka's voice erupted down the phone. He sounded stressed.

"Lakuna's been bleeding."

Mokoto heard those three words more clearly than anything else he had reminisced, as if they were more than just a memory. He could still feel his exact feelings; he could smell the scent of Lanka in the air...

"The baby's dead." He continued to stare at the floor as he spoke the words in his head once again. It was all he'd been telling himself for the past hour. Lakuna had lost the baby. He knew it. Even without being told he knew it. After spending months trying to get her pregnant... She really was useless.

XXI.

'Kala does not give up on unity and love. Sometimes Taka and Lanka will drive a couple apart, but Kala is resilient, and she will ring her bells and find her children someone new. When one half of a couple is lost, Kala will strive to replace them.'

-        Extract from the Gaiamirapon: 'The Identities'

*

Mokoto raised his head at the sound of footsteps. It was a doctor. No doubt one of the most skilled in the world. If anyone could save mother and baby from the coldness of Lanka's arms, it was this man. With his skills and knowledge, and with the money this man was undoubtedly making, he would have every reason to smile. Except now. Now was not the time to bask in his reputation. It had failed him. He humbly knelt before Mokoto, a look of sorrow upon his solemn face.

"Your Highness…" the man uttered.

"Is Lakuna alive?" Mokoto asked bluntly. He sharply gestured for the man to rise, and watched as he did so.

"Yes," the doctor answered. "She's stable – your wife will be okay. Your baby, however…" There it was. That look again. That pitiful, pathetic look. "I'm sorry, Your Highness. We did everything we could."

"She didn't." Mokoto stood up.

"Sir – I can assure you this was nothing to do with your wife. She didn't do *anything* to harm the baby, she just –"

"So it's just in her genes?" Mokoto looked coldly at the man. "Her biology is so useless she can't even carry a child? What the fuck am I doing with her then?"

"I –" The man's jaw dropped as he stared at Mokoto, gobsmacked that the matat could be so cruel. "I –"

"Tell her to sleep in her own room tonight. I don't want to look at her." Mokoto glared at the man and walked away, leaving the doctor to stand there in shock at what he'd just heard.

270

'On this occasion, the Gaiamira have chosen not to bless us with a child. That's all there is to it. I've been told it's not her fault. She did nothing wrong. The doctors said we can try again, so we'll try. We are hopeful, and we are praying. Whatever happens, she is still my wife. That will not change.'

-       Matat Mokoto, 20131G

*

Mokoto stared vaguely into space, his mind wandering slowly and steadily. He was alone in one of the common rooms. It was late at night and the rest of the family had gone to bed – Lakuna included. She'd been on her feet a few hours ago; she had tried to offer her apologies to Mokoto but he hadn't listened. He'd been too busy screaming at her. He'd hit Lakuna. Not for the first time. He'd harmed her plenty of times before, but it had always been with passion, with lust. This time, though… he'd wanted to damage her. He'd wanted to rip her apart and feed the pieces to the birds in the garden or the bugs in the earth. The only thing she was good for was making a child and now she couldn't even do that. Why was he with her…? They'd had a hurricane of an argument. He'd hit her, she'd hit him back. He'd called her names, sworn at her, called her useless, said he was wasting his time with her… She'd challenged him to go elsewhere and called him a spoilt brat that couldn't stand to be patient. Then he'd hit her a few times more… and he'd finally left the room when she was a bloody mess on the floor – and she'd still had the nerve to swear at him as he walked out.

That was what happened for weeks, every time Mokoto and Lakuna saw each other. After a while they'd become famous for fighting and the other members of the family avoided going in a room if they thought Mokoto and Lakuna would be there. He'd hit her, she'd hit him back; he'd say nasty, vile things to her and she would respond

271

with words just as foul… Mokoto was covered in cuts and bruises from the many times Lakuna had tried to defend herself, and she was far worse. He was angry a lot these days. In fact he was always angry. Lakuna was such a useless woman! It amazed Mokoto how there had once been a time when the very sight of Lakuna had turned him on. He used to adore her; she was a gorgeous, sexy Hiveakan woman filled with passion and charisma. Their sex life had been better than he'd ever had before and better than he ever could have imagined; she was so fiery and so reluctantly submissive that even the slightest touch of her claws or the quickest glance from her eyes could drive him wild. They couldn't get enough of each other when they were new… before she'd struggled to get pregnant. Mokoto only had so much patience in him and her lack of gestation had pushed him to the limit. The miscarriage was the final straw; he'd lost all interest in her. Lakuna was dead to Mokoto and he'd been looking for another woman for a week or so now, and as it happened a young servant had caught his eye.

Miama. It was her first name, and the first thing he'd learned about her. He'd first seen her dusting the furniture in his bedroom; he must have seen her a hundred times before, but it was only now that he noticed her. Even a beautiful face could go unnoticed by the man who could have whoever he wanted. He only tended to pay attention to the servants with red collars, until now. Now that he was actively looking for a new womb. Miama didn't wear a red collar… That was a pity.

"You would earn more money if you wore red," Mokoto said to her as he watched her move around his bedroom. He'd asked her to clean it while he was still inside. He wanted to watch her work; to watch how she moved, and how she composed herself… Technically, it was stalking.

"Oh…" Miama blushed slightly, and looked at him. "Um… thank you, Your Highness," she said. "But… I um…"

"You're shy?" Mokoto smirked slightly, drawing his own conclusions to label Miama in the way that he wanted. He wanted her to be shy, and quiet. The opposite of Lakuna. "I see. Well… maybe one day."

"Yes." Miama smiled awkwardly and continued dusting.

Mokoto watched her lustfully, his eyes moving up and down her frame. She wasn't dressed too pleasingly; she wore a long black dress with plain shoes and a dirty apron. Her autumn blonde hair was tied back unimaginatively, and her pale yellow skin was mostly covered by her clothing. What Mokoto could see though was her figure. She was a slim little thing underneath her clothes, very slight but well curved, and her face... she had a very pretty face. Very pretty. It wasn't painted too excessively, and yet she was one of the best looking girls he had ever seen. There was something attractive about her natural beauty... She looked so sweet. So innocent.

Mokoto smirked as Miama tensed a little. She could feel his eyes on her. Wasn't she used to it? That was a surprise... an attractive timid little thing like her should be used to the attention of a dominating Hiveakan male. Maybe she was used to it, but it frightened her anyway. Or maybe she fancied him. Mokoto hoped both were true.

"What is your name?" he asked bluntly.

"Um..." She looked at him and gave another small, timid smile. "Miama, Your Highness."

"As in the flower?" Mokoto questioned. Miama nodded, relaxing ever so slightly.

"They're my mother's favourite," she answered.

"What about your father?" Mokoto replied.

"Oh... I don't think he had a favourite." Miama shrugged. "Men don't, do they?"

"You speak about him in the past tense," Mokoto commented.

"Yes... he died. Three years ago." Miama lowered her eyes, her smile fading slightly.

"I'm sorry," Mokoto recited. Not that he particularly cared.

"Don't be. He had cancer – we knew about it." Miama smiled again. "It's just one of those things. I'm glad it's over for him now. He's with the Gaiamira."

"Mm..." Mokoto watched as she got back to her dusting, seeming a little less tense than before. He held his gaze on her for a few more minutes before uttering her name. "Miama?"

"Mm?" Miama looked at him. "Yes, Your Highness?" she asked politely.

"Would you like to have sex with me?"

"What!" Miama's jaw dropped, her eyes widening as she processed the question. "I – I –" Her body began to tremble slightly, then shake wildly. She was so nervous! Mokoto sniggered a little. He was turned on by her nerves, her fear. He liked how he'd so easily managed to catch her off guard. Even if she was an Outsider… Her extreme timidness was exhilarating.

"You don't have to." Mokoto shrugged. "But I'd like you to."

"Um…" Miama swallowed. "Do – do you mean –?"

"Right now?" Mokoto raised an eyebrow. Miama nodded frantically, her body still shaking. Mokoto exhaled deeply and replied. "Yes," he said flatly. "I'm not busy."

Miama stood there for a moment, stunned by his request. She managed to still herself somewhat, as she adjusted to the idea. Her wide eyes contracted steadily, moving from shock to surprise. Mokoto stared at her closely, instinctively studying every inch of her to try to predict her reaction. He didn't think she would say no. He didn't think she would feel comfortable saying no, even if she wanted to. He fully expected her to give in to his proposal even if it made her cry. What he didn't expect was what she would say next. With a huge gulp and a quick gasp for breath, Miama nervously and timidly stated her reply; "Can we go on a date?"

"Uh!" Mokoto choked at her response, so struck with disbelief he was sure he had misheard her. She hadn't just said that, had she? That hadn't just happened…? Had she really just – asked out the *matat* of Gaiamiráka?

"I mean afterwards. I want to see a movie…" Miama mumbled.

"Um…" Mokoto cleared his throat, but it couldn't be cleared. It was dry, and hoarse. His body was numb, as if the great God of War himself had just struck his sword right through Mokoto's soul. Never in his life had he felt so speechless. It was as if he were back in the Hive. "S-Sure…" Mokoto softly stammered, with absolutely no idea of what else he was supposed to say. He tried his best to banish the look of shock from his face, but he knew he'd failed. "Uh – whatever you want."

274

"Alright." Miama nodded, a deep blush forming on her cheeks. She put down her duster, and smiled sheepishly at Mokoto. "But... you'll have to be patient with me," Miama uttered. "I'm a virgin." "Wow...!"

*

'Fuck knows if he's dating again, he's not my son – and even if he was, I wouldn't know. I think you're grossly overestimating how much interest I have in my family.'

-      Malatsa Thoit, 20131G

*

"Was that okay, Your Highness...?"
"Yes. Very pleasant."
"Good. Then... can we go out tonight? You did agree."
"Okay." Mokoto would never forget how he'd felt after his first time with Miama. It was confusion, blunt and plain. Confusion over how to feel. He had never been in such a way before. Should he be shocked that a servant had dared to make such a demand, or should he be infuriated at her blatant disrespect for his position? Should he have her executed for treason, or presented to the Taka temples and honoured for her bravery? To this day, he didn't know. At the time he didn't know. He didn't know how to feel when she asked him out. He didn't know how to feel afterwards when she confirmed their agreement, and he didn't know how to feel that evening, when he paid an entire cinema to shut its business for the rest of the night so that he could go on a very secret date with a servant. He didn't know how to feel when he was sitting next to her, watching some shit that he would never dream of watching in a million years. Why was he here? Why wasn't Miama dead? Could he get away with slaying her now? He didn't even know how to feel when his father found out about it. Should he feel ashamed that he had stepped outside of the palace with an Outsider servant? Should he feel pleased in a sickening sort of way

that his actions would no doubt hurt Lakuna as much as she could possibly be hurt? Mokoto couldn't help but take pleasure in that. Should he feel proud that the beating he got from his father was something Mokoto's hardened Hiveakan body could endure? Should he feel guilty for causing his father to give him such a beating? Mokoto would spend his life never really knowing the answers, but regardless… Whatever the case and whatever Mokoto did or didn't feel, the events had still occurred… and they continued to. Even in Mokoto's mind.

Mokoto sighed deeply and ran a hand through his hair, fatigued in the moments when he wasn't distracted by his more appealing thoughts. He was sat alone at the table in one of the meeting rooms, working. He was only halfway through the paperwork his father had given him, and he'd already been reading for an hour. It didn't normally take this long. To be frank Mokoto was struggling to focus on the work; it was hardly captivating. Uncle Omota, the malatsa of the continent Haniaka was requesting a change in his continent's laws. The changes had to be approved by King Taka, who had virtually no time or patience for his extremist Outsider brother at the best of times, and especially not when Omota was once again trying to make his continent as Hiveakan-free as possible. Taka had ordered Mokoto to read through Omota's proposal and allow Omota to make some changes whilst keeping Haniaka's Hiveakan laws intact… which happened to be an impossible task. Everything Omota was asking for would result in making Haniaka less Hiveakan-friendly. Mokoto had no idea why the king didn't just tell Omota to fuck off; what did it matter what the people of Haniaka thought? Nobody liked Haniaka! Nobody liked Omota either – Mokoto had only ever seen him twice in his entire life. Still… this was what King Taka wanted, and therefore it was what King Taka would get. Of course. Mokoto read each word of Omota's proposal obediently, whilst half-heartedly attempting to fight off his frequent daydreams of Miama.

Miama… There was a pleasant thought. Mokoto had been having an affair with her for around two months now, and it surprised him how much he was enjoying it. It didn't make any sense. Everything he knew told him he should like Lakuna. Lakuna was attractive. She was a Hiveakan. She was strong, ambitious, aggressive, and apparently still perfectly able to conceive… and yet Mokoto could barely bring himself to look at her these days. To him she was a failure. She had taken too long to become pregnant, only to miscarry just a few months later. Miama was younger – only eighteen. She had years of fertility left in her and a big family. Three sisters and two brothers; Miama was the youngest. She was pretty. She was sweet, friendly, and energetic… Her skin was soft, completely free of scars or stains from a terrifying life, and she was so blissfully naïve. She whimpered so softly every time Mokoto bit her; she winced at his claws on her flesh, and on a few occasions he'd even made her cry. It turned Mokoto on that she was so obediently submissive and eager to do whatever he wanted, never arguing and never attempting to fight back. She was a timid prey; a frightened girl that had come along at a time when Mokoto had needed it most. When his Hiveakan woman had failed him.

That being said… Miama was not like any typical timid prey. She could never be boring. She was too unpredictable. Mokoto didn't understand it. He'd never seen anything like it, and he'd never thought he would. He never thought someone like Miama could exist until she was so obviously there. She was shy and timid, always obeying and never arguing… but, every so often, she would demand something. It was always something innocent, and always out of the blue. Out of nowhere she would suddenly demand that they go to dinner or see a movie, or that they slept in his room. It was amazing how someone so submissive had the courage to give Mokoto orders. The way she so blatantly told him what she wanted, and the way she stropped and sulked, glaring at him with all the rage of Taka when she didn't get her way. He found it… enchanting. To be frank the girl made his heart race; in fact the only thing more exciting than sex with Miama itself was wondering how she would react to his aggression, and what if any, demands she would make of him. Everything that was Hiveakan about him – no… Everything that was royal about him, everything that was self-respecting and proud about him told him that he should slit her throat every time she dared to ask him, Mokoto, the matat of Gaiamiráka, for anything more than permission to live… but, for some reason, Mokoto never felt the urge to kill her. In fact, he always became flooded with an overwhelming desire to keep Miama alive. Alive, and within his fierce and lustful grasp.

Mokoto looked up at the sound of the door opening. Speak of the ghost… Miama greeted him with a smile and bowed politely, holding a box of cleaning products in her hand.

"Sorry, I didn't know you were in here," she said. "I can come back."

"No, you have a job to do." Mokoto said. "Don't worry. You won't distract me."

"Then it must be very interesting." Miama laughed a little, completely comfortable with speaking to him in such an informal manner. She began cleaning the furniture, and Mokoto allowed his gaze to settle on her.

"Actually… you could do me a favour," Mokoto spoke, and met Miama's eyes as she looked up at him.

"Mm?" she uttered with another smile.

"Could you get me a drink?" Mokoto asked.

"Oh…" Miama moved her eyes to the jug of water that sat in front of Mokoto, drawing his attention to it.

"A real drink," Mokoto said. "In the cabinet." He reached into the pocket of his loose silk shirt and pulled out a key, tossing it to Miama. "Don't let Chieit look at it. She's into cutting keys."

"Really?" Miama sighed. "I thought she'd calm down with Gonta being here."

"He was the one that got her into it," Mokoto mumbled from his paperwork. "Apparently he's quite the artist. He can cut and carve anything with just one look."

"He's just experimenting with art," Miama smiled. "He's a good boy, he paints such beautiful pictures."

"Fine, Gonta is perfectly innocent. If Chieit learns how to make keys it won't be for the sake of art." Mokoto frowned slightly at the sound of Miama's laughter. What was funny? He was telling the truth. Gonta and Chieit were both intelligent in different ways; Gonta was bright, and he was a friendly good-natured boy. Chieit on the other hand was a genuine genius that entertained herself by building computers and decoding security systems. She was a liability, and a potential terrorist.

"I'll bring you something strong." Miama winked and left the room.

Mokoto sighed deeply and placed his cheek on his clenched fist, lazily turning onto the next page of Omota's proposal. Why had he spread this over so many pages? It was such a waste of paper. He could have sent over a holo-document... All official changes in law had to be written on paper, with the king's signature, but this was only a proposal. It wasn't official yet. Omota was just being difficult. Most of it was crap anyway; his actual request took up about a third of the document and the rest was just a lecture on Omota's own views and opinions of the current law, and apparently the views of 'his people'. How did he know that? He was describing the views of what, a few hundred? Out of the one million people that lived in Haniaka. What Omota failed to mention in his essay of a rant was that there were plenty of Hiveakans living in Haniaka who did *not* agree with what he was saying. Then again, they didn't want to live there anyway so maybe it was right that their opinions shouldn't be considered. The only people that ever left Haniaka were Hiveakans, the reason being that it was full of pathetic, idiotic Outsider extremists that made living there both tedious and irritating for anyone that knew how to throw a decent punch. Fuck this. Mokoto wasn't going to read anymore. He quickly scanned through the rest of the document just to make sure he hadn't missed out on any relevant points. He hadn't. He knew he hadn't. With another deep sigh, Mokoto opened a fresh document on his holograph laptop, and he began to bullet point Omota's requests. This wouldn't take long... In his unnecessarily long proposal, Omota only wanted a few things. He wanted less emphasis on combat in Outsider school gym classes; a heavier restriction on the type of firearms merchants could sell; a heavier punishment for Hiveakan offenders... that one might be acceptable, actually. Any Hiveakan that couldn't control his actions obviously needed more training. Then again... the death penalty for all Hiveakan offenders? Shoplifters as well? That was a little extreme... He could at least consider circumstances; Haniaka wasn't completely free of poverty, after all. Maybe if Omota stopped concentrating on

279

wiping out his Hiveakans and focused more on his own economy, it would be.

Interrupted, Mokoto smiled slightly at the sound of Miama's soft footsteps approaching him. "Here." Her voice came from his side, accompanied by the sound of Miama placing the cabinet key and a bottle of tetsa on the desk, next to Mokoto's barely touched water. "I wasn't sure how much you wanted."

"Hm." Mokoto's lips twitched into a small smile again as he moved his eyes to the bottle. "I suppose it's better to be over-cautious..." He shot her a teasing glance. "If you can't get it exactly right."

"I tried!" Miama frowned, genuinely insulted by his remark. Mokoto chuckled a little and downed the water in his small glass, replacing it with a large helping of the thick, dark alcohol. Miama's face twisted at the smell of it. "I don't know how you can drink that," she gagged.

"It's easy, darling. Try it," Mokoto replied. He was semi-serious. He'd never seen an Outsider drink tetsa before... He was sort of interested in her reaction, assuming he would water it down enough to prevent her dying, of course.

"No thank you," Miama refused; a look of disgust still upon her face as she stared at the liquid.

"Hm." Mokoto moved his eyes back to his document and continued typing. He could feel Miama's eyes on him, and his chest tingled a little with anticipation as he awaited her next move. Would she say anything? Would she go back to work? Or maybe she just wanted to watch him for a while... She did that sometimes. It was... somewhat unsettling. Mokoto hadn't yet managed to figure out why, and that in itself was annoying.

She moved behind him, and a soft appreciative purr escaped Mokoto's throat as he felt Miama's hands gliding themselves across his tight shoulders. Ah... okay. That was it. Her next move. It was the best thing she could have done. Well... maybe the second best.

"You've been fighting today," Miama commented.

"You can tell?" Mokoto smirked a little, somewhat impressed that she noticed. Then again... it was hardly unheard of.

280

"You're more knotted than usual," Miama replied. "You won."

"You can tell I won by how knotted I am?" Mokoto questioned.

"No." Miama laughed softly. "But you always win."

"Haha!" Mokoto uttered, grinning smugly. "That's true. Lanka tried to take my throne again."

"It's not your throne yet," Miama giggled.

"As good as," Mokoto arrogantly replied. He pulled his hands away from his work and closed his eyes for a moment, allowing himself to enjoy the massage. "Lanka's not even half as strong as me. She'll never take it."

"But she tries." Miama smiled. "Every day."

"Every day since I was thirteen…" Mokoto moved his head back to look at Miama. "Pathetic, isn't it? She's put her entire life on hold."

"It's admirable," Miama said. "She really believes she can do it."

"I don't think she knows how not to believe it," Mokoto replied. Miama simply smiled again, and looked back down at her hands on his shoulders, giving them one final squeeze.

It was over so soon? Well that was disappointing… But, Mokoto had work to do. He yawned and went back to his laptop, reaching for the glass of alcohol.

"You know… you look like your father, sitting there with that," Miama commented.

"So who does that make you?" Mokoto replied gruffly. Why did she say that? Was she supposed to have insulted him with that remark? It was a compliment!

"Your mother," Miama answered. "She was an Outsider too, right?"

"She was bad for him," Mokoto growled. "You aren't my mother."

"Was she that bad?" Miama reasoned. She ran her hands firmly down his bulky arms, leaning into his neck with her cheek against his. Mokoto could feel her smile. "She gave him a boy," Miama said. "A good one, too."

"Mm." Mokoto pulled his face away to look at Miama. "Is that what you want to do?"

"Uh…" Miama's eyes widened, and her hands suddenly stopped dead. Her body locked into place and her lips went dry; she was stunned. Did he… did he want her to…?

"Cute."

Mokoto and Miama both looked up to see Lakuna stood in the open doorway, her arms folded. Mokoto sighed in annoyance. Why did she have to be here? He was actually enjoying being in the company of a woman, something that never seemed to happen when that woman was Lakuna. Why did she have to destroy it? He had to talk to Miama as well… He had a terrible sense that she hadn't realised his comment just now had been a joke.

"What do you want?" Mokoto growled at Lakuna, eager to banish her from the room.

"I want to speak to my husband!" Lakuna hissed, moving towards him. She glared at Miama. "Last time I checked he only had *one* wife."

"I'm – I'm sorry." Miama's face went pale and she timidly removed her hands from Mokoto's arms, stepping a few feet back. "I – I should get on with cleaning –"

"Right, you should," Lakuna spat. "I don't see a red collar on you. Don't give it away for free, sweetheart."

"At least I'm not paying for faulty goods." Mokoto stared coldly at Lakuna, his fist clenching slightly as he became more angered by her presence.

"Oh. Sorry," Lakuna sniped. "You wanted a birth as well? You should have said."

"I… I should go." Miama whimpered, becoming frightened by the tense atmosphere between them.

"Fine," Mokoto grunted. He threw Miama a quick, soft glance before setting his eyes back to Lakuna, his shoulders tensing. Miama smiled at him quickly, and headed for the door.

"Bye." Lakuna smirked at Miama as the young girl passed her. "Try not to hurt yourself cleaning. Those bleach products can damage your skin."

"Thanks…" Miama mumbled and left the room, taking her cleaning things with her.

Lakuna sniggered slightly as she watched the door close, her back turned to Mokoto.

"Really?" she began, placing a hand on her hip. She smirked again at the sound of Mokoto getting out of his chair. "I'm not denying that she's pretty, but a servant? What would your father say?"

"Leave my father out of this." Mokoto's coarse, angry voice came from behind her. Close, behind her.

"Why?" Lakuna snapped. "You've made it personal. Do you think I wanted to lose it, Mokoto?" She turned her head slightly; she could just about see his arm positioned stiffly at his side as he stood behind her. What was he going to do, hit her? Hmph. Well, fine. "It wasn't strong enough," Lakuna continued on, not the least bit intimidated by the man that had the strength to kill her. She didn't think he would. She believed he wanted to, but she didn't believe he would. "The next one will be better, a true Hiveakan heir. We'd be halfway towards it by now if you weren't so busy fucking all the Outsider servants –" She gasped in pain as Mokoto suddenly grabbed her arms and pulled them back towards him, tearing at her shoulder blades.

"You think you're better than her?" Mokoto snarled. Before Lakuna could even reply he forcefully spun her around, keeping hold of her wrists and digging his claws into her flesh. He looked into Lakuna's eyes, smirking at the pain he saw in them. There was no fear, though… Not yet. He planned on changing that.

"Get off!" Lakuna hissed, trying desperately to pull herself free from his grasp. "You're breaking my wrists, you idiot!"

"I know," Mokoto replied. He tightened his grip on Lakuna further, keeping his gaze on her eyes. They were changing… steadily. Yes. There it was. That was what he wanted. Right now, it was what he craved. That look of restrained fear. Her pitiful mask was falling apart, although Mokoto was certain she still thought she was bulletproof. He had an overwhelming desire to prove to her that she was not. He wanted to hurt her. Truly hurt her. He didn't stop. He pushed his grip into her wrists, savouring the sound of her breaking bones and the

283

changing texture of her bruising flesh as he forced all of his strength into his hands.

"Mokoto!" Lakuna wailed. She closed her eyes and gritted her teeth, enduring the agony of him destroying her wrists. "Get the fuck off me!" She swung her leg out at him, catching his inner thigh as he made a half-hearted attempt to dodge her attack. Mokoto simply chuckled, holding the same tormenting smirk as he stared into her eyes. Why had she done that? Who did she think she was? There was no way in a million years she would ever get away with speaking to him like that. There was no way in a million years she would get away with chasing away his girlfriend, not ever in the Gaiamiras' world. He had a right to date Miama; he was the matat of Gaiamiráka! He could date, or fuck, or kill whoever he wanted! And nobody except King Taka or the Gaiamira themselves had any right to get in his way! Lakuna had no rights. None at all. She was nothing, and she would be even less without him. In the life of luxury that Mokoto had provided for her, she had obviously forgotten that. Mokoto felt a sudden urge to remind her…

"Lie down," he ordered.

"Why?" Lakuna hissed.

She was greeted with a harsh slap, one that she would have turned from if she hadn't taken the opportunity to claim back her hand.

"You're confused, darling," Mokoto snarled. "I don't answer to you." He glared at her. "Now. Lie down, and turn that disgusting face away from me." He waited for a second, long enough for Lakuna to realise what was going on. He wanted her to understand what was happening. He wanted her to know what he was doing to her. It would be a bad decision to kill her; for reasons that Mokoto couldn't understand the planet had forgiven Lakuna for the failure that she was. Killing her would do the palace more harm than good, and if he beat her the way he wanted to it would leave too many dark marks upon her skin. So… this was the best way. This was the best way to remind her, that her only purpose in life was to serve and obey him… and to never question the matat of Gaiamiráka.

"No!" Lakuna snapped. Her heart started to race as the sickening reality of what he was doing began to sink in, like bile in her

284

blood. She didn't want to feel afraid. She was repulsed at herself; she was disgusted by the fear she could feel in her heart... But she was trapped. She knew she wouldn't be able to get away. He was stronger than her; he could break every bone in her body, but it wasn't enough. Not for him. He didn't just want to hurt her. He was demanding something more; something he knew she didn't want to give. That was why he was doing it. He was going to rape her.

Mokoto briefly let go of Lakuna's other wrist to give her a chance to obey him – she didn't take it. Instead she used the few seconds she had to backflip away from him; she landed harshly on her feet and desperately raced towards the door. Ignoring the pain in her wrists she threw her hand out to push the door open, but she never even managed to touch its surface before he captured her again. Lakuna's heart stopped as she felt Mokoto's arms wrapping around her waist, pulling her towards him. She let out a scream, which was abruptly ended by his powerful hand. Nobody had heard it. Nobody knew what was happening to her. She was alone.

Still unwilling to surrender, Lakuna kicked her legs back against Mokoto, fighting ferociously as he dragged her towards the centre of the room.

"Stop squirming," Mokoto's low voice ordered from above her, followed by the vilest words she had ever heard in her life. "You'll make me come too soon." Lakuna's face twisted in disgust as she listened to his cold, dark laughter. It was almost ironic. In any other time and in any other place she would have wanted this. She would have enjoyed every callous action of someone she had once adored. But not now. Not now. She didn't want this. She didn't want this and he knew!

Mokoto positioned his arm across Lakuna's face to hold her in place while he reached down and unfastened his trousers. Lakuna growled loudly and began to move her head in a desperate attempt to break free. She managed to loosen his grip enough to allow her to open her mouth and sink her teeth into his flesh, as hard as she possibly could. Mokoto cried out in shock and flinched; he hadn't expected her to do that. In his brief moment of surprise he let go of Lakuna, just for a second. She reacted immediately, and threw her elbow into his ribs, pushing him back enough to give her a head start. She ran for the door again; her head pounding and her heart racing as a sharp, cold panic darted through her being faster than light. It pushed her forward, strong and weightless; she felt as if she were flying as she ran for the door. She was in a trance. She was in shock. She couldn't believe this. She couldn't believe this was happening. This couldn't be true. She had never thought he would do this. Even with all the hostility between them and with all the hatred he held for her in his heart, she had never expected this. Not from him. Her own husband. Her own matat. He was trying to rape her! Lakuna stared desperately at the door in front of her as she raced towards it, not daring to look away as if it would disappear if she did. She became closer and closer to it, close enough to believe she would escape. She was only a few feet away when an almighty blow slammed into her back and knocked her to the ground.

Lakuna coughed and spluttered as Mokoto's entire body weight fell onto her; her ribs crashed into his arms as they locked themselves across her chest. Lakuna winced in pain. Her ribs were bruised; her entire back and chest ached from the force of his weight, but she ignored it. She ignored her discomfort and struggled wildly to break free. She wriggled and kicked frantically underneath his body, using all her strength to try and push him up and away from her. Mokoto simply laughed, and slammed Lakuna's face into the floor, almost breaking her nose.

"You are a fighter, darling. You always were," he said. "Why couldn't you fight this hard for our child?"

"Shut up!" Lakuna hissed. "This is no fight! You're going to rape me! Do you really think you can call yourself a Hiveakan after this?"

"Yes," Mokoto purred, positioning himself on top of her as he returned to loosening his trousers. Lakuna closed her eyes and bit her lip as she felt him push himself against the bottom of her skirt. "A true Hiveakan never loses a fight." Mokoto looked down at Lakuna with a cold smirk and pressed his cheek against hers, roughly lapping at her flesh. He sniggered slightly when Lakuna pulled away from his tongue; he was delighted by her discomfort. He licked her lips, just because he

286

knew she would hate it, and he sank his teeth into her cheek. "I don't think I'm losing this one, do you?" Mokoto teased.

"Rapist," Lakuna snarled.

"Well. You said you don't want me fucking the Outsiders." Mokoto shrugged. "So I'll fuck you." His expression suddenly turned serious. Angry, even. He sat above Lakuna and glared down at her with the eyes of Taka. Dark and venomous; bloodthirsty and enraged. Then, he snarled, "And if you don't like it then I would suggest you keep your attitude to yourself – otherwise I can guarantee this will be the best thing that will ever happen to you."

"Mokoto, no!"

Lakuna let out one final scream as Mokoto lifted up her skirt. He held her in place with one hand, pressing firmly onto her back as he used his other hand to lower his underwear. He ripped Lakuna's off, causing her to yelp in pain as the fabric tore against her flesh and left a heavy burn mark upon her skin. With another dark snigger Mokoto attacked her, brutally and fiercely, wickedly smirking at the scream that escaped Lakuna's throat as she failed to protect herself.

"Mokoto!" Lakuna cried, trying in vain to get away. "Stop it! Please!"

"This is what you want, isn't it?" Mokoto roared. He threw his entire bodyweight down onto her back, grabbing her wrists to keep her in place as he continued his invasion. "You shouldn't have complained!" He closed his eyes and covered her mouth to mask her screaming. As much as he adored the pain she was in he didn't want anybody to hear what was happening in there. This was between him and Lakuna. Him and his wife. The woman that had promised him a child; the woman that had come to him with nothing. He'd given her a home, an education for her brother – he'd done more for Gonta in these past few months than he had ever done for his own niece in her entire life. Then how did Lakuna repay him? She'd taken as much of his money as she desired; she'd made herself at home in his father's home – in the king's home – and then she'd miscarried Mokoto's child… and all without a scrap of remorse. She just kept arguing with him. She blamed his child for being too weak to survive; she blamed him for bad DNA – as if he, the matat of Gaiamiráka had anything other than a perfect bloodline! She snapped at him for the way he spoke to her, as if he couldn't speak to her however he desired. She argued with him for looking elsewhere – when it was his right to look elsewhere. The most disgusting thing of all however, was the way she'd screamed at him for being annoyed about the miscarriage. As if the child had been nothing more than an insignificant parasite to her, a parasite that she'd been grateful to purge from her being. The way she spoke about it, it was as if she had prayed for the Goddess Lanka to take it herself.

Mokoto grew angrier the more he thought about it, and as his anger rose so did his desire to hurt her. He forced his attack on her fiercely, becoming more vicious with every movement. He sank his teeth into the flesh on her neck and he tore at her skin. He crushed her wrists in his hands and he clawed viciously at her flesh, so much so that his hands were soon coated in Lakuna's blood. He savoured the sound of her muffled cries and the feeling of her weak, injured body struggling under his. She never stopped fighting, but her fighting only made it worse. Good. He wanted this to be worse. He wanted this to be the worst thing that would ever happen in her entire life; he wanted her to be in unbearable pain and he wanted her to hate this. He wanted her to hate this so much that she would willingly go back and watch her parents die, just to end this. Never in his life had he felt so cheated by anyone; even *Lanka*, his worst enemy was a better friend to him than his own wife. It was no wonder he hadn't come near her; it was no wonder he had looked elsewhere – Lakuna was useless to him. *Useless*! Then she'd had the nerve to argue with him over Miama... He could see whoever he wanted; he could even marry someone else if he felt like it; he was the damn *matat*!

Mokoto closed his eyes as he listened to the blissful sound of Lakuna in agony. She hadn't thrilled him like this for months; he was going wild at the sound of her pain! The way her blood trickled over his hands, the way her skin so easily peeled away with his teeth... He was so enjoying causing this much damage to her. He was enjoying causing this much pain. He was enjoying *humiliating* her. Mokoto tightened his grip on Lakuna's flesh and uttered a low moan as he bathed himself in her pain. He smirked to himself when he noticed Lakuna had given up screaming. She was still struggling weakly under him, refusing to surrender completely, but her efforts were half-hearted and her eyes were closed. Closed tight. Mokoto moved his head slightly to look at her face. Her teeth were gritted and her brows were furrowed into a twisted frown. She'd surrendered. In a silent Hiveakan way. He'd defeated her. He'd *destroyed* her. Mokoto closed his eyes and locked a solid grip onto Lakuna's wrists as he finished his attack. He could barely remember the last time she'd given him such satisfaction. His chest heaved heavily as he took a few short, deep breaths. He'd done it... He'd done it. He'd shown her once and for all who was the dominant one; he'd shown her who answered to who... and she had better not make him show her again, because next time he wouldn't simply rape her. He would kill her. In front of her brother. Part of him felt that he should have murdered her this time, for her unacceptable attitude. She knew it was wrong. Bitch...

After a short moment of catching his breath, Mokoto raised himself up onto his knees and crawled off Lakuna, watching her reaction as he released her from his grasp. She lay motionless for a while, as if she were waiting for him to do something. Hm. What was she waiting for?

"Do you want a second round?" Mokoto sneered. "Like the old days?"

"What days?" Lakuna hissed. "Those were with a Hiveakan man. Not a criminal."

"A real Hiveakan woman doesn't get raped," Mokoto remarked as he began to dress himself. He stood up and looked down at her, fastening his trousers. "What next? You'll call me a monster? Tch." He glared at her in disgust, his face twisting at the very notion of such weakness. "It's that brother of yours. You're turning into an Outsider."

"Good," Lakuna replied flatly, her voice lacking any kind of emotion. "Maybe then you'll love me."

Mokoto responded immediately, by slamming his foot down onto Lakuna's back. Her spine cracked, so loudly its sound echoed off the walls and filled the room with the melody of breaking bones. Lakuna shut her eyes tight and battled against the pain that shot through her, forcing herself to hold onto at least some of her pride.

"I wouldn't bother," Mokoto uttered gruffly as he watched her restrain her screams. "There is nothing left of you to be proud of. You might as well cry." He kicked her in the side and made his way back over to the desk. "I have work to do," he uttered as he sat back down. He took a large mouthful of his tetsa and looked back at Lakuna, irritated that she still hadn't moved from the floor. "I know you can stand. Get out of here now before I *really* break your back."

Lakuna lay motionless for a moment. She kept her eyes closed and her body still, steadily gathering the strength to stand. She didn't want to, although she was fully aware that she could. She knew it would hurt, but she didn't care about that. Physical pain had never been much of a bother to her. What Lakuna was so reluctant to face was the inevitable humiliation of struggling to stand. It would take her a moment. A moment in which she would look weak and she would be weak because of him. He would be proud of it. She would look him in the eyes, to try and prove that she was not afraid of him. That he had not defeated her… But she didn't want to look at him. She couldn't bear the thought of it; it disgusted her. This was not Mokoto. This was not her husband. Her husband was a gift from the Gaiamira. He was a true Hiveakan man that believed in loyalty, honour and respect. He was a man that had made her happy to be a wife. This man wasn't him. This man was a monster. A bitter, cheating rapist that knew nothing of honour or loyalty or respect, or anything else that made a Hiveakan man. This man was… something Lakuna never wanted to lay her eyes upon for as long as she lived.

She had to, though. In this moment at least, she knew she had to. She bit her lip and fought against the pain as she leaned on her broken wrists to help herself stand. She slowly and steadily climbed to her feet, not daring to think what she must look like. How pathetic she must look. She could feel him watching her… She could see his sadistic smile before she even raised her eyes. She wasn't going to look at him. He didn't deserve it. She didn't respect him enough to poison her eyes with his image. Lakuna stubbornly kept her gaze away from Mokoto, and steadily made her way over to the door. Her back hurt more than she had been expecting. Her back, her wrists… Her whole body throbbed in pain, so much so that she felt as if she were about to pass out. She wouldn't though. She could handle this. She was almost gone. Just a few steps more...

"Aren't you going to kiss me?" Mokoto's mocking voice came from the desk. Lakuna stopped dead, her anger burning so much she wanted to vomit. She couldn't think of anything else to say to him, just two simple words...

"Fuck you." She slammed her hand onto the door, and pushed through the black dots that briefly dominated her vision as she almost fell into unconsciousness.

XXII.

'Taka has been known to change. To some he has appeared as a brave warrior, handsome and heroic. Though to others he has shown himself to be the embodiment of nightmares. Taka can be a comrade to those that follow him, but to those that go against him he can appear so frightening it will destroy their soul.'

\-   Extract from the Gaiamirapon: 'The Identities'

*

"Laku, open the door!"

"Just a minute!" Lakuna snapped from inside her bedroom as she desperately threw a scarf around her neck. She quickly looked at herself in the mirror. It was acceptable... She was wearing a long cardigan to cover the cuts on her arms – it was out of character for her but she had to do something. She couldn't let Gonta see what had happened to her. It would frighten him. He was too young. He was an Outsider. He wouldn't understand...

"Lakuna!"

"Alright!" Lakuna roared and marched over to her bedroom door. She unlocked it and harshly yanked it open, then glared at the young boy that stood there. Gonta. He had just finished his schooling for the day, and had come straight to her room. He was still carrying his school bag.

"Are you cold?" Gonta laughed, immediately noticing her excessive clothing.

"It's a type of training," Lakuna lied. "If you get used to being warm you can work for longer."

"Really?" Gonta looked at her suspiciously. He didn't believe her. He was a smart boy.

"Don't question me!" Lakuna kicked her brother lightly and allowed him into the room, closing the door behind him. She took a seat on the bed and watched as Gonta set his bag down on the floor. He always insisted on carrying a bag... It was what he'd had to do in his old school, where the pupils went home to a different building when the day was done. Now that he was being educated by private tutors Gonta could leave all of his things in the palace classroom if he wanted, but he never wanted to. It was partly because the bag was sentimental to him; he'd always been so reluctant to erase his old life... Even now Lakuna thought he'd preferred his old existence, even though he was so much better off in Meitona. He would learn, one day. When he wanted to buy a car or a house or a wife of his own... He would learn the value of wealth. He would appreciate that regardless of what happened to them here, their lives were still so much better in Meitona.

"I want to show you something!" Gonta beamed as he pulled a large sketchbook out of his bag, keen to show his sister his latest masterpiece.

"You've been doing hard sums?" Lakuna half smiled at the size of the book. He must be a genius to need so much space.

"Better," Gonta grinned.

Lakuna kept her eyes on Gonta as he jumped onto her bed to sit next to her, and keenly opened the book.

"Look," Gonta said. As instructed, Lakuna looked down at the pages, expecting to see some elaborate formula – the kind Chieit used to design her bombs or weapons, or whatever it was that she spent all day building with the tools her genius parents had given her. It wasn't a formula, though. Actually, there were no letters or numbers at all. Instead, it was pages full of drawings. That's all it was. Just... drawings. *Drawings?*

"Is this what you've been doing in your free time?" Lakuna growled.

"On my lunch break," Gonta mumbled. "And... in class."

"In class!" Lakuna yelled. "You're supposed to be paying attention!"

"I do!" Gonta protested. "I just do this a little – don't you like them?" His eyes began to glisten as he looked up at his older sister, his once bright pupils steadily dimming as the cold reality of Lakuna's anger struck him, as if he had done something really wrong. "It's Mum and Dad..."

Lakuna moved her eyes back down to the pictures. Hm. Well, they were accurate. She had to admit that. In fact it was amazing how well he'd drawn them; they could be photographs... but still. They were a waste of time!

"You can honour them by doing well in school, like they wanted," Lakuna stated. "Not by drawing pictures. Don't do that in class, alright?" She frowned at Gonta. "You can have two hours a week to draw – that's not including art class. Spend the rest of your time studying real things – otherwise I'm taking away *all* of your pens."

"I thought you'd like them..." Gonta quietly whimpered. "Chieit thinks they're good."

"Chieit?" Lakuna uttered, her tone softening a little as she watched a look of deep hurt sweep across Gonta's face, unrepressed and blatant, as if it were nothing to be ashamed of. Lakuna knew that look. He was about to cry. Gods; don't let him cry... she *hated* having to deal with his crying, and now of all times... She really didn't need it. "Have you drawn her?" Lakuna asked, trying to perk him up in whatever way she could.

"No." Gonta moved his eyes away from Lakuna, suddenly embarrassed by his drawings. He shut the book and firmly dug his claws into its shell.

"Do one of her. That's your next project," Lakuna instructed. "Two hours a week."

"You don't want me to," Gonta stubbornly huffed.

"Who cares?" Lakuna replied. "It's an order." She watched Gonta raise his head up, and she studied the expression on his face. He looked a little better. He was smiling, at least.

"You're not my boss," Gonta teased.

"Who said?" Lakuna raised an eyebrow. "You want me to beat you?"

"Is that what Mokoto does when you don't do what you're told?"

Lakuna froze. What in the Gaiamiras' world...? How did he know that? Fuck... Fuck, what was she supposed to do? She didn't want him to know... Lakuna had argued with Mokoto in front of Gonta, but she'd always made sure he didn't see any violence. He didn't need to see it; he wouldn't understand... How did he know?

"I'm worried about you," Gonta said. He reached for her scarf and attempted to pull it off.

"Hey!" Lakuna hissed, and batted his hand away. "Don't talk crap," she snarled. "Why would you be worried about me?"

"You're always covered in bruises," Gonta stated. "I'm not an idiot. I know he does that to you."

"It's not what you think," Lakuna said. "It's nothing bad. It's just..."

"Just what?" Gonta looked at her demandingly, his brows furrowing into a deep frown. Fuck, how was she going to explain this? What could she say...? Ah! Lakuna knew. The ultimate subject-changer. It worked in almost every situation, especially with Outsiders – and especially with young Outsider relatives. She smirked slightly at Gonta's expression. It was suddenly amusing, seeing that face and knowing exactly how he'd react to what she was about to say. Lakuna folded her arms and smirked at him, and calmly and casually spoke.

"It's how Hiveakans have sex."

"Ew!" Gonta's face twisted in disgust, his tongue flying out of his mouth in a gagging motion and his body dramatically wrenching as if he had fallen ill.

"Well, you had to learn sometime..." Lakuna shrugged.

"I'm never talking to you again!"

"Haha!" Lakuna sniggered at the look of sheer disgust that plastered itself all over Gonta's face. Phew. She'd escaped!

*

'Following her miscarriage the relationship between Lakuna and Mokoto became incredibly strained. He became verbally and physically abusive towards Lakuna, which caused some servants to fear for her life. Although Mokoto stood by her publicly, he seemed to blame Lakuna for what he considered to be the death of his child, and wanted little to do with her within the privacy of Meitona Palace. It is believed that is was due to the hostility between the couple that

295

Mokoto began his relationship with Miama; many historians have suggested that he would not have become involved with her, had Lakuna's child survived.'

-      Extract from history textbook: 'The Mokoto Era: 20103G - 20147G', 20160G

*

Lakuna spent days locked in her bedroom after Mokoto's attack, only coming out when it was necessary. She didn't want the world to see her like this. Bruised and scarred, but with dishonourable scars. These weren't battle scars. These weren't scars to show off. These were... deformities, caused by a Hiveakan who had gone wrong. As far as Lakuna was concerned he had even less of a right to show his face than she did. He did show it, though. Every day, boldly and proudly. Mokoto carried on living his life how he wanted, and it was mostly with Miama. More and more frequently, he found himself spending his mornings with Miama.

He steadily opened his eyes, reluctantly after a night of peaceful sleep, to the faint sound of birds. They always woke him up... There was a bird's nest above Miama's window, and unfortunately every single egg had hatched. Mokoto found the chicks' constantly high-pitched chirping irritating, but Miama liked it so they had to stay. Of course. What well-adjusted woman didn't want to be woken by the shrill cries of a group of overfed children demanding more food? Sometimes he regretted giving Miama her own room in the palace... Actually Mokoto had thought twice about doing it at all; he had needed the king's permission to give Miama a room and the king hardly approved of their relationship... In the beginning, at least. Eventually he had come round to it, and to Mokoto's complete surprise there had come a point when the king had thought Mokoto's relationship with Miama was a good idea. Apparently it would make the family look more in touch with the common people... Mokoto couldn't see how that was a good thing, but the king seemed happy with it and so that was that. There was one condition, though. Mokoto had to marry her.

296

Eventually, anyway. His relationship with Miama wasn't official public knowledge yet, but King Taka wanted it to be announced officially before it was discovered scandalously. It made sense... as cautious as Mokoto had been on their 'secret' dates, he couldn't deny that there was a possibility he would be seen by some disloyal citizen who wouldn't hesitate to go to the media. So... King Taka had given Mokoto a very clear choice; he could either end it with Miama and threaten to kill her and her entire family if she ever told anyone, or he could become engaged to her within the next month. It wasn't much time... but they had been seeing each other for four months already, and four months of an affair was plenty. In one more month Mokoto could grow bored of her and end it. Although... he wasn't bored of her yet. He had been thinking about it; if he married her he could get rid of her at any time, but if he ended it now that was it. So... perhaps marriage would be the best option. If she let him kill those birds.

"Isn't it sweet?" Miama's soft voice came from beside him.

"Mm..." Mokoto grunted. He turned his head to look at her. She was smiling softly, her eyes half closed as she gazed at him. They'd spent the whole night together, again. After Mokoto's 'incident' with Lakuna he'd finished his paperwork and gone to find Miama. They'd... stayed in. He thought they would go out; he thought she would name some ridiculous movie she wanted to see, or she would want to try a new restaurant that she wouldn't like, but she hadn't done anything of the kind. She'd wanted to stay in and just... be with him. Be with him. Be with him? What did that mean? Why did Outsiders always say that sort of crap? If he was there she was with him; it didn't matter if they went out or stayed in, she would still spend the exact same amount of time with him. Even so... it had been pleasant. Being 'with her'. They'd had a few drinks in her room, and talked... Miama had somehow known he'd done something terrible. Terrible by Outsider standards, at least. Not that she could understand... but as soon as she'd laid her eyes upon him she'd known. Mokoto didn't know how, and he'd had a reluctance to ask. She'd asked him if he'd hurt Lakuna, and he'd replied yes. Then she'd asked him if it was badly... and he'd said yes. Then she'd asked him if Lakuna was alright, and he'd said no. Then... she'd looked at him.

She'd looked at him so sweetly, so innocently… and with sympathy. Why? Why would she do that?

"You must be hurting." Mokoto recalled the words as clear as day. What did that mean? He'd asked her, of course. He'd wanted her to explain herself! *"Everybody has a reason to do things. She lost your baby, and she doesn't care. I don't think I could live with her either."*

Mokoto stared blankly at Miama for a moment as he remembered… that. She hadn't been angry, or shouted, or called him a monster… any other girl – any other Outsider would have gone crazy. They would have reported him to the authorities, and screamed at him, and run away… They would have made such a drama out of it and they would have told the whole world, but Miama had just smiled. She pitied him for it. She blamed his actions on a broken heart and wanted to do nothing more than comfort him. It was… somewhat pleasant. She was wrong, of course. Mokoto wasn't hurting; he didn't do that sort of thing! He was just angry. That was all. He was just an angry bastard that liked to settle things with violence; it was simple and plain, and Hiveakan. Just like him. Miama saw him differently, though. She thought there was more to him than that. She thought he was a complex creature, with a heart that could be broken and needs that could very much wound him if they were not met. Mokoto found it pleasant that Miama thought about him in that way. He found it pleasant that she was so blissfully naïve.

Miama giggled a little at Mokoto's response, and curled up against him. "Why don't you like them?" she asked.

"Why do you? They wake you up every morning," Mokoto growled.

"I know…" Miama sighed softly. "But they'll be gone soon, and then I'll miss them."

"I won't," Mokoto said. Miama laughed again, and kissed his cheek.

"You will," she replied. "You'll miss this. Lying here and talking about them."

"We can talk about other things," Mokoto mumbled.

"I want to call our baby, Toka," Miama said. Toka? It was the Gaiamirákan word for 'bird'. It was a very Outsider name… The only

298

reason Mokoto didn't call it ridiculous was because it was also the name of his uncle, whom he was morally obliged to respect.

"No." Mokoto yawned. "Anyway, we don't even have a baby. What makes you think I would let you give me a child? It would be tainted." He closed his eyes again and settled his arm around her, smiling slightly as she trailed her fingers lightly along his side. Outsiders had such odd fingers… They trimmed their claws down much further than Hiveakans; they weren't as dangerous. Actually, they weren't dangerous at all. Miama's claws didn't hurt… which only made her feel more innocent, and helpless. Mokoto couldn't understand how someone could choose to leave themselves so vulnerable…

"Mm…" Miama looked at him. Mokoto opened his eyes to meet hers, and frowned slightly as she continued to stare at him. What was wrong with her? Her lips slowly formed into a half smirk; somehow it was both soft and gentle, and wicked and gleeful. She stared at him unblinkingly, and meaningfully. Deeply, and knowingly…

Suddenly, Mokoto's eyes widened. His heart began to race, his body awakening with a start. What…? Seriously? She was – *what*!

"Are you serious?" Mokoto cried. Miama nodded; her semi-smirk growing and her eyes twinkling in excitement. She giggled a little, forcing herself to remain as silent as she could. She didn't seem the least bit intimidated by him – by his obvious rage! Mokoto almost choked on his own words. He struggled to get them out; he had no idea where to even begin! His body threw itself upright; he sat there straight and stiff, staring down at Miama's calm face. "Wha – Miama!" Mokoto roared. "Do you really think this is the best time to tell me?"

"I thought it was nice." Miama smiled.

"What about when you found out?" Mokoto yelled. "How far along are you?"

"A couple of weeks," Miama said. "Maybe more."

"*Weeks*!" Mokoto repeated frantically. How? How could she be more than a couple of days? Why hadn't she told him sooner? What was the matter with her? She was insane! The mother of his child was *insane*! How could she keep this from him? How dare she keep this from him! Him, the matat of Gaiamiráka! The father of her child! How could she – the bitch!

"It was raining when I found out," Miama sighed. "I didn't want it to bring bad luck by telling you."

"Wha –" Mokoto's eyes widened further; he clutched at his own hair in a desperate attempt to stop himself slamming his hands around her throat. What was *wrong* with her? Did she think this was a game? She couldn't withhold information from him at her discretion, he wasn't a mere servant! "Do you know who I am?"

"Yes." Miama smiled. "But I'm pregnant with your child now, so you have to be nice to me."

"What!" Mokoto felt like his head was about to explode; he was certain he'd never felt like this before. He didn't even know what this was. This - - cocktail of dysfunction! What had she done? What had she said? He wanted to do a thousand things; a large part of him wanted to kiss her and an equally large part of him wanted to smash her skull to pieces. Her devious, secretive, pretty little skull. He knew he should be angry, he knew it; it was a perfectly reasonable reaction... It was the only reaction – and a part of him was angry. A large part of him. The part that held his Footprints; the part that took pleasure in tearing apart anyone that did this sort of thing to him! But, amidst all that ferocity... this made him like her. Somehow, in the Gaiamiras' world, he liked her more now than he had when he'd awoken a few minutes ago. Why? Why did he like her? She was a traitor – she'd kept her pregnancy from him!

"I want to go baby shopping!" Miama beamed. "And I want to call my family."

"You don't want to see them?" Mokoto frowned slightly at his own question. Why had he just asked that? Of all the things in the world right now he cared about that the least – he didn't want to see her family. He could only imagine what sort of horrific people they were.

"No." Miama shook her head. "I think they'll be frightened of you. I'll go another time."

"Right." Mokoto put his palms down on the bed, vainly attempting to calm himself. He felt confused. He'd never felt that way before – not like this, anyway. He was always so certain. He was the matat of Gaiamiráka. He had earned the right to be here; he had earned his place in the world and he would earn his place on the throne. Things went his way. He got his own way. He made other people give him his own way, and they would be worse off if they defied him. This, though… This wasn't his way. Miama wasn't acting his way… and he could do nothing about it. This had never happened to Matat Mokoto before. This was like being back at the Hive. But she wasn't even strong enough to be a tutor…

He stared blankly at the bed sheet below him, as his frazzled mind tried to comprehend what was happening. She was pregnant… for two weeks. Maybe more. Maybe an entire month! An entire month and she hadn't said a word… He felt Miama's weight move from the bed.

"I'm going to feed the birds," she said from somewhere in the room.

"Mm…" Mokoto closed his eyes and sighed, throwing himself down into his dismay.

*

'Meitona Palace announced this morning that Matat Mokoto is to marry again. It was revealed by a spokesperson of the palace that the matat has been courting a young woman, who he plans to marry later this month. Details of the relationship are still unknown at this point, but it has been confirmed that she is an employee of Meitona Palace and provided support to Matat Mokoto and his wife Lakuna after their miscarriage last year. The palace has confirmed that the matat's marriage to Lakuna will not be affected by his second wife, and Lakuna is in full support of his marriage to the young woman, Miama, who she has come to call her friend.'

-    News report, 20132G

*

301

Lakuna's body froze at the sight of the single green line she saw before her. She couldn't deny this one. She knew she couldn't deny the first one, but she had hoped it to be wrong all the same... This was it, though. This was a certainty. Three tests couldn't be wrong. Not even the greatest doctor in the Gaiamiras' world could tell her what she wanted to hear. This was the cold, cruel truth. She was pregnant. Pregnant! Why? Why now? Under any other – *any* other circumstances Lakuna would have been thrilled, but this time... it was wrong. It couldn't be more unwanted. She hadn't even wanted to have sex with Mokoto, he'd forced her! She hadn't given him consent to come near her and this thing – this *parasite*... it didn't have her consent to grow. It made her sick. She felt physically sick, and mentally repulsed. Just the thought of it... all those months of trying in vain, desperate to have a healthy child but to no avail... and it had been this bit of rapist sperm that got her pregnant! Why was this happening to her? *Why*? Was the almighty Tangun mocking her? Wasn't he supposed to be a sweet, compassionate figure? He was supposed to be an Outsider deity! Maybe Taka was mocking her... maybe he was controlling Tangun. Maybe it was his idea to put this thing inside Lakuna, as punishment for her being weak enough to allow herself to be raped. It wasn't Hiveakan to be raped... perhaps the God of War had seen it as a betrayal.

Lakuna sighed, and grabbed her hair. She looked vacantly around the room, as if searching for something. She was searching for nothing, really. She was under no illusion that she would find anything in there. What answers could she possibly get? In this room, her own bathroom? The bathroom he had provided her, for the purpose of grooming herself to his expectations. Everything about the way Lakuna lived her life was dictated by Mokoto. She had never thought much of it before, but... really. What power did she have here? She was as powerful as she could influence him, and so she was powerless now. Obviously. If he had any respect for her thoughts or her status he wouldn't have put this unwanted thing in her womb. Her decisions were her own only when she was away from him, and even then she couldn't stray far without him knowing, and questioning her. It was a wonder he hadn't found out about this – she'd only managed to do this

302

test in secret because she already had a few spare kits, from when they'd been trying to conceive. Mokoto knew nothing about this. This was the only power Lakuna had. To be able to sit in her own bathroom, beside the toilet, with an array of discarded pregnancy tests and packaging in front of her. Why had she even checked? There had been thousands of times when she and Mokoto had had sex and she hadn't conceived. What had made her think this time would be any different? Maybe she'd noticed something about herself, something in her biology that didn't feel quite right… or maybe she'd felt Tangun's spirit looming over her like a lost cloud. A dark cloud. Either way, something had made her check. Then… suddenly, here she was. Here it was. The evidence of Mokoto's child. The child he had forced into her, against her will. Bastard…

"Bastard!"

Lakuna threw the pregnancy test at the floor and watched it smash into the others. She growled deeply and closed her eyes, wishing that she would just miscarry now and get the thing out of her. Just kill it. *Kill* it!

Actually… No. No… Lakuna smiled a little as a much more vindictive thought came into her mind. She could stay pregnant for a few months. Yes. She could carry this child. She could nourish it, and let it grow healthily and with promise, for just a few months. Just long enough for Mokoto to get excited… then she would abort it. In front of him. She would take a knife, or better yet her own claws, and rip the thing out herself. Mokoto could watch it bleed to death, on his bedroom floor. Or in front of his father's throne. That was it… that was her revenge. This parasite wasn't put here by Tangun. It was put here by Taka. It was a weapon, which Lakuna was to use to punish Mokoto for what he'd done.

She began to snigger slightly at the thought of it. Murdering her own child… now that was low, wasn't it? It was sick, and not something that any Hiveakan in their right mind would ever do. Perhaps her Footprints were made up of two left feet. Perhaps she and Mokoto belonged together after all. He might have two right feet in his soul. Ha! The notion of it made Lakuna laugh a little. This was sick… but it was right. Inspired, she half-cheerfully grabbed at the used tests and packets. She dropped them into the bin next to her and stood up to walk into the bedroom. Maybe she should even name the thing… that would be nice. Or better yet she could let Mokoto name it – and find out the sex! She could let him get to know it; she could let him get attached to it and create all sorts of fantasies of how strong it would be and how great a ruler it would make… and then she would take it away. Now that was a good idea…

Then again… Lakuna sighed and sat down on her bed. Did she really want to carry this thing for so long? This product of… rape! She'd been violated, beaten and humiliated… her body still ached at every inch, and she was afraid to leave the room in case someone saw her looking like this. It wasn't even because she was worried for Mokoto. Of course she wasn't worried for him. Fuck him. Fuck him, and his family and his reputation. She couldn't even say she was trying to protect him; she couldn't be that loyal or that honourable. The fact of the matter was that she didn't care if they locked him up or sentenced him to death for what he'd done… she just couldn't stand the *humiliation*. She couldn't stand people knowing what he'd done to her. What she'd let him do to her. She didn't want people to know how weak she'd been, or how powerless she was against him, or how easily he'd taken her and how she'd been able to do nothing to defend herself. She was wearing a ridiculous amount of clothing just to hide her injuries; if her ten-year-old brother noticed then everyone else would too, and they might not be so eager to believe whatever excuse she made for looking like this. She couldn't go back to work… everyone would notice something was wrong. A lot of them were Hiveakans; no matter how well she covered herself up they would still notice her scars. They would read her body language, her eyes… and as well as she might be able to fool the Outsiders, Lakuna wasn't sure if she could fool her own. They were some of the best minds the world had to offer; they were perfect at reading others; that was why Lakuna had chosen them to work for her. What if they realised something was wrong? No. No… they wouldn't! She shook her head angrily. This was ridiculous! Lakuna was an expert at putting on a front to the world! She could fool anybody, even them! How would they know what had happened? How would they know anything had even happened at all? She was hardly a nervous wreck; it was just a few injuries. She hadn't died. Gonta hadn't died. What else mattered? Just this thing… this child. This unwanted parasite. Should she even wait to kill it? She could do it right now, and she could tell him about it later. She could show him the pregnancy tests; she could prove it had once lived. It wouldn't be as fun; the less Mokoto grew attached to it the less he would suffer… but Lakuna didn't want it. She didn't want to spend another second with this thing feeding off her, and why should she keep it alive for him? She didn't owe him anything. In fact he owed her!

Lakuna looked over at her phone, distracted by the sudden vibrating on her dressing table. Shit! She sighed in frustration, and made her way over to it. It was probably one of the boys at work… they always worried when she didn't show up on time. What did they think could possibly happen to her? Lakuna looked down at the name on the screen. It was the king. Oh, what did he want? Why was he calling her? Why couldn't Mokoto and his bastard family just leave her alone? Lakuna clenched her fist, briefly composing herself, and she answered the call.

"Yes, Father?"

"Lakuna. Are you at work?" Taka demanded.

"No… it's my day off," Lakuna lied. "I'm here."

"Oh – sorry, dear. I would have come to see you if I'd known. I just wanted to let you know you have competition."

"Competition?" Lakuna frowned. Competition…? In what?

"Yes. You know Mokoto's… friend, Miama?"

"Yes…" Lakuna forced herself to not grit her teeth as she spoke to the king. She didn't want to hear that name. It had all started with that name!

"Well, she's pregnant. So naturally, he's marrying her within the month."

Suddenly, the world seemed to stop. Just for a moment… just while Lakuna processed those words. Pregnant…? Pregnant…

"You'd better start praying to Tangun, Lakuna. Maybe get yourself checked out – they said you're still fertile, didn't they?"

"Yes…"

305

"So do something. I don't want you to be upstaged by a servant; we both know I'll get a better grandchild from you," he scoffed, and grunted slightly. *"If he gives you any trouble, tell me. He knows I want you to be the mother of his heir."*

"Yes, Father..." Lakuna uttered numbly, only half listening to him.

"Don't let me down."

"I won't. Thank you." Lakuna heard Taka hang up as she stared into space, not looking at the phone. Miama was pregnant... Pregnant. Mokoto's cheap servant fling... pregnant. Lakuna placed herself down on the seat in front of her dressing table. Well... this changed everything. Just like that. Lakuna couldn't abort this baby now. She needed it to destroy Miama.

XXIII.

'A mortal was once brave enough to ask Tangun about Taka and Kala, wondering if they were married. Tangun did neither confirm nor deny, but the question seemed to please him.'

-        Extract from the Gaiamirapon: 'The Communications'

*

The sun's rays shone brightly into Lakuna's eyes as she stared up at the clear, cloudless sky. She didn't cover her eyes; she didn't mind if they burned a little. Why would she? It was a perfect day for Mokoto's Outsider wedding. He'd been lucky. The weather at this time of year could be so unpredictable... perhaps the Gaiamira were in favour of this wedding, after all. Or perhaps they were in favour of what Lakuna planned to do at it. She hadn't even spoken yet, but already she was amused by the details of the event.

It amused Lakuna how Miama had been in charge. Of everything, as far as Lakuna could tell. She'd chosen the temple, the prayers, the priest, the caterers, the decorations... Mokoto had let her arrange the entire thing, and there was not a single request he had denied her. Lakuna hadn't been particularly interested in planning her own wedding, beyond what kind of armour she would wear. Why Mokoto had even agreed to an Outsider wedding was beyond Lakuna. It was boring. All they did was stand there and say a few prayers, and then give each other an oversized necklace made from bells and Kala flowers. Kala flowers... they were called that, but they could be any flowers really. 'Kala' just meant they were blessed by the Goddess of Marriage. Kala's traditional flower was a foxglove, and as it happened Mokoto and Miama were using that flower in their wedding. Miama's idea, again. She wanted to keep it traditional, apparently. As well as the symbolic flower necklaces they'd also exchanged wedding jewellery – they'd gone for necklaces again. In addition to the Hiveakan-style chain he wore for his first marriage, Mokoto now wore a thick, solid golden chain, decorated with red stones. Red being the colour of Kala.

Not purple, the colour of the God of War and the Hive. These weren't purple stones like on his Hiveakan chain. These were red stones. This was an Outsider wedding chain. Miama, again. The bride in charge wore a similar thing; hers was thinner and more feminine. The underside of Miama's was decorated with some sickeningly sweet verse... Lakuna smirked as she wondered if Mokoto's was like that too. Lakuna never thought he would ever wear something like that, but now she was starting to wonder.

It meant nothing, of course. Lakuna knew that, as much as she was sure Miama didn't. She was sure that Miama, in all her Outsider innocence and naivety believed that Mokoto was giving her whatever she wanted because he loved her or cared about her... No. That wasn't the case. Miama may believe it, but Lakuna knew better than that. She knew Mokoto better than that. Mokoto didn't care about anyone but himself. He was only going along with what Miama wanted because he didn't respect her enough to argue; her opinion meant so little to him that he wasn't even going to validate it with one of his own. That was the kind of man Miama was marrying. That was the kind of life she would live. Lakuna would feel sorry for Miama, if she wasn't so excited about destroying her.

She looked around the palace garden at the gathering crowd. The ceremony had been in a local Kala temple, one that held some significance to Miama's family, and now the happy couple's relatives were returning to the palace for a few celebratory drinks. Outside. The 'outside' part was the only thing that would have been out of Miama's control, if she hadn't wanted an outdoor event herself. King Taka didn't trust Miama's family to go wandering around the palace, and therefore a large proportion of it was closed off to the guests. Miama's family were common people, who as a clan had achieved nothing that could earn the king's respect. King Taka didn't want them tainting the exquisiteness of his home. Hm. The snob.

It was just as well that today was a pleasant day; Miama had a big family... Lakuna had never seen so many Outsiders in one place. All of Mokoto's sisters were here, as well as Miama's many Outsider relatives. Some of the men were quite attractive actually, Lakuna had to admit… They were Outsiders though. Every single one of them. There was not a decent man in sight.

"Hey!" Gonta's chirpy voice came from somewhere below her, breaking Lakuna's focus away from the swarm of weaker beings that were steadily polluting Meitona Palace's grounds. Lakuna looked down to see her brother staring up at her with a small frown. "Who the shit are all these people?" he demanded.

"What?" Lakuna frowned. "Where did you learn language like that?"

"You." Gonta shrugged.

"Well… don't say it again. Not here," Lakuna ordered. "If Taka hears you saying that today he'll kill you."

"He always tries to kill me," Gonta sulked. "I don't like him!"

"Well, he doesn't like you. So you're even," Lakuna replied, holding back a smirk. It was immature, she knew… but she did take pleasure in knowing that Gonta disliked Mokoto's family just as much as she did.

"My hair's too short," Gonta complained as he started to scrub wildly at his new haircut, scowling at the length.

"Why? You look nice like that," Lakuna argued. It was much better than before! Gonta's hair had become a complete mess recently; he was starting to look homeless…

"I look nice anyway." Gonta winked. "Everyone likes me!"

"Taka doesn't," Lakuna remarked, and sniggered when Gonta stuck his tongue out at her. She moved her eyes back to the crowd, noticing that Taka was studying the guests as well. He had a drink in his hand… As always. That didn't mean much, but Lakuna could tell that he was judging the numbers, getting ready for the next event. Perfect… speech time! "Come on." Lakuna harshly kicked at Gonta's leg. "He's going to say something, so sit down. You don't want to keep your pregnant sister waiting, do you?"

"She's not my sister," Gonta huffed as they made their way towards a seating area that had been provided for Mokoto's family, far away from the riffraff that Miama had invited. Not far enough for Lakuna… "And she's not even showing!" Gonta protested.

"Well she isn't very far along," Lakuna reasoned. "And she's only small; the baby won't have much body to it."

"Yeah but he's huge…" Gonta mumbled. "Hey!" He grinned up at his sister. "Maybe he's not the father!"

"*Shh!*" Lakuna forced herself to hold back her laughter, but she allowed herself a small snigger and she pulled Gonta against her. "Don't say that!" she giggled. Gonta laughed with her and broke away from her grasp.

"Don't worry, nobody's listening. I'm not an idiot."

"Sit down." Lakuna smirked. She let Gonta go off and pick a table, watching him as he did so.

He didn't sit down. Typical. Instead he slid along the grass and came to a stop beside Chieit's seat, getting stains all over his new trousers. Lakuna scoffed in disapproval. Not an idiot? So why had he done that? He winked at Chieit and pointed his index finger at her slickly. She giggled at him for a short moment, before retching in disgust when she noticed the dirt he'd put all over his trousers. Lakuna sighed, and folded her arms. Great… now she would be getting daggers from Chieit's parents. She didn't need that. She didn't even like them! Lakuna reluctantly made her way over to the table, and smiled politely at Anaka and Raikun, who were of course already sitting there, quietly and politely, as if they were trying to set an example for everyone else.

"Sorry about him," Lakuna said flatly.

"Oh, boys will be boys." Raikun smiled, looking fondly at Gonta. Raikun was okay, actually. He was a rich snob, but he didn't seem to look down on others as much as Lakuna had expected. She didn't have anything against him. Other than his family, anyway…

"Mm," Anaka grunted, not seeming at all amused by Gonta's behaviour. Stuck up bitch.

"Hey!" Gonta dragged a chair round and placed it next to Chieit's. He hopped up onto it and put his arm around her. "Budge up, mate!"

"Gonta!" Chieit wailed. "Get off me! You've got dirt on your hands!"

"Oh – sorry." Gonta licked his palms and grinned at her. "Clean now – see?"

310

"*Ew!*" Chieit screamed as he shoved his hands into her pristine face. She turned her head away and fiercely swiped at his hands, gagging as he tried to touch her.

"Gonta!" Lakuna snapped. "Stop it."

"Tch." Gonta folded his arms and sat in an over-exaggerated sulk, as if he were genuinely annoyed that he had to sit down and be quiet. He sort of was... He was only acting like this because he didn't like the fact that Mokoto had taken another wife. What was wrong with Lakuna? Why wasn't she good enough? As far as Gonta was concerned, Mokoto shouldn't have married Lakuna if he wasn't happy with her.

He yawned dramatically and let out a sigh, making everyone fully aware of how bored he was. Lakuna ignored him and took the closest spare seat, beside Raikun.

"How are you, Lakuna?" Raikun asked her politely. "I haven't seen you much lately."

"No... work." Lakuna smiled at him. "You must know, being workaholics."

"Oh, actually I'm proud of myself!" Anaka insisted. She held up her phone. "I've only made *one* work call all day."

"Well done!" Lakuna almost laughed falsely, but she really couldn't be bothered. She'd never really had much time for Anaka... Anaka was the worst snob of all – she was completely stuck up, so much so that it was painfully obvious, but she was forever casting fake smiles and pretending like she actually approved of Lakuna and Gonta being in her life, making out like she didn't hate the fact that they, with all their commonness and dirt, were part of her precious rich family. Yes. The rich family full of scandals, murderers and rapists. Bitch.

"Mm..." Raikun uttered. He half-smirked at Lakuna. "Don't be too impressed. I've been holding onto her phone all day. She couldn't be trusted with it herself."

"Whatever." Anaka pouted and took a sip of her drink, then nodded towards her father. "It's starting."

Lakuna moved her head to look towards King Taka. Ah... there he was. At a table next to Lakuna's, he was standing proudly above the seated members of his family. What a pretty picture. His son and heir Mokoto with the beautiful Miama to King Taka's left, and to

311

his right his loyal wife Kaeila. That woman deserved an honour from the Gaiamira; Lakuna had no idea how anyone could stay in this family for so long – and an Outsider, of all people. Then next to her there was legendary Malatsa Thoit, who no doubt was under strict orders to behave himself. He was sitting beside his wife Keika Haliku, and their children Matat Nomizon and Meitat Teisumi, Teisumi's husband Sutan, and their daughter Meitin. There was a dog around here somewhere, possibly under the clothed table, Lakuna couldn't see. Thoit had a habit of bringing at least one animal with him whenever he visited. As company, perhaps. He never did seem to get along with his wife… Right now, Malatsa Thoit looked bored out of his mind. Oh well. Lakuna smirked a little. He would be entertained soon.

"Greetings to my friends and family…" Taka smiled as he began his well-rehearsed pile of bullshit.

"Thoit looks thrilled as ever." Raikun chuckled.

"Father banned him from smoking." Anaka smirked. "And he has to sit next to Haliku."

"If he doesn't like her why don't they get divorced?" Chieit questioned.

"That's a very good question, Chieit…" Raikun mumbled. "Your mother has been asking him that for years."

"Sometimes it's easier to stay married even if you don't like them." Lakuna shrugged, half listening to their conversation and half listening to Taka. Not long now…

"Easier for her, maybe. He has nothing to gain from that relationship," Anaka said.

"I suppose she makes him look good in the media," Raikun reasoned.

"Oh – since when has Uncle Thoit ever cared about *that*?"

"That's true…"

Lakuna tuned out of the conversation and stared at Taka. She patiently listened with a respectful smile on her face, seemingly moved as he congratulated his son and heir. How nice. It was a lovely speech, no doubt it would have been at the front of every paper and website in the world… if Lakuna didn't have something so much more interesting to say.

"Now, if you would all join me..." Taka raised his glass and smiled fondly at the crowd. Lakuna had to snigger at Thoit; he looked up at Taka and took hold of his glass as if he'd just woken from a heavy nap, and was now just copying everyone else to try and look like he'd been paying attention the whole time. Actually, that was probably accurate. Thoit didn't look like he'd listened to a single word of his brother's speech, and he was now staring at Taka, impatiently waiting for him to get this shit over with. Taka carried on. "I would like to wish the best of fortune upon Mokoto and Miama." He looked down at his son and new daughter, as if he could ever be proud that Mokoto had brought a servant into the family. "May the Gaiamira watch over you and forever protect you, your marriage and your children."

"Yes." With a sudden rush of adrenalin, Lakuna found herself standing with her own drink before the word had even left her mouth. She cleared her throat and waited a moment for the crowd to turn to her. She wanted all of them to hear this; every last one. She felt ever so calm as she looked at their surprised faces, and as much as she half-heartedly tried, she could not stop her lips forming into a large, victorious smirk as she spoke the words she had been waiting to speak all day. "And may the Gaiamira watch over my child – or should I say 'our' child, for eternity." She winked at Mokoto. "Here's to Moko Junior. Let's hope it's a boy." She downed her drink and listened to the sound of Uncle Thoit erupting into laughter, and with keen eyes she watched triumphantly as Taka's and Mokoto's faces became plastered with a twisted mix of shock and horror. *Bingo.* Now that's how it's done.

XXIV

'The doctor knew he had seen the Gaiamira, and he knew the child they had given him was theirs. They had asked him never to reveal her identity to anyone, and to raise her as his daughter. The doctor did so willingly, of course. He raised the child alongside his own, and when people asked he said he had chosen her name himself. As far as the other mortals were concerned, Aleisa was his child.'

-        Extract from the Aleisapon: 'The Exile'

*

"What the fuck were you doing?" The thunderous voice of King Taka echoed off the walls of his meeting room as he screamed at his son with all the rage of the God of War, his Footprints galloping to the front of his being as if they were about to kick the life out of Mokoto's skull. "Why is Miama carrying your child if Lakuna is pregnant?"

"I didn't know she was pregnant, Sire!" Mokoto insisted. He turned to look at the Hiveakan woman that was seated behind him, half-heartedly attempting to not look pleased with herself. The bitch... The lying, deceitful bitch!

It was shortly after the celebrations were over, and hours after Lakuna's catastrophic announcement. The family had spent the day smiling and acting as if nothing were wrong, as if they all knew that Mokoto had two children on the way... It was only after the guests had left and it was safe to raise his voice and unleash his Footprints that King Taka had summoned Mokoto into his meeting room. Mokoto, Lakuna and Miama... Uncle Thoit was there as well, against King Taka's wishes. Thoit had refused to leave, and eventually the king had run out of patience, so much so that he had none left to argue with. Now Thoit was sitting beside the women, smoking, and making as many mocking and argumentative remarks as he saw fit. At least the dog wasn't here; that was with Nomizon and the other members of Mokoto's family elsewhere in the palace. Mokoto glared at Lakuna.

Fiercely, as if he were trying to kill her with his eyes. She simply stared back with a satisfied smirk upon her face. She knew he couldn't hurt her. He couldn't touch her. It would be a crime against the God of Birth to harm a pregnant woman, and as if that were not motivation enough to keep his distance, they both knew that King Taka would kill Mokoto if he caused any harm to Lakuna's child. This child was a Hiveakan pureblood. Its mother was a valued member of society. This unborn child was worth more than Miama's life, and everyone in the room knew it.

"You didn't know?" Taka snarled. "Were you not educated in the Hive, child? Don't you know how a woman gets pregnant? Two unplanned children within weeks of each other, how can you be so careless?"

"Ha!" Uncle Thoit snorted, from behind the comfort of his tonito cigarette. "Fuck me," he remarked. "If that isn't the pot calling the kettle an even bigger fucking cunt than him."

Lakuna bit her lip, trying desperately not to laugh at Uncle Thoit's comment. He had such a brilliant way of putting things…

"Thoit. Stay out of this," Taka hissed. "This is my son, and my daughters. It is nothing to do with you."

"Oh, no. Not now, it's not," Thoit sniped. "But when they've got you into a hole and you come running to me for advice, then they're mine as well." He took another drag of his cigarette, and exhaled. "You are lucky he only has two pregnant wives. How many did you have at his age? And you were king. You were in no position to get away with it."

"*Thoit!*" Taka roared. "Yes, I am the king! I am the king and you are a malatsa, and I am *ordering* you to shut your mouth." He stared at Thoit fiercely, his face deadly serious. He was not playing. It was a real order, and he expected Thoit to comply. "You know the penalty for treason?"

"Thank fuck." Thoit sighed. "A reason to go against you, as if I didn't have enough."

Taka waved a hand at him, dismissing Thoit's very being as if he wasn't even worthy of dealing with. He turned back to Mokoto, and looked between him and Lakuna.

315

"I thought the two of you weren't getting along?" he spoke. "Isn't that why you found her?" He gestured towards Miama, not looking at the girl. Miama stared down at the floor timidly, not daring to look up. She was frightened. What was going to happen now? She feared for herself, and for her child. She knew Lakuna's baby would matter more to Taka. She knew she was nothing. She wasn't the general of an army, or a Hiveakan, or anyone important... She knew the world wouldn't care if she disappeared. Miama didn't know much about politics, but she knew enough to understand that this family would be in a better position without her and her baby. So where would that leave her...? "So where has this child come from?" Taka continued, looking at Mokoto. "Have you patched things up?" He moved his eyes to Lakuna. "Lakuna?"

Lakuna remained silent, unsure of what she should say. Her silence was enough. Her reluctance to speak and Mokoto's refusal to look at her... even an Outsider could work it out.

"Fuck!" Thoit spat. He stood up, and turned to his nephew, his shoulders hunched as if he were about to attack. "Who does that?"

"Thoit," Taka spoke. "Let me deal with him."

Thoit remained silent for a moment, quite obviously considering whether it was worth pushing his fist into Mokoto's skull. Eventually, he backed down, allowing his brother to take the lead. He took a seat beside Miama and sat ready to rise again, as if he were protecting her from the three ferocious creatures that could turn on her at any moment. "Lakuna," Taka began. "Do you intend to keep the child?"

"It is an offence to the Gaiamira to abort, Sire," Lakuna answered. That was true, it was an offence... but in modern society, not illegal. The God of Birth was said to forgive women in... 'certain' circumstances.

"That is not what I asked," Taka replied. He looked at her sternly, unblinking. "Do you intend to keep it?"

"Yes," Lakuna stated.

"Please," Miama whimpered.

She looked up at Taka pleading, the fear in her soul brightening her widened eyes. They were damp. She was coming close to tears. "Let me keep mine. I – I'll go," she stammered. "I'll change my name; I'll register someone else as the father. You'll never hear from me again, I promise –"

"You'll do none of that," Thoit interrupted her. "His father had to live with the consequences of his actions. He will as well." He looked at the king. "Won't he, Sire?"

"Of course," Taka stated, as if the answer were obvious.

Mokoto clenched his fists, fighting against his Footprints as he forcefully urged them to stand down. They wanted to kill her. He wanted to kill her. Lakuna. He wanted to rip her to shreds – how could she do this? How could she torment him and his family in such a way? If she had just conceived a healthy child to begin with, Miama wouldn't even be here! Lakuna had wasted everybody's time, and embarrassed this family in a way from which it would take years to recover. Why had she done this? If she had just got it right to begin with; if she had just conceived when she was supposed to... But what if she lost this one as well? She had created all this drama; she had embarrassed the family in front of the world, and what if it all turned out to be for nothing? It was unacceptable. She deserved to be sliced by the God of War – how could she do this to him?

"But I was punished, Thoit." Taka looked at Mokoto, and the younger man stiffened. He knew what was coming. Obviously. His father was about to beat him. Almost to death, Mokoto assumed. It was reasonable... "Get them out of here."

"Actually, Sire, I'd like to watch." Lakuna smirked, much to Thoit's amusement. He laughed, and took another drag of his cigarette.

"No, no... the child doesn't need to hear its father go through that," he sniggered. "Come on, dears." He stood up, and pulled Miama to her feet. She still looked terrified. "It's alright," Thoit assured her. "He'll be fine. He'll be a brat for many years to come, just like his father." Miama didn't dare answer; she was too afraid. Thoit gestured for the women to leave the room, amused once more by the look of disappointment on Lakuna's face.

Thoit followed them outside. He closed the door and told them to join the family; he would be along in a moment. He watched them leave, and he waited outside the room, his cigarette still alight. He smoked carelessly, listening to the sound of his only Hiveakan nephew being beaten. Broken bones, torn ligaments, repressed screams... Mokoto was quite a strong boy; Thoit hardly heard a noise out of him. Taka had screamed when his parents had beaten him over Kaeila's pregnancy. Then again, Taka had been much younger... not that it had made a difference. Kaeila was still a servant, and the child was still conceived out of wedlock, and a rushed wedding had followed... Hm. Thoit snorted. So history repeated itself, did it? Well, in that case... Nomizon was fucked.

He turned his head slightly when the noises stopped. Silence... Was it over? An Outsider would be dead by now. Perhaps Mokoto was dead; part of Thoit didn't give a fuck. He took another drag of his cigarette, and stepped into the room.

As he'd expected, Mokoto was a bloody mess on the floor. He hadn't tried to defend himself; he had allowed himself to be beaten by a figure of authority, as any well-raised Hiveakan would. The boy was panting breathlessly, most of his body shattered... it wasn't typical for the groom to be so bloodied at an Outsider wedding. It was because of choices, though. His responsibilities. It was all the boy deserved after what he'd done to Lakuna. Thoit grunted, and watched as Taka poured himself a drink of tetsa, leaning against his desk.

"Do you want a drink, Thoit?" Taka offered.

"Yes." Thoit nodded. Taka held his glass out to Thoit, and started to pour himself another. "Thank you." Thoit spoke politely, his eyes moving to Mokoto. "Well, you'll be no good tonight," he said. "But you understand this had to happen? It happened to your father – and there were two of them that beat him." He took a sip of his drink, and sniggered. "Your grandmother was a fucking lunatic."

"Thoit," Taka growled, shooting a stern glare at his brother. He hated Thoit speaking ill of their mother; even after all these years Taka remained convinced that she was listening, and that she would curse them if they ever said a bad word about her.

"Fuck it, let her take me," Thoit snorted. "At least it will be for something *I* did for a change."

Taka rolled his eyes, and allowed Thoit to continue uninterrupted. Thoit was going to say his piece regardless; it was pointless arguing. "The thing is," Thoit began, gazing down at his nephew. "I was responsible for your father's behaviour." Mokoto listened as best he could, through the ringing in his ears and the blood in his eyes. He spat his own blood out of his mouth for the sixth time; it was a miracle he still had his teeth. His father had been careful not to knock them out... Mokoto still had to look good in photographs. "So whenever he did something wrong, your grandmother blamed me," Thoit said. "Do you remember, Taka?"

"Yes." Taka sighed, taking a sip of his own drink. "What's your point, Thoit?"

"Whenever you got beaten, I would get beaten worse. Remember?" Thoit looked at Taka, and he watched the younger man steadily tense. Taka was not an idiot, and he knew his brother well. He knew where this was heading; Thoit had expected him to know.

"Thoit..." Taka warned. "*Stop.*"

Thoit downed his drink and moved closer to Taka.

"He's your boy. He's like you," Thoit said. "Your responsibility. Your heir – still your heir?"

"I'm not sure," Taka replied, throwing a stern glare at Mokoto. "He will have to earn it back."

"Well, that shouldn't be too hard. Unless Anaka becomes stupid enough to want the throne," Thoit replied. "Anyway..." He looked at his brother, and winked. "He's your mess."

Mokoto flinched as he watched Uncle Thoit drop his cigarette into King Taka's glass, and in one lightning movement the mountain of a man threw out his fist and knocked the king out cold. Malatsa Thoit didn't catch King Taka as he fell to the ground; in fact he moved out of the way to allow him to land. In a moment that seemed unreal, with an almighty *thud* that he was sure he had imagined, Mokoto found himself lying next to his unconscious father. His father, the King of Gaiamiráka. Named after the God of War himself. Knocked out cold. What... had just happened?

Uncle Thoit reached into his pocket, and calmly pulled out another cigarette. He lit it as if nothing had happened. He took a drag, and exhaled... and he looked down at Mokoto. "Sorry – do you want one?" he offered casually, as politely as a mortal could speak.

319

"I… I don't smoke, Uncle," Mokoto replied.

"No," Thoit answered. "You're better off just drinking and fucking, it never did your father any harm. He's a good boy, underneath the crown. You were right to copy him – but you do not need to copy all of him. You are a father now; you need to learn to behave." He calmly took a seat, and continued enjoying his cigarette, paying no attention to the bodies on the floor.

XXV.

'Tangun always appears as loving and kind, even to Hiveakans. He takes pleasure in welcoming new lives into the world, and he loves every child equally, because they are all his own. Whether they are blessed with the spirit of Taka or Kala, Tangun will hold a child in his arms lovingly, and his smile will always be the same.'

-       Extract from the Gaiamirapon: 'The Identities'

*

Mokoto swallowed his fifth shot of tetsa. Gaiamira, he was getting worse than his father! Nine long years had passed since Lakuna's announcement on his wedding day. Even now Mokoto could still recall so vividly how much he'd wanted to kill her... He'd hated her for it. He'd hated her for months afterwards; he'd spent every day wishing he could slit her throat... but then things changed. Lakuna had given him a son, a year after the wedding. On 12-02-20133G, the twelfth day of the second month, the month of Tomakoto, Matat Tomakoto Sota-Rokut was born. He was a strong, healthy boy. He was a big baby. He was aggressive. He'd bitten the midwife before he'd even opened his eyes. He had very dark eyes. Almost black. Frightening. Tomakoto was named after his birth God, the God of Achievement, Success and Ambition. It was also the name of a bitter fruit that was believed to enhance strength and determination. It was a popular legend, especially within the Hiveakan community, that Hiveakans named Tomakoto would become great leaders – and a great leader was exactly what Mokoto wanted from his son; his heir. Lakuna's boy was born only a month after Miama's son Tangun, who was named after his birth God, the God of Birth. It was a very Outsider name; Miama had chosen it. It was an acceptable name; any name taken from the Gaiamira was good enough... but Mokoto hadn't particularly cared about Miama's child. By the time Tangun was born Mokoto was so close to getting his own pureblood Hiveakan heir that he didn't have time for Miama's half-

321

breed. He let her choose the name, the toys, the yotuna temple… she'd been happy enough doing it and so Mokoto had washed his hands of the whole thing.

As for the rest of the family… Mokoto had no idea what the Outsider girls were up to, and he didn't care to ask, but Gonta had moved away. He'd never liked Meitona and had always vowed to go back home… Mokoto had never paid much attention to the stubborn ramblings of a bitter child, but when he'd reached adulthood Gonta had remained true to his word. At the age of fourteen Lakuna had got him a good job in the Meitonákan army in an attempt to turn him into a decent adult; she had hoped he would stay in Meitona, but by the age of fifteen Gonta was back in North Heikato, in his home town, only a few streets away from where he'd lived with his parents. He was still in the army, but as a low-ranked soldier with no real career prospects – not the kind that Meitona had to offer, anyway. His costly education was wasted; his potential to have a higher-class lifestyle in Meitona was thrown away. In many ways it was a pity; Gonta had actually turned into a very intelligent young man, with a good work ethic and the potential to do well in Meitona… but Mokoto had to admit, he hadn't been particularly upset to see the back of him. Gonta had never liked Mokoto, and Mokoto had never held much respect for Gonta. So, that was that.

Meanwhile, Anaka's clan had expanded, and was steadily populating Meitona Palace. Her Hiveakan children Aourat and Maida were out of the Hive now, and Aourat had a son. He was named Keizu, after the Hive and his great grandfather – King Taka's father. Aourat and his now wife Muzini had decided to raise him themselves in the palace, outside of the Hive… that hadn't gone down well. Nor had Aourat becoming a father at the age of eighteen. Anaka had gone berserk; actually it had been quite amusing to watch. Laughing over their sister's meltdown had been one of the few times when Mokoto and Lanka had shared a pleasant moment, briefly forgetting about the endless hostility they were destined to hold between them. There was always much more hostility on Lanka's end, though… Mokoto found it difficult to hold a hatred for someone who was clearly so inferior to him. Lanka wasn't a threat, and she hadn't been since he was a child.

How could he find her constant failure to kill him anything other than amusing?

In any case, Aourat had actually turned out to be a good boy, one that Anaka and the family could be proud of. Actually, all of Anaka's children had turned out well. Aourat worked in the Royal, as a dual mechanical engineer/test pilot for the Keizuakákan military – always an admired career for a member of the royal family. The public liked to see their leaders working to keep them safe. Maida had followed in her father's foosteps and become an infant tutor at the Hive, with the hope to becoming department manager in a few years. She was very good at her job and she was well respected by her peers, and the Hiveakan community in general. Chieit, once a terrorist in the making had actually blossomed into quite a fine young woman. She was now seventeen, and just like her parents she had gone into the world of science, working under her father at the Royal. She was intelligent, conscientious and socially popular. Actually, she had turned out to be the perfect child. Mokoto had been mildly surprised at that… but then again, he hadn't expected Anaka and Raikun to stand for any less. Raikun was doing well, considering. Not long after Chieit finished her education Raikun had lost his mother to cancer, and his father by suicide a few days later. Then his wife… Anaka wasn't in good shape these days. Earlier in the year Anaka, aged only forty-six, had retired. Raikun had forced her to do it. She'd been unwell for some time, only suffering from mild muscle aches and discomfort to begin with, but now she could barely move without being in pain. Even breathing strained her. It was an awful thing to see… Mokoto found himself unexpectedly troubled. Anaka was his friend. Not just because it made the family look good. He liked her. He respected her. He'd spent his childhood socialising with her and Raikun; Raikun was one of the few male role models Mokoto had, and Anaka… Mokoto had always felt a closeness to her. As close as he could be to anyone, at least. Now that he was older, he could look back and realise that. He could see that there were very few people he cared about, but Anaka was and always had been one of them. It was troubling for Mokoto to see her struggling to live. Nobody could help her. Nobody had the faintest idea what was wrong with her. Test after test came back negative; the greatest medics in the world with the finest technology given by the Gaiamira couldn't diagnose her. Of course, one of those medics was Anaka herself. She wasn't officially working anymore, but she still used all the hours in the day to go through Raikun's documents. In fact she worked so much from home the Royal staff probably hadn't noticed she was gone.

Anyway… that was Meitona Palace over the past nine years. Nine years… they had flown by, and yet many days had seemed to drag. For Mokoto they had come and gone like the tide in a sea of day to day tasks. He had spent them assisting his father in preparation for inheriting the crown, memorising every letter of the law, and untangling web after web of political bullshit and problems that never should have existed in the first place. Also maintaining his social status and relationships, trying his best to ignore his attention-seeking Outsider son whilst keeping on good terms with the boy's overprotective mother and Mokoto's Hiveakan wife. Constantly trying to keep Miama from Lakuna's harm and having to deal with the tediousness of Lakuna making Miama upset… Mokoto had been too busy balancing every great and trivial thing to notice that time had gone on without him, and now… it was nine years. Nine years since his second born had come into the world. Nine years since they had made eye contact. Now… at the age of nine years, Tomakoto was leaving the Hive.

Mokoto stared down at his glass, and in doing so he caught a glimpse of his hand. It was scarred, with a deep cut that ran down the length of his palm. Mokoto remembered getting that scar. He recalled every second, as clear as day… and he remembered what his father had said to him afterwards, on the night of Tomakoto's yotuna, when Tomakoto was secured within the cold depths of the Hive.

"So," King Taka had spoken, handing Mokoto a drink. *"You are father to a Hiveakan now."*

"Yes," Mokoto had answered proudly, as anyone would.

"You have your first parent scar."

"Parent scar?" Mokoto had repeated it questioningly, not wanting to sound rude… but he had no idea what the king was talking about.

King Taka had simply chuckled, and set his glass down. Then he'd raised his palm up to Mokoto, to point to four scars, wounds made by a yotuna knife a long time ago.

"Lanka," he'd spoken, pointing to the first scar. *"Anaka. Korana... for all the good it did."* He'd snorted; a look of disapproval upon his face as he touched upon his overlooked daughter's scar. *"And you."* Then he'd pulled his hand back, and picked up his drink. *"Your Uncle Thoit always said the other girls were Outsiders because I didn't have enough flesh to put them in the Hive."* He'd laughed. *"But, your Uncle Thoit talks shit. I had another hand – I just didn't want to waste the Hive's resources on their mothers' children."* He'd taken a sip of his drink, and chuckled, with a small smile upon his face. The sort of smile Mokoto had only seen from King Taka a handful of times... and always with the same person in mind. The slight pinch of jealousy Mokoto had felt was still clear, to this day. As irrational as it was. *"Anaka bit me. You probably can't see now..."* King Taka had raised his hand to his face, as if searching for the infant teeth marks that had faded over the years. He'd seemed somewhat disappointed that he couldn't find them, as if they were a trophy of some sort. Mokoto knew that was ridiculous, though. She was his daughter. Not his idol. *"She always did whatever she wanted, even when it came to me."* He'd laughed again. *"Nobody in the world would dare bite the king. I'm sure if she'd known enough to decide, she still would have chosen to do it."*

"Yes, Sire," Mokoto had answered, with the bitter taste of jealously in his mouth. It almost sounded like the king was permitting Anaka to defy him. Of course, Mokoto knew better than that. Anaka was good for the family. Her position in the Royal suited the family more than her position as heir to the throne... that was the only reason the king hadn't forced it upon her; it was not motivated by admiration for her. Mokoto had known better than that. Though... while they were on the subject, he'd felt brave enough to ask... *"Was I a waste of the Hive's resources, Sire?"* He'd looked at the king, not daring to break the man's gaze. Mokoto had only done that a handful of times in his life.

"I don't know," the king had answered bluntly, turning his attention back to his beverage. *"And I won't be around to find out. The*

success of your life will be determined by what kind of king you make, and unfortunately..." He moved his eyes to Mokoto. *"It is the nature of inheriting the throne that I will not be around to see it."*

"*So you will have to trust me then, Sire?*" Mokoto had spoken.

"*Yes,*" the king had replied. He'd extended his arm out to Mokoto, offering up his glass. *"I have to trust you."*

Mokoto had extended his own glass, and they'd touched into a vow.

"*I will not let you down, Sire.*"

Mokoto remembered the words vividly. How could he not? He'd meant them. He still meant them now, as much as he had back then. He couldn't fail, and to not fail as a son he had to not fail as a father. Although truth be told, he was shitting himself.

Mokoto sat tensed, swallowing down shot after shot of tetsa. What was he supposed to say to this child? He tried to relive over and over again the first words his father had said to him, but it didn't help. Mokoto had met his father under very unique circumstances – how likely was he to find Tomakoto lying on the floor, half-dead after entering into an unfair fight with his sibling? Maybe he shouldn't let Tomakoto see him right away... Mokoto recalled responding very well to having to wait to meet the king; it had made the king seem so much more terrifying when they had finally met. Then again... what excuse did Mokoto have to not see Tomakoto right away? His father had been busy, unable to tear himself away from his duties. Mokoto had been perfectly able to clear his schedule for this. Maybe doing that had been wrong. Why had he made such an effort for this child? He had nothing to prove! It was Tomakoto that had to prove he was worthy of being Mokoto's son, and of being the king's grandson.

Mokoto almost sighed at the sound of someone else entering the room. Who was this now? Why did people have to come in here and disturb him? There were plenty of other places in Meitona to be!

"Are you excited?" It was Teikota's voice... alright. That wasn't too bad. Still. Mokoto could do without him. He tolerated Teikota, but he hadn't forgotten what he'd done. Mokoto never would like him, not even after all this time. It was pathetic and unforgivable for a Hive tutor to lose control. He moved his eyes to his older brother, who was standing before him with his arms folded.

"Why?" Mokoto shrugged carelessly. "He's only a boy."

"Now he is," Teikota replied. He took a seat near Mokoto, looking at him. "You have to teach him. Mould him. Like your father did with you." He half smirked. "Like I did."

"Mm... I remember." Mokoto grunted. He poured more liquid into his glass. Teikota watched him do it, and held back a disapproving sigh.

"You shouldn't meet him drunk. You'll lose your power."

"I'm not drunk," Mokoto growled, insulted. As if Teikota would know. Teikota didn't drink. Ever. He didn't smoke, he didn't socialise... He really was a dark entity, one whose only purpose was to linger in the ghostly corridors of the Hive and attempt to murder its children for no reason at all. "What should I do?" Mokoto sighed, submitting to civility. If Teikota was going to be here... Mokoto might as well make use of him. It was a fact that Teikota had two graduates of his own. "What do you do with a new child?"

"Don't say he's new," Teikota answered. "That is a lie. He isn't new; he's been alive for nine years. He's been your property for nine years. That's all you need to remember. It's taken him nine years to become good enough to live with you."

"I'm well aware." Mokoto looked at Teikota. Why didn't he understand? The fact that it had only been nine years was the problem; Tomakoto was a fucking legend! His name had been all over the media for months; the whole world knew how much he'd excelled, and in what short a space of time. It was because of his yotuna, Mokoto was sure. It was common practice for a Hiveakan baby to be held by the Hiveakan members of its family during their yotuna, so that the family's Footprints may be passed onto the newborn... There had been plenty of Hiveakans at Tomakoto's yotuna, and therefore plenty of Footprints to inherit. Tomakoto had clearly absorbed them well into his soul. He'd been the youngest child to graduate in over fifty years; he was four years younger than Mokoto had been! How was one supposed to treat a child that was obviously better than them? The Hive could have at least kept him in until he was thirteen...

327

"Don't be put off by his age," Teikota said, immediately knowing what the problem was. It was obvious. Even if Mokoto hid it – it was perfectly rational to be unsure of what to do with such a blessed child. "You and I know that Tomakoto is good. He doesn't." Teikota took hold of Mokoto's glass and poured the liquid back into the bottle, then sealed the cap. Mokoto watched him do it, his fingers twitching slightly. He wanted to gut him. "As far as Tomakoto is concerned he's taken too long. He thinks children graduate when they are nine. He already believes he needs to make it up to you." He looked at Mokoto. Sternly. "Just remember that. He doesn't own you. You own him. He is terrified of you."

"Mm." Mokoto smirked a little. Teikota had a point... how terrified was Mokoto when he left the Hive? Everyone frightened him, and to some extent even the Outsiders. They were technically his superiors, after all. He was always so scared to speak in case he said something wrong. Tomakoto would be no different... In fact it would be amusing to see someone so afraid. Mokoto hadn't seen that in a while. He cleared his throat and took hold of the bottle of tetsa, staring at Teikota as he re-opened it. "Thank you for your advice, brother," he said. "But I'm not a child anymore." He re-poured his drink. "You can't take my food away."

"No, much worse." Teikota stood up and snatched the glass from Mokoto's hand. "I can take your drink. You can't raise a child when you are influenced by this sort of crap! You'll ruin him. Now pour it back in!" He slammed it down on the table and walked towards the door, not waiting to see if Mokoto obeyed him.

"Do you really trust me?" Mokoto said with a sadistic smirk as he stared after him.

"It's not a matter of trust, Mokoto. It's a matter of hierarchy," Teikota answered without looking back, and left the room.

Mokoto sniggered slightly and studied the glass on the table. Tch. Teikota. Hierarchy? They weren't in the Hive now. Teikota had no power here; his power was merely borrowed from Anaka, and she didn't even like him. Mokoto was Anaka's best friend. So there! Why would Mokoto listen to Teikota now? Cockily, Mokoto took hold of the glass and downed the liquid, sniggering to himself again.

"Certainly is a matter of hierarchy, brother," he said as he poured himself another. "I'm bigger than you now." He downed his drink and yawned. Teikota. The idiot. How many years had it been since he'd laid a finger on Mokoto? Now he wouldn't dare.

"Matat Mokoto, your son is home." A servant's voice came from the doorway.

"Great." Mokoto shrugged. "Tell him I'll see him tomorrow." Fuck it. Let the little brat wait.

*

'Ana was the worst queen that ever lived. Nobody has dared name their child 'Ana' since her execution. She caused one of the greatest wars in history; she almost wiped the entire planet out. She went against the Gaiamira. She took hundreds of thousands of innocent lives; she never should have been given the throne. She was the most shameful thing to happen to the royal family – they don't even acknowledge her existence. The same goes for Mokoto. It is nothing short of a horrific tragedy that history repeated itself in Mokoto. He was Ana, but on a larger scale. He didn't just start a war with Outsiders; he started a war with another world. He cost the lives of millions. Both of them deserved to be killed. Neither of them should have ever been given the throne. No child will ever share their names. History will spend forever regretting their existence.'

\-   Priest Donso Ten-Hora, 20147G

*

Anaka's face was fixed into a constant wince as she typed into her laptop. Her fingers had been hurting for an hour now, but she was keen to finish her work. Not far from her Mokoto furiously blasted through the paperwork his father had assigned him. He was allowed to write laws now and make decisions that would affect the world; all King Taka had to do was sign. In fact, Mokoto did quite a lot of the planet admin these days. King Taka was seventy-seven now… he had

329

another what, twenty or so years left? Thirty at a push. He intended to be king until the day he died, in accordance with tradition... but he would be an idiot not to prepare Mokoto for the possibility that the almighty Goddess of Death Lanka would claim the king in the next ten years. So... Mokoto did a lot these days. It was good practice for him; his position as the next ruler of Gaiamiráka was a certainty, and he was sure that even his sister Lanka didn't believe she would get the throne now. Not that it stopped her trying... How could she stop? This thing with Mokoto was all she'd ever had in her life, and Mokoto knew that. So he let her carry it on, in perhaps the only act of kindness he had ever done in his life... and even then it was done through a dark twist of pity and amusement. Oh well. It was a good enough distraction from the tedium of this paperwork.

Mokoto was sitting alone with his sister in one of the common rooms; she was lying as comfortably as she could across the sofa, and he was in a chair hunched over a desk, his head buried in legal terms. Neither had spoken in over an hour. They each barely remembered the other was there.

The door creaked open; neither sibling looked up. There were only a few people it could possibly be, and none were interesting enough to distract them from their work.

"My my, isn't this a pretty scene?" Hm... actually, that voice was unexpected. Mokoto raised his head to see Lakuna standing there, a hand on her hip.

"I thought you were at work?" he said.

"My deputy's keeping an eye on things." Lakuna shrugged. She perched herself on the end of the sofa. "Actually, he's leaving soon. I'm trying to get Gonta to take his job."

"Are you sure that's a good idea?" Anaka smirked a little, looking at her younger sister over the top of her laptop. "It's a long commute from Heikato."

"Then he'll have to move from Heikato," Lakuna sniped, gritting her teeth. "It's a shithole! He can do better than that – he's just a nobody soldier over there, dealing with nobody criminals. He can actually be somebody in Meitona!"

"You should give up pushing him…" Mokoto mumbled, getting back to his work. "Pushing worked for Chieit. Gonta's a lost cause."

"Shut up," Lakuna growled. She made her way over to him and trailed her arm across his back, settling it around his shoulders. "What do you care?"

"I don't," Mokoto said. He placed his arm around her waist and crushed his claws into her flesh, smirking when she purred a little.

"Hey!"

The couple looked up to see Anaka glaring at them, a look of disgust upon her face. "I don't have sex in front of you!" she snapped.

"How can you? You hate one husband and the other…" Lakuna smirked cruelly. "He can't get it up anymore, can he?" Her smirk widened at the sound of Mokoto's laughter, and he applaudingly squeezed her waist again.

"Actually, he can!" Anaka frowned, turning away. "It's me that can't. This stupid thing…"

"Oh, well…" Lakuna sniggered. "If he ever gets bored, Lanka's still single. She'd probably be up for it, just once."

"I think she'd prefer Teikota," Anaka giggled.

"Well, obviously." Lakuna replied. She considered adding 'who wouldn't', but in Mokoto's presence… she knew better.

"I think Lanka is waiting for you to die, darling," Mokoto commented, deliberately not addressing Lakuna's remark. "What does Uncle Thoit say? 'If you want to fuck a man up, give him a wife'," he snorted. "She can't kill me, but if we married she could destroy my soul."

"That's sick," Anaka scolded, but she was smiling in amusement all the same. "And isn't it 'give him a fucking wife and an ugly fucking son'?"

Mokoto started laughing again.

"Yes, that's it," he nodded.

"You know, I wouldn't put it past her, though," Lakuna said, looking at Mokoto. "She hates you enough to marry you."

"Well, a marriage is a marriage. At least it's a long-term relationship, that'd be a first," Anaka commented. Lanka wasn't much

331

of a fan of commitment – not to anyone except Mokoto, anyway. She'd had many partners over the years, but never an official boyfriend. As far as the world was concerned, she'd never even gone on a date. Anaka only knew she wasn't a virgin because Lanka had once disclosed to her that she liked to make use of the palace red collars from time to time. A handful of times in her life she'd had a very secret fling with someone in the royal family's social circle, but nothing had ever come of it and Anaka wasn't completely certain of any names. They weren't all male though, she knew that at least. Not that Anaka asked much about that… Lakuna probably knew more; their mutual dislike of Mokoto many years ago had caused the two women to become somewhat friends, and nothing had happened to break the friendship off. So at least Lanka had someone to talk to about… whatever. "Speaking of marriage," Anaka looked at Lakuna, swiftly changing the subject. "Gonta's twenty-one this year, isn't he? Has he found a girl yet?"

"Probably." Lakuna carelessly sighed. "He never tells me anything."

"Well, don't just ask." Anaka smirked. "You need to drag it out of them."

"What about Chieit?" Lakuna replied. "She's a good-looking girl. She must have found someone."

"She gets plenty of offers, but she works too hard," Anaka said. "She hasn't got time for that."

"Gonta works hard." Lakuna frowned.

"Mm…" Anaka grunted, and ignored Lakuna's attempts to murder her with her eyes. Lakuna certainly had a Hiveakan glare… Well, it wasn't Anaka's fault that Gonta was a nobody! Chieit actually had a future to think about.

"Stop worrying about them, they aren't children," Mokoto growled, quickly becoming bored. Why did he *always* have to listen to this crap? What was it about women that made them fuss over their offspring for so long? And why Hiveakan women, of all people? That didn't even make sense – and especially not Lakuna! Gonta wasn't even her child and she was more worried about him than Tomakoto! Then again, Tomakoto showed more promise… He was actually less of a concern. So perhaps Lakuna was in fact doing the right thing, on this occasion… "Tomakoto is the baby of the palace now – you do remember him? The third king of Gaiamiráka?"

"Is he?" Anaka giggled. "It's not even your crown yet and you're already trying to get rid of it – I'll tell Uncle Thoit, he'll be proud."

"It's just fact." Mokoto shrugged. "Who else would I give it to? You know…" He sniggered. "When Lanka finally kills me?"

The girls started laughing at Lanka's expense, until Anaka felt guilty enough to change the subject once more.

"Actually – Toma's not even the baby," she said. "Keizu is."

"The *Hiveakan* baby," Mokoto replied.

"Yes. Keizu." Anaka smirked back, playfully bickering with her brother. "He's been raised by Hiveakans – Toma was barely in there five minutes. I don't think that counts, you know."

"Haha!" Mokoto grinned proudly. "You think they should make a minimum graduation age?"

"If you want a Hiveakan ID then yes," Anaka teased. "The rest of us had to suffer into our teens."

"The rest of us weren't my son." Lakuna winked, her face quickly becoming as brightly lit as her husband's.

"My son." Mokoto nudged her harshly, taking the credit for their remarkable boy.

"Actually, I think it is definitely Mokoto's genes. Sorry." Anaka looked at Lakuna. "Our family makes the best Hiveakans."

"Oh, you mean like Aourat?" Lakuna retorted, her eyes laced with accusation. It was no secret that Anaka adored her son. He was her first child and her only boy, so already held an advantage over Anaka's daughters. Well, Maida. Chieit would always be Raikun's child and therefore cherished by Anaka like a signed trophy. Plus Aourat was a favourite of the media, and he worked in the Royal, and he was charming and attractive, and he was intelligent, and he was interested in technology… It would be an insult to Anaka's narcissism if she did anything but adore the male version of her.

"I never said anything!" Anaka protested, straightening her posture in defence. She winced as a sharp pain shot through her; she'd moved too quickly.

"You say things with your eyes every second of the day," Mokoto said. "You think he's a gift from the Gaiamira. I think he's a pain."

"So do I," Anaka replied. "But so are you, and you're getting the throne."

"Well…" Mokoto got back to his paperwork, a small smirk on his lips. "I'm charming too." He listened, and sniggered along as the girls started to laugh.

*

'My father was a good man. I believe that. He was flawed, obviously… but he was a good man.'

-       King Tangun, 20147G

*

"Hey, Father, what do you think of this?" It was a few hours later and Mokoto had come to visit Miama in her bedroom. Unfortunately, Tangun had been there… Mokoto never would have bothered if he'd known that. The boy was always so clingy; it was tiring. Tangun smiled as he showed his father his latest piece of artwork; he had a passion for painting and drawing.

"Mm," Mokoto uttered, lazily glancing over the piece. "Did you paint that?"

"Yes!" Tangun grinned. "It took me four hours."

"Four hours?" Mokoto's eyebrows rose. Four hours? *Four*?

"It's good isn't it?" Miama smiled from her seat. She stood up and approached the boys, fondly stroking the back of Tangun's head. "We've got a real artist!"

"Mm. Well, he certainly is creative," Mokoto remarked. "He's found yet another way to waste four hours of his life."

334

"What?" Miama looked at Mokoto, stunned.

"You don't like it…?" Tangun mumbled.

"Tangun. You aren't an idiot. Actually, you aren't even useless." Mokoto looked at the boy, his face coated in disapproval. It almost pained him to see his own blood wasted on such an Outsider child. "But at the moment you are worthless. Do you understand?"

"Yes, Your Highness," Tangun said. "Every word." He slammed the painting down, as dramatically as he could manage, and he stormed out of the room.

"Tangun!" Miama gasped. She went to run after him, when Mokoto grabbed her arm.

"Leave him," Mokoto snarled, glaring at the doorway in anger. The insubordinate little shit… How dare he act like that towards his father! "I'll find him, and I'll break his legs for talking to me like that. What kind of child are you raising?"

"He's *our* child!" Miama yelled back, yanking her arm away. "And how else was he supposed to talk to you? That was a horrible thing you just said to him!"

"Oh, shut up," Mokoto growled. He couldn't be bothered with this crap. "He wouldn't have cared if he wasn't such an Outsider."

"*I'm* an Outsider!" Miama wailed. "You never had a problem before! Before Toma came out!"

"Don't be absurd." Mokoto pushed past her, and made his way over to the door. He wasn't getting into this. Again. She was tedious, and not even worth beating.

"Absurd?" Miama raced in front of Mokoto, blocking his path. She stared at him firmly; her eyes were filling with tears and her breathing was rapid and uneven. She was angry, and a little scared, the combination of which made her out of control.

Mokoto sighed deeply, and looked his wife up and down. He clicked his tongue and clenched his fist. Really? Why? Why did she have to be like this? It was all the time these days!

"Why are you always so fucking moody?" he demanded.

"Because you don't give a damn about us!" Miama cried. "Your son loves you. *I* love you. I love you with all my heart!"

"Oh, Miama –"

"All you care about is *him*!" Miama screamed. "Ever since Toma came out you haven't spoken to Tangun once! He did that picture for you!"

"Good. He should be trying to impress me," Mokoto stated. "Just not with paintings."

"You hate who he is," Miama sobbed. "Tomakoto's the favourite. Tangun knows that."

"So?" Mokoto snorted. He folded his arms and shrugged, failing to see any reason why she should be so upset. She was insane. "My father has favourites. He likes Anaka more than me. He likes me more than Lanka. We know. We don't care. We deal with it. I don't know what your problem is."

"My problem is that you're trying to be like your father," Miama whimpered softly, her body timid and unsure. Even as she spoke the words, she was wondering if it was worth it. If it would make a difference to him... "I don't love your father. I love you. I want you to be you."

"This is me!" Mokoto snapped. "It's not my fault you were wrong! If you don't like it you don't have to stay here, there are plenty of women who can replace you." He glared at her, infuriated by her arguing. Why could she never just accept things the way they were? "Plenty of women like what I am."

"Hiveakan women," Miama replied.

"Yes, actually," Mokoto nodded. What of it? What was her point?

"Lakuna..." Miama smiled a little. It was a sad, needy smile. The kind that Mokoto had seen from her much more than he would like. "I used to be the favourite wife. Now you barely look at me either. Me and my son... are we really so disgusting to you?"

"What are you talking about?" Mokoto growled. He was getting bored of this now... it was the same every time they were together! It was even worse if Tangun was there; was it any wonder Mokoto hated seeing the boy? All Tangun's presence meant was that he'd have to deal with more of this bullshit! That wasn't what Mokoto wanted from a son! Or a wife... Maybe he should just beat her. She wasn't worthy of it, but maybe it was the only way to make her understand that she had to stop this shit. Telling her obviously wasn't working. Or he could just break her voice box… That would solve everybody's problems. "I look at you all the time," Mokoto continued to argue, giving her one last chance to shut up. One more chance than she deserved. He had no idea why he was even entertaining her; he was never so lenient on anyone else. Perhaps it was because he knew what a drama she could make if she didn't get attention. "I slept in here last night!"

"Yes, your body is always here," Miama said. "But not your heart."

"Oh, for – what the fuck are you talking about?" Mokoto roared. Gods, he wanted to rip her head off! Why did she talk such crap? "My heart was never here, Miama! Listen."

Miama let out a sharp yelp as Mokoto grabbed her, pulling her away from the door. His Footprints wanted to harm her, but he restrained them. He pushed her against the wall, but not hard enough to hurt her. Just fiercely enough to make her listen. "I don't have a heart! I don't love you! I never loved you! And I never fucking will!" He stopped for a brief moment to look at her. She was a pathetic sight, even for an Outsider. Her breathing was frantic. Her eyes were wide and innocent, flooded with hurt and sorrow and… whatever else. Tears were pouring from them; they stuck to her cheeks like some kind of badge, as if to emphasise her sadness. She looked so injured.

"I…" Miama choked, trying her best to hold back her tears. She didn't do a very good job. She couldn't stop herself crying. "I…I thought you loved me."

"Yes, well…" Mokoto grunted. "You think a lot of things, don't you, Miama? Most of it is horse shit." He yanked his hands back from her, and marched out of the room. He made his way down the corridor, not looking back, towards his own bedroom, and he locked himself inside. Gods… what was wrong with her?

Mokoto lay down on his bed and sighed. She was a nightmare these days. An absolute nightmare. What had happened to her? He remembered a time when she wasn't like this. He remembered it vividly; a time when he enjoyed her company – enough to seek it out. He used to make time for her. Time to spend with her, just the two of them… and he never used to like it when that time was over. Now, being alone with Miama was horrific. It always ended up in some sort of crying or complaining or whatever else Mokoto couldn't be bothered with, and all for no reason except that he was a Hiveakan man that was acting *exactly* like a Hiveakan man should. It never used to bother her – actually, didn't she used to like the fact that he was a Hiveakan? She'd certainly seemed to at the time, and it didn't feel like that long ago. It was, though. Nine, ten years ago. Things changed when Tomakoto was born. Miama got jealous. Now she was desperate to be the most important thing in Mokoto's life. It wasn't going to happen. Ever. Miama used to be content with knowing Mokoto could never love her. It was hardly his fault if she'd decided to change her mind now.

He should kill her. He knew he should. Neither of them were happy; at least if he put her out of her misery it would bring the pair of them peace. He'd killed before. He'd killed his own sister; he'd raped and almost killed his own wife… Actually, Mokoto wasn't particularly proud of that. At the time he'd been pleased with himself, of course, but the older he got the more he could find flaws in who he once was. Still. It didn't change the fact that he *could* kill Miama if he wanted to. So why not? The thought was perfectly rational. She was making his life a misery and she was spoiling their child – Mokoto's child. That could be classed as treason, if Mokoto was willing to say that he considered Tangun to be his heir. Not that he was willing to do that… She wanted Mokoto to love her though – she tried to make him, and that was definitely treason. If the king found out he might insist on executing her himself. The king wouldn't find out. Something in Mokoto told him to make sure of that. Something told him to keep her alive; to keep her with him. His memories, maybe. She had been fun before. Perhaps she could be fun again. Perhaps he could look forward to her company again… It had happened with Lakuna. People changed, and they changed back. They went from exciting to disappointing to… okay? Was that how he would describe it? Mokoto and Lakuna were on good terms these days, but it wasn't anything like it had been. Now that he thought of it… the blissful days with Lakuna were gone. Maybe things with Miama wouldn't be like they were, even if they improved.

It was worth finding out though. Something in Mokoto told him that. Something told him to wait. For now at least, he had to keep her alive. As annoying and frustrating as that was. At the very least, she would keep Tangun out of Mokoto's way.

Mokoto sighed. Fuck it. His marriages were a mess. That was the only thing that was though. He was rather pleased with his position in the world, and very pleased with his Hiveakan son. Not that those facts stopped him feeling frustrated and desperate to harm somebody at a time like this. Mokoto sat up on his bed and yawned, submitting to his agitated Footprints. Time to kick the shit out of Lanka again.

XXVI.

'A mortal child who had moved between continents missed their old home. They prayed to the Gaiamira, and looking for comfort, they asked them if they ever missed Earth. Kala answered the child first. She said it is easy to miss something, even if it does you harm. It is better to miss something that is gone, than resent it for still being in your life.'

- Extract from the Gaiamirapon: 'The Communications'

*

Mokoto waited outside his father's meeting room, his body slightly tensed. He'd been summoned only a few minutes earlier; his father's aide Rozo had come to Mokoto's room and told him the king wished to speak to him immediately. Rozo hadn't said what it was about; the king hadn't told him. All either of them knew was that King Taka had some news that couldn't wait. News that had to be reported to Mokoto first. To say the least, it was troubling. Mokoto was the king's heir, and he was becoming increasingly involved in the planet's politics, so for him to be summoned like this… This sounded like a war. Or at the very least, some significant change in the global laws or world hierarchy that would have a drastic impact upon Gaiamiráka. That was what Mokoto assumed. As wild as he allowed his imagination to be, it was very limited, really. It was limited to this planet. Limited to this world. As much as he imagined, he only ever imagined this would involve the Gaiamirákans alone. How wrong he was.

He stared at the dark wooden door to King Taka's meeting room in anguish. Rozo had gone in a few seconds ago, to inform the king of Mokoto's arrival. It didn't often happen like this. Normally Mokoto was permitted to walk straight into his father's meeting room, but it seemed that now the king needed a moment to collect his thoughts. It was unsettling. Just what sort of thoughts were they? Already Mokoto's personal issues were looking embarrassingly small.

The more he allowed himself to think about it, the more likely it seemed that the world was about to end. *Click.* Snapping Mokoto from his thoughts, the door opened, and there stood Rozo.

"Your Highness." Rozo bowed. He stepped out of Mokoto's way and gestured for him to enter the room. "Please."

Mokoto didn't make a sound as he rose to his feet. He straightened his clothing, quickly composing himself and banishing his unwanted nerves. Of course he had to look completely calm and fearless in front of the king. He stepped past Rozo, into the king's meeting room, and he cast his eyes upon the tall figure that stood in its centre. His father. As soon as he saw the king, Mokoto knelt down, and he heard the door close behind him, with Rozo still outside. He and the king were alone, without a chance of anybody seeing them talking. Not even the king's loyal aide. Now this was formal…

"Rise," Taka uttered, his deep voice landing with what felt like a *thud* upon Mokoto's head.

Mokoto stood at his father's command and met eyes with the king, in a territorial display of confidence. He tried to read the king as he looked at him. His father was difficult to read, the owner of a perfect mask… but he was not wearing it completely. He was allowing Mokoto to realise… Something wasn't right with the world. Something had happened. Something extreme. Taka made his way over to his lounge table and sat down, gesturing for Mokoto to do the same. Mokoto obeyed. The fact that they weren't at King Taka's desk was puzzling. King Taka liked to do business at his desk. This wasn't business… So what in the Gaiamiras' world was it? Mokoto continued to watch his father in silence, waiting for permission to speak. Taka started by gesturing to the botte of tetsa on the table, and two glasses filled with ice. "Do you want a drink?"

"Yes?" Mokoto answered as if it were a question. What he meant was; would he *need* a drink for this?

"Good." Taka grinned, and proceeded to pour them a glass of tetsa each. He handed Mokoto his drink, and watched the young man. Mokoto stared back awkwardly, unsure of why he was being studied. Was he supposed to be doing something now…? With nothing else he could think of, he took a sip of the tetsa and nodded.

341

"Very nice, Father," he spoke, his discomfort high in his voice.

Taka started laughing, which took Mokoto aback even more. He had absolutely no idea what he was involved in. It was as if he'd walked into a practical joke.

"Thank you." Taka sniggered, taking a sip of his own. "Mokoto…" He looked at the younger man… fondly? No. That wasn't a word that could be used with King Taka. Not when it concerned anyone except Anaka, anyway. Still… he looked rather proud. Happy. Yes. That was it. The king looked… happy. "My son." Taka grinned once more; the frequency was disturbing. "I would like you to know, I am not disappointed in you."

"Thank you, Father," Mokoto uttered, his jaw dropping slightly. Had the king just admitted… pride? Mokoto didn't know what to say. Why would the king do that…?

"Can you keep a secret, boy?" Taka asked. Immediately, Mokoto was pulled from the moment. Whatever he might have thought or felt about King Taka's last remark, and however Mokoto might have responded… it was killed now, with this question. This was it. This was the business. The troubling reason why Mokoto was here.

"Of course," Mokoto answered loyally, bracing himself for what he could only imagine would be a disaster… Although, the seemingly cheerful mood of King Taka was slightly confusing him.

"Good!" Taka exclaimed. "Well then, keep this one for me. You are not to tell anyone, do you understand?" He looked at Mokoto sternly, and all at once he reverted back into the terrifying and deadly King Taka, Mokoto knew so well. It was slightly comforting. "Mokoto?"

"Yes, Sire." Mokoto nodded. "Of course."

"Good boy." Taka took another sip of his tetsa, and smiled. More than that. His face brightened significantly, more than Mokoto had ever seen. It was as if he had just been brought to life. "The Gaiamira have spoken to me."

"Spoken to you?" Mokoto uttered flatly, stunned. Of course he tried to understand it right away, but he couldn't… Was the king trying to say he'd had a religious dream? Mokoto had heard it said that the Gaiamira could communicate with mortals through their dreams, amongst other ways. It was so rare for the dreams to be genuine, though... they were often just the creations of an imaginative and hopeful mind. A naïve one, to put it bluntly. The king wasn't naïve. Why would he be talking about such things...?

"They started in a dream," Taka said. "One which I wrongly ignored, so they sent another. Eventually, I had to talk to your sister."

"Beina?" Mokoto questioned, immediately knowing to which sister the king referred. It had to be Beina. The nun. She had a connection with the Gaiamira; she was the only resident of Meitona Palace that could verify divine communications.

"Yes." Taka nodded, the light never fading from his face. "She said they were real, and then she recommended prayer... They were real, Mokoto. My son... The Gaiamira have spoken to me."

Mokoto remained quiet for a moment. He was... confused. To begin with. He couldn't quite believe it, but even if he did... Why would the Gaiamira contact his father...? As soon as he asked himself that Mokoto reminded himself that it was no business of his, but an honour to his father. A great honour. It was the single greatest thing a mortal could hope to have in their life. Contact with the Gaiamira... If it was real, it was better than taking the throne.

"You are not to tell anyone," Taka spoke, pulling Mokoto from his thoughts once more. His face was stern again. He was serious. "Only Lanka and Anaka. They haven't permitted anybody else to know the details at the moment, only those involved."

"How many people are involved...?" Mokoto mumbled. He was starting to become unnerved; this was starting to sound like a major event. One that required people, and secrecy... Mokoto's heart pounded rapidly inside his chest. What was happening here? Mokoto didn't know how to feel. If this was as real as he was starting to believe it was, he knew he should feel honoured and happy for the king. The Gaiamira speaking to King Taka, it was truly a blessing for Meitona Palace, and Mokoto knew he should be excited... and he was, to some extent. He was excited and elated... but those feelings were shadowed by nerves. What was going on...?

"They told me to take a hundred soldiers," Taka answered.

"A hun – what for?" Mokoto gasped, his eyes widening. Now he couldn't believe it! A hundred people? *Soldiers*? What! What were they getting into?

"Just a simple exploratory mission," Taka said. "The soldiers are just a precaution, in case we are greeted with hostility, but the Gaiamira have assured me I will not be harmed. This is a peaceful mission." He took another sip of his tetsa. "But still, I need you to get a list of Lakuna's strongest soldiers. Don't tell her it is anything to do with the Gaiamira, just tell her I want it. I need a hundred names, in order of merit. Do you understand?"

"Yes…" Mokoto nodded. His chest felt tight. He felt like he would stop breathing at any moment. The king was serious, wasn't he? This was really happening… his father was becoming an einjel – a servant of the Gaiamira. Mokoto didn't know what to say… Normally he would feel honoured – he should feel honoured – but he couldn't bring himself to share his father's obvious glee. He was too unnerved. He just wanted to know… Before he could feel anything he knew he should, there was one question Mokoto had to ask.

"Why?" Boldly, Mokoto looked at his father. "Why do they want you to go? Where is it, Sire?"

"The beginning, Mokoto." Taka smiled. "Earth."

"Earth?"

Again, Mokoto was stunned. Earth? *Earth*? As in… *Earth*? The home of the Gaiamira…? Every Gaiamirákan child knew the story. Earth was the place of the Gaiamiras' birth; it was a world filled with corruption and confusion, so much that the Gaiamira had chosen to leave, and start anew somewhere else. If this was truly real, and the Gaiamira had spoken to the king, why did they want him to go there…? Did they hope to… move back to Earth? No… No, they couldn't! The Gaiamira were the very foundation of Gaiamirákan society, and everything that was birthed from it. The planet would die without them. They couldn't leave! "Father –"

"Don't worry," Taka spoke, holding up his hand. "They just want to see how they are doing, that's all. They want me to observe, and report back."

"Why...?" Mokoto asked hoarsely. "What do they plan to do with the information?"

"Mokoto." King Taka looked sternly at his child, the kind of look that made Mokoto feel like he was back in the Hive. It was terrifying. "It is not our place to question. We trust, and we obey. Whatever the reason, do you think even I would have the right to refuse? I am above every mortal on this planet. I am not above them. Do you understand?"

"Yes," Mokoto answered quietly. The king was right... it really didn't matter why the Gaiamira were sending him away. Nor was it anything to be afraid of. If they had assured the king he would not be harmed, then he would not be harmed. He was their child. He was the one they had seen fit to lead their people. Of course King Taka could trust the Gaiamira with his life.

Taka chuckled a little.

"You have every right to be concerned," he said. "Mokoto... would it help to know that your sister has been there?"

"S..." Mokoto looked at him, his eyes widening once more. His sister? To *Earth*? Who was it? Beina... Yes, it had to be. She was the only one who had a relationship with every member of the Gaiamira – if the word was allowed she could even be considered their friend. It had to be her... Why had she gone? How had she gone? *When*?

"Yes." King Taka nodded. "Anaka. She went when you were still in the Hive; she never told you because they ordered her never to speak of it. They asked her to gather information, the same as me. I was never permitted to know exactly what sort of information, but I suppose it was similar to this."

"*Anaka!*" Mokoto gasped.

He suddenly felt sick. Nauseous. In fact, he had to fight against his body to stop it shaking. This was ridiculous. Ridiculous, and so unfair! Why did Anaka always get everything? Mokoto wasn't thinking about King Taka anymore; in that split second the entirety of his attention had been diverted to *Anaka*! Anaka – she was an einjel! She'd been to Earth... of course she'd been to Earth. Of course, of all the residents of Meitona Palace it had to be her. Typical! As well as being the biggest living tourist attraction in Meitona she'd been the first einjel in the palace – and before Mokoto was even out of the Hive! He never had a chance. No wonder she was the favourite. Whatever repressed feelings of jealously Mokoto had, they were running wild now. All of a sudden, he felt like he could never possibly hope to compete with her. It was no wonder she didn't want the throne. Why would she waste her time being the leader of mortals, when she could call herself a servant of the Gaiamira?

Taka started to laugh, which made Mokoto feel even worse. It was embarrassing, if nothing else. The king could obviously hear Mokoto's silent screams. Did he know Mokoto wanted to smack his own skull against Taka's lounge table? Or better yet, into his own glass?

"Don't look like that," King Taka smirked. "This was nothing to do with it, I assure you. I always was fond of her, even before the Gaiamira were." Mokoto had to try so hard to stop his jaw dropping. Why… why would the king say that? Surely he couldn't have expected Mokoto to feel anything but worse? "So… as you can see. You will have to try harder now, my child. You not only have to surpass a greater king, but a greater heir. It is truly a boy worthy of the throne, who can rise above two einjels."

"Yes…" Mokoto mumbled. No… No, he didn't like this. He didn't agree with this! Try harder? He had tried hard enough! He had already done so much to deserve this throne, why did he have to do more? Was he being punished? For his complacency? For the way he taunted Lanka about it? Or the way he treated his wives? He had been a poor husband, and an unwilling father to Tangun… Perhaps the Gaiamira were punishing him for that. Was that what this was about? Shit!

"Anyway… I am leaving in three days; it should take me about ten to get there. I'll be home by the end of the month," Taka spoke. "And I will be an einjel, my son. Ours will be a palace of einjels."

"Yes, Father." Mokoto nodded. He felt bitter. So bitter, and so angry and jealous… but he knew what he should be feeling, and he knew how he should behave. So like the well-trained Hiveakan boy that he was, he raised his glass. "To einjels," Mokoto spoke, a fake

346

smile upon his face. King Taka grinned, and touched his drink to Mokoto's.

"To einjels." They downed their tetsa, with unmatched feelings. The king was so obviously excited, and his excitement wasn't at all tainted by the bile he could sense within his son. Actually, a part of him found it amusing. At least Mokoto was trying to behave as he should. "Oh…" the king uttered, pouring them another drink. "Mokoto – if you see Lanka or Anaka you can tell them about this, but don't go into detail. Just tell them to see me, and nobody else must know. Do you understand?"

"Of course." Mokoto nodded, and obediently drank with his father.

He didn't stay long after that. A few short minutes passed, and Mokoto left the room to allow the king to get on with his work. He steadily made his way down the corridor, his mind racing with a thousand thoughts of Anaka, and his father. Well… it was an honour. Mokoto had to realise that. Even through his bitterness, he did realise that. Of course. He wasn't a fool. As devastating as the news of Anaka had been, Mokoto was starting to appreciate its implications more and more with every second that passed. Steadily, he allowed his mind to once more move onto what this would mean for the planet. For Meitona Palace, and for the royal family. The world would have a hundred einjels, and his father King Taka would be their leader… There was no denying it; this event would go down in history. His father would be documented as one of the greatest kings that ever lived, and Mokoto would be remembered as his heir… Heir to an einjel. Being worthy of the throne was an even heavier burden now than it had ever been before, but it was a burden that Mokoto was willing to carry. One that Mokoto would be proud to carry – and one that he *would* carry, with success. He was determined to make his father proud. King Taka would be remembered throughout history, and Mokoto would spend the rest of his life making sure that he ended up the same. Actually, as he thought more about it Mokoto's soul started to tingle with the warm buzz of excitement. He couldn't believe what this would do for the family. It wasn't just Anaka, or King Taka, or Mokoto… the whole family would be changed because of this. In the eyes of history they would be made immortal, forever remembered by everyone that walked the Gaiamiras' world for the rest of time. Mokoto's children, and grandchildren, and great nieces and nephews and cousins and every descendant they made... they would all carry the blood of einjels. They would all be blessed by the Gaiamira, more than everyone else in the world, and it would go on like that for as long as the royal bloodline existed. It was fantastic... *fantastic*!

"Hey."

Mokoto looked up to see Anaka slowly approaching him.

"You are walking today?" he teased, suddenly forgetting about his jealousy. It was difficult to feel jealous towards someone who was obviously so frail. All Mokoto saw before him was a broken einjel, one who would benefit his and the family's reputation without being of any threat to him at all. Looking at the image of her, Mokoto couldn't help but smile.

"Shut up," Anaka growled. She stopped a few feet in front of him and leaned against the wall, taking a deep breath and biting her lip. "Trying to..." she mumbled. "Whoever diagnoses me I'm going to kill them for taking so long."

"Do you need help?" Mokoto offered. It was a sincere gesture; his friendship with Anaka was claiming its place in his soul once more.

"No... today isn't that bad..." Anaka replied. She closed her eyes, and took a few more deep breaths before looking at him. "Anyway. What are you so happy about?" she asked. "You aren't getting married again?"

"No," Mokoto smirked playfully, unfazed by her taunting. "Father has some good news."

"Mm?" Anaka uttered, rolling her eyes. She seemed rather sceptical of that. "Who's pregnant now?"

"Better than that," Mokoto sniggered. He looked around to make sure nobody else could hear him. No... They were alone. He turned back to Anaka, and allowed a wide grin to form upon his face. "They've spoken to him."

"Who?" Anaka frowned.

"*Them,*" Mokoto answered.

348

He moved his eyes to the floor, gesturing towards the beings that resided in the centre of the world. His excitement was escalating; now that he was telling someone it seemed more real, and all Mokoto seemed capable of thinking about in this moment in time was what this meant for him and his family. They would be legends! His heart skipped a beat as he uttered the words, his excitement never failing to grow with every second that danced by. "The Gaiamira."

"What?" Anaka's eyes widened, at the same time that her face grew pale. In one short moment the colour drained from her; her face hardened, and she started to look unsettlingly serious. Worried, in fact. Even... scared. "What did they say?"

"Well... you can't tell anyone," Mokoto answered awkwardly, slightly taken aback by her manner. He had expected her to be elated; she'd done this herself had she not? Was she worried that Mokoto may find out about her visit? Perhaps she didn't realise he was permitted to know... Or perhaps *she* was jealous. It would be typical of her to be jealous of the king. Ill feelings were not permitted towards their father, but trust Anaka to break the social rules. "They're sending him to Earth," Mokoto told her, as boldly as he could manage. "Anaka – don't worry, I know you went. He's going for the same reason. He said he'll be back by the end of the month. You should speak to him –"

"What...?" Anaka's face continued to fall, at an alarming rate. She looked sick and ghostly, so much so it was as if the Goddess of Death would take her at any moment. Her entire body became tense, and yet it still managed to tremble. She looked terrible...

"It's okay – don't worry!" Mokoto assured her, taking hold of her shaking frame. "They gave me permission to know. I won't tell anyone else. Do you know what this will mean for our family –?"

"*Shit!*" Anaka shrieked. She clasped her hands onto her face, in such a tremendous panic that her claws were digging into her own skin. She didn't seem to notice, nor did she seem to care that she was harming herself. "Has he left yet?" she demanded.

"Anaka – what's wrong?" Mokoto frowned. "You of all people should feel honoured! Father is an *einjel* –"

"I don't want him to be a fucking einjel!" Anaka screamed. "Where is he?"

349

"He's in the meeting room –"

"*Is he leaving now?*" Anaka's voice grew louder, her breathing shaky and frantic.

"What's wrong with you?" Mokoto snapped, and as quickly as Anaka's face had changed his excitement turned to rage. Why was she being like this? She was so disrespectful! It was disgusting! "Aren't you happy for him? Do you have *any* idea what this will do for our family?"

"I don't care about that!" Anaka yelled. "Fuck the family, he's going to die!" She yanked herself away from Mokoto, taking him by surprise. As weak as she was, she wasn't weak now. Suddenly she was full of life and fire, her dormant Footprints waking and racing to the front of her being as if she had been possessed by the God of War. With a fierce shove she pushed past Mokoto and started to run down the corridor.

"Hey!" Mokoto barked and ran after her, violently grabbing her arm. "What's wrong with you? Don't talk like that!"

"Mokoto, let go of me!" Anaka snarled. She glared at him with an anger Mokoto had never seen in her before. It was unnerving; such ferocity had never been present in Anaka's eyes. He didn't understand why it was here now. Stunned, he let go of her arm and she immediately ran. Within seconds she'd hurled herself down the corridor and into their father's meeting room, without a warning to the king and without a single trace of the pain she must have felt. Mokoto stood there, in a state of disbelief. He vaguely wondered if he should follow her… but she was with the king now. What good could Mokoto do? And more importantly, *what* had gotten into her? Mokoto's fists clenched in anger, his foot tapping against the softly groomed carpet of the palace. He was disgusted at her behaviour. How could she be so disrespectful? Their father had been presented with the greatest honour possible and, she was… angry? Unsupportive? How dare she say such blasphemous things! How dare she burst into their father's meeting room like that! She was not above their father! She had no right to behave in such a way! What in the Gaiamiras' world was wrong with her? Mokoto scoffed in anger and made his way back to his room, hoping their father would beat some sense into Anaka.

350

XXVII.

'Taka found the traitors that had turned against him, and they were afraid, because they knew they had betrayed him. He told them they would be punished, because the Gaiamira must never be betrayed. Just like a parent must always be respected, honoured and obeyed, so must the Gaiamira, because the Gaiamira are the parents of mortals.'

-     Extract from the Gaiamirapon: 'The Communications'

*

"No! Please!" Anaka's screams echoed through Mokoto's mind, over and over like a sickness; a plague in his blood. *"Please, Father! Please don't go! You'll die! I'm telling you you'll all die!"* It had been horrifying to hear. Truly. Why had she said those things? How could she say such things? It was sickening. It was all Mokoto had thought about all day. Eventually the king had knocked her unconscious, offended by her maniacal shrieking. It was a wonder he didn't have her executed for blasphemy or treason; Mokoto wouldn't have blamed him if he did. Anyway… she was in her room now. It was the night before King Taka's departure. Anaka had been begging and pleading for two days, creating a disturbing atmosphere within the palace. It had unsettled everybody. The king had ordered her not to leave her room; he feared she would curse his journey if she continued to openly scream her opposition. So Mokoto hadn't seen Anaka for a couple of days, nor had he wanted to. If she was going to behave like that… Apparently even from her room she kept phoning the king and sending servants to him with messages. It was unacceptable. It angered Mokoto actually; he had no idea how she could bring herself to behave in such a disgraceful way.

    Anyway… that was Anaka. Doing her own thing as always, while the rest of Meitona Palace – particularly Mokoto – continued to be supportive of the king. Now he sat in one of the common rooms, accompanied only by his father, sharing a last drink with King Taka before he left. They'd talked about many things. The mission, their

351

family, Meitona… now they were both sitting, with a comfortable silence between them. King Taka had his eyes closed. He wasn't sleeping, just relaxing. Enjoying the home that he was about to leave. Of course, the world knew he would come back a changed man.

"Let me ask you something…" King Taka spoke from the comfort of his chair, not moving anything but his lips.

"Yes, Sire?" Mokoto replied.

"Miama." Taka opened his eyes, to look at Mokoto. "What's happening there?"

"What do you mean, Sire…?" Mokoto asked cautiously, genuinely unsure of what the king meant. Or rather, what he was insinuating… The king had that disapproving look about him, one that Mokoto knew well. One that Mokoto had been raised to understand.

"Do you love her?"

"L…" Mokoto practically choked. He was gobsmacked that the king had even asked him such a thing. Love? *Love*? No! "Of course not!" he protested. "Sire –"

"It's fine if you do," Taka said calmly, as if they were talking about something perfectly normal. "It cannot be helped – even the Gaiamira have said that. 'Love is a weakness, but it is not a curse. A good Hiveakan is not one who never falls in love, but one who overcomes it'." He recited the Gaiamirapon perfectly; it was a line that every Gaiamirákan knew – particularly Hiveakans. It was a quote from the God of War. "You remember that, don't you?"

"Of course. But I'm not in love, Sire," Mokoto answered forcefully. "I never was."

"Really…?" Taka uttered. He didn't seem convinced. Why not? "Well, it is none of my business. The public like her; I would like you to keep her. Just… be careful. It can happen, without you realising." He paused for a moment, as if he was deciding whether or not to continue, but the decision had already been made. Before he had even started this conversation. It was obvious… the king had something he wanted to say. "It happened to me."

Mokoto looked at his father, his lips slightly parted. He didn't know how to respond. He felt quite uncomfortable; Hiveakans

shouldn't talk about this sort of thing. They shouldn't admit it, either…
What was the king doing? Why was he saying this…?

"It's late, Sire," Mokoto said. "Perhaps we should call it a
night."

"We should," Taka answered with a small smile. "I have a long
journey tomorrow." He poured a little more tetsa into his glass, clearly
refusing to leave. Mokoto's heart sank. This was happening, wasn't it?
They were definitely going to talk about this. Shit. Taka took a sip of
his drink and continued on, fully aware of the fact that Mokoto didn't
want to. Well… things had to be said, from time to time. This was such
a time. "This woman…" Taka sniggered. "Your uncle Thoit would say
was the 'fucking love of my life. Fuck, shit…'" He raised his fingers to
his lips, imitating smoking a cigarette. Mokoto had to laugh at the
impression. It was flawless. "Fucking… heartbreaker." Taka started to
laugh to himself, continuing his imitation of his brother. He seemed
eased by it, as if it made this conversation less awkward. Why was this
conversation even happening? Mokoto couldn't understand the need
for it. Still, though… the king was obviously nervous about tomorrow.
Mokoto let him say his piece, in peace. If it was what he wanted?
Surely it wouldn't take long. "I met this woman…" Taka continued.
"Not my first."

"Really?" Mokoto answered with a small smirk upon his lips,
almost teasing the king.

"No," Taka laughed. "Really, not my first. If you can believe
it?" He laughed, and took a sip of his tetsa. "She was… she was a
friend. Beautiful, and my age. We got along well, and my parents liked
her. The planet liked her, your uncle… everyone. Especially me." Taka
let out a sigh, his eyes unfocused as he watched the memories pass by.
The memories of… what, happiness? It seemed hard to believe. For
both men, actually. Mokoto couldn't imagine his father being truly
happy any more than Taka could remember it. Still… Taka was certain
it had happened, in a very distant part of his life. "We got married. I…"
He laughed again, very slightly. Very quietly. "I couldn't wait to marry
her – and we had a good marriage. She gave me two children…" Taka
cleared his throat. "Then she betrayed me."

"Oh!"

Mokoto looked away. He understood now. This was why the king was talking about love to Mokoto; it was relevant to Mokoto. The king was talking about his mother. Teima... Mokoto knew very little of her, but he knew enough. She had been a good wife who had given the king two children, and then she had been executed for treason. Mokoto had been taught all about it in the Hive. She had tried to change the king; she had tried to make him lose his brutality, and from what Mokoto could gather she had tried to make him fall in love with her. It was an unforgivable act, one that deserved death... Mokoto had never put much more thought into it than that, but now it was clear. She had been successful in her efforts, hadn't she? That was what this was about, wasn't it? It was brave of the king to admit it; not many Hiveakans would. Such bravery was only deserving of a Hiveakan king. Was he worried about Mokoto? Worried that Miama may cause the same harm as Teima? The quiet Outsider, destroying the brutality of the king... That was why King Taka was talking about Miama; perhaps he could see it going the same way with Mokoto. Well... Mokoto appreciated the warning. Very much so. He would keep an eye on his relationship from now on.

"I must apologise, Mokoto." The king's voice took him by surprise, and Mokoto raised his eyes to his father once more.

"Apologise, Sire?" he questioned.

"I killed your mother under false pretences. I didn't realise until after she was dead. After... my mind became clear," Taka spoke.

"I don't understand, Father," Mokoto uttered. "My mother tried to change you."

"Hm," Taka snorted. "No. She didn't. She was innocent. I didn't realise at the time. This woman..." He sighed. "I suppose she was jealous of Teima. She put the idea in my head – like a fool I let her. Can you believe that? That was how strong my love for her was." He sniggered again. Spitefully, at the sheer patheticness of his own forgotten heart. "I loved this woman so much she managed to convince me I was in love with someone else. Can you imagine that? The power she had over me... I believed everything she said. My thoughts weren't my own – she could have told me there were only six members of the Gaiamira and I would have believed her. She told me your mother was

354

a traitor, and I didn't question it." He looked away, and took a sip of his drink. "Your Uncle Thoit tried to warn me. He could see her for what she was, but I didn't listen to him. It was only years later that I realised. By then it was too late, of course." He turned his head towards Mokoto, and looked at him with the deepest sincerity Mokoto had ever seen. "I am truly sorry, my son. You are not the child of a traitor. Anaka is."

Mokoto's heart stopped. A sharp, cold pain struck his chest as it finally hit him about whom his father was talking. Not Teima... He didn't mean Mokoto's mother. He meant... that woman. The one whose name was not permitted to be spoken in Meitona Palace. The korota... "She made me very happy. I... I can't tell you how much. I've never been that happy since. Never." The king went quiet for a moment. Mokoto didn't know what to think. The king didn't seem himself. He seemed... Mokoto couldn't describe it. If it were an Outsider, Mokoto would use the word 'sad', but... that word wasn't fitting of the king. This was just... not himself. "But it was dangerous," Taka spoke briskly, purging his face of the uncharacteristic expression that had stained it. Whatever kind of trance he had allowed himself to fall into, he'd pulled himself out of it now. "I did something that cannot be undone. That is the power of love. You must be careful of it," he spoke. "If you catch yourself appeasing Miama – or either of them – ask yourself why. Otherwise..." He smiled slightly. Humbly, even. It was a look Mokoto had never seen before, not on the king. He seemed... lesser, somehow. "I am sorry you never knew your mother," Taka uttered. "It was because of my foolishness. Do not think I will ever forgive myself for it. Teima was very loyal to me."

"Forgive yourself, Sire," Mokoto answered. "Even if I had known her, she always did sound soft to me." He smirked a little. "I might have ended up like Tangun."

"Ha," Taka sniggered, and returned to his drink. "No. I wouldn't have allowed it. I would have influenced you myself," he scoffed. "But then, I tried to influence Anaka – Anaka never met her. I thought I could make her my child... but that hasn't worked out. She has her mother's blood, even after all this time."

355

"She will apologise to you, Sire," Mokoto said. "If she isn't a fool."

"Maybe," Taka half-heartedly replied. He didn't seem to care. "You are a good child, Mokoto. Please do not change."

"Yes, Sire." Mokoto nodded. "Of course." He took a sip of his own drink, and they sat in silence.

*

'Above all else King Taka was remembered as the first monarch to ever travel to Earth. His mission was not made public knowledge at the time, at the request of the Gaiamira, but it was this mission which led to the Gaiamiráka-Earth War of 20144G.'

-        Extract from history textbook: 'Inside Meitona Palace, A History of Monarchy', 20171G

*

It was the night before his departure, and King Taka had finally retired to bed, in the room of his first wife. He let himself in, not particularly caring if he disturbed her at this late hour. He had a right to be in here as much as she – more so, actually. It was his palace. He found Kaeila sleeping, but she stirred at the sound of the door opening and closing. She didn't wake, though. She simply rolled over in bed, and settled once again. Taka removed his clothing, and slipped into the bed beside her.

"Kaeila," he spoke through the darkness. She moved, but again she didn't wake to his voice. "Kaeila," he spoke louder, to drag her attention towards him… if she didn't wake up now he would scratch her awake. Fortunately, she did. His loudened voice pulled her into consciousness, and she turned towards its sound. Slowly, she opened her eyes… and she let out a sigh.

"Hello, Sire," she mumbled, her annoyance at being awoken clear in her tone. "Were none of the young ones free?"

Taka started laughing, which caused her to frown. She hadn't expected that snippy remark to amuse him.

"You were a young one once," he spoke, settling down beside her.

"Mm..." Kaeila sleepily grumbled, and closed her eyes again. "Those days are long gone."

"Yes, they are." Taka stared up at the ceiling, at the familiar blackness of the night... Into his memories. Early memories. Memories of a young attractive girl, one that fancied him when he was a young attractive boy. Not a brain cell between them, not a chain upon them... They were idiotic, and naïve... but they were free. Free, and as far as they knew they had a terrific life to come. Well... the life hadn't been bad. Not for Taka, anyway. Kaeila probably had a different opinion. Still... she had stayed, hadn't she? Taka had come to appreciate that over the past couple of days. He'd had eight wives in his life, and they had given him thirteen children. One child of which was not here now; seven wives of which had died in misfortune or as traitors... Not one of them had lived to see what had become of him. Not one of them were here beside him, when he was becoming an einjel. Not one, but Kaeila. The woman who had stolen his youth, and the woman whose life the mistakes of youth had destroyed. If it had been up to him, he would have let her go the moment Maika was conceived. It hadn't been up to him, though. The future king was still but a matat, and against his father Matat Taka hadn't had a scrap of power to his name. It was different now, though. He was an einjel, and he was the king... and as king, he could release whomever he wanted from any prison in the world. "You have been a good wife to me," he spoke into the darkness, aware that Kaeila was still awake at his side. "And a good mother to my children."

"All twelve of them," Kaeila growled, obediently not acknowledging the child who had been killed. She had perished so long ago it was not even worth remembering her name. "What's your point, Sire? It's late."

"You have served your time," Taka said. "You stayed a loyal wife – even though you didn't want to marry me." He sniggered slightly at that, amused by the fact that his one remaining wife had

357

never even wanted to marry him at all. It was ironic, really. Taka was certain the others would have all wanted to be here today. "Should something happen to me while I am away," he continued on, "I want you to know I would not think ill of you if you decided to leave." He turned his head to look at her through the darkness, and he smirked a little to see that her eyes were open now. What he'd just said had probably surprised her. "You wanted to go travelling, didn't you? I'm giving you my permission to do it. If I'm gone, you have no need to stay here."

Kaeila stared at him for a long moment. Taka watched her in curious fascination; Outsider emotions were pathetic, and not something that Taka liked to see, but Kaeila's misery had hardened her so much over the years that she seldom displayed them. So it was quite amazing to watch her now. Her eyes were glistening. Even through the darkness, Taka could see them release just a few tears. Really...? He couldn't remember the last time he had made her feel anything more than spite. Or rather, anything at all... Kaeila had become quite dead to emotions. It was a wonder she remembered how to cry.

"Thank you," she whispered. "But..." She wiped her eyes, becoming embarrassed by her display. She agreed with him; it was pathetic. "I'm not young anymore. I'm quite used to this lifestyle, Sire. I wouldn't want to change it now."

"I see," Taka said. "Well then. Should I die, then by all means stay. I'm sure my heir would keep you in the lifestyle you are used to."

"Yes." Her answer was short, but there was no need for anything more. They had an understanding, as they always had. They were thrown together against their will. They were a fling that went terribly wrong, each one bound to the other, reluctantly and eternally... and they had both become too accustomed to it to change. That was them. That was their life.

King Taka closed his eyes and extended his arm, and amidst the darkness of sleep he felt a warm body lay against his.

XXVIII.

'Tomakoto appears as a young boy, energetic and bright. He is always smiling, and always thinks of the future. He looks into a mortal's soul and he knows what they want to achieve, and he believes it is in their power to achieve it. Tomakoto does not doubt that great things can happen to those that believe.'

-      Extract from the Gaiamirapon: 'The Identities'

*

Mokoto paced nervously around his room. It had been ten days since his father had left and he hadn't heard a single word back. It was late; the king and his army should have arrived by now. He should have made contact with Gaiamiráka, but nothing. Mokoto hadn't been worried at first, but the king's ship was being monitored by the Royals' military team, and reports on its activity indicated that the king had arrived on Earth. So, now Mokoto was worrying. There was no reason why Mokoto shouldn't have heard from him. Why hadn't he made contact? Maybe his communication devices were broken – the devices that were checked meticulously by the most qualified engineers in the world before the king's departure... Or maybe Anaka's negative energy had cursed him. ... No. Mokoto couldn't think like that. He battled that thought every time it entered his mind, and it entered many times. His mind was constantly racing through all the possibilities of why the king hadn't made contact. Perhaps he was lost or captured... but maybe there was something wrong with his communication systems; Mokoto kept thinking of that. It was one of his more favourable ideas. As much as they had been checked and tested, such devices had never been used over such a long distance before. It was the sort of technology the people of the Royal had been developing for years, but the Gaiamira had never given them permission to use it – not to this extent, at least. Nobody had been permitted to travel beyond Gaiamiráka's moons before. Nobody except Anaka, and that was... what, almost thirty years ago now. So maybe that was it. Maybe King

Taka's technology had failed. Or maybe he was dead. That idea always came at some point. As much as Mokoto reasoned with himself, and went through all the perfectly plausible, safe possibilities, that thought always returned. The king might be dead. Anaka might have cursed him after all... No. No, no, she couldn't have. Mokoto couldn't think that! He took a seat on his bed, his foot anxiously tapping against the floor as he tried to decide what to do. His father had told him to wait a week before he took the throne... not that Mokoto wanted it to come to that. Not that it would come to that. There was no reason to believe it, even though it was a thought that repeatedly forced its way into Mokoto's mind.

Knock. Mokoto leapt to his feet at the sound – was it news of his father? He made his way over to the door and keenly opened it... Then his face dropped, and he sighed in annoyance at the person he found standing there.

"What do you want?" he growled, offended by her presence.

"Nothing now." Anaka pushed past him into the room, wincing as his arm touched one of her many injuries – injuries that she had received from the king for speaking her objections. Mokoto hadn't spoken to her since their father had left; he couldn't bring himself to put his anger into words. It would be an insult to his father and to the Gaiamira to grant her the honour of his words. He was repulsed by it... the thought that King Taka was an einjel, and she couldn't even pretend to be happy for him! The thought that she had screamed her opposition so loud it might have cursed their father... it made Mokoto sick. Even looking at her filled his being with hate. "I wanted to see if you'd heard anything," Anaka said, taking a seat on the bed. *His* bed!

"Nothing," Mokoto replied. "So you can leave now."

"In a minute!" Anaka frowned. Her muscles were half tensing and she squinted a little; she seemed to be in a lot of pain.

"No. Now," Mokoto spoke, coldly and impatiently. "You're a Hiveakan. Deal with the pain."

"I'll deal with you..." Anaka mumbled. She sighed, and steadily struggled to her feet. "I'll be in my room. Let me know if you hear anything."

360

"Fine." Mokoto refused to look at her, even though he knew she was looking at him. He could feel her eyes on him. Her lying, treacherous eyes. He refused to acknowledge her; he simply waited, and he felt her walk past him and out of the room in silence... Then he keenly closed the door.

He sighed deeply and went to lie down on his bed. He would have the sheets changed before he slept in it. He didn't want her treason to spread onto him while he was sleeping. Perhaps he would stay in Miama's room tonight. He couldn't believe what was happening... Above all else, above everything that was going on, Anaka had surprised him the most. She had shocked him, even. Of all the people in the world he had never expected Anaka to betray him. Not him and especially not their father. She had always tested the king, and she hadn't always been as respectful towards him as she should, but she had always been loyal. Always. She even did as much as to marry Teikota and conceive two children with him – just because the king had told her to. She'd always seemed to adore him; she'd always seemed to admire and respect him... What had happened to make her change? Mokoto closed his eyes, as if it would help. Perhaps this illness was affecting her brain... perhaps it was changing her judgement. Or, perhaps she was just a bitch. Mokoto sniggered slightly. That seemed more likely, somehow. Perfect Meitat Anaka... King Taka's favourite child, the love of Meitona, the only Hiveakan daddy's girl in existence... had let the entire family down. Mokoto's chest tightened as his anger grew stronger, his Footprints stampeding through his soul. Why was she the favourite? Why had she ever been the favourite? She was disrespectful, and ungrateful, and she had betrayed their father! She had betrayed him! Mokoto would never do that, never in a million years! No matter what he felt – even if he didn't agree with the king he would support him to the very end; that was what a good child was supposed to do! That was what Tomakoto did, it was what Maida did, what Aourat did and what Chieit did and what everyone else in the palace did! And it wasn't just a question of loyalty towards their father.

This mission was a command of the Gaiamira, and by opposing it Anaka was opposing them. That was unacceptable. As

361

unacceptable as disloyalty towards the king was, disloyalty towards the Gaiamira was far worse. It was eternally worse, and they would eternally punish her for it. Actually, it angered Mokoto that he'd been friends with her for all these years. That was perhaps the thing that he hated the most. He'd been so naïve. He'd never once seen her for what she was, and he hated it. He absolutely *hated* it. It gnawed at him, like a parasite feeding on his soul. He should have known better; he should have been intelligent enough to see it. He shouldn't have been so trusting that he could not see it. She didn't honour their father, she didn't honour the Gaiamira and she didn't honour the family or Meitona – or the world, actually. Not a single one of them mattered to her – *nothing* mattered to her. Nothing except her own ill-formed opinions and her own ludicrous ideas. How had it taken Mokoto so long to realise it? She didn't deserve to live in the palace. She didn't even deserve to live in the Gaiamiras' world, and she certainly didn't deserve to be King Taka's daughter. King Taka didn't need her. He had his heir. Mokoto wouldn't let him down. He was a better child than Anaka ever was! He could see that now, as clear as day.

Buzz. Suddenly, Mokoto tensed at the sound of his phone ringing. The Royal's engineers had set it up to receive calls from King Taka's ship, via the communication devices in the Royal. Every time his phone rang Mokoto was on edge, hoping that it would be him. Immediately, Mokoto dove his hand into his pocket and yanked out his phone.

"Yes?"

"Mokoto!" A sharp, white coldness shot through Mokoto's heart when he recognised the voice, and he desperately leapt to his feet.

"F-Father!" he gagged. It was him… It was the king. Finally! He wasn't dead. Of course he wasn't! He was King Taka! "Did you land safely, Sire?"

"No. Listen to me…" King Taka breathed. He sounded… not how Mokoto had expected. He was speaking quietly, but his tone was frantic. It was unsettling. Something was wrong; Mokoto could sense it in the king's voice. He could feel it. Immediately, he started to panic. Immediately, he started thinking the worst. Mokoto was suddenly convinced that the engines of the king's ship had failed; he was convinced the king was stranded there. Shit! Shit! Anaka! "I'm not coming home."

Mokoto's heart stopped. His hand loosened a little, and just for a short moment his breathing ceased. He found himself unable to process the words right away, and once they were processed he didn't believe them. He didn't know what his father meant, but it couldn't be the traditional interpretation. He must mean that it would be a while before he returned home. Well, it made sense. By the time the Royal built another ship to rescue him, and by the time they got it to Earth and back... Yes. That was it. Of course that was it. The king had uncharacteristically made a poor choice of words, but that was what he meant. What else could it be? "Mokoto!" King Taka's voice came once again, yanking Mokoto's attention towards it.

"Yes, Sire?"

"They've attacked us," Taka stated. "They destroyed our ship."

"What?" No. He still didn't understand, and he couldn't think of anything else to say. Mokoto couldn't imagine what the king meant. He knew it couldn't be literal, obviously. That was impossible. The Gaiamira had assured the king he wouldn't be harmed. He was King Taka; of course he wouldn't be harmed. So Mokoto didn't understand...

"The humans attacked us," Taka spoke. "I've taken shelter, but they'll find me soon. Your soldiers sacrificed themselves to protect me – you make sure the world knows that. They were loyal. All of them. You will make sure the world knows that?"

"What?"

"*Mokoto!*"

King Taka's voice thundered through the phone with all the passion and rage of the God of War, and for the first time Mokoto started to believe him. It was as if King Taka's Footprints had struck him, knocking into him the horrific truth behind their vessel's words. The plain, simple, literal truth. Suddenly, Mokoto understood it. The king had been attacked. The humans had attacked him. They had destroyed his ship. He wasn't coming home. King Taka was going to die there.

"What's going on?"

363

Mokoto snarled at the sound of Anaka's voice. Again! Why did she have to be here? What was she doing here? He turned towards the door and saw her standing there; in his shock Mokoto had barely heard the door open. She softly closed the door behind her and looked at him, her face already panic-filled even though she didn't know what was going on. Or... she did know what was going on. With her face the way it was, it certainly seemed that way. How did she know...? How had she known...? "I picked up a signal in my room..."

Mokoto ignored Anaka. He refused to acknowledge her presence. He refused to let her distract him; he refused to allow her to take him away from – this. Whatever this was. King Taka's last call, or... shit! Shit! That was what this was. Shit! Shit! Shit! Shit! Shit! No. This wasn't it. Mokoto refused to believe it. The Gaiamira wouldn't allow this. They never would have sent him if it could have possibly turned into this! This was blasphemy!

"Mokoto, is Anaka there?" Taka asked.

"Yes..." Mokoto answered, his anger rising at the question. No! No no, this was wrong! Anaka shouldn't be here! The king didn't want her here – he was angry at her. He had left being angry at her – she had done this! She had cursed him! She had no right to be here!

Mokoto stepped towards Anaka, preparing himself to quite literally throw her out of the room. He knew that was what the king wanted. He knew it was what the king was about to request. Mokoto would spare him the time.

"Let me speak to her."

"What?" Once again, Mokoto's heart stopped. Once again, he entered into a state of disbelief. He must have misheard...

"I have to speak to Anaka! Put me on to her!" Taka demanded. He suddenly sounded desperate, as if speaking to Anaka was the last thing he had to do before he died. As if it was the only thing he wanted to do; as if he had a need to do it... Why...?

"Sire..." Mokoto spoke quietly. "What do you want me to do with the throne?"

"I don't care! It's your throne now!" Taka roared, his voice thundering once more. "I'm going to get found any minute, *put me onto Anaka!*"

364

"Yes, Sire."

Mokoto didn't understand. Once more. Any of it. He felt confused, and dazed. He didn't understand why this was happening. He didn't understand why his father had been sent there, nor did he understand why he had been attacked. He didn't understand why he was going to die. He didn't understand why... of all the people in the world, of all his children, King Taka was choosing to speak to Anaka in the final moments of his life. Anaka, the traitor. Anaka, the one who had opposed him. The one who had cursed him. The one who didn't even respect King Taka enough to take his throne. Why Anaka? When she had betrayed him? Why, when Mokoto was King Taka's heir? Why... any of it? Mokoto didn't understand. He was realising that now. Actually, it was starting to feel as if he had lived his entire life blind. Blind, and blindly loyal. He was a good heir and a good son... and yet, here he was. In his blind loyalty, in his last ever talk with his father... he was handing Anaka the phone.

She took a seat on the bed and held the phone close to her lips, closing her eyes. Of course she would do that. Of course she would make this dramatic. Of course she would look like an Outsider. Even in his final moments, Anaka could not bring herself to behave in any way except her own before the king. Why did he want to waste his time on her...?

"Father..." she uttered softly.

"Anaka..." Mokoto didn't need to hear their father to know exactly how he sounded. Somehow, he knew. He had been blunt and cold and angry with Mokoto, but he wouldn't be with her. Mokoto couldn't hear the king screaming; he couldn't feel his Footprints through the phone. He wasn't using them on her. He wasn't screaming at her. So what was he doing? What was he saying...?

"Don't worry." Anaka smiled feebly. "You don't need to apologise. I would have done the same." Mokoto's stomach turned at the sight of her wincing. No. No, he had *not* just heard that. She scrunched her eyelids, and bit her lip. "Of course I forgive you. You don't need my forgiveness!"

Mokoto felt sick. A jolt of something cold and sharp shot up through his spine. It cascaded through his body and burst into his chest making his heart race and making him gag. He was hearing words that he knew could not possibly be spoken. Anaka's face was riddled with emotions that he knew she couldn't possibly be feeling, because if she was feeling such emotions then it would mean the king was saying something he couldn't possibly be saying... Mokoto knew it was not possible. He knew none of it could be happening, and yet he was seeing it. He was hearing it, and feeling it... and all with the most horrific sensation tearing through his soul. There was not a word for it. For this... bile that plagued Mokoto's being. Such an emotion had never existed in the world before today. Such an emotion hadn't had a need to exist. Why...? Why was King Taka choosing *her?* Why was he apologising, why was he demanding forgiveness? He had *nothing* to be sorry for! Why was he talking to her? "Thank you..." Mokoto watched as Anaka opened her eyes slightly. They were glistening. Was she *crying?*

"What is he saying?" Mokoto demanded.

"Father... you –" Anaka laughed a little and wiped her eyes. "Alright. I won't." She smiled again, a little sadly. Why...? "You know me. I have too much to do in the Royal." Mokoto's heart sank. No. No, not sank. It didn't have time to sink. It crumbled away into nothing. He knew what was happening; it was obvious. King Taka was asking her to be his heir. Of course. He'd always wanted her, hadn't he? Even now, after all his hard work, and loyalty, and dedication, Mokoto still wasn't good enough. Even after all these years... it was her. It had always been her. Why was Mokoto even here...? "I will." Anaka glanced briefly at Mokoto before turning back to the call, and smiling faithfully as if her father could see her. That short glance angered Mokoto; it got his back up, and his body tensed in defence. They were talking about him. What were they saying? "I promise. I promise, Father." She sniffed a little and shut her eyes in an attempt to force back any tears that were trying to pass through. Tears... *tears?* She was crying – she was performing a weak, Outsider, *unacceptable* display of emotions, and still... the king had chosen her. Why? Why? Why, why, why? " Goodbye, Sire."

"*What!*"

Mokoto's eyes widened. He watched in horror as Anaka hung up the phone, not even asking if he wanted to talk! That bitch. That treacherous *bitch*! "That is my father!" Mokoto screamed. He stormed over to her, towering over her smaller frame like a beast readying to attack. He tore the phone from her hand and tried desperately to call the king back – but nothing. Of course nothing, this ridiculous technology created by those alleged geniuses at the Royal could only allow the king to call him, not the other way round! Why was it so primitive? Was the king dead? Mokoto had no idea! He hadn't been given the opportunity to ask! He glared back at Anaka, his teeth bared and his Footprints bright in his eyes. He wanted to kill her. He wanted to rip her apart! Why shouldn't he? He could think of no reason not to destroy her – all of this was her fault!

"I'm sorry!" Anaka looked up at Mokoto pleadingly. She wasn't afraid. As terrifying as he looked, she wasn't in fear of her life. Still, it didn't keep the tears from her eyes. They were damp. Not with fear. With guilt. She wasn't pleading for her life, she was pleading for his forgiveness. Did she know this had all happened because of her? Did she ever expect Mokoto to forgive her for that? Or even so much as pretend to? "They found him."

"Who?" Mokoto exhaled sharply, briefly allowing himself to be ignorant of the truth. Of course, he knew the truth. Refusing to acknowledge their name would not change what had happened, nor would it erase Mokoto's knowledge of it. The king was dead now, wasn't he? He had died on that world. His soul... was on that world. He would be trapped there, away from the Gaiamira. Unable to travel to the Gaiamirarezo, unable to be reincarnated... He would be lost, forever. In the world of the lost. Why...?

"The humans," Anaka answered, wiping away her tears. "They found him. He was the only one left."

"Why didn't he speak to me?" Mokoto demanded, his rage suddenly returning to its greatest height. "I'm his heir!"

"It's nothing personal, Moko." Anaka spoke the words so perfectly, so calmly it almost made Mokoto wonder if this was all just some horrific joke. Perhaps his father would walk in at any minute and say this was a test of character, or perhaps Anaka would giggle and say the phone call was fake. Perhaps that would happen... or perhaps this was real.

"Personal?" Mokoto spat. "I'm his heir and he wanted to talk to you. *How* is that not personal?"

"He had nothing left to say to you," Anaka mumbled. She smiled a little. It was a difficult smile; Mokoto couldn't read it. She sounded sad – sympathetic, even... but she looked... happy. *Happy*? What was wrong with her? "He spent so much time with you when he was here, he taught you everything. He already told you everything. You're the only one he wanted a future for."

"You piece of shit," Mokoto snarled. "Do not talk to me like I'm an Outsider, and don't look at me like that! I don't need your fucking pity!" He gestured towards the door, his Footprints pounding against his palms, desperate to break out and do some serious harm to her. He wanted to. He wanted to rip off her limbs and drain the life from her useless body... but he wouldn't. She wasn't worth it. Their father – his father... he wouldn't have wanted it. If he did, he would have asked. "Go. Get your crying face out of here – tears aren't allowed in this room. Leave before I kill you."

"Moko –"

"*Out!*" Mokoto grew angrier at the sound of her sickeningly sympathetic tone. Why was she doing that? Why was she behaving like she pitied him? She was the pathetic one! She was the one who was weak and frail, and crying like an Outsider. Why had the king spoken to her?

"What's your problem?" Anaka growled.

"My problem," Mokoto glared at her, "is that my father is *dead*, and the last thing he wanted was to speak to you. Now *get out!*"

"Ow!"

Anaka screamed in pain as Mokoto yanked her up off the bed, digging his claws deeply into her arm. "Get off me!" Anaka yelled. She swung her palm out and smacked him across the face. "He was my father too!"

"How do you know?" Mokoto roared. "You must have inherited the traitor's gene from somewhere, how can you be sure your mother wasn't a liar?"

368

Anaka froze. She stared at him in horror, her eyes widening. "How…?" she choked. "How can you say that?"

"Well…" Mokoto snorted viciously, glaring into her eyes. "You certainly didn't get it from him."

"How can you *say that?*" Anaka screamed.

She flung her arms out and began wildly thrashing at him, ignoring her own burning pain as she destroyed herself to harm her brother. "You little piece of shit!" she wailed. Her Footprints were burning; all of a sudden they were lively and bright in her eyes. She actually looked like a Hiveakan. For the first time in years, she looked dangerous. "Don't you ever compare me to her again! She was a traitor – I am nothing like her! Don't ever mention her to me!" She slammed her clenched fists into Mokoto's chest, causing him to gag at the impact. His eyes widened when he heard one of his bones crack, and a shooting pain accompanied what seemed to be a very real injury. How? He stared down at Anaka, shocked. He didn't understand this! How had she managed that? Where had she found the strength? She must be in tremendous pain now, to give such an attack… In a way it was admirable. Anaka stared back at him furiously, her thrashing had ceased. She was panting. Her powerful attacks had drained her; her Footprints had demanded more from her body than it could give. She barely had the strength left in her to stand. "I'm sitting down outside," she mumbled, tiredly but stubbornly. She was refusing to appear weak, though just moments ago she had been quite comfortable with crying.

"Fine." Mokoto shrugged. He turned his back to her. "As long as it's out of my sight. Fuck off!"

"Our father is dead."

"Yes." Mokoto gritted his teeth. The words scraped through him as if he were under torture. Why had she said that? What was she hoping to achieve? He was fully aware. He had witnessed it – but he had not heard it, thanks to her. Her and her sickening, treacherous presence. Mokoto didn't look at her. He couldn't stand to. She wasn't worth it. She would never be worth it. "Thank you for talking to him on my behalf."

"Mokoto –"

369

"Leave." Mokoto spoke the word coldly and fiercely, and listened for the sound of movement. She was obeying him… at last. He heard her shuffling towards the door. Slowly, and painfully… Mokoto could imagine the agony she was in. Good. He wanted to imagine it. She deserved it. She deserved more. He heard her leave the room, and he heard her close the door behind her. At last.

Mokoto sighed and placed a hand firmly on his chest, frowning at the pain that shot through his muscles. Fuck! She had broken something. How she'd managed to, he had no idea. He would have to see a doctor. Later. His injuries were his lowest priority; he had more important matters to attend to… like arranging a funeral. Shit! Shit! Mokoto closed his eyes and sat down, running a hand through his hair. Shit! This wasn't real. Why was this real? This *couldn't* be real! … He'd lost his father.

XXIX.

'Donso and Mokuya present themselves as the perfect king and queen. When the people of Gaiamira need a strong leader they are warriors, and in times of peace they are mild and wise. Sometimes they are two separate entities holding hands, and sometimes they are conjoined. The closer these deities, the more the world needs its leader.'

\-   Extract from the Gaiamirapon: 'The Identities'

*

"Matat Mokoto," the voice of a priest echoed above Mokoto as he knelt with his head down in front of the large statue of Donso and Mokuya, God and Goddess of Kings and Queens. Of course, Mokoto had been crowned immediately; Gaiamiráka could not survive for even a day without a king. The public had been told of King Taka's death only a few hours after he had spoken his last words and reports of King Taka's ship confirmed it had been destroyed. The people of Gaiamiráka were told a part truth. They were told that King Taka, along with one hundred of their friends and relatives, was sent to Earth to gather information, and unforeseen circumstances led to their deaths. That was all. There was no explanation of what such circumstances were, nor was there any explanation of whether it could have been prevented, or whether there was anyone to blame... It was frustrating for the people, of course it was, but the Gaiamira had to be obeyed. They did not want the details of King Taka's mission to be known, and known they were not. The king had died. A hundred soldiers had died... and only a select few members of the royal family knew why. Needless to say, the public were angry. Angry, and frustrated, and they wanted answers... but they would not get answers. Mokoto would not get answers, nor would he get closure. He would get a better title that was all. The relatives of those hundred einjels would get life insurance pay-outs, and a rare story to tell to their children. The world would move on... it had already started to move on. Much more hastily than Mokoto could have ever imagined.

371

He listened loyally to the words of the priest that stood behind him, holding his crown. It was a new crown… King Taka had been wearing the family crown when he died. It was one of the few pieces of jewellery that had been in the family for centuries; Mokoto had always thought he would wear it someday. Why would he assume anything else? It devastated him that he wouldn't. Those people – those creatures… they had taken that away from him. They had taken his birthright, and the birthright of his own heir, and their heir and their heir… generations of kings and queens would be forever denied their family crown, because of those things. "On behalf of the Gaiamira, I crown you King of Gaiamiráka, before our almighty God Donso and Goddess Mokuya," the priest proclaimed. "May your reign be long, may you always know victory and may you lead our people to greatness… and may Donso and Mokuya always guide you, watch over you and protect you, for as long as you are king of their people, and may Tangun protect you for an eternity afterwards." He carefully placed the crown on Mokoto's head and stepped back. "Now… rise, Your Highness." Mokoto obeyed, never taking his eyes off the statues. It seemed disrespectful to look anywhere else. "Turn, please." Obediently, Mokoto turned, to find the priest on his knees. He and everyone else who had been permitted to view this historical event, in the temple of Donso and Mokuya. There had to be thousands of people here, all with cameras and smiles. Mokoto paid no attention to any of them. He didn't want to. They shouldn't be here. He shouldn't be here. "Sire…" The priest spoke from his position on his knees, his head bowed before Mokoto. Before… the king. "King Mokoto. Welcome to the throne."

*

'The crowds are gathered outside Meitona Palace, awaiting King Mokoto's first address. There are mixed feelings in the air; many are still devastated over the sudden, and frankly shocking news of King Taka's death, but at the same time it's fair to say that everyone here is excited to witness this historical event, and we are all looking forward to what will no doubt be inspiring words from our new king.'

- News report, 20142G

*

"Try not to appear nervous, Sire. These are difficult times, but they cannot be difficult for you. You mustn't seem like this has come as a shock." Rozo's voice came from beside Mokoto, as he stood on the third floor of Meitona Palace, before the glass door that led onto the Royal Balcony... The balcony where he would make his first speech as king. He had only worn the crown for a few minutes before he was driven from the nearby Donso and Mokuya temple back to Meitona Palace, where he would officially address his people. His people. Not his father's. His people now. Rozo was here... speaking to him. Advising him, as if he were getting paid for it. Mokoto could have sworn Rozo's job was not to be Mokoto's aide. It wasn't this morning...

"You are treating me like the king, Rozo," Mokoto remarked. "You never called me 'Sire' before."

"Well... Yes, Sire," Rozo answered awkwardly. "You... you are the king, now."

"So people keep saying," Mokoto replied. He looked down at Rozo, with an expression that was impossible to read, even for the most skilled codebreaker in the world. "Then if I am king I am a Hiveakan king, and I do not need your advice. Even a Hiveakan matat knows how to conduct himself."

"Yes, Sire." Rozo nodded, lowering his eyes. "I apologise. Please... forgive me. I... I'm not as strong as you. I'm not handling things as well."

"Hm." Mokoto snorted, a small smirk forming upon his lips. "I am sure you are."

He turned his head towards a... person. Mokoto wasn't sure what they were. Some sort of associate of the media he assumed; one who would let him know when their colleagues with cameras were ready for Mokoto to step onto the stage. Unbelievable. After all his hard work, Mokoto had finally become king and yet there was still

373

another mortal telling him what to do. So far the crown had only served to restrict Mokoto's freedom even more. "Are you people ready yet?" he demanded.

"Um…" The woman looked at him nervously, and desperately turned her attention to Rozo.

"I believe we are waiting to hear back from security, Sire," Rozo answered for her. "You will be vulnerable out there; we need to make sure it's safe first."

"Somebody would dare shoot me on my first day as king?" Mokoto sniggered. "Then I suppose my reputation isn't frightening enough. Perhaps we need to tighten the laws on gun crime."

"Yes…" Rozo uttered, not entirely sure how to interpret that. For a start, he couldn't tell if King Mokoto was joking. "Maybe… don't mention that in this speech, Sire."

Mokoto chuckled a little, amused by the traces of fear he could sense in Rozo. Was Rozo shitting himself right now? Was he wondering what sort of maniac had taken the throne? Well, nobody wanted this. Nobody had planned it, and yet here they all were. So that was that. It was just another issue to be dealt with now. Mokoto closed his eyes, allowing his thoughts to roam as they pleased.

"This is your music?" The memory of many years ago entered Mokoto's mind. The memory of a young matat, looking at his sister Meitat Anaka with an overly-repulsed expression upon his face. *"You know you are technically a Hiveakan, right?"*

"Shut up!" Anaka had smirked back, watching him in her bedroom mirror as he went through her music collection, while she fiddled with her hair. *"I like that stuff."*

"It's all… love and boyfriends – this stuff is marketed for Outsider teenage girls." Mokoto had frowned.

"I don't listen to the lyrics," Anaka had insisted so genuinely Mokoto had believed her. He'd always believed her. After they'd become friends, Mokoto had always listened to every word she'd said. Like a fool… *"I just like the beat. There's a karaoke one in there that Uncle Thoit bought me – he knows I don't listen to the words."*

"Oh!" Mokoto had grinned, finding the gift. Then he'd laughed. *"That was nice of him."*

374

"Well, he is nice." Anaka had giggled.

"Sire," Rozo's voice broke into Mokoto's thoughts. "We are ready now."

"Thank you," Mokoto uttered. He didn't need to be told again, and he didn't hesitate once. As if he had done it a thousand times before, King Mokoto stepped outside.

He made his way down the Balcony, almost deafened by the thunderous sound of the crowd that had gathered on the streets below. There were thousands of them; many more than there had been in the temple. They were already cheering. His presence alone had set them off; it was enough to make Mokoto wonder if such cheers were genuine, or if their support was motivated by pity. Did they start wailing like animals the moment they saw him simply because they felt they should? Well, they shouldn't. He didn't need their pity! He made his way towards the end of the Balcony, their cheers growing louder with each step he took. What was wrong with them? He found himself at the end, and he looked down at his feet. He had to be careful where to go, so that he didn't step on Ana's footprints. The spot where Queen Ana used to stand on the Balcony had been highlighted, so that no future king or queen stood in that spot. If they did, she would curse them and their reign. King Taka hadn't stepped on them, had he? By accident? Or maybe it wasn't a mistake in where he'd stood. Perhaps his mistake was in giving his child Ana's name. Perhaps he had been cursed from the day Anaka was born.

Mokoto stared down at the people below him, and listened as their mindless howling began to soften. They were going quiet, for him. They were waiting for him to speak. Well... fine. This was it. Mokoto's first speech as king. "Thank you," Mokoto spoke, his tone ever so polite despite the lack of gratitude he felt. Why were they cheering...? "Thank you, for coming to see me at such short notice. I understand many of you are upset. Many of you..." He closed his eyes for a brief moment. Distracted. She was here, he could sense it. He could feel her eyes on him. Anaka... "Many of you have lost loved ones."

"This movie is terrible." Lanka's voice echoed through his mind, as he became engulfed in memories once more. He had

375

memorised his speech so perfectly his mind could afford to wander, and wander it did. Into yet another thing that had happened a long time ago. *"It's unrealistic – this wouldn't happen. You can tell it was written by Outsiders."*

"It's a Hiveakan falling in love with an Outsider and not being embarrassed by it. Of course it was written by Outsiders," Anaka had replied, as she sat between Mokoto and Lanka. The three of them were watching a movie, on one of the few occasions that they had all informally been in the same room. *"I'm watching it for him."* She'd nodded towards the lead actor, a very attractive man.

"What about you?" Lanka had looked at Mokoto with a small smirk. *"Are you watching it for her?"*

"Actually," Mokoto had taken his eyes off the lead female, a beautiful actress, to look back at Lanka. *"Aren't you?"*

Anaka had laughed, enough to almost spill her drink, and she'd looked at her sister, eagerly awaiting Lanka's comeback.

"No," Lanka had replied, calmly, confidently, and completely unfazed. *"Been there. There's a reason she doesn't strip in films."*

"Whoa!" Mokoto had practically choked, his eyes widening, while Anaka's laughter had become uncontrollable. "Please let me apologise, on behalf of our fallen king," King Mokoto spoke. "I can promise you, he did not know he would be lost. He did not know his einjels would be lost…" Mokoto paused, as another vision appeared before him. It was a memory, yet again… but a still memory. An image. One of his father. Mokoto could see him now, as clear as day. The family crown upon his head, his dark eyes as terrifying as he himself was fearless. He looked immortal. King Taka had always looked immortal; he had always felt immortal… so much so that Mokoto had almost forgotten he was not. "He wanted to come home, and he wanted to bring his einjels home." Mokoto stared down at the crowd. He could see their faces from here; they were hanging on his every word. They were so quiet. So loyal… but to whom? Why…? "But still, we lost him, and we lost his einjels – and they were einjels. They are einjels. They will always be einjels!"

The noise was unbelievable. The crowd were cheering – screeching, like feral birds. It was amazing how such few words could cause such noise. They almost seemed happy. Mokoto could already see the stories they would tell their families; they were all so proud to be here. They were excited to be here. They were honoured to witness this, the crowning of a new king. They were thrilled to hear King Mokoto's first speech themselves. In fact, they were so happy they would not even grieve. Not really. Why would they grieve over their einjels, when they could brag about being here today? What good were einjels alive when they could be honoured and talked about, and used for fame and money when they were dead? The world knew about King Taka's mission now, only because it had failed. These people… these people that should be grieving, if they had no reason to grieve then the world had no reason to know their einjels' names. They would be a secret, forever. Clearly, a famous death was more important than a secret life. That was apparent now. That was what King Taka had meant to them. That was what those one hundred soldiers had meant to them. Mokoto felt such a deep anger within his soul. It was a wonder his Footprints didn't kick the Balcony to the ground. All Mokoto wanted was for these people to stop cheering. To stop applauding the fact that King Taka was dead – didn't they understand it? He had died on Earth, away from the Gaiamira! His soul would be trapped there forever, he would never be reincarnated! He would never reach the Gaiamirarezo; he would never become one with the Gaiamira and with the world. Why were they fine with that?

"And we will remember them, forever," Mokoto continued on. "*I* will remember them forever. As your king, as King Taka's son, I promise that with my life. They will not be forgotten, as long as there is life in my soul." More cheering… "And I will continue my father's work. I will rule this planet the way he wanted it to be ruled. I will continue his legacy. I will be a king worthy of his throne, and I will make him proud." Still, they cheered… but their cheering had softened slightly. Some people had gone quiet. Why? Why had that been the only thing that had silenced them? Were they not satisfied with how King Taka had run this world? Was the lack or war, or poverty, or crime not to their liking? Were their comfortable lives not comfortable enough? The animals! The traitors!

Mokoto wanted to scream; his Footprints were stampeding inside of him so violently he thought he would vomit them out. He had never been so angry. At everything. At his father's death, and his father's people, at his sister, at Earth… at this fucking brand new, costume jewellery crown. "I promise, Gaiamiráka… in the name of the Gaiamira, I will devote my life to being your king," Mokoto spoke. "And I promise you, my people…" He stared down at the crowd, and it took all the strength and willpower in Mokoto's being not to let his Footprints show in his eyes. "I will not forget this day."

Then the crowd cheered.

21755190R00223

Printed in Poland
by Amazon Fulfillment
Poland Sp. z o.o., Wrocław